THE PASS PROTECTION

ALEXIS BUXTON

Editor/Proofreader: My Brother's Editor
Cover Designer: Mel D. Designs
Publisher's Name: 419 Publishing, LLC.
Publisher's Address: 1978 Havemann Rd, #161, Celina, OH 45822

Other Titles

CTU Eagles

The Late Hit

The Christmas Scramble

The Change Up

Playlist

Self Care - Mac Miller
Trouble - Cage The Elephant
bloody valentine - mgk
The Spins - Mac Miller, Empire Of The Sun
Car Radio - Twenty One Pilots
Stay Away - Nirvana
I Wanna Be Yours - Arctic Monkeys
You Give Love A Bad Name - Bon Jovi
Perfect - Simple Plan
All We Have - mgk, Anna Yvette
Amarillo Sky - Jason Aldean
el Diablo - mgk
Dreams - Fleetwood Mac
Relapse - Warren Zeiders
Party On Fifth Ave. - Mac Miller
Come a Little Closer - Cage The Elephant
Creep - Radiohead
Secrets - OneRepublic
We're Going to Be Friends - The White Stripes
Last Night - Morgan Wallen
Float On - Modest Mouse
Howlin' for You - The Black Keys
Seven Nation Army - The White Stripes
jawbreaker - mgk
Nikes on My Feet - Mac Miller
Thunder - Imagine Dragons
Wild as Her - Corey Kent
mirrorball - Taylor Swift
Ain't No Rest for the Wicked - Cage The Elephant
Would That I - Hozier
Slow Hands - Niall Horan
21 - Hunter Hayes
Birthday Song - 2 Chainz, Kanye West
Mr. Brightside - The Killers
Better Together - Jack Johnson
The Search - NF
The Boys Are Back In Town - Thin Lizzy
Best Friend (feat. Doja Cat) - Saweetie, Doja Cat
Memories (feat. Kid Cudi) - David Guetta, Kid Cudi

Playlist

Slow Burn - Kacey Musgraves
Chemical - Post Malone
Real Love Baby - Father John Misty
feelslikeimfallinginlove - Coldplay
Thriller - Michael Jackson
Lose Control - Teddy Swims
Better - Khalid
Stolen - Dashboard Confessional
Livin' On A Prayer - Bon Jovi
Home - Daughtry
Good Life - OneRepublic
Livin' The Dream - Morgan Wallen
bellyache - Billie Eilish
Cigarette Daydreams - Cage The Elephant
Stolen Dance (Acoustic Version) - Milky Chance
Enter Sandman – Metallica
I Will Follow You Into The Dark – Death Cab For Cutie
body bag (feat. YUNGBLUD) – mgk
Somebody Told Me – The Killers
Control – Halsey
Nightmare – Halsey
Let You Down – NF
Haunting – Halsey
Carry on Wayward Son – Kansas
The Night We Met – Lord Huron
What Was I Made For? – Billie Eilish
Home – mgk
Work Song – Hozier
Let Her Go – Passenger
Fight Song – Rachel Platen
The Alchemy – Taylor Swift
Earned It – The Weekend
One Call Away – Charlie Puth
Die A Happy Man – Thomas Rhett
For the complete soundtrack, listen to 'THE PASS PROTECTION'
on Spotify

Before You Read

This book does feature a few trigger warnings. Please read on with caution as these triggers may be considered spoilers.

This book contains adult material including mentions of the death of a parent (off-page), emotional/psychological abuse (from an ex, off-page), stalking, mental health struggles with a strong mental health representation, and mentions of suicidal thoughts. The Pass Protection is an open-door romance with explicit sexual content, strong language, as well as college-aged main characters drinking.

It is my hope that I've handled these topics in the care that they deserve. Readers, please be advised.
Your mental health matters.

To my high school self,
It got better.
Love Always,
Alexis

CHAPTER 1
Bret

They say a woman who changes her hair is about to change her whole life. Well, I guess I'm about to change the world with how drastically I've changed my appearance over the last few months.

Not only have I dyed my golden-brown hair with natural blonde highlights—the color people pay big money for—black, but I just packed up my Jeep and moved nine hundred miles.

All without telling my parents.

Can you say college crisis?

Or maybe it's not a crisis.

Maybe it's me finally taking control of my own life and doing the things I want to, the way I want to do them.

For as long as I can remember, I've done everything right. I've been the perfect daughter, sister, friend, student, and girlfriend. But the problem with trying to be perfect in everyone else's eyes is that along the way, I lost myself.

The traits I thought made me who I am are not actually *my* traits but the characteristics that people around me want me to be. At twenty years old, I've spent so much time pleasing everyone else that I forgot to please myself. I have no idea who I am or what truly makes me happy.

A couple of weeks ago, I was on the phone with my older broth-er—by fifteen months—he was filling me in on what's new at CTU for the upcoming school year. Grant briefly mentioned one of his buddies on the team was in a lurch for a fourth roommate since someone who was supposed to move in had bailed. Grant is a wide receiver on the college football team, where my dad is the head coach. When he mentioned Tyler Harris, the quarterback, was the one needing a roommate, I filed that information in the back of my mind.

Lying in bed after a particularly rough day, I searched for Tyler on Facebook. There was a post on his profile inquiring about a roommate, and I noticed it was still open. After a brief war in my mind, I decided to shoot my shot and send him an email. Praying my last name was common enough and that my dad and brother hadn't mentioned my real name, I hoped it was enough for him not to put two and two together. Hitting Send, I locked my phone and waited.

Forty-eight hours later, after a few back-and-forth emails, Tyler was sending over the lease agreement. I mean, I was the perfect candidate. What group of athletes wouldn't accept a sports management major who plays intramural basketball, has a zero policy for drama, and whose favorite movie is *The Fast and the Furious*? Once that acceptance notification hit my phone, I quickly filled out the transfer application from the University of Arizona to Central Texas University.

Should I have specified that I was a female? Yeah, probably. But what's the fun in that? And it wasn't like there was a spot on the form for me to mark my gender. So, I mean, whose fault is it *really*?

Anxiety coursed through my veins as I signed the form with my electronic signature. Never in my life have I made such a big decision without my family knowing, but I've got to get far away from Arizona. I've got to escape the fear and crippling worry. It's time to run from the monster chasing me.

It's time I join my dad and brother and become an Eagle. I'd much rather soar like an Eagle than roar like a Wildcat.

Turning down the radio, I lean forward in my seat as I gaze above my steering wheel, searching for the entrance to the apartment complex. For some reason, having the volume off makes my concentration and vision so much better. My GPS says I only have a few hundred feet to go, but all I see are rows and rows of buildings behind a black metal gate.

Glancing down at my GPS, my eyes bounce from the screen to the road. Ah, there is the opening. I flick on my turn signal as I step on the brakes, causing the car behind me to honk and shout at me.

"Sorry. Sorry," I mumble, knowing the person behind me can't hear me, as I turn onto the road that leads to the parking lot.

The black metal gates welcome you into the complex with a sign stating "Eagles Landing Apartments." Continuing down the paved road, I pass a white brick and black-roofed community building with an in-ground pool beside it. The pool is overflowing with residents inside the water and lounging in chaises around the pool.

And wait, I lower my sunglasses for a better view, is that a DJ?

"The apartment complex doesn't hold back," I say, shaking my head and letting out a soft chuckle.

Pressing down on the accelerator, I pass cars and people walking as I try to find the road where my new home awaits. I can't get over how clean this complex is. Each building has flower beds with fresh black mulch, trimmed green shrubs contrasting against the mulch, and a few other blooming flowers. The bottom units have small covered porches, while the upper units have balconies in the back.

Taking in each building, I feel a sense of warmth. I can see myself happy in these units. I hope my roommates aren't too mad about the fact I'm a woman. But if they really wanted to know, they should have had a specific spot on the application to state whether the applicant is male or female.

At least, that's the defense I'm going with.

Turning right and following the main road, I find building eight and pull into a vacant spot. Shifting the gear into park, I rest my face against my steering wheel, taking a few deep breaths in the grounding exercises I've been working on. I hope at least one of my roommates is home. I'm arriving a few hours later than anticipated.

Here's to a fresh start.

A new you.

You can do this, Bret.

I slowly release the air with one last deep breath and push the ignition button off. Reaching for my purse, I step out of the Jeep and walk to the back to grab one of the two suitcases I brought.

The moving company I hired to move all my belongings from Arizona to Texas isn't picking them up until tomorrow. Thankfully, Olivia, my former roommate and best friend, is an angel and was willing to help make sure they get everything.

For now, it's just me, my Jeep, two medium-sized suitcases, my backpack with my laptop, and of course, my favorite basketball. There was no way I was leaving Spalding behind. We've been through too much.

Wheeling one of my suitcases toward the steps, I hoist the heavy bag by the handle toward the third floor where unit eight-thirty-four awaits. The area where this building is located is quiet. The only noise is my feet echoing in the enclosed space as I climb the wooden stairs. It's a good thing I'm all about exercising because climbing these stairs would get old quickly if I wasn't in shape.

Reaching the top of the stairs, I glance to my left and right and see that unit eight-thirty-four is on the right side of the walkway. Taking another deep breath, I try to center myself and my nerves before my feet carry me toward the awaiting door. The rolling vibrations of my suitcase wheels against the wood are the only soundtrack to the next chapter of my life.

This is it, girl. Here's to the new you. Gone are the hard days of living in Arizona. Your new future is behind this door.

My knuckles rap against the metal as I wait for my new roommates to answer. The white door swings open, and my jaw nearly hits the ground. Maybe I didn't think this whole living with guys situation over enough.

Standing before me is a god. He's tall—having five to six inches on my five foot ten frame—and has golden-tanned skin on full display thanks to his lack of shirt. My eyes trail down his six, no wait, eight—eight? I pause, counting the indents again. Yes, eight-pack abs. And stop at his very defined v that leads to what I can only assume is...

"Not that I don't mind the blatant eye fuck, but can I help you?" he says with a chuckle interrupting my, well, blatant eye fuck.

"Oh shit." I snap my eyes back up to his, where a waiting smirk is spread across his face. "I'm Bret Campbell, your new roommate."

I watch as that sexy smirk morphs into a straight line of confusion. "I'm sorry. Can you say that again?"

My mouth opens to repeat myself when I'm interrupted by a loud, albeit familiar, voice in the background. "Yo, Harris. Who's at the door?"

Harris? Taking another long look at the man in front of me, recognition dawns. Tyler Harris, the CTU Eagles star quarterback and one of my brother's close friends. *Shit.* Tyler slides away from the door and opens his body so that the guy shouting his name gets a clear view.

"Addy?" His voice was a shocked whisper, and my eyes quickly widened.

As I stand there, Tyler's god-like presence is suddenly overshadowed by the Herculean Adonis approaching us. His disheveled blonde hair and mocha brown eyes command attention, and I question my decision to be here. Crew Riggsby and I have a history, not in the romantic sense, but in the 'we met once and sort of became friends' kind of way. I never expected to see him here.

God, seeing him in person, I forgot how much his looks affect me. Not only is Crew model-worthy attractive—like he deserves his own Sports Illustrated cover—but he's a big, powerful guy. His six foot five inch frame towers over me, making the apartment's entryway tiny. His muscles bulge from his two hundred and thirty-plus pound athletic build without needing to flex. He's the perfect body type to be a starting tight end for the football team.

And dear lord, those athletic shorts do nothing to conceal the outline in his shorts. Crew has been blessed in the big gene department...everywhere.

"Hey, Crew—"

"Wait?" Tyler interjects. "I thought you just said your name was Bret?"

Both guys stare at each other and then back at me. I watch Crew's eyes rake over my body, which heats along his path. From my red, white, and blue Nikes, his eyes lick up my tan, toned legs from hours spent running up and down a basketball court. They skim over my distressed denim shorts and pause at my chest.

My eyes widen as I mentally palm my forehead and realize why his gaze lingers. I completely forgot that I removed my bra during the two hours I was stuck on the interstate in standstill traffic. The underwire was digging into my skin so badly I couldn't take it anymore. I needed to free the ta-tas.

And now I'm standing before two hot-blooded males wearing a skin-tight white cropped top with my new piercings on full display.

Does dying your hair black and getting your nipples pierced signify a crisis or a rebellion? Asking for a friend.

Refusing to cower under their assessment, I steal my shoulders and wait for them to stop gawking.

Tyler is the first to break. His eyes snap to me and widen as the realization hits. "Wait? Addy like Addy Campbell? Oh, fuck. Like Grant's sister? Coach's daughter?"

I point to myself and say, "Bret Addison Campbell. Not that I don't mind the mini-interrogation. I knew it'd be coming, but do you mind if we do this inside? It's been a very long day of traveling."

Both guys jerk to the side, making way for me to enter the apartment. Taking a step in, I enter a small hallway. A wall-mounted coat rack sits empty since it's the middle of Texas heat. There's another smaller key rack next to the coat rack. It's simple, but I didn't expect a fancy entryway in an apartment filled with college football players. At least the place smells good. Fresh. Not like dirty gym bags.

Walking a few more steps into the entryway, there's a galley kitchen to the left. It's closed off from the rest of the apartment and smaller than my last place, but that's fine—cooking isn't my specialty.

Diagonal from the kitchen is the first bedroom. My eyes peek inside, and I notice the unmade bed. The hallway opens to the living room, where there is a black leather sectional, and a big-screen TV is mounted to the wall. Yes, this is definitely a guy's apartment, considering how big it is. I think it's at least seventy inches and takes up most of the wall. No doubt this TV sees a lot of video games and Sports Center.

A sliding glass door sits at the back of the room and opens to a balcony with a view overlooking the green space toward the clubhouse. I can't make out much else from where I'm standing.

Wheeling my suitcase off to the side near a dining table behind the living space and the kitchen, I turn toward the guys who follow on my heels.

"So let me get this straight, your name is *actually* Bret?" Crew asks.

"I'm so confused," mumbles Tyler.

Life should come with thought bubbles above people's heads, like in comics. I'd love to read the thoughts that are no doubt swirling inside his head. This way, I can figure out how best to reassure people that, yes, my name is Bret.

Bret Addison Campbell.

A female.

Here's the thing. I like my name. It's cool and unique and fits my personality perfectly. The thing I don't like is the dumbfounded look everyone gives me. Or them constantly asking if I said Britt. No, Bret. B-R-E-T.

As if naming me after my uncle wasn't confusing enough, Mom decided to drop the second 't' because she thought it'd be more feminine. Turns out it isn't. It led to more explaining in my life.

Pulling out a wooden chair, I sit at the dining table and watch the guys follow my lead.

"I was named after my dad's brother, his best friend in life, who passed away when my mom was pregnant with me. Evidently, it was a whole debate between the two of them. She wanted to name me Addison after her grandmother, and Dad wanted to name me after his brother. So they compromised and spelled my name with only one 't' because it made it more feminine, whatever that means."

"Okay," Tyler draws out. "That explains the name, but what are you doing at CTU? I thought you went to school in Arizona."

Chewing on my lip, I look around the table at the two guys who need more answers than I want to give. Crew's eyes dart away when I make eye contact with him.

Seeing him in person is weird. Last Christmas, when I was visiting, Grant invited me to the Football House where his buddy Quinton lived. Crew was there, and the two of us kind of hit it off. Not in the romantic sense—I had a boyfriend at the time—but there was some kind of spark between us.

It's hard not to be drawn to Crew. There's something about his personality that welcomes people. He's the goofiest of my brother's friends, but that's what drew me to him most. I firmly believe that people come into your life when you need them the most. Last Christmas, I was in a really dark place, hell I've been in a dark place for far too long, but Crew's beaming smile, jokes that had me curling over with laughter, and flirtatious attitude that had me blushing and my brother scowling was not what I needed.

Since then, we've kept in touch by sending random text messages and liking each other's pictures on social media before I deactivated my accounts. But the vibe he's throwing my way is not the same one we've been sharing the last few months.

Shit, does he think I, like, stalked him, and now I'm forcing myself onto him? Of course he does, Bret. This whole situation is quickly turning into a mess.

"I didn't know you were Tyler's roommate." I point the words to Crew, who looks taken aback by my outburst. "Seriously. Grant filled me in on the roommate situation during one of our phone calls. He has no idea I'm here, and I had no idea you lived here. I'm not like stalking you or anything, if that's what you think."

Crew shakes his head and scoffs but doesn't say anything. Tyler is the one doing all of the talking, and I can see that he's freaking out internally. "This just keeps getting worse. Your brother has no idea you're here? I assume your parents know, right?"

I wince, and he curses. "Look, it's a whole story, one I really don't want to get into right now. In the past two days, I've driven from Arizona to here. I'm honestly exhausted. I promise I'm cool, and I won't cramp your bachelor lifestyle. Bring back all the girls you want, I'm not about to be a cock block. I needed to get out of Tucson and find someplace where the rent wasn't insane. I clean up after myself, don't do drama, and have no problem keeping to myself in my room."

"You don't do drama, but this sounds like a lot of drama," Tyler says, and I can't fault him for it. Yes, it sounds like drama at this moment, but once I talk to my family, it'll all be okay.

"How do we know we can even trust you? For the past seven months, I thought your name was Addy. Jesus, I've been talking to a stranger." Hurt laces Crew's voice, and it kills me. It was never supposed to go down like this.

"You two talk?"

Putting my hand in the air, I attempt to halt the spiral around the table. "Okay, let me sum everything up. My mom and brother call me Addy, while my dad *always* calls me Bret. It's confusing, I know, but it is what it is. I needed to leave Arizona because some...stuff...happened, and I haven't told my family I moved here. I needed to be closer to my family."

"Are you okay?" Crew's eyes lock on mine, and it's as if he's reading me for a lie.

With a tight-lipped smile, I nod. "I will be."

Turning to look at Harris, I find him watching me intently, too. It's very intimidating to be under their stares, and I also can't help but be a little turned on by the two gods sitting across from me shirtless. It's been a really long time since I've been this close to two very attractive guys.

For the past four months, I've been a hermit in my apartment. Since classes ended last April, I have only left the apartment to go to the gym and the grocery store—but never alone. My life has been really depressing, so much so that I've collected six tattoos from my roommate, who is an apprentice at a tattoo shop. She needed someone to practice on, and I was a blank canvas begging to be touched.

Clapping my hands together, I snap my attention back to the matter at hand. "I promise to tell my family this week. It's all a little unexpected, but I have a car to unload if we're done with the chit-chat."

"Yeah, we're good, Bret. Don't make us hide the truth for long. I don't need tension on the team," Harris says in what I can only assume is his football captain tone.

"I promise." I smile at the guys before reaching into my pocket and fishing out a fifty-dollar bill. Slapping it on the table, I slide it toward the middle. "Pizza and beer are on me tonight."

"Yo," a voice shouts from the hallway. "I was talking to Rick downstairs, and he said some babe was rolling her suitcase up the stairs. Looks like there's some fresh—" his words trail off as he rounds the corner to where the three of us are sitting. His eyes widen before they land straight on my chest. I really need to grab a bra.

"Uhh, what's Coach's daughter doing in our apartment?" The guy says, and I recognize him instantly. Jeremiah Prince, or JP to everyone, is a defensive back on the football team and another of my brother's closest friends. I also met him in person at the Christmas party last winter, but I've heard a lot about him over the years.

"Hey, roomie!" I greet my new roommate as cheerfulness drips into my words.

"Grant didn't say anything about you moving. How's it going, Addy?" he asks me before turning his attention to Crew and Tyler. "I thought we were getting some dude named Bret?"

"And that's my cue. You boys fill him in while I carry my stuff up from my Jeep," I say, standing from my seat and adjusting my clothes, which had ridden up from sitting. All three track my hands, sliding down the denim cutoff shorts and adjusting my crop top.

You need this fresh start, Bret. It'll all be worth it.

I'm halfway to my car when I feel him approaching.

"What the fuck, *Bret*?" Crew's words cut through me like ice.

Instead of stopping at his words, I continue to my Jeep, hitting the button on my fob to unlock the doors. Opening the back, I reach inside for my other suitcase. I'm about to pull it out when large arms move me out of the way. My body tenses at the contact as my back goes ramrod straight.

"Sorry," Crew grumbles, lifting my bag and placing it at our feet. He watches me, curious about my reaction.

Hello, trauma, it's been a while.

I hope there's a time in my very near future when the sudden contact of someone else won't have me crawling out of my skin.

"It's fine." My voice wobbles as I grab my black backpack. Tossing it on my back, I adjust the straps so it's not digging into my piercings. My nipples are still a little sensitive to the metal.

Warm-brown eyes bore into me, and I want to crumple right here in the middle of our parking lot. But I won't do that. I can't be that weak girl anymore. I left her in Arizona.

"I'm sorry I didn't tell you my real name was Bret. I didn't think it'd be an issue."

"You didn't think it'd be an issue? All these months, what were they?"

"I don't know, Crew. What do you want me to say?"

"I think I want you to be fucking honest with me, Ad—*Bret*—whatever the fuck you want me to call you. Do you still have a boyfriend, or was that a lie?"

I halt my movement and turn toward him. We're nearly chest to chest, and I can feel his frustration vibrating off of him. Reaching up, I place my hand on his bare chest, next to the cross tattoo he has over his heart. Electricity zaps between us, but I fight not to let the spark of our connection ignite.

"Crew, I'm sorry. It's Bret or Addy; call me whichever you want. No, there's no boyfriend—not anymore. And yes, I can be honest with you. I know I don't deserve your trust, but please trust that I will tell you everything when I'm ready."

His eyes soften, and I feel it. I feel that there's hope that we can move forward from the lies. "Just tell me one thing."

"I'll try."

He brings his hand up and cups my cheek. I only flinch slightly at the contact, which he no doubt notices. Brushing his thumb across my cheekbone, he asks, "Who hurt you?"

And I melt into his touch. Out of everyone in my life, I know it's going to be Crew Riggsby who will be the one to break down the walls I'm trying so desperately to build.

CHAPTER 2
CREW

I can't believe she's here. I haven't been able to get those emerald-green eyes out of my head for seven months.

I close my eyes and see her smile.

I close my eyes and hear her laugh.

She's like a drug, and I'm an addict who can't get enough.

But now she's my roommate.

What did I do in my past life to deserve this karma?

Not only have I been fighting feelings for an unavailable girl, but she's also my teammate's little sister and my coach's only daughter.

After I carried the few belongings she brought to the empty room in our apartment, we both went our separate ways. The guys are waiting for me in the living room, and *It's Always Sunny in Philadelphia* reruns are playing on the TV. I graciously accept the beer Harris has waiting for me.

"Bro, what the fuck?" He sighs and rests his head on the back of the couch, a cold beer in his hands. "I had no clue the Bret Campbell that applied was a girl, let alone Coach's daughter."

"I think that was her plan this whole time. She's hiding something."

"I texted Grant." Both Harris and I snap our heads in the direction of JP who is sitting on the opposite side of the sectional.

"Why?" I ask, bringing the beer to my lips for a long pull. I savor the cold, hoppy liquid as it slides down my throat.

This beer is much needed. Not only because of the new roommate situation, but practices have been brutal as we gear up for the start of our season. Coach has high expectations since we brought home the hardware last season by winning the national championship. Now that we've tasted success, we're all desperate to bring it home again.

Today was a scorcher in Texas, and I wanted to head to the pool, but the impromptu party prevented me from doing so. Football, partying, and farming are a few of my favorite things, but a pool party after the most brutal practice was not what I was in the mood for.

"He needed to know." JP shrugs. "Grant always worries about his sister, but lately, he's been even more concerned about her. The fact that she dropped out of the University of Arizona, drove solo thirteen hours, and moved in with a group of guys would have any big brother concerned."

I nod, resting my head on the back of the couch, and close my eyes. I know he's right, but a small part of me wants to be the one she turns to. I know it's absolutely ridiculous to be her sounding board, but I want to protect her. It's my job on the field to protect the passing game, and I guess that need to protect has seeped over to her.

There's just something about her that draws me in. The attraction hasn't changed, even though her appearance has completely changed. I noticed all the ink on her perfect olive skin. Her brown hair is now jet black. And damn, don't get me started on her new piercings. I couldn't help but stare at them.

"Did you order the pizza?"

Harris nods his head. "Yeah, should be here in about ten minutes," he says, glancing down at his smartwatch. "I stuck Bret's money in the drawer of the entryway table. She's not buying on her first night here, but I didn't want to start a fight, so I hid the money."

"Smart thinking," I say with a chuckle.

Silence falls over the room as we all turn our attention to the TV as a familiar beat reverberates off the wall separating the living room from Ad—*Bret's* room. Shit, it's gonna take a minute to get my brain to call her Bret.

Honestly, hearing that her name is Bret makes so much sense. Addy felt too common for her. She's too fucking cool.

A beer cap hits my chest as Harris's chuckle fills the space. I look up and find JP shaking his head at me.

"Dude, you've got it bad," JP says.

"What do you mean?"

"You literally said 'she's too fucking cool,' like out of the blue," Harris adds.

"Shit, I didn't mean to say that out loud."

There's a knock at the door, and Harris jumps up off the couch and heads down the hall to answer.

"Where the *fuck* is my sister?" Grant storms into the living room. If this were a cartoon, steam would be shooting out of his ears. His attention whips in my direction, and his eyes narrow. "Did you know about this?"

"Yeah, Campbell, I knew this whole time," I retort sarcastically. His glare has me quickly changing my tune. "No, man, I'm just as blindsided as you are."

Grant runs his finger through his hair, and I can practically feel the turmoil radiating from him. Whatever problems Bret's dealing with is making her brother stress the fuck out.

Another knock on the door has Harris turning back around to answer. Hopefully, it's the pizza this time.

"Did she seem okay?" he asks. I'm not sure what Campbell knows about my friendship with his sister. There honestly isn't much there. A few videos were sent to each other on social media, a liked picture here and there, and the occasional text. He warned me off of her last winter, and I've done my best to honor that. Of course, I felt a connection, but damn, that's my Coach's daughter, who is clearly going through some shit. I need to tread lightly, very lightly.

I'm about to respond when her door swings open. "Is the pizza…" Her words trail off as her eyes widen at seeing her big brother standing outside her door. Since she's entered her room, she's tossed on an oversized hoodie with her high school basketball logo across the chest. Thank God she covered up her tits.

Shock crosses both of their faces as his sister's appearance literally takes Grant aback. "What happened to your hair?"

She scoffs. "Well, hello to you too, brother." Her eyes narrow as she bounces her gaze from JP to Harris, who's setting our pizza order down on the table, and then they land on me. The glare she gives me is glacial. And reminds me way too much of the glare her brother just gave me.

I raise my hands, one still holding my beer. "Don't look at me like that. I didn't say shit. If you want to blame anyone, blame the jackass on the other side."

Her head quirks as she props her hands on her hips. "Oh, so this is how it's going to be, roomie?"

Grant goes to grab Bret's arm, and she freezes. Her back goes ramrod straight as fear covers her face. It's the same reaction she gave me in the parking lot when I questioned who hurt her. At that moment, every guy in this room knew she was hiding something. Someone fucking hurt her. Call it male instinct, but a protectiveness went through each of us.

"Don't," she says, her words soft. "I'm fine, Grant. I just missed the family and wanted to be an Eagle like you."

He pulls her into his arms, and I'm jealous that I'm not wrapping my arms around her. He whispers something in her hair, and she grabs him tighter. He pulls away with a quick peck to the top of her head. "We'll talk about this more."

She gives him a terse nod before he steps away from her. Heaviness weighs on his shoulder as he stares at his sister.

"Wanna stay for some food?" Harris asks, tossing paper plates next to the pizza boxes. It looks like he ordered Cousin Jimmy's, a staple around campus. They're the only place on campus that stays open until four a.m. Their pizza is super greasy, super tasty, and super cheap. When the late-night drunk munchies hit, they're the go-to. Somehow, they even cure hangovers. They also have a helluva deal of an extra-large pizza, ten breadsticks, and two large drinks for ten dollars. You can't freaking beat it.

Grant shakes his head. "Nah, man. You sure you're good, Addy?"

"Yeah, and don't be mad at them," she says. Her green doe eyes sparkle as she looks up at him. "I did everything under Bret Campbell. They had no idea."

"I still don't like it. Why didn't you call me? You could've taken my extra room."

"Some things need to be done on my own."

He eyes her, much like a parent would search their child for any traces of a lie. When he seems satisfied with her answer—at least for the moment—he pulls her in for one last hug. The two are close. I'm jealous of their relationship. I have an older brother and a younger sister. My sister and I are somewhat close, but she's quite a bit younger than I am. And as much as I wished I was closer to my brother, we've never had the chance to be close.

He's four years older than me, and when he was in high school, he was quite the shithead. Trouble always seemed to find him, so I never got much opportunity to grow close to him. Then, after he graduated high school, he enlisted in the Army. My dad would have been proud of him. He would have been more proud if Jett had followed in my dad's footsteps and enlisted in the Air Force, but I guess the Army is the next best thing.

For the past six years, he's been serving overseas. Building a relationship with someone who never wants to come home is hard. It's not like I'm at home in Ohio either, but we aren't even in the same country. The two of us email back and forth, and he tries to catch replays of my games when he has the chance. But it isn't the same.

Maybe once I graduate, he'll be ready to leave the service, and we can both be home together. Dad's dream was always for the two of us to take over the family farm since my younger sister never had any interest in it—at least, she didn't when I lived at home.

"See you guys in the morning," Grant says as he reaches into his wallet and pulls out a card for his sister. "Here's my keycard to get into the practice facility. We have practice from six to nine. You have until ten to talk to Dad, or I'm doing it for you."

Bret takes the card from Grant and nods her head. With that, Grant leaves us alone for our first dinner with our new roommate.

Dinner went smoothly. We watched *It's Always Sunny* reruns before Bret beat JP in a game of rock, paper, scissors, and the winner got to choose the movie. The three of us all sat on the edge of our seats as we waited—eyes closed, per Bret's request—for the movie she selected to start playing. It turns out that Bret is a big fan of action movies. We all sighed in relief that it wasn't a chick flick.

However, halfway through the movie, I glanced over and found a sleeping Bret. She had curled up in the corner of the sectional and fallen asleep. Her hood was up, her hands folded underneath her head, and her legs curled in the fetal position. It was at that moment I saw a genuinely relaxed Bret. Her walls weren't standing tall. She seemed at peace.

When ten o'clock rolled around, the guys and I were ready to call it a night. We've been waking up at five in the morning to make sure we fuel up before our morning workouts, which meant early bedtimes. Harris nudged Bret awake, and the four of us went our separate ways.

Now it's after two, and I'm staring at my ceiling knowing only a bathroom separates us, not hundreds of miles. I can't get her out of my head. Her pitch-black hair hanging long down her back and her toned-athletic framed body. Those eyes remind me of summer days on the lake in my hometown. The tattoos she now wears have me wondering if she's hiding more under her clothes, which has me begging to explore her body more than I already did. And dear lord, those piercings on her perfect, perky tits.

Rebellion looks good on her.

My body is exhausted, and my eyes are heavy, but my brain won't quiet down to allow sleep to consume me. I've tossed and turned enough times tonight the sheets are no longer tucked underneath the mattress. Rolling over, I tap the screen on my phone to check the time. Deciding a glass of water might help me go back to sleep, I toss the covers from my bed and lazily stumble across the hallway to the kitchen.

With heavy lids, I barely make out a lone figure sitting across from me on the counter with a bowl in her hand in the dimly lit room.

Without thought, I stride across the cool linoleum floor and close the gap between us. My hand wraps around her head as I tug her toward me. Our lips meet, and she lets out a small gasp in surprise. My tongue takes the opportunity to plunge inside as cinnamon sugar hits my taste buds. She startles at the contact as her hands find my bare chest, and she pushes me away.

"Shit!" I gasp. "I'm sorry, I thought maybe I dreamed you were here in my apartment."

"Nope," she says, popping the p. "I'm here, Crew."

Running my fingers through my hair, I stare at her. "Yes, you are."

Tipping the bowl toward me, she adds, "I'll buy another box for whoever has the Cinnamon Toast Crunch. I had the late-night munchies."

Reaching into the cabinet, I pull down a glass. Holding it against the built-in water dispenser, I glance toward her. "They're mine. Help yourself whenever you want."

Turning, Bret swings her legs out in front of her rather than where her feet had rested on the countertop. That's when I take in what she's wearing in the low glow of the under-the-cabinet lighting. She's in a green tank top and a pair of panties.

Fuck me.

Leaning with my back against the counter, I do my best to avoid looking at her. I know if I give into the temptation that is her, I'll end up staring at her tits as I trail down all of her exposed flesh. Her perfectly toned olive skin.

Shit, I can feel the blood rushing to my cock right now with the brief thought of her body.

"Are you still upset with me?" Her words are low and timid, and I hate that she's shying away.

Taking a deep breath, I tilt my head in her direction. "I'm not mad exactly. But did you think we'd never see each other again?"

"Honestly, I didn't think so. I never come to CTU, and I figured you'd lose interest eventually. You can't honestly say you'd carry on a friendship with someone you never see. Come on, Crew."

"You're right. I guess I was living in a delusional world. I thought we shared a moment at Q's at Christmas. You told me you had a boyfriend, and I respected that, but I felt something between us. Didn't you?"

Her eyes drop down to her lap as she turns away, avoiding eye contact with me. Bringing my glass to my mouth, I chug the water. I empty the contents in seconds before placing the glass into the kitchen sink.

I guess that's my answer.

Turning, I start to storm out of our kitchen, but my name on her lips has my steps faltering. Glancing over my shoulder, I watch as Bret quickly erases the space between us. Her hand lands on my arm as she turns me back toward her. Our chests brush, her threadbare tank against my bare chest, as her hands find a home behind my neck.

Before I can react, she's pulling my head down and crashing her lips against mine. I groan at the contact. Her plush, perfectly pink lips are smashed against mine. It's a feeling I've thought about way too many times. As if I hadn't just had her lips against mine.

Her tongue flicks against the seam of my lips, and I grant her the entrance she's begging for. Our tongues brush against each other, and the shock that flows through my body has my dick growing rock hard. I know she can feel it, but I refuse to break the kiss.

I should not be kissing my teammate's sister, hell, my coach's daughter, but my brain refuses to step away from her.

Her hands slide up my neck, fingers tangling in the hair at the nape of my neck as I pull her closer to my body before sliding my hands down her back, over her tight ass, and down her thighs. In one quick motion, I'm hoisting her in the air, and her legs wrap around my waist. My erection presses into her core where I can feel moisture pooling in the thin panties she's wearing.

She grinds against my length, and I struggle with every fiber of my being not to carry her into my bedroom. But instead, I use my brain and halt our movements.

Her face heats as she scurries down my body. "I'm sorry about that."

"Don't apologize," I beg.

"I had to kiss you one last time."

Wait, what? Who says this has to be the last time?

She must read the confusion on my face because she's answering the questions I never spoke aloud. "We can't do this, Crew. I need a place to live, and you're my brother's friend. We can't cross this line."

Reaching forward, I skate my thumb down her cheek before brushing a strand of hair behind her ear. "But—"

"No, buts. This can't happen again. I-I-I'm not ready to be in a relationship, and I don't want to complicate things. It's bad enough already."

Blowing a frustrated sigh out of my nose, I lean forward, planting a soft kiss on her forehead. "Whatever you need, Bret."

And with that, I turn and walk back to my bedroom. Crawling under the covers, I toss and turn some more and will sleep to take me. But it never does.

Instead the images of her in my arms, her tongue down my throat, assault my mind.

She never answered if she felt something for me like I did her. Was it all a game to her? Did she come here over Christmas break and play me? She doesn't seem like that type of person, but that girl I met months ago is no longer the girl on the other side of this wall. Something happened to her because she's changed drastically. I want so badly to believe she feels the connection, the zap of electricity that sparks every time we touch.

Even if she feels the same way as I do, what can I possibly do about it? She's right that she's not only my teammate—and friend's—sister, but she's my coach's daughter.

Am I going to risk losing playing time in my junior year because I want to sleep with my coach's daughter? Hell, I want more than that. I want to date her. But I can't even say that she feels the same way toward me.

Is it worth it? I can't risk having a bad relationship with my coach because he found out I was messing around with his daughter.

Dammit. This isn't how this year was supposed to play out. It was supposed to be simple. Play football and continue getting good grades. I only have two more seasons left until reality comes crashing down on me. Two more years of playing the game that I love before I fly home to Ohio and take over the family business. That's always been the plan.

Even though thoughts of playing in the NFL plague me, especially since I've watched my friends go on to get drafted. Last season, Quinton Boyd took me under his wing, and in the spring, he was drafted into the NFL. It was a dream come true for him. I've never given the NFL much thought. It's never been a dream of mine, as a kid we'd play in the yard like we were professional football players, but that's all it ever was.

After watching Quinton leave CTU for Denver, his parting words have struck a chord deep inside. He told me I had what it takes to make it to the league. That if I keep working hard this season, the scouts are going to notice.

But is that what I want? Do I want to play professionally, or do I want to go back to Ohio and help lower the stress on my mom? If my brother was around, I could talk to him or at least feel him out for what his future plans are. But of course, he's off playing hero to avoid his reality.

And now there's Bret.

So much for easy. It looks like this year just got a whole lot more complicated.

CHAPTER 3
Bret

I heard the boys leave an hour ago. A lot of noise came from the living room and kitchen, with a mixture of shushes as they all tried not to wake me.

Good news for them...I hardly ever sleep.

Last night, I was wide awake at 2:07, which is the same time every night. I wake in a cold sweat, unable to fall back asleep. No matter how hard I try to exhaust myself, I'm never able to escape the nightmares that come calling in the late-night hours. Bravery is a trait I'm working on building, and after an internal pep talk about how I was safe and far away from Arizona, I stood from the heap of blankets I had piled on the floor in search of a late-night snack. Something about pouring a large bowl of cereal in the middle of the night calls to me. Knowing I was living in an apartment full of boys, I assumed my odds of finding cereal would be high.

Lucky for me, I was right.

Inside the large pantry were five boxes of cereal. I was even surprised to see my favorite brand sitting there. After preparing the delicious cinnamon sugar treat, I climbed on the counter and enjoyed the serenity. The only noise in the apartment came from the whirring of the refrigerator. It was peaceful. For the first time in a long time, I felt genuinely safe inside the four walls that made up my home—as temporary as it may be.

Seeing that it was the middle of the night, I didn't put any thought into my state of undress. But as soon as Crew walked in from his bedroom, I instantly regretted my choice of not putting on pants.

Crew Riggsby has been on my mind for nearly seven months. And there he was, standing in the doorway of the kitchen we now shared in a pair of tight boxer briefs that squeezed his strong thighs and no shirt. Every ridge of his was on display, and I had to fight with all my might not to give away the reaction he was causing me.

Everything between us has been amicable. I dumped him in the friend zone, and it wasn't a hard decision since I was dating someone. But I won't lie. When we are near, there's a current that runs through us. There's a spark, an instant attraction. I mean, who wouldn't be falling to their knees before him?

As a tight end for the football team, Crew isn't just tall, but he's freaking built. At six foot, five inches and two hundred and thirty-five pounds of pure muscle, he makes me feel tiny. And I'm not a tiny girl. Height runs in my family, and I'm five foot ten inches and athletic.

Did his build instantly attract me? Absolutely.

But there's so much more to Crew than tanned skin, muscles, the perfect amount of blond hair dusting his chiseled face, and his dazzling smile.

Crew Riggsby is like a golden retriever puppy. He bounces around with his jovial personality. You can't help but smile when he's around.

Which is why I found myself needing to escape the tight galley kitchen. He makes me want to tear down the walls I've been trying so desperately to construct over the last few months. But then my idiot self had to go and kiss him. I practically climbed him like a tree, like a magnetic force field pulled us together.

If I thought there was a connection before, there is no doubt there is one now that our lips have touched. His tongue stoked a fire deep inside me and had me wanting to beg him to take me right there.

But I'm not ready for that. I'm so far from ready.

This year, I'm supposed to be focusing on myself. Figuring out who I am. I'm not jumping the first guy who fires up my engine.

Shaking my mind from last night's encounter, I leave the confines of my room, the very dull and very empty room. I seriously cannot wait until the movers arrive so I can slowly transform this drab apartment room into my hidden sanctuary. I have a feeling I'll be spending a lot of nights in here not to take away the bachelor vibes of the apartment. No guy wants to bring a girl back and have to explain that they live with a girl. I figure I should stay out of sight and out of mind.

Walking a few steps from my bedroom to the living room, I reach for the remote and turn on the TV. I scroll through the apps, hoping one of the guys uses the same workout app I do. It's my lucky day. I find the black icon and click it open, scrolling through the programs until I find the one I'm searching for. Gearing up for the yoga and meditation workout I like to do in the morning, I sit on my floor.

Time to nama-*slay* this day.

Locking up the front door, I jog down the stairs with my backpack and forever trusty Spalding—the basketball I carry everywhere. I realized I forgot to pack my gym duffel in the items I brought from Arizona, which means I'm juggling a basketball, a lanyard with my keys and wallet, a phone, a protein shake, and a water bottle.

Hitting the bottom of the steps, I spot a guy sitting on the wall that separates his porch from the flowerbed.

"Hey, are you Rick?" He turns toward me and nods slowly. "Cool, I'm Bret, the new tenant in eight-thirty-four. JP made it sound like you sit outside and monitor the parking lot frequently."

"Yeah, I guess you could say I do," he says, and I can see the nervous energy radiating off of him. His uneasiness makes me want to chuckle. Rick's probably afraid I'll tell him off for running his mouth to JP about how a "hottie moved in" or whatever he said.

"Listen, can you let me know if you see anyone wandering around the apartments? Like they're scoping things out or looking for someone?"

He eyes me quizzically, but he must sense the seriousness based on my tone and the expression on my face because he doesn't question me. "Yeah, I can do that."

"Thanks, Rick, I appreciate it." I give him a small smile, and that's when I see the CTU golf logo on his polo. "You golf?"

"Yeah, I'm on the CTU team."

"That's sweet. Good luck this season."

"Thanks," he calls after me as I turn and walk toward my Jeep.

Unlocking the doors, I toss my basketball onto the passenger seat and situate the rest of my things in their places. Climbing in the driver's seat, I start the engine and quickly hit the button to retract the roof and roll down the windows. It's another scorcher in Texas. You'd think I'd be used to the heat coming from Arizona, but I swear it feels hotter here.

My phone connects to the Bluetooth, and Mac Miller starts playing as I pull out of my parking spot. Something about his music gives me the mood boost I'm always searching for. It's like a hit of serotonin. Too bad he was gone way too soon.

Ten minutes later, I arrived outside of the football facility. My mouth gapes open as I stare at this insane building. The facility has a massive red brick exterior and floor-to-ceiling windows in the center. I've seen pictures, of course. Dad sent a selfie on his first day coaching, but to see it in person is remarkable.

Closing the roof and windows on my Jeep, I climb out with my large water bottle in hand, already finishing my shake on the drive over. Maybe Dad will let me use the weight room while I'm here.

Digging into the side pocket, I pulled out Grant's ID and swiped it on the keypad next to the door. If I thought the exterior was impressive, I was thoroughly wrong. This lobby would have me signing up to play for CTU in a heartbeat. Which I guess is the point.

Unlike its exterior, the lobby is modern, with a large open staircase and multiple large screens hanging from the ceiling with scrolling images. One of the screens has highlights from what looks like last season. It's cool to see players flash across the screen with the highlights.

Trophy cases line the walls underneath the screens and are filled with awards from over the years. In the center case stands the national championship trophy from last year in all its glory. It is a beautiful sight to see.

A reception desk sits off to the right, manned by a woman wearing a CTU polo, and her graying hair is perfectly coiffed. "Hi honey," she greets. "Is there something I can help you with? The facility isn't open to the public at this time."

I step up to the desk and flash her a warm smile. "Hi, my name is Bret Campbell. My dad is Derek Campbell."

Her eyes widen, and she straightens her spine. I guess tossing out that my dad is the head coach is like announcing you're part of the royal family. "The team is on the practice field right now. Do you know how to get there?"

"Honestly, I have no idea, but if you're busy, I can figure it out."

"I don't mind at all. It's easy to get lost in this building. I'm Ruth, by the way. I'm typically the one here during the day. Hank comes in around 5:30 if you're ever here in the evenings."

She leads us down a hallway where more video screens line the wall. Videos flash highlighting NFL draft picks, and I recognize a famous number thirty-one. Quinton Boyd is among the most recognizable NFL draft picks to come through CTU in recent years.

"That screen is on a loop. You'll see videos from the season, NFL combine, highlights from players playing in the NFL, and everything in between. It's fun to stand and watch."

Ruth doesn't stop to talk, she simply speaks over her shoulder as she leads the way. I assume she needs to hurry back to the desk in case anyone else comes in or tries to come in.

She leads us past the weight room, and my eyes widen at the equipment lined up. There are tons of machines, all in pristine condition.

Yeah, I want to work out in here.

"Here you go, honey," Ruth says, pausing outside the glass doors where I can see the team practicing.

My eyes widen as I take in the room. "Wow," I say, my voice filled with awe. The room before us has a full-length football field surrounded by large windows. The white ceiling somehow manages to let in lots of natural light. There's room on the side of the field for the team to stand, but there isn't much else inside.

Ruth chuckled at my slackened jaw, and what I could only imagine were stars in my eyes. "It's an incredible facility," she says, following my eyes. "The inside is temperature controlled too. We don't want any of our players passing out from the heat."

All I can do is nod. Not only am I impressed by the state-of-the-art facility, but my anxiety has crawled up my chest and settled in my throat. My nerves are all-consuming, and I'm terrified to walk through the doors.

How is my dad going to react? Is he going to be upset that I transferred? Or will he be more upset that I drove across the country by myself?

Suddenly, my need to please everyone else constantly is screaming at me to turn around and not face my problems head-on. I'm such a daddy's girl, and I can't face the fact that he may be upset with me.

I startle at the contact of Ruth's hand on my forearm. Glancing down at our contact, my eyes bounce up to find her watching me, reading me. "He'll be happy to see you, honey. Your dad talks about you all the time. Whatever it is that has you coming here, you're in the right place."

"How-how did you know?"

"Oh honey, I was young once. I recognized the hesitancy as soon as you walked in those doors. But whatever it is, it'll all work itself out. One day, you'll wake up and be sixty-six, and you won't even think about your troubled past."

"Really?"

"Really. Put on that brave smile I saw earlier and surprise your daddy." With a final pat on my forearm, Ruth leaves me alone.

Steeling my shoulders, I take one last big inhale, hold it, and slowly exhale the breath while reciting the mantras my therapist has had me practicing.

You are strong.

You are brave.

You are worthy.

You are fearless.

And I'm pushing the doors open.

The room must be entirely soundproof because the noise is the first thing that greets me. The sound of fans cheering and roaring from the sound system is painfully loud. It's like experiencing an actual game. I guess this is good practice for what they can expect in a week.

Slowly, I make my way down the wall, trying to hide. Glancing across the sea of players, ocean-green eyes find mine.

Grant.

Of course, he would be the first person I saw. Flicking my hand up, I give him a quick, subtle wave from my hip, not wanting to cause a scene.

Luck wouldn't be on my side for that.

"This is a closed practice," shouts a voice from the field, garnering everyone's attention. Heads whip in my direction, and I feel my cheeks heat from all the curiosity.

Eyes wide, I scan the group of guys. I find Grant shaking his head, his expression set in his signature stoic look. He needs to find some way to release his grumpy attitude. It wouldn't kill him to smile every once in a while. Still scanning the crowd, my eyes latch on warm-brown eyes. Crew is standing off to the side, helmet clutched in his hand as his sweat-soaked face stares at me. His expression is unreadable, which is not an expression I'm used to seeing on his face.

"Bret?" my dad's voice booms over the field. My eyes move to find him. My dad is standing diagonally from me on the sidelines, dressed in his signature coaching outfit of mid-thigh navy athletic shorts, a moisture-wicking CTU football T-shirt, and a cap.

A huge smile breaks free, and I watch him push his way through a line of players. Before I can think about it, my feet carry me to him.

"Hey, Dad," I say, barely above a whisper as my nerves struggle to strangle me. I know he can't hear me, but I'm sure he's reading my lips as he tries to figure out my body language. I could never hide anything from him. His brows furrow, and his shock morphs into concern. Yep, he's definitely reading me like a book.

The two of us meet on the field, and he pulls me in for a hug. "Bretster, what are you doing here?"

"Can't a girl come see her favorite dad?" Extending his arms, he keeps his hand on my biceps as he pulls away to get a better look at me.

"Of course you can, kiddo." His voice is lined with worry, and I hate that I'm putting more stress on him as he gears up for the start of a new football season.

Mustering up all my strength, I paste on the biggest, brightest smile I can and hope my dad can't see through me. His soft chuckle tells me he knows I'm full of shit.

Swinging his arm across my shoulders, he pulls me into him as he starts steering us toward the sidelines. "Stand over here and watch the guys, and we can chat afterward."

I squeeze the arm wrapped around my dad's back and fall in step with him. As we approach the sidelines, one of the coaches makes his way over to us.

"Sorry, Derek, I didn't realize she was your daughter."

"No worries, I didn't know she was coming." His eyes snap down to me, and there's a slight twitch in the corner of his lips. "And she decided to change her entire appearance."

My eyes widen, and I bring my lip between my teeth before looking at the field before me. As much as I try to fight the pull, I'm a weak bitch. As subtly as I can, my head turns until I find the deep brown eyes, the ones attached to my new roommate.

Life sure loves to throw a plot twist your way.

CHAPTER 4
CREW

"Riggsby, are you planning on catching a ball today, or would you like to stand on the sidelines watching everyone else?" Coach yells from behind the line where he's watching us perform.

Shaking my head, I tap my hands on my helmet, hoping to clear the funk I've found myself in. Is it not bad enough I have to share an apartment with Bret Campbell, but now she's showing up at practice? And after our awkward encounter last night.

Jogging into the huddle, I chance a quick peek at Harris, who is already watching me. His eyes bore into mine, and I can feel him telling me to focus.

Harris calls the play, and we all run to our positions on the line. My fingers twitch at my hips as I wait for the play to begin. The ball is snapped, and I take off straight down the field before faking right and going left in a diagonal route. The defenseman is on me, and I'm not able to shake him. I know the ball is in the air, and with a quick spin move, I jump into the air just as the ball hits my fingers. Curling my fingers, I pull the ball into my hands, securing the pass.

"That's what I like to see," Coach yells, and I can't hide the excitement any longer.

An excited roar rips through my chest as I break out in a bit of a celebration dance. I'm feeling it right now. Jogging back to the huddle, wide grins greet me.

Coach blows the whistle twice in quick succession, signaling the end of practice. Helmets come off as we all move toward the fifty-yard line. My gaze moves past my teammates as I search for the raven-haired beauty. She's standing alone on the sideline, dressed like she's ready to hit the gym, and all I can think about is how good her legs looked dangling from our kitchen counter.

She's the beautiful fruit dangling from the branch that is just out of reach. We've all been warned to stay away from her, but her sweet temptation is overpowering. It's a craving I feel in every fiber of my being.

"Great practice, boys," Coach praises from the center of the huddle, interrupting my thoughts about his daughter. "Be sure to check the schedule in the locker room for each position's team meetings. Tomorrow, we'll have all the details finalized for next weekend's first game in Ohio."

Our first game is quickly approaching. And as luck would have it, we are playing a team that isn't far from my hometown.

It's been a long time since I've played in my home state, and I'm excited for my family and friends to catch one of my games in person. Last week, when I talked to my mom, she said she was busy planning something big. But true to her, she wouldn't spill the secret. My mom loves nothing more than surprising her kids and making us feel special. Has she always been the one to spoil us? Absolutely.

I follow the line of my teammates as we head off of the practice field, but not before giving her one last glance. It's like she can feel the magnetic field because our eyes lock. At this moment, I can see the turmoil raging a war in her mind. Her smile doesn't shine, and her eyes are filled with something I can't quite put my finger on. Is it fear?

Who hurt her?

"Goddamn, Coach's daughter is fine as fuck," one of my teammates says inside the locker room.

Taking a deep breath, I ignore the jackass mouthing off about Coach's daughter. I'm trying so hard to keep my cool and not show my cards. That's not my style. A loud commotion sounds behind me as I reach for the sports drink bottle I left in my locker.

Looking over my shoulder, I watch Grant storm across the floor, fists clenching at his side. I make the hasty decision to step in line right behind Grant as he reaches the guy who was mouthing off. Before he can hit him, or whatever his plan, I'm sliding between the two.

Grant's eyes widen at my interference. His hand flies above my shoulder as he points to our teammate. "Don't you fucking talk about my sister like that again. I swear, I'll kick your ass if I hear anything come out of your mouth again."

Our teammate raises his hands in surrender as Grant's chest heaves.

"That goes for all of you. My sister is *off limits.*"

This altercation should clear the air if anyone has questioned his protectiveness toward his sister.

This is another reminder that I must keep my hands away from Bret Campbell.

She's. Off. Limits.

Pulling into the parking lot, Harris has to park further away from our building than usual due to a moving truck taking up most of the road. Bret's things must have arrived. Climbing out of the car, Harris and I walk toward our unit.

We step aside to let two of the movers through and overhear their conversation. "Damn, I would've killed to be those guys in college," one guy says.

"Especially with a girl who looks like that, shit," said the other.

Moving into their path, I allow my shoulder to bump into one of the douchebags. On contact, the guy stumbles to the side. "Oops, my bad," I mumble, sarcasm dripping from my words as I continue toward the steps. Harris chuckles from behind me as he follows me up the stairs.

"What the hell?" Harris questions from behind me as we land at our floor. In front of us are piles of boxes and pieces of furniture. The door to the apartment stands wide open as music blasts from inside.

"She better not get us a noise complaint," he mutters, pushing his way into the apartment.

I follow behind him and add, "It's mid-morning, Grandpa. I think she'll be fine."

Tyler Harris is one of my closest friends here at CTU. And while I value his leadership on the field, sometimes he forgets that he's a college-aged student with his constant need to parent us.

Last year, Quinton, our running back who was drafted into the NFL, took me under his wing and helped morph me into the friend group. Harris and I are in the same year, and while he's the starting quarterback, I was on rotation with the other tight ends. His leadership on and off the field has really helped me improve and take the game more seriously.

And since we are roommates this year, I'm hoping my never-too-serious personality rubs off on him so he can have some fun. The dude needs to relax. He lives a high-pressure life between being a quarterback and a kinesiology major.

If we thought the boxes outside the door were terrible, it's even worse on the inside. Cage the Elephant is blaring from a Bluetooth speaker, the patio door stands wide open, half-open boxes scatter around, and Bret is nowhere to be seen. Tyler doesn't let her lack of appearance detour him. He marches straight to her bedroom door, which is cracked open.

I'm right on his heels as he barges into her room. She's lying on a makeshift bed of blankets on her floor in what looks like a bird's nest. Headphones are in her hair, and she appears to be on a FaceTime call.

Glancing to her left, she practically jumps out of her skin at the sight of a steaming Harris.

She screams, clutching her heart and nearly dropping her phone on her face. "Yeah, Liv, I'm fine. My roommate just scared the shit out of me."

Bret tells whoever she's talking to that she'll call them back and hangs up, turning her glare toward us as she gets to her feet. "What the hell is your problem?"

"My problem is this entire apartment is full of your shit, and you're sitting on your ass with all the doors open and music blaring," Tyler shouts. Her body language shifts at his raised tone, and I instantly want to step in. It seems like anything that has to do with Bret Campbell has me wanting to step up and be a protector.

"They literally just dropped my shit off, and I was on the phone with my friend thanking her for getting everything organized and sent my way. But fuck it, maybe I'll let it sit a little while longer." Bret shrugs and goes to turn away, but Tyler's following words have her freezing.

"Or maybe you should find another place to stay." With a long sigh, Tyler pauses. "I-I don't think this is going to work out."

Fear streaks across her face. I see it, and so does Tyler. "Guys, c'mon. Let's just take a deep breath. Everyone's tired, everyone's overwhelmed."

"Sis?" Grant calls from behind us. We all turn to see him standing in our hallway, twirling his keys. He eyes the mess before him before rubbing the back of his neck. "This is a lot of stuff."

A soft chuckle escapes, but I watch Bret's facial expressions morph again. "Yeah, Liv is moving into the studio above the tattoo shop, so she sent me some stuff she no longer needs. Do you have room for some of the furniture? Or can you at least let me store some stuff in your spare bedroom until I can get it to Mom and Dad's?"

Grant looks around the space again. "Or you can just move in with me?"

"Grant," Bret groans as she places her hands on her slender hips.

With a frustrated sigh, he runs his hands through his hair. "Yeah, I'll store some of your shit, but you can't keep it there for long."

Bret's shoulders relax as I speak up. "All right, roomie, now that that is settled. Make us your bitches and tell us which boxes to haul to his truck."

Tyler groans, but the small smile that curls the end of Bret's luscious lips makes the additional workout worth it.

It's officially been forty-eight hours since Bret moved in. To say things in the apartment are tense is an understatement. JP has barely been home, but much of that is due to the shifts at the bar he's been squeezing in between practices. Tyler is still worried about the fact that Coach's daughter is living with us. And I'm trying to keep the peace.

Honestly, I'm surprised we haven't had Coach call us out on living with his daughter. There's no way he wouldn't have a conversation with us if he knew where she was living. Hell, maybe she fed him a line about where she was staying. Bret's clearly hiding something. What's one more thing? For the past day, I haven't seen her leave her room. Grant took all the extra furniture and boxes she didn't need, and since then, Bret has been avoiding everyone.

This morning, I passed her on the steps as I was coming home from practice, and she was leaving in workout clothes with her basketball. I tried looking her up on social media to see if there'd be any clues on what she's up to, but since being here, she's deactivated everything except her Facebook page. Her last post was a post she shared from the college basketball tournament.

Unable to take the tension any longer, I reach inside my pocket and pull out my cell phone.

> **Me: When will you be back?**

> **JP: Heading home now.**

> **Me: Cool. We are having a video game tourney.**

> **JP: *thumbs up emoji**

Closing out of my messaging app, I pull up the Cousin Jimmy app and order two Jimmy specials and an additional large pizza. I have no idea what kind of pizza Bret likes, but she doesn't seem like a weirdo who would put pineapple on pizza or anything.

Getting up from my bed, I head out to the quiet apartment. Flicking on the TV, I turn on Sports Center to fill the noise while I get everything set up for game night. I remember Grant telling us that he and his sister used to have epic video game battles so I know she can play.

In the kitchen, I pull down napkins and paper plates before grabbing the tote in the pantry, which is full of junk food. Is it the best thing we should be eating tonight? Nope. But desperate times call for Doritos and Red Vines.

Once the supplies are gathered, I drop them off at the coffee table before walking to Harris's room. With a quick knock, I wait for him to answer.

The door swings open, and Tyler stands scowling in front of me. "Roommate video game tournament in fifteen minutes."

Tyler goes to protest, but I stop him. "We need this. She needs this. C'mon."

With a deep sigh, I watch as he finally accepts. "I'll be right out."

I nod before going to Bret's room. I can hear music playing softly from behind her door, and my heart hurts at the fact that she feels like she needs to hide away. Rapping my knuckles against the wood grain, I wait again for my roommate to open the door. It takes her longer to come to the door, but when she finally opens the barrier separating us, my eyes widen as I take in her appearance.

My eyes trail down the woman standing before me. Her olive-tanned skin is fully displayed. Scanning up her legs, I take in the muscular calves and thighs only someone who works out possesses. I stifle the groan when my eyes lock on the tiny navy boy shorts she's wearing before my blatant perusal climbs her tight stomach. Are those abs peeking out? Her arms are folded across her chest in annoyance, but I can't help myself. I'm obsessed with her.

Her naturally plump lips are the perfect shade of pink but are set in a firm line. I trace the curves of her face with my eyes and land on the bright green eyes that magnetize mine.

"Are you done? Or would you like to take a picture?" she snaps, and I can't fight the sly smirk that spreads across my face.

"Is a picture an option?" I ask, leaning my forearm against her doorframe. I'm six foot five, and Bret stands more than half a foot shorter than me, hitting me around my chin.

She surprises me back, gently slapping my stomach as we both laugh.

"Oh my gosh, Crew. You're terrible." It's brief, but I take in the smile that warms her face. It's like a curtain falls, and her face hardens. "Did you need something?"

"Yeah, roommate video game night is starting." Just like with Harris, she starts to interrupt me, but I stop her. "Don't even, we're all doing this, and your brother has let it slip multiple times that you kick ass at gaming."

She bites down on the corner of her lip, and I know she's trying hard to keep from smiling. With an eye flutter, she turns, tossing out, "Fine. Let me change."

Stepping away from her door, I will myself to head to the living room where Tyler and JP are waiting. The apartment is bathed in a golden hue as the sun starts setting on our last night of freedom. Tomorrow starts a new school year, and this weekend is our first game. The summer went by too fast, and with all the new tension since Bret arrived, I knew we all needed a fun night. A night where we can relax, steal a couple of cars—on Grand Theft Auto, of course—and veg out before our chaotic schedules have everyone running in opposite directions.

Sinking onto my spot on the couch, I adjust the pillow underneath my elbow until I'm at the maximum level of comfort while still being able to handle the controller. Opposite me, JP tosses me a controller while Harris gets situated in the corner of the sectional. Somehow, the three of us have worked out our positions on the couch, and each of us has dubbed those positions our spots. Out of the corner of my eye, I watch Bret leave the solace of her bedroom in a pair of loose-fitting fleece shorts that resemble cutoff sweatpants and a longer sports bra.

We all must be staring at her—I know I am. I can't keep my eyes off her—because Bret pauses her steps as she quirks an eyebrow at us.

"What? You guys can parade in your shorts and no shirt. Well, so can I." She pauses, her gaze never leaving ours. "Anyone have a problem with it?"

"N-no," Harris splutters.

Bret nods while mumbling, "Good," as she takes her spot between Harris and me. Tyler stretches his hand to her, holding the extra controller. With a hesitant sigh, she takes it from him, and I watch as she brushes her fingers across his skin. She shifts awkwardly on the couch, her stiff body moving back and forth as she tries to find a comfortable position. The cushions do nothing to alleviate her uncertainty as she worries her lip between her teeth.

What I'd give to take a peek inside the mind of Bret Addison Campbell and figure out who in their right mind could hurt such a beautiful person.

"Dammit!" JP yells from the couch. "Why am I always the one being chased by the cops?"

"Maybe because you drive like you just stole a car—oh wait, you did. Right in front of them, dumbass!" Bret retorts, chomping down on a Red Vine.

Harris nudges her shoulder as he laughs at her sarcasm. We've been playing GTA for the past hour. Pizza and Doritos are long gone, and so is the ice that froze the mood in the apartment.

"Don't worry, JP, I'll hire you legal counsel when you get your ass thrown in jail," Harris adds.

Bret clicks away on her controller, her eyes never leaving the screen. "You'll be the only one able to afford legal counsel, Mr. Next Number One Draft Pick."

With a glance so he doesn't crash, Harris flashes his gaze toward the raven-haired beauty who is currently kicking our asses. Grant said she was good, but I didn't think she was this good. Maybe we should be concerned about how well she navigates all these heists.

"You mean that?"

She looks over at him, her eyes softening as a subtle, earnest smile spreads across her lips. "Of course I do. Your accuracy and arm strength are one of the best in college football. And your work ethic and football IQ are both out of the world."

The room is silent as we all stare at the bombshell sitting next to us. "What?" she muses.

"Damn, I didn't think Harris's ego could get bigger," I chime in. Harris chucks a Red Vine at my head, and it bounces off my cheek. "Ouch!"

Laughter fills the room as our attention is drawn to the game before us. The sun has fully set and the glow from the television illuminates the space, casting shadows across our faces. Sometime in the evening, someone puts on a classic rock station that plays through Bluetooth in the room.

Game night was the perfect idea. Except somewhere during the night, Harris lowered his guard, and now there seems to be quite the bond blooming between him and Bret. Don't get me wrong, I'm glad he's done being a dick about her living here, but I don't want them to have a spark.

A faint knock comes from the front door, and I bounce my head up to see if anyone else has heard it or if I am hearing things. My eyes find JP's, whose eyebrows are quirked. Pausing the game, I leave the couch and go to the front door. Without looking, I flip the lock and open the metal door.

"Coach?" I greet, eyes wide. Standing before me is a very intimidating man dressed in slacks and a button-down shirt, but the woman standing at his shoulder has me pausing. "Mrs. Campbell."

She doesn't spare me a glance as she brushes past me. Stepping aside, I watch her retreating form as Coach crosses the threshold.

"Bret Addison Campbell," she shouts as she storms down our hallway. A faint 'mom' comes from the living room.

And just like that, our peaceful evening has gone up in a burst of flames.

CHAPTER 5
Bret

"Mom?" I gasp, eyes widening as I scan the room.

Shit! Shit! Shit! This cannot be happening.

I knew I'd have to have this conversation with my mom, but I couldn't imagine having this chat like this. Both my parents are at the apartment I share with three guys. As she storms in, her anger is palpable with all of us in limited clothing.

Standing from the couch, I take tentative steps as I navigate the tight space between the couch and the coffee table. Mom stands before me as I'm rounding the edge of the sofa.

I inherited my height from both of my parents. While Dad and Grant are around the same size, my mom and I are similar in height. She is about an inch shorter than me, meaning we are practically at eye level.

Shock crosses her features as she takes in my new appearance. "What have you done to yourself?"

My shoulders sag as the disappointment weighs heavily in her voice. Looking past her shoulders, I see both Crew and Dad standing in the small opening next to our dining table. Dad's arms are folded across his chest while Crew's are tucked in the pockets of his athletic shorts. Meanwhile, I can feel the gaze of my other two roommates watching everything unfold.

"Your beautiful hair? Tattoos? And are those nipple piercings?" she whispers the last words in disgust.

Shuffling sounds from around us as an uncomfortable mood settles in the room. "Can we please have this conversation in my room?"

Mom must realize we are far from alone because her eyes bounce over my shoulder to where JP and Tyler are sitting. "Hello, boys. I'm sorry to interrupt your"—she glances around the space—"game night, but imagine my absolute shock when I was informed that my daughter drove across the country to transfer schools and didn't bother to tell her mother."

"Emily, let's take this to her room," Dad says from behind. I give him a small smile, hoping the look in my eyes portrays my thanks. He gives me a tight nod before quirking his brow at Crew.

"It's that one," Crew answers, pointing to the room directly to Dad's right as if he knew what he was asking. I guess that's part of what makes my dad a good coach, his ability to read his players and their ability to read him.

I move to step around Mom, and that's when she must see more tattoos on my skin. She sucks in a small breath, and I swear I hear her heart breaking. No words leave her mouth as she follows me into my room.

Crossing the room, I sit on the bed with my legs folded underneath me, and my back resting on the headboard as I pull a pillow into my lap. Dad leans against my dresser while my mom sits at the foot of the bed. Silence falls over the room, and I instantly feel like a little kid again.

"Mom—" I start before she cuts me off.

"Bret, what's going on with you?" The anger from earlier has disappeared, and only concern laces her voice.

Inhaling deeply, I look through my lashes and find tired, kind eyes much like my own staring back at me. "I wanted to be closer to home."

"Sweetheart," she begins, as her shoulders relax, and she reaches for my hand. "You know we want nothing more than for you to be home near us, but this isn't how you do those things. Can you imagine my shock when your father asked me how you were settling into the move while we were eating dinner with boosters?"

Warily, I turn my attention to my dad, who still hasn't moved from his spot near my dresser.

"I'm sorry you were blindsided, but I was going to tell you. It's been a busy couple of days trying to get settled."

"I can imagine. Can you also picture my shock when I walk in and find my daughter's appearance nearly completely changed?" She pauses, looking over my body. "Tattoos, Bret? You know how much I hate them."

One thing my mom despises more than anything is tattoos. She doesn't understand why anyone would want to mark their skin permanently. While I know her feelings on the matter, it's one of our generational differences. And at the end of the day, I need to live for me. Every single one of the designs I've had inked into my skin means something to me.

"Are we going to ignore the fact that I walked into this apartment to find my daughter and her roommates half naked?" Dad glances at me, his face laced with concern.

With a heavy sigh, I fiddle with the pillow resting on my lap. "Dad, please, we were only playing video games. I refuse to be fully dressed when it's socially acceptable for men to walk around without a shirt on. It's not like I was topless. Besides, you know these guys. You know they're good people."

"Yes, they are, but you're—"

"No, buts," I interrupt. "This is my home, and I refuse to be uncomfortable in it."

"Sweetie." Mom's voice cuts through the tension that is starting to build. "I think it's great you wanted to move home to be closer to us. Your room is still yours at the house, and I think it'd be best for you to come home—clearly, something isn't right in your life. Dad has to be on campus early every morning so you can commute with him. Or better yet, move into Grant's extra bedroom."

"No, absolutely not." My eyes bounce from my mom to my dad. "I appreciate the offer, I truly do, but I'm twenty years old. I'm not moving home with my parents. And there's no way in hell Grant and I are living together again. As much as I love my brother, we'd kill each other."

"Bret," Dad starts, but my glare cuts him off.

Standing from my spot on the bed, my chest heaving with the overwhelming sense that they are about to force me to move home. "I signed a lease, and this is where I want to be. I want to live here. I love you both, but right now you're treating me like a child."

"And we love you, sweetheart." Mom's voice wobbles as I watch moisture gather in her eyes.

Unlike most kids, I have an incredibly healthy relationship with my parents. Some days they're overbearing, but it's only because their love for me and my brother runs deep. At the end of the day, they only want us to succeed in life.

Are some of their views on life a little old school? Yes, but I don't fault them for that. Growing up, we were fortunate to never go without. Our life wasn't extravagant, and even though my dad has been a high-profile coach, they taught us the value of money. We moved around a lot—it was the hazard of my dad's job. But no matter where we went and the people we met, our family was the most important. It was the one thing in our life that would never change. It's why Grant and I are so close. We were each other's best friends because finding and keeping friendships was tough.

Even now, I know their concern stems from love, and if I'm being honest, I didn't put their feelings first. If I had, I would've given them the heads-up that I was transferring and moving in with a group of guys. But there are some things I need to do on my own. I need to make adult decisions and live with the consequences.

"I promise I'm okay, or at least I will be. Life is hard, and I'm learning that. But you both raised Grant and me right. We know the difference between right and wrong, good and bad. You just need to trust that the lessons you've been teaching us along the way will get us through life." I pause, giving them a small smile. "Besides, I know if I need anything, your door is always open."

"Always, Bretster." Dad crosses the room and pulls me into his chest. "I love you, kid."

"I love you, too, Dad."

Lifting his head, his voice grows louder. "And I'll kick anyone's ass who hurts my baby girl. I don't care if they're on my team or not."

My chuckle is smothered by his chest. I have no doubt the boys heard him from where they're probably eavesdropping in the living room. The walls in this place are ridiculously thin.

Mom sidles up next to us, and I pull her in for a group hug. "We know you're a big girl, but it's hard for us to wrap our heads around it sometimes. We trust you, Bret, and want you to be safe. There are days and moments when I'm hard on you, but I hope you know you don't have to keep things from us. We'll always support you, sweetheart."

Popping a kiss on my mom's cheek, I squeeze her harder.

Our hug breaks, and everyone takes a step back. Swiping underneath my eyes, I gather the tears that have started to pour over my lids.

"If you're sure you're good, we'll get out of your hair." Dad assesses my face.

With a reassuring expression, I nod. "Yeah, I'm good. I need to get ready for bed anyway. You know, big first day tomorrow."

"You've got this, Bretster," Dad muses, rubbing his hand on my head like he did when I was a kid.

I grumble under my breath, and he chuckles. Mom gives me one last hug before they turn to leave the room. I follow behind, watching the guys startle and try to make it look like they weren't eavesdropping.

With a knowing smirk, I watch as they all try to hide their grins. Harris is in my direct sight line and gives me a smirk with a wink.

"Take care of my girl, or you'll be doing burpees every practice for a month." Dad's stern coach voice comes through as he threatens my roommates.

All three of them nod and say in unison, "Yes, sir."

I watch my parents slide out the door, and with my arms crossed across my chest, I sigh. It feels like a weight has been lifted off my shoulders.

I can do this.

Junior year in a new location is what I needed.

"There she is," comes from my side. Turning, I notice all the guys are watching me.

Quirking my brow with confusion, I tilt my head. Harris speaks first. "Happy looks good on you."

I feel my cheeks heat, and the smile he just complimented me on softens. "Good night, guys."

"Night," they say in unison, and I turn my attention to Crew, who has been surprisingly quiet. Only when my eyes snap to him do I find him already watching me. "Thanks for organizing the game night. I needed it."

And with that, I turn and head to my room.

The blaring sound of my alarm wakes me from sleep. How can it possibly be morning when I feel like I just fell asleep? Last night, like every other night, was filled with restlessness, leading me to my two a.m. bowl of cereal.

Factor in the nightmares and the night before the first day of school nerves and I was wired.

Even starting my third year of college, I still experience that dreadful first day of school nerves. Something about starting a new school year, especially at a new school, sends my nerves on a wild ride. The anxiety creeps in, and my stomach flutters with the unknown.

Silencing my alarm, I toss the covers off and let out a long yawn. My back feels stiff, and I'm in desperate need to stretch out. Making my way from my room to the bathroom right outside my door, I pop my head out to the main area and notice that no one is home. I'm not surprised since the guys usually have a six o'clock practice.

Running through my morning routine quickly, I head to the living room for a few morning stretches on the workout app. After the quick ten-minute video, I find a morning meditation. Reaching for a pillow off the couch, I use it to sit on since I need to order myself a new bolster. Back in Arizona, my roommate and I shared one, or we'd use the supplies from the yoga studio we frequented.

Living with Olivia was the best decision I made for our sophomore year. She taught me the importance of self-care. Where I thought a good workout and shooting hoops was all I needed, she showed me the importance of talking to my inner self through meditation. I was the biggest skeptic and thought meditation was silly, but I'm glad to say I was wrong.

We've been taught that eating a well-balanced diet and exercising are vital parts of living a healthy lifestyle, but struggling with inner suffering makes you crazy, or we're told to just get over it. Somewhere along the way, someone deemed mental health was a taboo topic. But it couldn't be further from the truth.

I learned that the hard way.

After an extremely hard day, I found myself seconds away from a mental breakdown. The thoughts racing through my mind were thoughts no one should ever have to deal with, let alone by themselves. Olivia found me in the bathroom with a pill bottle in my hand as I stared at the mascara-streaked girl before me.

She saved me that day in more ways than one.

Mental health is a war everyone battles at some point in their life. We're not crazy. We're not making it up. We're not making a bigger deal out of something that shouldn't be.

Olivia didn't leave my side the rest of that day, and the next morning I attended my first yoga and meditation class. During the final few minutes of Savasana, I couldn't fight the sobs any longer.

Shaking my head from the thoughts of the past, I focus on the red-headed instructor on the TV. A calming melody fills the screen, and I follow her instructions on how to get myself comfortable on my pillow. It's not long, and she's instructing us to focus on the first word that comes to mind and use that word to focus on throughout the session.

Peace.

My mind instantly connects to the word peace, and it couldn't be a better word.

There's nothing more I want in life right now than that. I want to feel like my life is mine again. No more looking over my shoulder, no more nightmares controlling my sleep, no more fear. I'd give anything for calmness to enter my life and erase all the fear.

Focusing on the word peace, I allow the instructor's soft voice to infiltrate my mind while shutting out everything around me.

"The world outside can be filled with chaos, but within you is a space of tranquility. Focus on your word as you allow the distractions to melt away. Trust in your word and allow it to help navigate you through the noise."

Slowly, my shoulders start to relax as the tension evaporates. My back stands taller as I let in a long inhale before exhaling. There's a heaviness in my limbs as I ground myself while keeping my focus word at the front of my mind.

"As we come to an end of today's practice, take a moment to feel gratitude for this practice and for allowing yourself time to work on your true selves. May your word continue to bring you focus and tranquility, not just in meditation but in every moment of your life. Carry it with you, and let it be a constant reminder of the calm within."

The video ends as a sense of tranquility falls over me. I've learned that starting my morning with fifteen to twenty minutes of meditation makes all the difference.

Now let's make today my bitch.

Lunch rolls around, and my stomach is growling. Even though I left the athlete life in high school, unlike my brother, my body still prefers to be on some sort of training schedule. This means exercising and eating with a routine is a must.

Walking through the quad, I let my gaze wander over the passing students hustling to and from class. The updated buildings still have the original design and the cobblestone walkways. Central Texas University has a gorgeous campus. Even being 150 or so years old, the campus feels modern and like you've stepped back in time.

Jogging up the steps to the Union, I smile and thank the guy who held the door open for me. Inside, it's loud and chaotic, as crowds of hungry students walk through the cafeteria, searching for food or tables to sit at. With a quick scan, I realize most of the tables are occupied, but that's fine. I don't have a problem finding a bench outside to eat at.

Even if it's a hundred degrees.

Taking my time, I make sure to walk all around the cafeteria to see what my options are. There's a grill in the back with burgers, sandwiches, and fried sides. A sub station and pasta bar are on the opposite corner. In the center of the cafeteria is a stir-fry bar where you can create your own concoction, not to mention a variety of other food options throughout the space.

I'm standing in line for the sub station, minding my business, scrolling on my phone, when someone shouts, "Campbell." Seeking out the voice, a confused look passes my face, and that's when I see my brother standing a few people in front of me.

Grant gives me that typical guy head nod as he greets me. "Little sis."

"Big brother." I smile at him. I still can't get over the fact that I'm living in the same state as him.

Once I make it through the line, I turn and find Grant standing off to the side, waiting for me. He throws his arm around my shoulder and lets a sports drink rest on my shoulder. "How's your first day of class going?"

"I can't complain." Setting my food on the counter, I wait for the cashier to ring me out.

"Hi, dear." The cashier has a warm smile with an even more welcoming aura. She has a personality that can turn any bad day into a few minutes of good.

Reaching into my backpack, I search for my wallet. My fingers brush against it, but my brother's arm comes into view before I have a chance to grab my student ID, which is loaded with money.

"I've got both of ours, Tina."

The cashier smiles.

"That's sweet of you, Mr. Campbell. I thought you might be together. It's not very often I get to see a real Grant Campbell smile."

Grant chuckles. "Please, Tina, you only ever get my smiles."

I roll my eyes as my brother innocently flirts with the older cashier. "I'm Bret, his sister."

Her eyes widened, and I didn't think her smile could get more expansive. "It's so nice to meet you, Bret. I'm Tina. If you ever need anything, swing over to my line. You two enjoy your lunch."

With a smile and a thank you, I leave the line and turn toward the exit.

"Where do you think you're going?" Grant asks, pausing with his food in hand.

Pointing over my shoulder, I shrug. "I was going to try and find a bench outside."

Grant rolls his eyes at my comment, which only stirs something inside me. "You're sitting with us."

I scoff. Who does he think he is? The last time I checked, I was my own person, and if anything, the last few months have taught me that I am capable of being on my own.

"I don't need your handouts."

"Stop, come sit. It's hot as fuck outside." If there's one thing Grant and I share, it's that we both want to be in control. As the oldest, he always wanted everything to be his way or the highway. The older I got, the more I tried to push his buttons and how he constantly needed to be in control. It used to drive our mom crazy because I would continuously torment him for the fun of it.

Shoulders deflating, I turn on my heels and follow him to the tables in the back corner. Heads turn as we walk between rows of tables. No doubt everyone wants to get two seconds with the hot-shot football player. But as I'm walking past a group of guys, I make awkward eye contact and get a wink in return. I swear I hear my brother growl from in front of me. The grump typically only communicates in caveman sounds.

Large, athletic guys surround three long tables. A few girls are in the mix, most of them on the laps of guys, and I can't help scrunching my nose up at them. It's the cafeteria, not a bar, so why not sit in your seat? Scanning the table, my eyes stop on a girl with honey-blonde hair, her nose stuck in a book as if she can't even be bothered with the group of rowdy athletes. She looks like my kind of person.

"Campbell!" some of the guys greet my brother as he goes to sit in a vacant chair. There's an empty seat next to him, and he pushes the chair out for me to sit in.

With a glance, I realize it's the last one left, leaving me no choice but to take it.

"Little Campbell," the guy across from me greets.

With a tight-lipped smile, I correct him. "It's Bret."

"No, right, of course," the guy begins to backpedal his choice of name, and all I want to do is be alone. There's a chill that runs through me as anxiety creeps in. I hate being the center of attention, and right now, I can feel eyes scanning me up and down. The girls are eyeing me skeptically as they try to figure out where I fit into the group. I can't handle it. I've spent months in practical isolation, and this is all too much.

"Can you not be such a brat?"

My head snaps in the direction of my brother. "I'm not being a brat. I'm just letting him know what my name is."

"Yeah, and you were pretty fucking rude. What's going on with you? Our parents are worried. Mom called me in hysterics last night."

"Hysterics is a little dramatic, don't you think?"

"No. Their only daughter decided to move across the country. On a fucking whim without telling us." His nostrils flare, and I know from experience he's not letting up anytime soon.

"I thought you were fine with everything. Why would you help me move my things if you had a problem with me being here?" I grit the words between my teeth as I notice the attention he's bringing to us.

"I don't know, Addy. Maybe I had time to finally wrap my head around you moving here. Something has clearly happened, and I want to know what's going on with you."

"We're not doing this here."

"Then when?" he demands.

"How about fucking never? You know what, I think I'm going to go." I begin to gather my things and feel Grant eyeing me. If I'm not careful, he's going to figure out that something bigger is going on with me, and all the months of hiding and healing are going to come crashing down.

"Hey, roomie."

I startle as seats shift next to me. From the corner of my eye, I recognize the figure who sat down beside me.

"Hey, Tyler. I was just heading out." I direct my words to my brother and start to stand. Tyler's eyes lock on mine, freezing me in my seat as I feel him trying to work out what he just interrupted.

With a quick nod, he gives me a small smile. "Okay, see ya back home."

Quickly grabbing my stuff, I don't waste any time. I'm up and out of my seat, leaving that conversation behind, but the words from Tyler's mouth stick with me.

"We've got her, man."

And if anyone will crack the layers I've been building up, it'll be my roommates. Even though our game night was interrupted by my parents, the four of us were having a breakthrough. Everyone might think that I'm an idiot for moving in with three guys after my history with men, but there was something about these guys that I knew I could trust.

I only hope they don't let me down like all the others.

Slamming my backpack down on the kitchen table, I have never felt more relieved to be home in my apartment. Today has been the first day of hell. Navigating campus was a challenge. I managed to get myself lost and turned around not once, not twice, but three times. Not to mention, I had to explain my name no less than ten different times.

I'm exhausted and starving. I should have grabbed something on campus because I'm a horrible cook. I feel bad for my future husband because I'm definitely not one of those women where cooking comes naturally.

"Hey." I startle with a small scream at the voice behind me. "Shit, Bret. I thought you heard me open my door."

"I was lost in my head." The words tumble from my lips sheepishly.

Tyler's eyes never leave mine as he closes the distance between us. My heart races, and my breathing stutters as he gets near.

He's not him. He's not him, Bret. You're safe.

Tyler's arms wrap around my shoulders as he pulls me into him. My arms dangle at my side as my face presses into his shoulder. His hand rubs circles on my back as his fingertips graze the skin exposed by my tank top.

"What's this for?" I question, my face pressed into his collarbone.

"You look like you needed a hug." The softness in his voice is enough to break me. Before I can stop them, moisture is gathering and spilling from my eyes. Tears coat my cheeks, and I work to keep in the sob that is so desperate to break free.

The truth is, I needed that hug. I have needed strong arms wrapped around me for weeks. There's no doubt I'm strong enough to handle anything life throws at me, but there's something about trusting someone else to carry the load, even if it's brief.

And while the feeling of being in Tyler's arms is everything I need at that moment, there's a fleeting thought that he's not whose arms I'm desperate to have wrapped around me.

CHAPTER 6
CREW

"Hey, sweetie," my mom's voice comes through the phone as I place it against my shoulder to unlock the door to the apartment.

Pushing open the door, I'm met with a savory scent from the kitchen. Walking forward, I pause in the doorway. Harris and Bret are in the kitchen. She's sitting on the counter, towel in hand, as she dries the dishes Harris hands her. There's almost a domestic vibe coming from the two of them. I won't lie and say that jealousy doesn't course through my veins.

"Crew, honey." Mom's voice pulls my attention away from the kitchen and back to the call.

"I'm here, Mom. Sorry, I'm just getting in from classes." My voice interrupts the two in the kitchen.

Bret's head snaps up as a blush creeps up her cheeks. Her emerald eyes warm and soften as she spreads a sheepish smile across her pouty lips. The same lips I can't stop thinking about. They are soft and pillowy. Luscious and full. A natural pout that leaves everything about her alluring. As I'm busy watching the vixen in the kitchen, Harris gives me a nod in greeting, snapping my attention away from her.

Moving from the doorway, I step into my room, closing the door behind me as I toss my backpack on my desk chair. My navy bedding is tossed haphazardly across my king-sized bed. What's the point in making my bed when I'm only going to sleep in it later?

"How was the first day of class? Are you getting excited for football season?"

"Classes were fine. It's going to be a busy semester, but I'm used to it now." Laying across my bed, I rest my head against my bent arm, keeping me propped up. "We have a new roommate this year."

"Oh, that's great, sweetie. I'm glad you could find someone to fill the empty room." Mom's voice is cheery, but if I listen closely, I can hear the hint of exhaustion she is trying to hide from us kids. "Is this young man on the football team too?"

I chuckle. "No, Mom. She is not on the football team."

"Crew Ryan Riggsby, a *girl* is living with you? Who is she? When did she move in? These are things a mother should know."

I chuckle at her onslaught of questions.

"This isn't funny, mister."

"I mean, it's a little funny, Mom." Images of Bret flood my brain as I try to find the right words to describe her to my mother. Where do I even begin? It doesn't matter what I say to Mom. She's going to read me like a book. It's the one gift she's always had. Dad would come down on punishments, but Mom always wanted to know the root cause of everything. She started picking up our ticks and cues for when we were lying when we had crushes, and everything in between.

"Where do I even start, Mom? Her name is Bret. She transferred from the University of Arizona and arrived on Sunday. We all thought we were getting another guy as a roommate."

Mom's soft chuckle fills the other end of the line. "With a name like Bret, I can see where there's confusion."

"Yeah, it was quite the shock. But she's really cool. She kicked our asses in Grand Theft Auto the other night, which was a fun surprise.

She's captivating with her love for sports and action movies and her unique sense of humor. It's like she's one of us but a girl."

"You sound smitten, my boy."

"Nah, it can't be like that."

"And why not? Because you're roommates? That's foolish."

"It's not just that. It would be awkward in the apartment if we were to pick up something and it didn't work out. The guys would be stuck in the middle. She's also a Campbell, as in Coach's daughter and Grant's sister."

"The heart wants what the heart wants, Crew. Don't forget that."

"So you've told me before. She's hiding something. I can feel it."

"That may be the case, and if she is, you should be there when those walls come crumbling down. Believe me, sweet boy, she will need someone strong if her world implodes. Be the gentleman your father and I raised."

"Always, Mom. Now tell me, is Grandpa still working himself to the bone?"

"You know that man will never settle down. Just this morning, he was running through the yard trying to gather the chickens when the rooster caught sight of him. That damn bird chased him all over the yard." A loud laugh bursts from me as a knock sounds on the other side of the door. I call out for whoever it is to enter.

Onyx locks contrast against the white-painted door as Bret pops her head into my room. My pulse thumps as my heart races whenever I'm in her presence.

"Hey." Her soft voice fills the space. "Sorry to bother you, but we have dinner ready whenever you are."

"Thanks, Bret. I'll be out shortly."

"Bret?" my mom's voice practically shouts from her end. Bret's eyes widen as she must hear my mom call her name. "Switch me to FaceTime, Crew."

"Mom, I don't think now is the best time."

Bret's head shakes as she waves her hands, mouthing no.

Ringing in my ear has me pulling away the phone to see the Face-Time request from my mom. Tipping my head against the headboard, I accept her call. "Hi, my handsome boy. As much as I love looking at my son, turn me around so I can meet your new roommate."

Doing as she requests, I turn the phone and watch Bret's face morph into shock before she runs her fingers through her lengthy black hair.

"Oh my goodness, Crew, she's stunning."

"Th-thank you, Mrs. Riggsby," Bret replies, fumbling over her words as she strides closer to the bed. Sliding over, I make room for Bret to sit on the bed next to me. She does, and what she does next surprises me even more. Instead of sitting on the edge of the bed, she brings her body closer to mine so that we are flush. Our backs against the headboard so my mom can see both of us in the frame.

Mom watches as Bret gets comfortable, moisture glistening in her eyes. I swear she better not cry right now. I love my mother, but she's an emotional woman. I've seen her cry more than imaginable. If she's feeling uneasy, she cries. If she's happy, she cries. If she's sad, she cries. If she's overwhelmed, you might as well forget it, as she'll find herself shedding all the tears until she can't breathe.

"Honey, call me Nora. Mrs. Riggsby is my mother-in-law."

"It's nice to meet you, Nora. You've raised a good one over here." Bret nudges her shoulder against mine as she smiles up at me.

"Well, aren't you a sweetheart? It was really nice to meet you, too. Now, you both go on and enjoy your night. Bret, I hope to meet you next weekend at the game. Crew, call your mother more, and don't forget what we discussed." She gives me a pointed look before softening her gaze on Bret.

Bret smiles at the camera and nods while I roll my eyes. "Yes, Mom, I'll call you more. Love you."

"Love you too, sweets." Hanging up on the call, I toss my phone before rolling my head to face Bret. Only by doing that, it brings our faces even closer together. My eyes find those full lips. Her bottom lip is more plump than the top. The perfect size to quickly suck into my mouth like I did that first night when she arrived.

It's her that moves away first. Her hand slaps my thigh as she stands. "C'mon, let's go eat dinner before Tyler gets cranky or we let the food go bad."

Following Bret to the dining table, Harris placed all the food out and was scrolling on his phone, waiting for us. "It's about time, assholes. I didn't make all this food for it to go cold."

"Yeah, yeah, yeah. My mom wanted to meet the new roomie." Sitting in my seat, I reach for a roll, which is still warm.

"How's Mama Riggs?" Harris reaches for a steak before passing the platter to Bret.

"She's good." Taking a bite, I let the warmth of the buttery pastry melt against my tongue. Hawaiian rolls are the superior roll. Reaching for the asparagus, I pause midair. "Wait, did Bret make anything?"

Her vibrant eyes shimmer as she rolls them. But it's Harris who speaks as he cuts his medium-rare steak. "She put the asparagus in the oven."

I nod. Okay, that should be safe. Her brother has told me on more than one occasion that Bret is the worst cook and no one eats anything she prepares. It's either burned, disgustingly bland, or highly over seasoned. Spearing a spear of asparagus with my fork, I shove the whole thing into my mouth. As soon as the spear hits my tongue, I'm instantly regretting my decision. Quickly chewing the green vegetable, I try to rush the process and swallow the disgusting thing in my mouth.

As Harris reaches for the asparagus, I knock his fork out of the way and shovel more spears onto my plate. "Jesus, Crew."

"So good," I mumble around the disgusting, oversalted vegetable.

Bret eyes me skeptically, but I just smile.

She stands from her chair and heads into the kitchen. Meanwhile, Harris is eyeing me as I work the chewed food down my throat and immediately reach for my water.

"What's with you?"

"It's awful," I whisper. "Don't let her salt anything."

He shakes his head. "You've got it so bad."

"Shut up," I mutter, cutting into the steak as Bret returns.

A look of disgust is plastered onto her face, and she gives me a soft punch in the shoulder as she walks by. "You jerk! The asparagus is disgusting!"

Laughter breaks out around us as she sags in her chair. "I can't believe you ate that and said it was good."

"I didn't want to hurt your feelings."

"No, you thought you'd risk a stroke by spiking your blood pressure with all that salt. It's like drinking straight from the ocean." She shivers, and I lift a shoulder.

CHAPTER 7
Bret

A little over a week has passed since I moved to Texas. It still feels a little surreal that this is my life now. The guys have been busy with football to the point where I never see them. But it's okay. I didn't move here to be dependent on anyone. I moved here for a fresh start and to rediscover myself.

This is why I stare up at the Central Texas Athletic Center. The large brick building is home to the university's gym, sports, and recreational facilities for students. The main entrance is for those attending sporting events, graduations, concerts, and other events at the main gymnasium. The back of the building is the entrance for students. This is where all the recreational activities take place. However, the main wellness center with weights and cardio machines is inside the Union.

Climbing the stairs, I swipe my ID card and enter the student entrance. It's a generic space with a long, minimalist hallway with signs directing you to whichever space you want. A large bulletin board hangs underneath a TV where flyers are placed. Walking toward the board, I notice a signup sheet for intramural basketball, which is precisely what I'm looking for.

I might have hung up my shoes on playing competitively, but the love for the game still runs deep. There's a number listed to send a text to sign up, which I quickly do as I make my way down the hall to the open gym.

The sounds of shoes squeaking against the polished hardwood floor and dribbling basketballs echo off the walls, filling the space with a cacophony of rhythms that is my version of a symphony.

Spalding and I walk into the doorway as I take in the massive gym made up of four basketball courts with a walking track suspended in the air above the courts. Only one of the courts is occupied by a group of guys playing two-on-two. Not wanting to be bothered, I head to the vacant court in the far corner.

Placing the few items I brought with me on the bleachers, I lean down to lace my well-loved basketball shoes before tightening the ankle strap. A tingle runs through my veins; it's the same feeling I always get when I'm in a gym. With the determination to pour my sweat out onto the hardwood, I let the thrill pulse through my veins. Some people get the rush of adrenaline by jumping out of planes or riding bulls. I feel it between the painted lines—the need to push my body to the limit and test my endurance.

With a flick of my thumb, my workout playlist begins with the thrumming beat of a popular hip-hop song whose beat matches the pulsating in my veins.

Jogging onto the court, I start with a few warm-ups, allowing my muscles to push and pull in that delicious feeling one can only feel when stretching. Each movement is slow and deliberate as I focus on warming up my cold muscles to prevent any sort of injury. I've had my fair share of strained muscles, and I'm not looking for a new ache right now.

Once my body feels like it's ready for the battle I'm going to put her through, I stand on the out-of-bounds line underneath one of the baskets as I prepare for my first cardio session. Jogging to each end of the court, I slowly build up my pace before I sprint each line as I reach down and touch the foul line, half-court line, opposite foul line, opposite end line before returning. The sound of my shoes squeaking mixes with my music in a perfect melody that only spurs my confidence to run faster and be more precise with my movements.

Sweat pours down my face as my ponytail swishes with each movement. With my heart rate pounding and breathing heavy, I move on to the next challenge of my workout. Starting at the lower block, I shoot ten baskets before moving to the next hash mark. I continue the routine until I make my way around to the opposite block. The bumpy grip has been worn off my trusty Spalding basketball, but my movements are still as fluid as ever. Each shot is simple as I let the ball roll off the tips of my fingers. The sound of the net swishing is drowned out by my music, but I can still envision the sound filling my ears.

Shot after shot, I find my rhythm and move to the three-point line, where I start in the corner and make my way around just like I did with the key. The added distance is a welcome challenge as I find my confidence to hit shot after shot like I did when I played the shooting guard position from junior high through high school. After each shot, I jog to the net to retrieve the basketball before returning to the line.

Muscle memory takes over, and I relish how my body remembers the routine of lining my fingers up to my sweet spot as I bend my knees and allow my ankles to work their magic by jumping off the floor. My arms hang perfectly as the ball arches in the air.

Swish. Over and over again.

As I make my way around the arc, the stresses of life start to slip away. My mind evaporates everything that is causing me problems. No thoughts of my parents or brother. No thoughts of Crew and the way his lips felt against mine. No thoughts of my haunted past that had me running nine hundred miles. Only the strain of my muscles and the thrill of hitting shot after shot fill my mind.

Basketball has always been my sanctuary, my safe space. A place where I can blast music, clear my mind, and reconnect with myself. It's different from the meditation I do every morning. Meditation allows me to sit in silence before the day's chaos takes over. It's a time to surround myself with a calm environment where I connect with my inner self as I sift through my thoughts and emotions. I can let go of chaos and noise as I find clarity in the moments of stillness. Meditation is my mind's way of hitting the reset button to find a sense of peace and strength that I carry with me throughout the day.

But basketball? Now, that's a whole different kind of therapy. As soon as I lace up my sneakers and step out on the court, I'm immediately transported to my oasis. The instant I feel the smooth leather as I dribble the ball, everything else melts away. The game's energy, the rhythmic thud of the basketball hitting the floor, and the swish of the net—all of it grounds me. It's an active form of therapy that allows me to channel as much energy as I need to express my feelings and release tension through physical activity.

Before I know it, an hour and a half passes as my phone's alarm alerts me through my headphones, nearly giving me a heart attack. My arms feel like jelly as I return to the bleachers to gather my things.

I'm halfway to my Jeep when someone behind me yells out, "Yo! Nice moves back there."

Turning around, I take in the two guys coming out of the building. I recognize them as two of the four from the opposite court. Much like every guy I seem to come into contact with at CTU, these two are tall—a few inches taller than me—with athletic builds. Was this a prerequisite for getting into CTU?

"Thanks!" I say with a jerk of my head.

"You looking for an intramural team to play on this fall?" the taller of the two asks. His dark ebony skin glistens in the sun from the sheen of sweat he accumulated in his game of two on two.

Brushing a loose strand of hair out of my face, I hitch Spalding higher on my hip as I cradle it between my elbow and hip. "Yeah, actually, I just texted the number on the board."

"Cool. My buddy is in charge of setting the schedule up. If it's cool with you, we could use another player on our team."

"Count me in." The guys move closer and the slightest surge of uneasiness washes over me. I hate that I have this reaction to strangers. It has nothing to do with these two guys, it's the fact that trauma surges whenever I'm alone.

"I'm Kyrie, and this is Dylan. How have we not seen you in the gym before? Your shooting skills are unreal."

"Thanks, I'm Bret. I transferred in this semester."

Dylan stretches his phone toward me. "Care if we grab your number?"

"No problem." Taking the phone from him, I type in my number and send myself a text. "I sent myself a text, so I have yours too. I've gotta get to class, but thanks for inviting me to join your team."

"See ya around, Bret." As I slide into the driver's seat, the guys wave and go their separate ways.

Once the door is shut and locked, I reach for my gym bag and pull out a case of cleansing wipes. Rubbing the damp fabric down my arms and armpits, I give myself a quick cloth bath before applying fresh deodorant. The clean fragrance from my extra-strength deodorant fills the space.

Reaching for the gearshift, my phone dinging has me pausing. Pulling it out of the cup holder, I smile at the name across the screen.

Liv: I just tattooed a butterfly on some girl and now I'm depressed.

Liv: I miss you, bitch.

Me: I miss your face.

Liv: How's life in Texas? Boring and miserable?

Me: Totally. I mean, I'm living with three hot guys. It's downright miserable.

Liv: Such a horrible life.

Me: They are great to look at, especially when they cook shirtless, but it's not like living with you.

Liv: I hear you. Maybe I should come for one of your dad's games. Check out Daddy Campbell and these men in your life.

Me: Gross. Don't call him that.

Me: But let's plan something. Maybe for Halloween?

Liv: My favorite holiday. Count me in.

Liv: Gotta run. My next client is here.

Shaking my head, I toss my phone back in its designated cup holder as I shift the car into drive and head toward campus.

One thing I've learned in my twenty years of life is how hard it is to make friends, especially growing up the way that I did. We moved whenever Dad got the call that something bigger was taking shape. I never resented him for that because I think it's essential for parents to keep chasing their dreams even after having kids. The one thing that always sucked about moving was leaving behind friends and the struggle to make new ones.

But when I arrived in Arizona, Liv was the first person I met in our dorm. She was on the same floor as me, and we had roommates we didn't relate to. Which meant the two of us became fast friends. Her unique personality encouraged me to get out of my comfort zone. She hung out with people who I wouldn't have necessarily gravitated toward. They were more of the loners who smoked pot in the quad with their skateboards tucked under their arms. There isn't anything wrong with the skater lifestyle. I wasn't accustomed to it, especially living in the Midwest, where the farm boys constantly surrounded me.

Liv taught me how to see color in a black-and-white world, how to get out of my shell, and how to experience life. Best of all, she taught me what it was like to have a real, genuine friend—the kind of friend who picks you up off the bathroom floor and cries with you.

Olivia Reed is one of the good ones, and I can't wait to introduce her to my people.

It's a little after seven when I'm leaving my last class for the day. The campus is blanketed in beautiful golden hues as the sun slowly descends for the night. My body is starting to feel it in my muscles from today's gym session. It's been a few weeks since I've been able to hit the court as hard as I did today. While it felt good at the moment, my body is a little angry with me.

Entering the glass doors of the Union, I notice the groups of students sitting around the tables for dinner. Deciding not to take my chances at home after last week's disaster meal, where I completely screwed up the asparagus, I follow the line of students into the cafeteria. I've spent the last couple of days trying different options, and I've found that the sub station has the best chicken, bacon, and ranch sub.

Once my order is placed, I grab a bottle of Coke from the refrigerator while I wait for my sub. Scanning the people around me, uneasiness washes over me, causing the hair on the back of my neck to stand up. Roaming the faces again, no one with ice-blue eyes catches my attention.

You're safe. He's not here.

"Campbell," the worker calls, interrupting my internal panic. With shaky hands, I reach for the paper-wrapped sub and thank him.

Moving swiftly, I make my way through the checkout line and start to hastily walk down the hallway toward the central area of the Union. As I turn the corner, I run into a muscular chest. Letting out an oof, hands grab my shoulders to steady me.

"Bret?"

Looking up, I find deep emerald eyes that mirror mine. "Dad?"

"Hey, kiddo, what's got you in a hurry?"

Steadying my breath, I paste on a smile. "I'm starving and ready to head home."

His appraising eyes scour over me before he wraps an arm around my shoulder and moves next to me. "Great, I'll walk you to your car. Have you talked to your mom today?"

"Not yet. I saw she texted me a little bit ago, but I've been in back-to-back classes."

"How are you settling in?"

"I really like it here. I can see why you and Grant decided to make this university your home."

"Good, I'm glad you're liking it too. How's the roommate situation?" He grumbles the last part of that question. The guys told me he's been giving them extra shit at practice. It's harmless, but he's making it a point to ensure they're on their best behavior. Which is absurd considering the three I'm living with are probably the best three on the team, excluding Grant.

"Dad, everything is fine."

"Honey, I love you, but you're a terrible liar." He squeezes my shoulder as we walk out of the Union and follow the sidewalk leading us to the parking lot.

"I mean with the guys. The roommate situation is good, and everything else will work itself out. I promise. A girl needs a little room to breathe between you and Grant and now the guys."

"As long as you promise to come to one of us if you really do need some help. No matter how old you are, I'll always be here for you, Bret."

"I know, Dad."

"Okay, good. Now that we have that settled, I want to talk to you about this weekend."

Quirking a brow, I look up at him. "I want you to come with the team to Ohio. Your mother is flying with us, and now that you're here, I want you to join us, too."

"Are you sure?"

"Of course I'm sure. I wouldn't have asked you if I wasn't. Plus, we have a surprise for the team."

"Spill!"

He chuckles. "Not a chance. You live with my team—ew, I didn't like that coming out of my mouth—but no, I can't risk them finding out. Not until we land in Ohio."

"Fine, fine. Keep your secrets. I didn't want to know anyway."

"Liar. Seriously, you would think years of teenage angst would have made you a better liar."

"What can I say? I hate lying to my old man."

He gasps, and it's my turn to chuckle. "Who are you calling old?"

"I mean, you are looking a little gray, Dad."

"It's stress from dealing with two children plus an additional hundred and fifty college kids who act more like children than the adults they're supposed to be."

"Whatever you say, Dad." Reaching into my pocket, I pull out my fob. The Jeep's headlights blink as the doors unlock.

Before I have a chance to open my driver's side door, I rotate until I'm pulling my dad in for a giant hug. His arms instinctively wrap around me as I'm smashed into his front. Since our height isn't that far off, my nose smashes into the crook of his neck, where I inhale his sweet, citrusy scent from the Old Spice aftershave he's used all my life. He squeezes me tight before pulling away.

"I love you, Bretster."

"I love you, too, Dad."

Dad reaches past me and opens the door. He waits as I toss my backpack into the back seat before climbing inside. Sitting my sub on the passenger seat and my bottle of Coke in the cup holder, I start the engine.

"Spalding still treating you well? You know I can always get you a new one."

I gasp. "Don't speak such cruel things. Spalding is perfect."

I've had this basketball since my freshman year of high school. It's one my dad bought me for my birthday right before I started playing high school ball, where I was one of three freshmen to make varsity. This basketball has seen all the hours in the gym where I've worked my butt off to perfect my jump shot and where I'd shoot free throw after free throw until I couldn't lift my arms. I can't imagine heading to the gym without my trusty sidekick.

The Bluetooth connection activates, and the last song I listened to starts blaring from my speakers, interrupting my train of thought and startling me back into the present.

Dad shakes his head. No matter how often he's tried to tell me that I need to lower the volume before turning off my car, I've never listened. I'm always in too big of a hurry and want to jam out for as long as I can.

"Drive safe, and I'll see you later this weekend on our flight to Ohio."

I wave goodbye as Dad shuts the door before stepping away and waving back.

Shifting into reverse, I back out of my spot and tap the horn twice before sliding into drive.

What kind of surprise could my dad possibly be planning?

CHAPTER 8
CREW

❜Twas the night before we traveled to our first game of the season, and all through the apartment, not a person stirred as everyone was tucked in their beds as visions of touchdowns danced in their heads.

Oh, who am I kidding?

The rest of the apartment might be tucked soundly in their beds, but my nerves have allowed sleep to evade me as I've spent the last three hours tossing and turning. Whenever I think I'm about to drift off into a peaceful slumber, visions of me fumbling the ball come crashing into my head. As if that wasn't bad enough, the visions switch to me allowing the ball to slip through my fingers and into my defenders for an interception.

Letting out a deep exhale, I pull the string on my lamp. The room cascades in a warm glow before I reach for my phone, which is plugged in on my nightstand. It's nearing one a.m., and a new text message sent five minutes ago is waiting on me. It's from Brynn Wilder. She's Quinton Boyd's girlfriend—well, wife. I guess that makes her Brynn Boyd, but I haven't switched her name in my contacts. The two decided to elope with a surprise wedding last spring before Q was drafted into the NFL. It would be an understatement to say it was quite a shock to all of us back at CTU.

Since sleep is evading me, I swipe open her message. The bright light from the screen illuminates the room, and I squint to read her text.

Brynn Wilder: Hey, family dinner is on Sunday night at our house! Keep me updated on the team's travel schedule, and we will have dinner waiting! Oh, and bring Bret! Can't believe I haven't run into that hottie on campus yet. Good luck, Riggsby!

Me: Thanks, Brynn. I'll keep you posted, and we'll be there.

Tossing my phone on my comforter, I fling the navy bedspread off my boxer-clad body and reach for my sketchbook to distract me. Sliding out my pencil from the sketchbook spirals, I flip the pages, passing over drawings until I find a blank page. Hopefully, the movements of lead against the crisp pages will help calm my nerves.

Bringing my legs up until they are bent in front of me, I rest the notepad against my thighs and adjust my body until I'm sitting up comfortably. My grip on the pencil is loose as I let my mind melt away as I conjure up an image to draw. The pencil almost moves on its own accord as the rhythmic sounds of the lead against the paper create a soothing, scratching sound.

Within minutes, I begin losing myself in the details—the sharpness of the beak, the strength of its wings, and the freedom of its flight. I chuckle as I realize the image my mind conjured is no other than an eagle soaring through the air. Clearly, I cannot escape the call of the eagle.

Growing up, when my dad had some free time in his day, which wasn't common since life on the farm was demanding, we would load the small Jon boat onto the trailer and head to the lake. We'd leave the boat ramp, and the two of us would navigate the aluminum boat down a channel to search out eagles. Once he realized I enjoyed sketching, he encouraged me to bring my sketchpad and pencil to draw the wildlife we encountered.

He was always so proud of my drawings. Once I got into middle school, he pushed me to enter the school's art fair. After winning my school's art fair and then the district's, Dad was the first person to say, "I told you so" when I questioned if I had what it takes. No matter how much I loved drawing, I knew pursuing it in any way would either not pay the bills or would take the enjoyment out of it. This is why I find myself sketching wildlife drawings as a guilty pleasure hobby.

Bringing my attention back to the image on the paper, I focus on the fierce expression I'm creating with each stroke as I bring the eagle to life. The eyes show a menacing gaze, while the wings are powerful with layers of feathers. Large wings showcase the eagle's gracefulness as it soars through the sky.

Minutes seem to turn into hours as time passes before my eyes. A soft knock and my door widening catches my attention, startling me. My heart races in surprise and then quickly races for another reason.

"Hey." Her warm voice fills the quiet room. "I saw your light and thought I'd check on you."

"Couldn't sleep."

Nibbling on her bottom lip, I take the opportunity to scan the goddess in front of me. She's dressed in an oversized black tee with a skull on the front and the name "Machine Gun Kelly" in pink font. Her long legs are on full display, and her jet-black hair is on the top of her head in a messy bun.

"Want some company?"

Shuffling over, I pat the spot next to me, inviting her into my space. She tentatively places one foot in front of the other as she closes the door behind her. She scans the walls as her feet carry her toward my gaze. With soft touches, her fingers trail across the surfaces she passes. The first thing that catches her eye is my framed jersey on the wall.

"How did I not notice this the other day?" Amusement laces her voice as she takes in my signed jersey. It's from a fan-favorite tight end who is now retired but once played for a popular northeastern NFL team.

"You were too busy meeting my mom."

"She's so cute."

"Don't tell her that. You'll become her favorite, and I'll be booted to the curb." Bret flashes me a warm smile over her shoulder.

"Don't worry, your spot is safe, Mama's Boy." She points to the jersey. "Was he your favorite tight end?"

"He was. He was incredible on the field and his personality was the best—the things he would say and do. I loved watching him. My parents—they, uh…" I pause, rubbing my hand down the back of my neck. "They got me the signed jersey for Christmas. It was the last Christmas I had with my dad."

Her beautiful smile morphs into sadness, and I hate that I was the cause of it. "Oh my gosh, Crew, I had no idea." Her movements are rushed as she climbs into bed beside me and flings her arms around my shoulders. The embrace she wraps me up in has her clean fragrance mixing with the cinnamon sugar of her favorite late-night treat, enveloping my senses.

Reluctantly, she pulls away, and her emerald-green eyes stare back at me, a soft sheen covering them. "It's okay, Rebel. It happened a long time ago."

"Rebel?"

"Yeah, your rebellious streak looks good on you, Bret."

She slides away from me, creating space between us, as her cheeks pinken. I instantly hate the space she made between us. "You know, I kind of like that nickname."

Moving my sketchbook from my lap, I lean over Bret to place it on my nightstand. Her hand reaches out and stops me. "Crew, did you draw this?"

It's my turn to blush as I hold the notepad before me. "Yeah, I couldn't sleep, so I thought I'd sketch for a bit and get my mind off the game."

"May I?" she asks, reaching her hand out.

I hand her the sketchbook and watch her analyze the eagle. "This is incredible. I had no idea you drew."

"It's nothing." A hand slaps my stomach as her jaw drops.

"*It's nothing*," she mocks. "That's bullshit, and you know it. This literally looks like a black-and-white photograph."

Closing the cover, she sets it on the table before turning to face me. Rocking back and forth, she lowers until her head is resting on her hands on my pillow. "Tell me more about *the* Crew Riggsby, the legendary tight end on the CTU Eagles."

Mirroring her, I slide until our bodies are at the same level. "What do you want to know, Rebel?"

She hums, tapping her finger against her chin. "Tell me about your family. Are you excited to see your mom at the game this weekend?"

"Yes, I'm very excited to see my mom. As you pointed out, I'm a mama's boy. Well, to be honest, everyone is a fan of my mom. She's the sweetest, most thoughtful person. But I'm the middle child of three. All of us are four years apart. Jett, my older brother—"

"Wait," Bret interrupts. "Crew? Jett? I'm sensing some kind of military vibes with your names."

"Yeah," I answer with a chuckle. "My dad was in the Air Force. He served for twelve years and loved his unit. I'm just glad he didn't name us Goose, Iceman, or even Maverick."

Bret's laughter fills the space at my *Top Gun* reference. The sound of her laugh is intoxicating. I could get drunk on it alone.

"Okay, do you have, like, a sister named Delta?"

"Ha. Ha. No, my sister's name is—" I pause and let the moment build. "Saylor."

"Jett, Crew, and Saylor, cute." She smiles as she shifts closer to me. "How old is your sister then?"

"Saylor is sixteen, and she's going through a bit of a rebellious stage. Like a pretty raven-haired girl I know." I wink. "But luckily for my mom, she had to deal with Jett. He gave my parents a major run for their money. So much so, my dad left him with an ultimatum to either get his shit in check or join the Air Force. He joined the Army to piss my dad off. Since he enlisted, he hasn't been home except for the occasional break. It's hard on my mom, but she handles it well."

"Your mom is a saint."

"You have no idea."

The gap between us has slowly disappeared to the point where we are almost touching. Silence falls over us as I stare at her emerald eyes, I can't help but trace the golden hues that mix with the forest green swirls. Her eyes are mesmerizing.

"What, uh, what happened to your dad?"

Clearing my throat as the emotion builds, I stare at her eyes and allow the green to calm me. "He was in a farming accident. It was the summer after Jett graduated high school. We were moving equipment, and a distracted driver forced him off the road."

"Oh my god." Her voice is a whisper as I watch tears form in her eyes. Dad's accident was a tragedy and one that could have easily been avoided if only people would respect farmers on the road.

Fingertips trail the stubble lining my chin, and I fight the urge to kiss her. But I don't have to fight the moment for long. Bret's eyes bounce between mine, and I can feel her hesitation. Something is holding her back from kissing me, and I think it runs more deeply than the fact I'm her dad's player.

"Rebel," I say her nickname in a whispered plea. Her eyes widen, and I see the moment she accepts the pull between us.

Her soft touch trails up my jawline, under my ear, until her hand is gripping the back of my head. With a slight tug on my blonde hair, she's erasing the gap between us as my heart rate spikes. Her plump lips find mine, and I melt into our connection as her body sags in relief. Everything about this kiss feels right. Having Bret in my bed feels like a dream, and in one minute, I'm going to wake up just like all of the other times I've imagined this scenario.

But it's not a dream as I feel Bret's warm, wet tongue flick against the seam of my lips. Granting her the access she desires, I wrap my arm around her back and pull her on top of me as our tongues tangle. Her legs land on either side of my naked torso. The only thing separating us is our underwear. She feels so good on my lap.

So *fucking* good.

I have no idea what we are doing, but I know I don't want to stop—not now, not ever.

Her teeth graze my lip as she bites down, pulling my bottom lip. My lip pops out of her mouth as she rides my erection through our clothes. We're making out and dry-humping like horny teenagers.

She reaches over and flicks the lamp off cascading us in darkness. "I don't want anyone to be alerted if someone comes out of their room."

I hum in understanding as I run my hands up her back, beneath her oversized tee, as I move them toward her front. Cupping her perky tits in my hands, I squeeze gently as I pull them toward me. Brushing my thumbs against her peaks, I flick the metal piercings. I've never been with a woman with nipple piercings, and it's so fucking hot.

Our lips separate as she lets out a long moan, her head tilting toward the ceiling. I'm quickly smashing my mouth against hers to quiet her noises. As much as I want to hear her moans, I can't let the guys know that we're in here together. Bret's the first to break the kiss—pieces of her hair have escaped her messy bun, framing her face as her chest heaves.

"Of course, I felt something Crew. I haven't gotten you out of my head, but we can't do this. We can't be more than roommates."

Finally, she answered the question I had asked her on her first night here. It's the answer I've been desperate to hear, but then she had to add a "but." Of course, I understand her reasoning, but it doesn't mean I have to like it. My ego feels like a deflated balloon.

"How can you say that when we fit together so well? You've spent the last ten minutes riding my dick while your tongue was down my throat."

Her shoulders sag, and I hate that she's feeling this turmoil. "Tonight is a one-time thing. It has to be."

"So, if you're saying tonight can never happen again, I don't want you to leave here without coming first."

"One time, Crew." The words no sooner leave her lips, and she reaches between us, gripping the hem of her shirt and tugging it over her head.

"Fuuuck, you're gorgeous." I palm her tits in my hands, pulling her toward me where our lips find each other again like two magnets.

Her hands slide down my chest as she digs her small, dark painted nails into my skin. The pain of her scratches is a welcomed feeling, especially when she glides those nails over my abs and reaches below my boxer briefs to free me. I feel her hand wrap around my shaft, and it's my turn to moan into our kiss.

Pulling away, her heated gaze slides down my face. "This has to be quick."

"Believe me, the way you're pumping my dick, I'll be coming in no time, but not before you." I thrust my hips upward into her hand. "But you have to be quiet."

She scoffs. "How do you know I'm not a silent screw?"

"I bet you're a screamer." I tweak her nipple as my words leave my lips, and she moans in pleasure, proving my point.

Flipping her onto her back, I kneel between her legs. Gripping her panties, I slide them down her legs. My fingers glide over her wetness, and she flinches. Snapping my eyes to her, I pause.

"Is this okay?"

She gives me a stiff nod, and it's not the reassurance I want. "Rebel, we don't have to do this."

"N-n-no, I want this, Crew." She stammers over the words.

"If you want me to stop at any point, just say the word, and I'll stop. I don't want you to regret this in the morning."

"I don't think I can regret you, Crew Riggsby." Her soft and earnest voice has my heart pumping faster.

Trailing kisses across her hip bone and down the apex of her thighs, my nose brushes against her wet center. With an inhale, I moan as her arousal fills my nose. I'm desperate for this woman who has driven me wild.

Her fingers latch on to the longer strands of my hair as she guides me to where she wants me.

"Feisty girl."

"We have to be quick, Crew," she whispers, thrusting her hips in the air, begging for my touch. "Taste me already."

I groan as I do what she says. My tongue flicks out as I lick her from seam to center. Her legs shake as my tongue comes into contact with her bundle of nerves.

Reaching out, I position my body so that her legs are draping over my shoulders, and my hands are gripping her tight ass as I feast on the delicious pussy spread out for me. She moans and writhes as I devour her. Fingers tangle in my hair as she guides my head exactly where she wants me.

Her back bows off the bed, and I grip her hips to keep her in place. "Yes, oh god, right there."

Removing a hand from her hips, I slip two fingers inside her tight, wet pussy. Flattening my tongue, I apply pressure to her clit as I pump my fingers deep inside her. Bret's legs squeeze my head, and if this is how I'm going to die, then I'll die a happy man.

"Fuck, Crew. I'm going to come."

She tries to pull away, but my hand on her hip holds her in place as I work her clit until she's clenching my fingers as pleasure erupts from her. Her hips ride against my face as the orgasm crashes over her like waves. Sitting up on my knees, I stare at the beautiful woman sprawled out beneath me. Her face is flushed and perfect. She leans on her elbows, nibbling on her lip as she stares at me.

With a crook of her finger, she beckons me to her. "You're pretty good at that, Riggsby."

"Pretty good?"

"*Very* good." I chuckle as my lips find hers. Hands roam down my body. Her fingertips kiss against my skin until she's slipping long fingers beneath the band of my boxers.

"These need to go," she mumbles against my lips. She doesn't have to ask twice. Breaking the kiss, I stand and slip out of my boxer shorts. Bret watches as my hard cock springs free, and I watch as her eyes widen.

"Are you sure?"

She nods, and I groan.

"Rebel, use your words."

Letting out a huff, Bret nods again. "Yes, I'm sure."

Reaching down, I stroke my cock as I watch her naked and perfect in my bed. My dick aches, and I can't wait until I slide inside her. Fumbling in my nightstand, I pull out a condom before gripping it in my teeth. The foil packet rips, and I glide the rubber on. Bret's eyes track the movement, and the way she's devouring me with her eyes makes me ready to come on the spot.

Leaning forward, I let the tip of my dick rub against her entrance. She moans at the contact, but before I have a chance to press her down into the mattress, she's pushing me away.

"Lay on your back."

Eyes wide, I do as she says. Bret tosses her leg over my hip and straddles me. My hands cup her perky tits as my thumb grazes over her piercings. She hovers over me before reaching below us, where she grips me. Guiding my cock against her soaked pussy, she uses the tip to hit her clit.

My hands reach around her back as I pull her toward me. Sucking a nipple in my mouth, I bite down as she rubs herself against me. "It feels so good."

"Imagine what it would be like when I'm fully seated inside you." She groans as she guides my cock to her entrance. I flick her pebbled nipple and work the metal as her pussy swallows my cock. She's so tight, her walls squeezing my thick erection. I have to take a deep breath before I come.

"That's it, Rebel. Ride me. Let me play with your pretty tits while you fuck me." Rocking forward on her knees, Bret begins to quicken the pace as she grinds down. Her clit grazes the base of my dick. She whimpers each time she skims my skin.

Our eyes meet, both reflecting dark desire. Everything about this moment feels so perfect. How am I only going to be able to have her only one time? I don't think I'll ever get enough of Bret Campbell.

Her pussy squeezes me, and I can feel the orgasm building. "I'm going to come."

"Thank fuck," I grit out. "I don't think I'm going to last long. You feel so fucking good, Rebel."

Removing my hands from her breasts, I grip her hips and help her movements. A low animalistic growl leaves my lips as she bares down faster and moves up and down. On her knees, she rides on my cock, and I stare at her, the bounce of her tits and the way they graze my skin. I can feel my balls tighten and my thighs stiffen. My orgasm is building.

"You're so deep. Oh my god, I don't think I've ever had someone hit that spot." Bret's head is tilted back, eyes fluttering close as she keeps one hand on my stomach while the other slides over her mouth to help muffle her moans.

"You're so perfect. This pussy is made for me. So tight. So wet. So perfect. How will I ever go on now that I've had you?"

Shock flashes across her face, and I hope I haven't ruined this moment. Bending over, her lips sear against mine as I grip her hips tight, gliding her up and down my cock. Her legs shake, and her pussy clenches so hard it almost hurts.

"Come, Rebel. Come for me."

My thrusts become deeper and rougher as we both use each other to seek out the release we're so desperate for. She screams in my mouth as she explodes. It's hot, it's animalistic, it's everything.

Chests heaving, we both collapse on the bed. Her legs tangle with mine as her black strands escape her messy bun. Turning my head, I stare at her flushed cheeks from the orgasms. But before I can pull her to my side, she's sliding out of my bed as I roll over to my side to watch her. I know she needs to leave. We can't get caught, but I hate watching her search my room for her shirt and panties in a rush to leave.

And I hate that our one time is over, and it had to be quiet and quick.

I take another glance at her perfect ass as she slides her panties up her legs. Too quickly, she's dressed and ready to escape to her room. Leaning over me, she bends down and kisses me. It's a softer kiss than the heated ones we shared earlier. This kiss isn't welcoming. It's almost like she's saying goodbye.

Which I know she is.

We can't do this again. That was our agreement.

Even though now that I've had her, I never want to let her go.

CHAPTER 9
Bret

"Let's roll!" JP yells from the kitchen.

I stumbled into my bedroom around three in the morning and fell blissfully asleep until my alarm went off at six. We need to be at the football facility by eight to catch the buses to the airport for our ten o'clock flight.

Even though I was going with the team, there was no way I was missing out on my morning routine. It's the first time the guys and I have had to navigate the apartment together in the morning. Typically, someone sleeps in on the weekends or is off doing their own thing.

While doing my morning meditation this morning, I was surprised to have Tyler join me. He does his form of meditation before games and wanted to do a class together, so I welcomed him.

Crew and I spoke a few words. He's mostly been avoiding me without making it obvious he's avoiding me. It's a weird vibe and not something I wanted to happen.

God, last night was incredible. I hate how much I'm drawn to this man when I promised myself I would not get involved with anyone. But no matter how often I tell myself to stay away from Crew Riggsby, his alluring personality draws me closer. And at the end of the day, I know he's not like he-who-shall-not-be-named.

In fact, I've slowly started to forget about he-who-shall-not-be-named as I adjust to life at CTU. I'll never fully let my guard down because that's when bad things happen, but slowly, I'm learning that having some fun is okay.

Speaking of fun, all of us are dying to know what the big surprise the coaching staff is keeping from the football team is. Whatever it is has to be big because my parents refuse to even tell Grant or me.

A knock sounds on my open doorway. "Baby girl, let's get a move on. If we are late, you can explain it to your dad."

"Baby girl? Really, JP?"

He shrugs.

Out of all the guys, JP is the one who never seems to be home. Between classes, practices, and the part-time job he picked up, JP seems to always be passing us as we are coming home for the night. I hope everything is okay with him. Tyler told me JP has younger siblings he helps support. I think it's admirable, but I hope he isn't burning himself out.

"Need help with your bags?"

"Nope, I've got it." Slinging the duffel bag over my shoulder, I check out my appearance one last time.

The team is required to wear its team-issued sweat suits, which are CTU powder blue with a team football tee underneath. The joggers hug all their athletic legs tightly, and I can't help but admire JP's physique. As a defensive end, JP is tall at six feet five inches and two hundred fifty-plus pounds. And while he's big, it's all muscle. The man takes up most of my doorway.

Not wanting to stand out against the team, I opted for a pair of black leggings and a CTU T-shirt I cropped. My long hair is left down in loose beachy curls, and my makeup is done minimally, much like always.

"Uh, Bret," JP muses as I'm grabbing my phone off my dresser.

"What's up?"

"You choosing the hippie life and going barefoot?"

Glancing down, my white-socked feet stare up at me. Chuckling, I drop my duffel, and JP groans at the delay. Digging through my closet, I'm on the hunt for the red, white, and blue Nike Dunks I purchased for football games. I had them on when I first arrived at the apartment, and I've been meaning to organize my closet since I have an overwhelming amount of sneakers, but my shoe rack broke, and I haven't ordered a new one.

A shadow falls over me followed by a low whistle. "Damn, girl. I thought Q and I had an excessive number of sneakers. You might have us beat."

"What can I say? I'm a girl who loves a good sneaker." The sound of a photo being taken has me glancing over my shoulder. "Did you just take a picture? And who has their sound on, Boomer?"

His booming laugh has me laughing. "Fuck, *Boomer*, now that's some good shit. But yeah, I took a picture. Sending it in the group chat."

It's not long before two more people are piling into my room to check out my massive shoe collection. "Holy shit, it's like Foot Locker threw up in your closet."

"Oh my gosh, you guys are ridiculous." My eyes snag on something red and blue, and I sigh in relief—my other shoe. Slipping the sneakers on my feet, I start lacing them while the guys discuss different athletes' shoes.

While guys care about the brand, the designer, and the drop, I care about the color and how good I'll look in them. A lot of times, I'll aimlessly wander the shoe wall until a pair calls my name. My collection is not that deep.

Sliding past the three guys, I grab my duffel and walk toward my door. "You guys coming or what?"

"Shit," JP mutters. "Bret, you got me all distracted."

Moving through the living room, the guys grab their gear while I pass out bottles of sports drinks to their waiting hands. "Everyone have everything?"

"Yes, Mom," the boys say in unison. Glaring at them, I double-check all the lights in the apartment are off before following the three behemoth men out the door. Tyler locks up as the rest of us head down the stairs.

"Shotgun," Tyler yells as he jogs up behind us. We're all tossing our bags in the bed of JP's pickup.

JP turns his attention to Tyler with his hands on his hips. "Listen, I know you're our quarterback and everything, but we have a female among the group."

"Yeah, so?" Tyler stares at me as I place my hands on my hips, eyeing him back.

"Harris, I thought your mama taught you better."

"Don't bring my mother into this."

"Whatever. We don't have time for this. Bret gets shotgun, so get over it, QB," JP interrupts our childish squabbles.

Climbing into the passenger seat, I shoot Tyler a wink, and he smirks. Crew has already climbed into the back seat behind JP. Fastening my seat belt, I pull out my phone and find no new notifications, which isn't surprising, especially since I deleted social media.

"Mind if the Passenger Princess controls the music?"

"As long as it isn't country." JP taps the screen as he reverses out of the parking spot. He starts driving us out of the parking lot as I connect to his Bluetooth. Thumbing through my playlist, I find the perfect song. "Party on Fifth Ave" by Mac Miller starts playing through the speakers, and I reach over and turn the dial making the music louder.

"What's your obsession with Mac?"

Lolling my head to the side, I watch JP as he drives. "What's not to love? His music is universal. It's open to anyone to interpret the meanings behind his songs, which I love. Whether it was through his beat or lyrics, he just wanted to spread positivity through his lyrics. And no matter what mood you are in, Mac's songs are perfect for the moment."

"Damn." JP flicks his signal as he pulls us out onto the main road on which will take us a few minutes to get to the football facility. "I dig your music taste. It's unique."

"I'm glad I've got your approval, JP." He flashes me his megawatt smile.

Once we're parked in the lot, the four of us climb out of the cab. Crew reaches inside the bed and begins pulling bags out for us. Everything about our movements feels so natural, like we've been doing this for years when in fact this is our first time.

Three large charter buses wait outside the facility to take us to the airport. Each bus is emblazoned with the team's logo and glistens in the Texas sun. An additional truck and trailer are parked behind the buses, and the equipment team scurries around to make sure the team has everything it needs.

A sea of blue spreads before me as the team members who are traveling with us wait outside the facility to board the buses. It's quite a sight to witness. So much talent in one space. This is all my dad's doing. A warm, fuzzy feeling spreads through my veins as happiness for my dad consumes me.

Crew bumps my shoulder drawing my attention. "Ready for this, Rebel?

"So ready." A bright smile spreads across my lips, and I watch him watch my lips. Hunger and desire flash through his mocha eyes, no doubt he's remembering images of last night like I am.

Tyler's arms drape over both of our shoulders as he interrupts our moment. "Let's go."

And go is what we do.

Four hours later, we touched down in Ohio. The flight was smooth, and I took full advantage of the inflight movie playing on the commercial plane the university chartered. Mom kept me company as she sat next to me and read one of her latest Christian romance novels.

We chatted for a while, but both of us were looking forward to the uninterrupted time on the flight. She's been busy being a dutiful college coach's wife by attending events and planning fundraisers. Mom handles the pressure to be the perfect wife for the media well. But my favorite time is when she is her true self at home.

Once we landed in Ohio, we were on to another set of charter buses. This time they would be driving us to our hotel on Western Ohio's campus. They're a large university in the middle of nowhere, Ohio. The nearest airport is two hours away, which is why I find myself crammed between my brother and another player.

Grant bumps my shoulder, and I pull out my headphones, giving him a questioning look. "Are we going to have that talk yet?"

"Sure, let's have a deep conversation on a bus surrounded by dozens of ears who would love to learn more about the mysterious coach's daughter."

"Do you have to be such a smart-ass about it?"

"Yeah, I do. Last I checked, my problems were mine." Reaching up, I start to slip my headphones back in, but Grant's large hand stops me.

"Chill, I'm just letting you know you're not alone."

"And I've told you I appreciate it, but you've got to let me breathe, G."

With a tight-lipped smile, he leans the side of his head against mine as he squeezes my knee. "I'm trying, Addy. Call it brotherly intuition, but I'm worried."

"I love you, big bro."

"Love you too, sis."

We've been traveling on this two-lane highway for over an hour with nothing but farms, cornfields, and small towns to look at. The bus is stopped at a light with only a Dollar General and Tractor Supply Store in the middle of the country. As the driver begins to accelerate, movement on the bus has everyone rustling in their seats.

Grant nudges my shoulder and points out the window to a makeshift billboard up ahead. Hanging off a lift are the words, "Welcome Home, Crew."

My head whips toward the back of the bus as I find a slack-mouthed Crew staring out the window.

Following the winding road, we come across a wetland where one of the guys points out eagles in the tree. As we near another town, more billboards and signs welcome us. The signs say everything from "Congrats Eagles," "Welcome CTU," and "We Missed You, Eighty-Eight."

Moisture gathers on my lids as I flip my head to the back of the bus to watch Crew and read more signs. But it's the green corporation limit sign that catches my eye.

Silo Bay.

We're driving through Crew's hometown. Emotion clogs my throat as an overwhelming feeling washes over me. Is this what Dad's big surprise was?

The bus rounds a curve as we continue driving into Silo Bay. Coral, yellow, turquoise, mint, and white buildings capture my attention as we drive into town. The beautiful townhomes have me feeling like I'm driving through a Florida beach town and not an Ohio lake town.

The squeaking of brakes causes the bus to slow down as it turns right onto a road next to the lake on a bank. A large lighthouse welcomes us as we drive by the blue-green water. The buses stop outside a turquoise and red building with metal sheets and synthetic thatch details.

"I need everyone's attention." Dad's booming voice fills the confines of the bus as everyone's attention snaps to him. "We've been invited by some of the lovely citizens of Silo Bay to enjoy a team dinner. This has been in the works since the schedule came out last spring. Riggsby, welcome home. I believe there's a woman out there who has been working her tail off to make sure you have a great homecoming."

My eyes find Crew's, and I can see that he's fighting his emotions right now. He looks over, and our gazes lock as I flash him a grin.

"Sunset Shore Resort and Grill has prepared a meal for all of us. I expect everyone to behave respectfully. I know this is an unusual dinner, but we should be honored to be invited. No drinking. No disrespect. And no wondering off.

"Past the stage, if you follow the boardwalk you will find a green space of turf. Under the shelter house will be tables of food and coolers of drinks. Feel free to eat wherever you want as long as you are on Sunset Shore property." Dad claps his hands and turns to exit the bus.

Chatter erupts around us, but I don't hear anything. I'm busy watching the man who has torn through the walls I've desperately tried to keep standing. But he's weaseled his way in, and this afternoon I get a glimpse of the town that made Crew.

And to meet his mother.

This resort is incredible. The grill is two stories high with an outdoor balcony on the second floor. The main level is connected to an outdoor patio which leads to a turf-covered surface underneath a large tent with the sides rolled up. A wooden stage is set on the far end with a local band playing music. Behind the tent is a huge wooden deck with a tugboat in the center of it. The boat has been turned into a bar and wood-fired kitchen.

The team spills out all over the property. While a handful are inside, most are scattered around underneath the tent or sitting on the deck. Some are at picnic tables in the green space where the food was set up. Small shacks line one side of the marketplace while a large sand volleyball court sits on part of the open space.

I can see why Crew wants to come back home and help on the family farm. This place is incredible.

While my parents have been visiting with our hosts and Crew has been chatting with his mom and sister, I've had the opportunity to roam and snap pictures. Reaching into my pocket, I pull out my phone and send Olivia a picture of Silo Bay.

Olivia is from Ohio and has been trying to get me to come home with her for the holidays since I've known her. It never worked out, and it feels so weird being in her home state without her. She's told me about Silo Bay, but she didn't grow up here. Her small town is only an hour away.

Within minutes, Olivia is messaging me back as I feel the notification vibrate in my pocket. Leaving the team behind me, I cross the road and climb down the stairs to where the sidewalk meets the lake. The water is a little greener than I expected, but it doesn't take away its beauty. I walk down the gray composite wood docking that bounces with my step as it floats above the water.

Turning down one of the tie-offs, I sit at the edge. Removing my shoes and socks, I place my feet over the ledge. My feet hang and don't quite touch the water, but I had to be cautious not to get my shoes wet.

Once I'm settled, I pull out my phone to read Liv's reply.

Liv: OMG are you in Silo Bay?

Me: Yeah, Dad surprised the team with a pit stop. Crew's hometown organized this huge dinner for us.

Liv: And which one is Crew? Is he the hot quarterback? The hot defensive guy? Or the even hotter tight end, who happens to have a very tight end?

Me: OMG! Stop! But he's the one with the very tight end I got to feel last night.

Liv: Bret Addison Campbell! You hussy!

Staring out past the manmade stone pathway, I can't help but get lost in the serene beauty of the scene before me. Pontoons and jet boats glide through the water, creating their wake and disrupting the glass-like waters. The small town on one side and the wooded area on the other frame the lake like a painting. The sounds of the band mix with the seagulls flying by. Everything about Lake Drummond and Silo Bay offers a sense of seclusion, of tranquility.

Nibbling on my lower lip, I lean back on my hands and try to envision myself living in a town like this. Can I leave behind the city and embrace life in a small town with tractor jams and where everyone knows your business?

The idea of joining this community, with its simplicity and charm, tugs at my heart. After graduation and everything is said and done, do I still want to live in Texas with my family? The thoughts linger as I watch pontoons drift and the trees sway, contemplating a future that feels foreign but alluring.

A future with Crew and Silo Bay.

Wait? What?

Panic starts to build as a future with Crew infiltrates my thoughts. Damn, these small towns and all their charms.

"Penny for your thoughts, Rebel?"

Glancing over my shoulder, I nibble on my lower lip and watch Crew stride across the dock. All of his confidence and swagger oozes out of him. He sidles up next to me before sitting down. Our shoulders brush as he sits and butterflies take flight in my stomach.

CHAPTER 10
CREW

A surprise trip to Silo Bay was not what I was expecting when the coaches informed us that we would be making a stop along the way to Western Ohio. In fact, this whole day wasn't what I had expected.

Since waking up with the smell of Bret on my sheets, in my room, hell, even in my stubble, she's all I can think about. It felt so surreal that I wondered if I had dreamed the entire thing. When I tossed and turned all night, I didn't expect Bret to climb into my bed and for us to end up having sex.

And it was good. So *fucking* good.

Unlike most of my teammates, I haven't let the celebrity of being on the football team become my advantage. I might joke about women and hooking up, but it's all a façade. The truth is, it's been seven months since I slept with someone and even longer before that.

When Bret offered a one-night, I almost said no. I'm not that guy, and I don't want to be that guy with her. I can feel the connection between us, even though she keeps saying there isn't one—or at least, she's fighting it.

Bret Campbell isn't the girl you have a fling with. She's the girl you bring home to meet your family.

With the surprise visit to Silo Bay, I now have the perfect opportunity to introduce Bret to my family under the guise of being my new roommate.

Sunset Shores has come a long way since I left for college. When I left town, it was a restaurant working on a facelift. Now there's an entire mini-village with a covered tent, and a deck around the tugboat which was transformed into a bar and outdoor kitchen for pizzas. There are shops, turf-covered green space for people to sit and mill about, and the cottages and townhomes they've built resemble a beach town. It's quite the addition to Silo Bay, and I can only imagine the tourists it'll bring in. It's about time someone put Silo Bay on the map with all our hidden gems.

Stepping off the bus, I'm hit with a burst of nostalgia. The smell of the lake hits my nose first, resurfacing all of my childhood memories. With its mix of fresh water, light aquatic plants, sun-kissed rocks, and the slight tangy scent of algae, the lake smells like home.

"Riggsby, this is where you grew up?" one of the guys on the team asks.

With a nod, I sidestep the others as they gawk at the lake. Striding down the boardwalk-covered sidewalk, I move around bodies as I head toward the space where Coach informed us the food was. My eyes scan the crowd, looking for a petite brown-haired woman who is most likely wearing jeans and a Riggs Cattle T-shirt. No matter the temperature outside, Mom is always dressed in jeans. She says she's been wearing them for so long she doesn't even notice how hot the denim can be in the summer.

Sure enough, my mom and sister, Saylor, are standing off to the side near a small, turquoise shack. A wide grin spreads across my face as I close the space between us.

"Surprise!" Mom yells as I embrace her. Her face smashes against the CTU football logo on my shirt. When she hugs us, it's obvious that we didn't get our height from her.

She chuckles, and I fight the emotion wanting to spring free. "I can't believe you planned this."

"Nonsense. It's not every day your son comes passing through town." She smacks my stomach, creating space between us. Saylor is quick to replace Mom's spot.

"Big brother!"

"Hey, sis." She squeezes my middle tight before letting go of me. Standing back, I notice how much she's changed. At sixteen, Saylor isn't so little anymore. Her looks have morphed from awkward teen to almost adult. An ache in my chest settles as I realize how quickly she's grown up and how I haven't physically been here for her.

"So, where is she?" Saylor bounces on her feet, looking around at the people who are filing in line from the buses.

"Where's who?"

"The *girl*," she mocks.

My eyes find Mom who dares to look amused. A smirk plays across her features as if she was saying her work here is done. As soon as she told Saylor that she met my new roommate, who happens to be a female, over FaceTime, she knew Saylor would do her younger sister's duty to pester the hell out of me until I spilled the beans.

Two days ago, there weren't any beans to spill, but after last night, well, let's say my poker face better be in check because Saylor will sniff out the truth like a shark sniffs out blood in the water.

And I cannot let Grant catch onto his sister and me being more than roommates. Coach, now, if he found out, I *might* be able to talk my way out of that situation. But Grant? Grant wouldn't have second thoughts about kicking my ass. Hell, I think he'd do it in front of everyone to prove that his sister is off limits.

"Come on," Mom says, saving me from the interrogation she sicced my sister on. "Let's go get you some food."

This entire afternoon has been incredible. I didn't know how much I needed to breathe Silo Sky air until I was here. A local cover band has been playing hit after hit as my two worlds collide. It was an incredible gesture for the Sunset Shores company to treat us as we passed through. The hometown pride showed through with every thought-out detail, from the food to the music to the CTU-colored decorations sprinkled throughout the property.

While I've enjoyed catching up with family and a few family friends who work for Sunset Shores, I've had the most fun watching Bret. A lightness has fallen over her as she roams around without a care in the world. A smile has firmly been in place since she stepped off the bus. And it's her real smile. The one she allows to slip free when she's in the comfort of the apartment. It's not the fake one that she forces as she walks through campus.

It's almost as if she's lowered her battle shield and allowed herself to be fully immersed in her surroundings. I've noticed how she looks over her shoulder as she walks through campus and how she's constantly scanning the crowd. For what? I have no idea. But I'm glad Silo Bay has given her the sense of freedom she's been desperately searching for.

Excusing myself, I climb out of the picnic table, which is a feat for someone as tall as I am. Cutting through the crowd, I let my legs carry me to the giant manmade lake. Lake Drummond is Silo Bay. Our town revolves around the lake as it's the center of our town. Businesses are built on the shores, and many people enjoy walking on the shoreline. Crossing the road to the sidewalk on the sea wall, I spy a familiar jet-black-haired girl sitting with her back to the chaos. Climbing down the few steps, I slowly walk toward her.

"Penny for your thoughts, Rebel?"

Glancing over her shoulder, she nibbles on her lower lip, and it immediately takes me back to last night when her pillowy lips moved over mine. A flashback of how her teeth grazed over my skin, eliciting goose bumps to break free. Slipping my hands into the pockets of my joggers, I subtly readjust myself as my blood runs south, settling in my cock.

Bret Campbell drips with sex appeal, and I don't even think she realizes it.

This woman is going to be the death of me.

Sitting beside her, I bend my knees as I settle on the composite dock beside her. My legs dangle near the water and I notice she's stripped her feet bare.

"This place is incredible, Crew. I can't believe you grew up here." Her eyes never stray from where she's watching boats glide across the water.

"I love this town. Although this"—I wave my hand in the direction of Sunset Shores—"wasn't here when I grew up. The restaurant was, but it was a dive compared to what it is now."

"It's like a secret resort in Ohio." I chuckle because that's precisely what Silo Bay is. It's an oasis only the locals seem to appreciate, or that used to be the case. "Is this where your dad would take you out on the boat?"

"There's a boat ramp at the edge of this road." I point in the direction to my right. "We'd launch from there and follow the lake until we reached a channel down the way."

"He'd be proud of you." Her soft voice whispers five words that have my chest seizing as an onslaught of emotions hits me like a tidal wave.

The sound of the tugboat horn fills the air with three rapid blows, interrupting our line of conversation. A voice sounds over the microphone where the band was performing, announcing that it was time for the buses to roll out. My shoulders sagged at the thought of leaving home, but I promise I'll try to get home during winter break.

Pushing up off the dock, I reach my hand out for Bret to take, which she does, and I help her to her feet. Rubbing my hand down my neck, I mull over a thought. "Would you like to meet my mom in person?"

Her head snaps up, and she smiles wide. "I'd love to!"

We fall in step together. "Okay, but I should probably warn you, my sister is here too, and she's a little annoying."

Her shoulder nudges mine as we climb the stairs from the sidewalk to the road. "I am the annoying little sister; I know how this works."

Standing by the first bus, Mom and Saylor wait for our goodbyes. Mom's eyes glisten in the late afternoon sunshine while Saylor bounces on her toes.

"Bret, this is my mom, Nora, and my younger sister, Saylor."

Warmth spreads across Bret's face as her smile spreads wide, crinkling the corners of her eyes. I watch as Bret steps forward and what she does next surprises the hell out of me. She lifts her arms and envelops my mom in a hug. "It is so nice to meet you in person."

Mom wraps her arms around Bret, hugging her back. "You too, sweetie." She breaks their embrace first and holds Bret at arm's distance as she takes in her appearance. "You are so much prettier in person."

"Mom," I grit as Bret's cheeks flame.

"I'm Saylor!" she screams as she pushes Mom aside to hug Bret. An oomph leaves Bret at the contact before chuckling.

Returning the hug, Bret says, "I've heard a lot about you."

"What, that I'm the annoying little sister?" Bret glances up at me, and I raise my brows in an 'I told you so' way.

"I'm the younger sister, too, so I know all about that."

"Oh yeah, we met your parents. They told us you were the youngest and how you transferred to CTU." The words tumble out of Saylor's mouth.

A hand taps my shoulder as Harris stops next to us. "Mama Riggs!"

"Tyler!" He pulls her in for a hug while Saylor talks Bret's ears off. "It's so good to see you, honey. Good luck this weekend."

"Will you be at the game?"

"Saylor and I are heading up in the morning with a small caravan." My chest warms at her admission. It feels so good to play in my home state and have so many people who mean a lot to me at the game.

Harris flings his arm around my shoulder as he taps my chest with his opposite hand. "I bet this guy is excited about that."

"I am."

Mom's lips curl in a small smile. I know she has to be thinking about Dad right now. She always gets a far-off look in her eyes. "Well, we've got to get loaded. Ready, roomies?"

"I am so jealous you get to live with him," my sister not so quietly whispers.

With one last final round of hugs, Bret, Harris, and I say our goodbyes as we load onto the bus. Bret sits in the empty spot next to her brother while Harris and I find spots toward the back of the bus.

As the driver starts the ignition, pulling us away from Sunset Shores, I watch as all the locals line the boardwalk waving as we leave. And I say goodbye to my home.

CHAPTER 11
Bret

"Oh my gosh, you guys were incredible last night." I can't contain my excitement as we climb the stairs to our apartment. It's mid-afternoon when we arrived back on campus. Last night, the boys crushed Western Ohio forty-two to three.

The drive home from the football facility was unusually quiet. As I looked over my shoulder at the three guys trailing behind me, I saw their exhaustion.

"Thanks, Rebel."

"Rebel?" I can hear the accusation in JP's voice at Crew's slip of the nickname he gave me. I busy myself with unlocking the front door because the blush on my cheeks would give a few things away.

"Uh, yeah, you know she kind of rebelled and moved here." His explanation is full of holes.

"What's that?" Harris interrupts. He reaches above my head, where an envelope is taped to the door. I was so busy trying to unlock the door that I didn't even see it. "It's got your name on it, Bret."

Dread settles in my stomach like a lead weight as fear creeps through my skin, causing my body to tremble. This can't be happening. "Whoa, whoa, whoa, you all right Bret?" Tyler's right by my side.

Clearing my throat, I take the envelope out of his hands and push open the door. "Yeah, I'm fine."

"You sure?" JP asks as they follow me inside. I can feel their silent questions.

"I said I'm fine." Moving through the hallway, I grip the envelope tighter as I step inside my room.

As soon as I step into my room, relief and security wash over me, as false as it may be. I could feel the panic wanting to pull me under like waves crashing in a hurricane. The midnight blue comforter and vibrant, jewel-toned floral pillows on my full-size bed seem to absorb my distress. The greenery from my faux plants offers some semblance of peace. The drawn blackout shades block out the chaotic world, allowing my room to be the haven I'm desperately searching for.

Tossing my duffel bag on my floor, I take off my sneakers before climbing into bed. Cocooning myself between my soft sheets, I close my eyes and practice a few breathing exercises. I can feel the heaviness of not knowing what's inside the envelope weighing down on my safe place. But I'm not ready to open it. I'm not ready to face the reality that I'm not safe here. He'll always find me no matter how many miles I put between myself and Arizona.

A knock on the door startles me as I flicker my eyes open. The breathing exercises must've done the trick. I didn't realize I had dozed off.

"Come in." Clearing the sleep from my voice, I bring my arms over my head, stretching out the stiff muscles.

Familiar blond hair is the first thing I see as the door opens. "Damn, it's like a cave in here. Are you secretly Batwoman?"

"Shh, don't tell my secrets."

His lip tips up in a smirk, but he hesitates to step inside the door. I follow his movements as he places his hands in his khaki shorts pockets sans shirt. Reaching over, I flip on the lamp from my bedside table. The light cascades the room in a warm glow.

"Holy shit," I gasp as my eyes land on the enormous black and purple bruise on his rib cage underneath his cross tattoo.

He hisses as he glances down, running a finger over the bruise. "Yeah, that last hit hurt like a bitch."

Late in the fourth quarter, Crew jumped to catch a high throw from Tyler when the defender came out of nowhere and drilled him in the rib cage. It was a brutal hit, and Crew hit the ground even harder. He was on the ground for a few minutes as he regained the wind that had been knocked from him.

Crew shifts his weight from one foot to the other before running his hand down the back of his neck. I've noticed that's a tell of his when he's feeling nervous or uncomfortable.

"Just spit it out, Crew."

His eyes bore into mine, and I fight the urge to cower underneath my asylum of blankets. "What the hell was that earlier? What was in the envelope?"

Shit, the envelope. I fell asleep and never opened it.

Scanning the room, I find it on the floor beside where I tossed my duffel. Crew's gaze follows mine as it lands on the white paper.

He's bending down and picking up the tainted letter in two strides. Flipping over the envelope, he inspects it as if he has x-ray vision and can see inside the sealed envelope. Crew's long legs eat up the space separating us, and before I know it, he is hovering above where I am still sitting in bed. White envelope in hand, he stretches his arm out for me to take the letter. With jerky movements, I do just that.

Nibbling on my lower lip, my fingers tremble as I slide one between the sealed paper. The crinkling of the seal breaking has my nerves completely frayed.

Breathe, Bret. Breathe.

The mattress dipping has my attention snapping up. Crew is sitting opposite me, watching me. There's comfort in knowing that I'm not alone. When my mind is screaming to run and not trust any man, Olivia pops into my head, reminding me that they aren't all like him and that I need to listen to my gut. If I get the ick from someone, then I need to trust that, but if there's the tiniest bit of spark, I need to listen to it.

Being in Crew's proximity is like igniting a volcano. My emotions pour over like hot lava. I can't get enough of him. There's something deep inside of me that is tethered to him. I knew it at Christmas, and I knew it when I saw those mocha eyes the day I showed up on this doorstep.

The seal gives free, and hesitantly, I slip a finger inside. Pulling out the contents, my body sags when I realize it is nothing—absolutely nothing to be concerned about. A tri-fold pamphlet with all of the details surrounding the intramural basketball league I applied for and our game schedule sits inside. There's a sticky note attached to the pamphlet explaining that the student in charge of intramural sports lives in the complex, and he decided to tape it to my door to save a stamp and the delay in mailing it.

"Okay, I'm going to go ahead and assume that's not what you thought was inside the envelope?" Crew's deep voice startles me. I was so concerned in my head that I forgot he was sitting in front of me.

I shake my head but don't say anything else. I know what's coming, and I don't think I can avoid it now after my reaction. And the thing is, I want to trust Crew. I mean, I do trust him. I wouldn't have slept with him the other night if I didn't feel an emotional connection.

"How much time do you have?"

He glances down at his smartwatch. "We need to leave for family dinner in an hour."

I nod. An hour, I can purge my fucked-up story and still have time to get myself together before I'm forced to attend a dinner with a bunch of people I don't know or barely know.

"My ex-boyfriend has been a bit of a bastard since we broke up in the spring."

Crew's fists tighten, and his body goes rigid. "Did he hurt you?"

My heart warms at the protectiveness he exudes. He's a lot like my brother in that regard. They both carry around BBE, Big Brother Energy. As much as I wanted to yell out, "Yes, he hurt me," I couldn't bring myself to say that. Call it denial, but he's never physically hurt me. But the mental toll he's taken over me, now that shit hurts.

"Chad and I met at the beginning of the semester last fall at a party."

"Wait, his name is Chad?"

"Yeah, it should have been my first red flag, right?"

His brows raise as in an "obviously" remark.

"Anyway, we met at the party and kept bumping into each other the following week. It felt like fate..." I let the words trail off as I reminded myself that Crew was the one in my room. Chad isn't here and didn't send me the envelope that caused this spiral.

Sliding higher on the bed, I rest my back against my headboard and pull a pillow into my lap, stroking the fabric. I need something to keep my hands busy.

"Everything started great. He was attentive, always wanting to go on dates and spend time together. He'd drop off little surprise pack-ages with my favorite treats or a black coffee in the morning. I really started to see a future with him." I pause and let out a huff of air through my nose. "Hell, I even gave him my virginity."

Crew shuffles in his seat but doesn't interrupt, and I appreciate his silence.

"It wasn't like I was saving it for anything special—the time had just never risen to lose it. Growing up, we were always moving, or Grant was overprotective whenever I was around a guy I met, and I never felt comfortable losing it. But Chad kept pushing until one day, I finally gave in. To say it was underwhelming would be an understatement." Clearing my throat, I pick at the pillow in my lap. "Anyway, us sleeping together must have triggered something in his pea-sized brain because that's when the raging jealousy and controlling started. He planted these seeds of doubt and insecurity, which I soon started believing."

The words feel vile coming out of my mouth. I still struggle with how naïve and stupid I was to let this *boy*, because let's face it, that's what he was, control me. But when someone you're attracted to starts to water the inner voice inside your head, those insecurities start to grow until they bloom. He would see the way that my mom would talk to me. Even though she was loving and supportive, she still disapproved of some things.

Chad picked at those conversations by telling me that my parents wanted to have control over me and that I was their little puppet who did whatever they told me. How they didn't appreciate me for who I was and how I needed to loosen the strings between us since I was no longer under their roof.

And the weak part of me that wanted to be in a relationship, who wanted to know what it was like to have a boyfriend, started to think he was right. I put distance between my parents and brother.

Once the first seed was planted, he started in on my friendship with Olivia. Everything spiraled out of control from there. Chad was doing everything he could to isolate me from everyone else so that I would only rely on him.

I hated myself for it. I thought I was stronger than that, but I was blind. Utterly oblivious to his manipulations.

"He manipulated me into isolating myself from my parents, Grant, and friends, especially my roommate, Olivia. When Grant and Dad visited me last fall, I was a shell of a person. They met Chad and instantly disapproved of him. Grant tried talking to me about him, but I was already too far gone. Chad's words replayed in my head that Grant didn't want me to be happy. Grant and I had our first major blow-up. Sure, we fought, you know what it's like to have a younger sister, but this was different."

With a shaky inhale, I tilt my head to the ceiling. This next part still hurts. It still makes my chest crack as the guilt and humility come back in force. Tears spring in my eyes, and as they trail down my cheeks, I don't brush them away. I let the pain wash over me as I allow myself the opportunity to feel the pain. Because feeling it is a reminder that I'm still here. I'm sitting on a bed, and I'm not alone anymore.

I can feel Crew's energy vibrating, and I hate that I'm dumping all of this trauma on him, but for some reason, I trust him. From the moment we met, I knew there was something special about Crew Riggsby. I thought I knew fate when I met Chad, but I was clueless.

"Eventually, the dates turned into nights at his apartment. He never wanted to go out anymore. Our time together was always spent isolated in his apartment, where we would do nothing but sleep together no matter if I was in the mood or not. He would use his smooth-talking words and my fragile state of mind to coerce me into sex. It was never rape, he never forced himself on me in that regard because I always gave in, but it was like he had me under some kind of mind control. I can't explain it.

"One night, after a particularly rough day, I decided I couldn't take it anymore. I hated who I had become. I hated how my friends had abandoned me, and I couldn't blame them. My relationship with my family was almost nonexistent, and I was starting to lose Olivia. I wanted it all to end."

Sobs erupt as the pain cuts through me at the memory. Crew's large arms wrap around me as he pulls me into his chest. My cheek hits his warm skin as I let my tears pour over him. His large hand rubs circles on my back in slow, calming movements.

With Olivia's help, I've been working on rebuilding myself for the past four months. I started therapy, and Liv took me to yoga and meditation classes. She helped me see that I wasn't broken and encouraged me to fight back. I'm no longer that weak, naïve girl anymore with fragile mental health, which is why I hate that I'm allowing Crew to see me break.

I'm stronger than this.

Letting out one last shaky breath, I sit up as Crew's arms drop away from me. I can't explain it, but I instantly miss the warmth of his embrace.

"Jesus, Bret. That's some fucked-up shit." His voice is soft, but I can hear the anger underneath. Crew reaches up and wipes the tears from my mascara-streaked face.

A dark chuckle escapes. "That's not even all of it."

"There's more?" With wide eyes, he runs both hands through his blonde hair as his head shakes.

"The day Olivia found me in the bathroom with a bottle of pills in my hand. I was ready to end it. To swallow away my demons and drift off to another world. She saved me that day. We sat on the bathroom floor and held each other while we both sobbed. Liv helped me see the light, and she helped me end things with Chad.

"But it didn't stop. Even after ending things with him, he would still pop up out of the blue. Gifts, flowers, pictures, you name it, were left outside our apartment or on my windshield. I'd see his car drive by the apartment and even places I frequented. Everything escalated until I found myself turning into a hermit. I never left the house alone. I quit going to the court, getting groceries, and everything.

"For two months this summer, I kept to myself. The only way I could think to get out of the situation was to leave. Finally, luck was on my side. Grant told me about his friends needing a roommate, which brought me here. So when I saw that envelope, I thought he had found me."

A long sigh escapes Crew, and for a moment, neither of us says anything. For a moment, I think that the bubble we've found ourselves in has deflated. But leave it to Crew Riggsby to surprise me. In a flash, he's cupping the sides of my face in his strong hands and pressing his lips to mine. At first, I don't move, the shock paralyzing me. I thought for sure he'd run for the hills. But with every step of the way, Crew Riggsby surprises me and sweeps me off my feet.

The moment ends before I can react, but he doesn't go far as he presses his forehead against mine. "I'm so glad you're still here." His words are a whisper.

I'm so glad I'm here, too.

Deciding I can't take this vulnerable state any longer, I slide out from beside Crew and stand on my feet. With my palms, I wipe the moisture from my face.

"Okay, enough of that."

Crew turns his large body, which looks surprisingly good on my bed until he's facing me. His muscular legs stretch out on the ground. "For now. I will need to know how to find this fucker and break his neck."

"Later. Right now, I need you to keep this information to yourself."

"Rebel," he groans my nickname, and the words heat my insides. "Promise me you'll tell your family, tell Grant, sooner rather than later."

"I will." He eyes me skeptically. "Really, I will. But right now, I want to go see what this whole family dinner is about."

Because the truth is, I miss having friends and a place I can feel comfortable in. I know my past won't stay behind me, but I need to pretend right now.

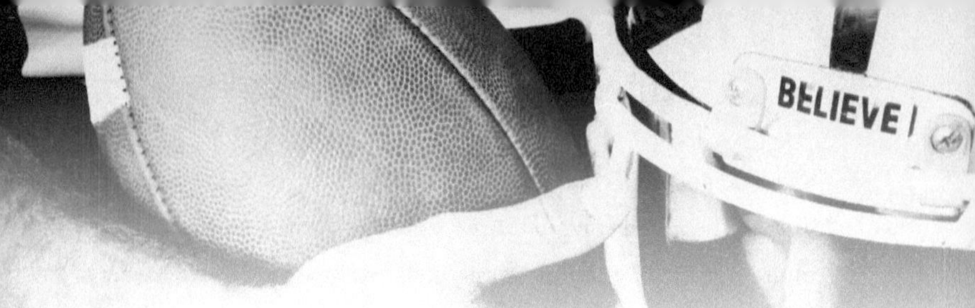

CHAPTER 12
CREW

What the actual fuck?

My mind is still spinning over Bret's revelation. I knew she was keeping a secret, and I knew someone had hurt her. But that? I never could have imagined that to be her story.

What kind of sick fuck preys on someone like that? Like *her*?

No woman should ever be used and manipulated, especially Bret. She has such a good character and a heart of gold.

Bret Campbell is the type of girl you bring home to meet your parents.

Blood boils in my veins as I fight the urge to catch the first flight to Arizona and find *Chad*—such a small dick name for a douchebag. I want to introduce him to my fist, and I'm not that guy. Now, my brother, he's the type of guy who speaks with his fist, not me.

But right now, I could make an exception.

The entire ride to Brynn and Chloe's townhouse has been silent. Bret has sat with her head lolled against the window as she stares out at the passing scenery. Harris hasn't said much but keeps finding my eyes in the rearview mirror. And JP, well, JP is *JP*. He's had his nose in his phone with a smirk playing at the corner of his mouth, probably organizing some kind of hookup.

A few minutes later, we are climbing the walkway to the townhouse. Harris leads the way, with JP behind him and Bret following him. I eat up the space between us and nudge her shoulder. Her green eyes shine up at me, but they aren't as bright as they have been. No, they look more like how she arrived weeks ago, which I'm not surprised about.

"Ready for this?"

"Totally. Who wouldn't want to spend an evening with people she barely knows after confessing her fucked-up past?"

Reaching my hand out, I gently grab her forearm and feel the shock between us. "Rebel, we don't have to go in there."

She shakes her head. "No, I'm fine. Sorry, that was a bad attempt at a joke."

"If that was your attempt at a joke, we have a lot of work to do."

"Crew!" a booming voice sounds from behind me. "Quit hogging our girl!"

A wide smile takes over Bret's face as she finds Brynn. With a pat to my chest, Bret's moving past me, our bare arms brushing. Her eyes find mine over her shoulder before she calls out, "You coming?"

I'd follow her to the end of the world.

Stepping foot inside the townhouse, my senses are hit with the delicious aroma of fresh-baked bread and garlic. Italian must be on the menu for tonight's dinner. Brynn and Chloe both live in a two-story townhouse near campus. It's a newer complex with higher-end finishes and neutral colors throughout.

The two started hosting dinners with their other friend, Macy, a few years ago. Even though Macy moved out to live with her boyfriend, Gregg, Brynn and Chloe have continued the tradition. Luckily for us, Chloe cooks all of the food. Her dad is a Michelin-star chef, and she acquired his talent in the kitchen.

"Okay, before we get this whole thing started," Brynn's energetic voice carries me back to the present. "I've gotta know what the hell I should call you. I had no clue you were like a double agent with your multiple personas."

Bret chuckles softly. "Grant, and occasionally, my mom will call me Addy. I'm Bret to everyone else, but you can call me whatever."

"Be careful, or she'll give you some stupid nickname." Speaking of her brother, he chimes into the conversation as he steps in from the kitchen.

Brynn rolls her eyes. "Bret it is. Welcome to my house. Ignore your brother. He hates me."

"He's a grump to everyone," Bret adds, turning to hug her brother. "Isn't that right, big brother?"

Grant scowls at his sister and then Brynn. The two have history, not romantic history or anything like that. Brynn was a wildcard until last year when she got with Quinton. Speaking of Quinton...

"Q here?" I haven't seen him since he moved to Denver in May. Last spring, the Denver Mustangs selected him first in the NFL draft. The two of them quickly found an apartment to rent in the city, and Q moved west. Brynn spent the summer with him, so the start of this school year is pretty much one big family reunion.

"Did someone say my name?" Quinton appears at the top of the stairs. I can't help the surprise that washes over my face as he hops down to where we're standing. With a quick kiss to Brynn's temple, Q sticks his hand out, and I grab it firmly. We pull each other in for a quick, one-arm hug as our shoulders bump, clapping each other's backs. Stepping back, I can't wipe the smile off my face.

"How's it going, man?"

"Good. Glad to be back for the weekend." Quinton drapes his arm around Brynn, and she beams up at him. Both of them glow. Happiness looks good on them. "Nice game yesterday."

"Food's ready," Chloe shouts from the kitchen, interrupting the conversation. Q and Brynn turn, and we all follow them into the kitchen.

"Chlo, you've got to meet Bret." Brynn's energy vibrates as she reaches over the counter and snags a tomato out of the salad bowl.

Bret stands at my side, her brother moving through the kitchen. Chloe kicks the fridge door closed with her foot as her honey-blonde hair flies in her face, and she turns, bringing salad dressing bottles to the counter.

"Oh, hey! You're the girl who was at the lunch table on our first day." Bret's smile widens before she steps around me, moving closer to the kitchen. The two chatter as I move outside the patio door.

"You and Campbell?" Q steps out on my heels.

"Grant and I are fine." Lifting the top of the cooler, I shift around the ice until I find a bottle of water and Coke for Bret.

Quinton reaches inside and pulls out a bottle of water. "Not Grant, Bret."

Twisting the cap, I take a sip, busying myself as I scan the small backyard where tables are lined up. "Just roommates."

"Yeah, okay." Q nods to the guys sitting around the table. "Use your brain."

The creak from the sliding door has us turning our attention. The girls are piling out with hands full of plates. Quinton and I step out of their way before following them. The white plastic tables are decorated with a few ceramic vases with fresh flowers, and clear holders hold small white-lit candles. Each table setting has a clear plastic disposable plate and napkin-wrapped silverware set. The girls always make sure the dinner feels special.

"S'up, man." Cody nods next to me. Cody Jacobs is a pitcher for the university's baseball team, which just won *their* first national championship. It's been a good year for CTU athletics, and I hope it continues. He and Chloe started dating last spring. The two of them have a sordid past they kept a secret from our friend group. But it's all worked itself out. I feel it won't be long until they say 'I do' like Q and Brynn. Only this time, I hope we're all invited to the wedding and not that surprise elopement bullshit.

I nod, taking in the spread. "Chloe, the food looks amazing."

She leans forward from her place next to Cody. "Thanks. I thought you boys could use a good meal after last night's game. How are the ribs? That hit looked nasty at the end of the game."

"Oh my gosh, you should see the black and purple bruise on them," Bret adds from her place across from me.

"And how would you know?"

Bret's eyes roll. "My roommates walk around without shirts, Grant."

"Yeah, Grant. A girl's got to get it where she can. And hell, I don't blame her for looking."

"You're extra spicy tonight, B." Grant leans forward on his elbows. Here we go. "I thought you'd be a delight with Q here."

"It's all my freaking—"

"Who wants salad?" Quinton interjects, and Brynn glares at him.

Heads whip at Q's random outburst, and Brynn slinks in her chair, her cheeks reddening. Something is off with those two.

Once the salad is passed around, everyone helps themselves to the Italian dishes spread around the table.

"Oh my gosh, this lasagna is amazing," Bret moans around a mouthful.

"Thank you," Chloe says, her smile warming her face. Over the last year, I've learned that Chloe loves to feed people. Call it her love language, but she exudes joy when she sees people enjoying the dishes she prepares.

Bret angles her shoulder toward Chloe. "Seriously, if you guys ever need any help preparing dinners—"

"Please don't ask her." Harris cuts off her words.

Bret's perfect mouth flies open as her eyes widen. "That was so harsh."

"Harsh was you trying to kill us." The mouthful of food muffles Harris's words.

"Dude, you didn't let her cook?" Grant shakes his head.

Harris raises his hands. "I didn't know."

"It wasn't *that* bad," I add.

Harris scoffs. "It wasn't *that* bad? Dude, the ocean has less salt than that asparagus."

"Hey, assholes, I'm sitting right here." Bret crosses her arms across her chest and purses her lips.

"I know," Harris says, flinging his arm around her shoulders, which has my blood tingling. "Which is why I'm letting the girls know that if they ever need help in the kitchen, maybe you bring something premade."

"Or cups and ice," JP adds.

We all let out a chuckle on Bret's behalf, but the taken aback mixed with the offended face she makes is priceless.

"Grant, you're my big brother. You're supposed to defend my honor."

"Not on that one. Cooking is not your thing. I feel sorry for the man who marries you." He takes a bite of his lasagna as Bret's eyes find mine. Her cheeks take on a pretty pink hue as she blushes slightly. Does she feel the way I do?

Brynn comes to Bret's defense as she points her fork at Harris. "All right, leave my girl alone before she decides she never wants to hang out with us again."

"Nah, she's stuck with us now." JP nudges her shoulder from where he's sitting next to her.

As much as I miss home in Silo Bay, these family dinners make the homesickness not as severe. The way we all can bust jokes at the expense of others and have the evening feel like a real familial bond makes everything worth it. Bret fits in like she's always been a part of our CTU family. These dinners feel like a family reunion when your favorite cousins surround you. The ones who make the large events worth it with their jokes, but at the end of the day, you know they'll always have your back.

"Okay, now that we know that you are to stay away from the kitchen," Brynn muses as she cuddles into Quinton's side. "Tell us more about you."

Bret rocks in her chair. An uneasiness settles over her as attention is once again returned to her. "Is this like speed dating?"

"Oh, that could be fun." Brynn sits up higher in her seat. "What's your major? Your hobbies? Favorite music? Movie? How many piercings do you have? I totally noticed the nips, and you go, girl."

Grant groans, rolling his eyes as he sips from his Coke.

"She's pretty much the girl version of Grant. That is why she was easily accepted as our new roommate. Boy, were we fooled." Harris's tone is dry.

Bret shrugs. "Once again, it was your fault for not having a gender box."

"I didn't think a girl would want to live with three guys."

"Oh my gosh!" Chloe is practically vibrating from her seat. "Do you have some like reverse harem fantasy?"

Coughing sounds around the table, as I'm pretty sure each one of us guys just choked on whatever we were ingesting. Brynn's laugh fills the air as it's swept up in the late summer Texas breeze while Bret's cheeks flame red.

"I swear to god, you better not answer that question," Grant mumbles from where he's still cleaning up the Coke he spewed across the table.

"I haven't given it much thought, but never say never."

"Addy!" Grant's voice is harsh. Meanwhile, Brynn gives a, "Thatta girl!"

And I'm over here avoiding looking at the girl who just confessed she'd never say never to a threesome. Or more. What the hell is happening?

"Hey! Sorry we're late," a voice comes from the patio, and everyone's attention moves away from the topic of discussion. Thank God for the interruption, or I'd be passing out from all the blood rushing from my head to my dick.

Gregg and Macy step out of the townhouse with their dog, Boone, at their feet. Macy used to live here with Brynn and Chloe, but after her boyfriend, Gregg, had a stroke last fall, she moved in to help with his recovery. It was a whole ordeal with drama between the girls, but they eventually sorted things out. Boone takes off running across the yard before sniffing around the table, looking for any scraps. He's a small brown and white Cavalier King Charles Gregg gave Macy as a Christmas present.

"Hey, guys!" Brynn stands and hugs Macy before turning to Gregg. "You have to meet Bret. She's Grant's sister and the guys' new roommate."

Macy's gaze flits over the table as she looks for the newest group member. "Oh my gosh, you're gorgeous!"

"Uh, thanks," Bret shies away from the compliment.

Macy chuckles. "I'm Macy, and this is my boyfriend Gregg."

"Nice to meet you both."

Boone jumps up and places his front paws on Bret's lap. "Oh, sorry about him. That's Boone."

"Hi, Boone," Bret greets the pup, scratching behind his ears.

"Grab some food," Chloe instructs, gesturing to the table with plenty of food. I swear Chloe thought the whole team was coming.

Macy and Gregg walk around the table and begin filling their plates. "Before I forget, there are two cheesecakes in the fridge, and each group has a plastic container of sugar cookies I baked. They have red and blue sprinkles in them."

"Hell yeah." Drool practically slides out of Harris's mouth.

Conversation soon takes over the table. Hours seem to pass as the late summer Texas sky morphs into shades of orange and pink.

The start of a new school year is here.

And I'm determined to make it the best.

CHAPTER 13
Bret

Stepping foot outside the rec center, the hot Texas sun bakes my sweat-soaked body, leaving almost a crust on my skin. An afternoon on the court was exactly what the doctor ordered.

It's been eleven days since I shared the big secret with Crew and we had dinner with his friends. The girls have merged me into their little group, and I'm officially one of them since they added me to the group chat. And that chat is unhinged. One minute, they'll be talking about some reality show, the next, they're sending links for clothes, wondering if they should buy them. But as chaotic as the chat can be, I'm glad to be a part of something.

Don't get me wrong, hanging with the guys at home is great, but a girl needs girlfriends.

Tossing Spalding into the back seat, I climb into my Jeep as Kyrie, one of the guys on my intramural team, pulls in next to me. Rolling down my window, I scroll through the group chat messages while waiting for him to leave his car.

Bestie Babes

> **Chloe: Cody wants to go to The Eagles Nest.**

> **Brynn: Possibly!**

Macy: Can't tonight...boo!

Chloe: Seriously, B?

Brynn: I'm going to FaceTime Q.

Chloe: You can FaceTime him when we get home, and it won't be late because of the time zone.

Brynn: Let me think about it.

Macy: Are you two seriously talking like both of you aren't home?

Chloe: She's in her room, and I'm baking.

Brynn: ^^^ Facts

After catching up on the many more messages that were left waiting for me to open, I quickly type out a reply. I've heard of The Eagles Nest, but I'm not quite sure about its details. An onslaught of messages quickly follows my text.

Me: What's The Eagles Nest and why tonight?

Brynn: OMG hi, new bestie! I thought we were going to have to send out an SOS.

Macy: Hey, girl!

Macy: A silver alert?

Brynn: No, you can send out an SOS for someone who is missing.

Macy: Really?

Brynn: Chlo, back me up.

Chloe: You're both right.

Me: Hello, back to me, please.

Chloe: Sorry...The Eagles Nest is the campus bar. They always have Thirsty Thursday specials typically on beers and seltzers, and there's almost always a live band that plays.

Chloe: I heard Ecstasy is playing!

Brynn: They're my favorite!

Chloe: Which is why you should go!

"S'up, baller." Kyrie's voice startles me as I lock my phone and toss it in my cup holder. I'll no doubt have a million messages waiting for me. As much as I love to be included in the group chat, it's a lot. Like a lot, *a lot*. And to make matters worse, Brynn types each thought out and sends it in a separate message.

He gives a nod as he hoists his gym bag over his shoulder. "Make any grown men cry today with your jump shot?"

"Nah, not today."

He runs his hand down his tight black beard. "Good, good. Saving it for next week when we have our first game."

"Oh, for sure. I'm itching to play again."

And that isn't a lie. It's been since high school since I played a legit basketball game. As much as I love the game of basketball, playing in college was never an option for me. I knew it'd feel more like a job than being fun, and I really didn't want to risk the chance of losing the love for the game. This is why I still train like I would if I were playing and use it as my favorite form of exercise and therapy.

Kyrie rests his arms on the window frame as a smirk spreads. "Yeah, I totally get that. There's just something about running the paint and making people your bitch as you pound the lane."

"Spoken like a true lover of the game."

"Damn right. What are you up to the rest of the night?"

Tapping my phone screen, I watch as text after text rolls in as I glance at the time. "I think I'm going to The Eagles Nest?"

"Don't sound so sure, Campbell."

Tipping my head to rest on my headrest, I chuckle. "Well, the group chat says that's what we are doing, but I've never been."

"Girl, it's a wild time," he says as he taps the plastic frame. "Ecstasy is going to be there, and they're fucking awesome."

"Yeah, that's what my friend, Brynn, said."

"Well, I'll probably see ya tonight."

"Have a good workout."

And with a salute, he walks away and heads toward the building. Slowly but surely, I'm starting to build a new life here, and it's so much better than I thought it would be.

Before reversing out of my spot, I scan the fifty-seven messages. *Jesus.* Most of them are between Chloe and Brynn as they debate on if

Brynn's going out tonight. At the same time, Macy interjects with the occasional message.

> **Chloe: Wear something cute and come with the guys. I need a new best friend.**

> **Brynn: Shut up, bitch. You know I'm still your favorite.**

> **Brynn: Bret—don't listen to her.**

> **Brynn: But wear something hot and get you some!**

I love their messages and toss my phone aside as I reverse out of my spot.

Guess I'm going out tonight.

It's after ten when we pull up to The Eagles Nest. There's a line of people waiting for their chance to be allowed inside while another smaller line is off to the side where a bouncer checks IDs. Luckily, Olivia knew a guy at her tattoo parlor who hooked us up with some epic fakes.

Tonight, I'm Sarah Swisher, a twenty-one-year-old from Missouri.

Harris holds the door open as music comes pouring outside while JP takes the lead, and I fall in behind him with Crew trailing me. It's like the guys sandwiched me between them so I don't get lost in the crowd, which I could see quickly happening. This place is packed.

The Eagles Nest is nothing spectacular. It's just a dive bar on campus which is everyone's place to go, or so I've been told. Worn, tiled flooring and wood-paneled walls make up the interior. Since TVs hang everywhere you look, I imagine the place is just as packed as it is tonight on game days. High-top tables are scattered about while a small section has black vinyl booths. Straight ahead of the entrance is a large L-shaped bar. Following the long part of the bar is the stage.

Heads turn as they watch the guys stride through the dense crowd. The guys' height and looks definitely draw attention.

Fingers graze against my exposed skin, and I glance over my shoulder. I'm dressed in light-washed denim jeans that hang baggy off my frame, the knees ripped out. A tight black short-sleeve cropped top hugs my chest sans bra. The shirt shows all of my tattoos, and my ears are filled with silver hoops from my cartilage to my lobes, exposing the ink behind my ear thanks to my slicked-back ponytail. A pair of white and green sneakers sit high on my ankles, completing the look. I'm dressed like me but still cute and sexy. Brynn and Chloe should be proud of me.

Crew's dark-chocolate eyes blaze as he gives a subtle wink in my direction. His wink sets butterflies free in my stomach. Someone bumps into my shoulder and rocks me off balance. Crew's hands glide around my waist keeping me from tumbling over as the guy who bumped me apologizes. The guy starts to speak to me, but I don't hear him as Crew's voice fills my ear.

"You look amazing tonight." Warmth spreads through my body. "We have a private room to the right."

Finally, I reach the private room, and shouts ring out as JP enters. The room fills the entire right side of the bar as multiple glass doors, which are propped open, separate the private room from the rest of the bar. Inside are large tables, which are overflowing, a pool table, dart boards, and more high-top tables that people lean against.

Guys from the football team, including my brother, sit at a long table in the middle. High-top tables are spread around the room where others mingle. Girls line the room, some standing next to the guys while others are on their laps. Two women flock to JP as he pours a glass of beer from the pitcher on the table.

"Babes! You made it!" Chloe stumbles over to us with Cody hot on her trail.

"I told you I'd be here." I smile, wrapping my arms around her shoulders. "You look so cute."

After only a few encounters with Chloe, I've noticed our style is completely different. Where I'm a mixture of edgy and casual with an athletic flair, Chloe is soft and feminine with her array of dresses and skirts. She's dressed in a mauve spaghetti-strapped mini dress with tiny white flowers which flow around her waist. Her honey-blonde hair is curled down her back, and a clip secures the sides of her loose waves at the back of her head. While our style might not be the same, we both have a shared love for sneakers. Her white low tops give her a casual vibe.

"She's had a few shots already," Cody tells Crew from where the two are standing next to us.

"Shhh, babe, don't tell my secrets." Chloe wraps her arm around my waist and starts to lead me away. "Let's go find you a drink."

My feet falter as I try to pump the brakes so Chloe can't lead me out toward the bar. "Oh, that's okay. I'm fine for right now."

Uneasiness pricks my skin as the fear of becoming intoxicated and letting my guard down rises. As much as I loved going out and dancing to music, it's something I did in the past. In the before. My eyes find Crew's, and he reads the panic across my face.

Cody must sense the change because he's stepping into Chloe. His arms wrap around her neck as he stands behind her. "Come on, Wildflower. Let them breathe."

"Fine." Her lips stick out in a pout. "It's just Brynn's not here, and I just want to dance with my friends."

He kisses the top of her head, and the gesture is so sweet. "Save me a dance!"

She nods excitedly before Cody pulls her over to a high-top table where other guys are standing.

"You good?" Crew's voice cuts in from beside me where he puts his hands in his dark jeans pockets. He's wearing a solid dark green tee which brings out his deep brown eyes and his sun-kissed tan skin.

My eyes find my brother, who is watching and scrutinizing me. It's suffocating to be under a microscope.

I nod. "Yeah, I-I'm just not sure I want to drink. I don't know if I'm ready to let my guard down."

His shoulders turn rigid as he purses his lips together. "Let me watch over you tonight."

My eyes fly up to his. Is he serious? And why do those words make me want to melt on the spot? I'm not able to reply because, instead, my big brother comes and interrupts us.

"What's up, little sis?" His tone is deep, and he doesn't look at me. No, Grant eyes Crew as if he's reminding him I'm off limits. Which is barbaric.

Rolling my eyes, I brush my shoulders against Grant's. "I'm going to get a drink."

If Crew's going to promise to watch over me tonight, I'm going to have myself a drink. But just a couple. Tonight is about taking baby steps.

Two hours later, sweat pours down my body. The dance floor is packed with people on top of each other. Everyone is moving to the alternative music Ecstasy has been playing for the last few hours.

When everyone was saying Ecstasy was good, they weren't kidding. Their vocals are perfect for the alternative music they cover. They've played popular songs from the '90s, early 2000s, and into today's alt music. Cody and Chloe have been dancing beside me all night while guys from the baseball and football teams filter in around us. I've been nursing a few beers which I've either gotten myself or watched Crew get. Speaking of Crew, he hasn't moved far from my sight all night. Grant has been close by as well, he's been dancing on and off with a brunette, who Chloe told me was their friend, Savannah.

Overall, the night has been good. Except for the fact a raging surge of jealousy courses through my veins and mixes with the alcohol every time I watch a girl approach Crew to dance. It's like a revolving door of women wanting to dance with him, and I can't say I blame them, but for some reason, it makes me feel itchy.

Some girls he dances with, and others he politely declines their offers. I appreciate how kind he is with his rejection, it shows the type of person he is. Glancing over my shoulder, I can't help the red-hot jealousy that pumps through my system. Even though his hands are on someone else, his eyes never stray from mine. But I can't take it any longer.

Excusing myself from the group, I find a long hallway where the bathrooms are located. Should I be going alone? No, but fuck it. I need a minute. There's a glass door at the back of the hallway which I can tell leads to the outside. I'm almost to the door when a hand reaches out and grabs my elbow.

"Where are you running off to, Rebel?" His deep voice is husky, which isn't helping the whole ache between my thighs.

A scream escapes, but a hand is quickly placed over my mouth, silencing me as he shushes me. The panic subsides as I whirl around, and I'm met with my favorite mocha-colored eyes. Crew stands before me, sweat glistening on his skin. His blonde hair is mussed from his fingers running through it while his chest heaves as his gaze trails over my body. Electric shock burns through my system as I fight the ache building between my thighs.

Crew Riggsby looks devilishly handsome tonight. He moves us into a closet across from the bathrooms. Supplies line the shelves as the outside is silenced. The only sound in the room is the click of the lock.

Crew's large frame leans against the door, arms crossed over his chest, allowing his muscles to bulge.

"Needed some air." Crossing my arms over my chest, I try to mock his stance. I fail miserably as Crew tracks the movement.

"And why's that?" He's pushing and waiting.

We both know why I'm running.

"Because I can't take the sight of other girls dancing with you. It's making me unexplainably jealous."

He hums as his eyes never leave mine. "I think I can explain it."

Waving my hands out before me, I beg him to explain. "Please, explain it to me then."

"I think you want me, but you're afraid to want me."

Damn this man.

With a lean and raised eyebrow, I stare back at him, refusing to let him see any more inside of me.

"And so what if I do?"

In slow, calculated steps, Crew starts erasing the space between us. "I think maybe you should start living your life, Rebel."

My heartbeat rapidly increases. My blood pumps in a drumming noise as if I was still standing in front of the band playing in the other room. Each beat and pulse feels like it will bounce right out of my chest as the nerves and excitement of having Crew this close to me escalate. The air becomes thick as tension swirls around us. My breaths become ragged as I watch his warm eyes darken, the rich hue intensifying, almost taking on a black intensity as desire flashes through his irises.

Fuck it.

Reaching out, I grip the cotton material of his moss-green T-shirt and tug him toward me. Stretching on my tiptoes, our lips meet as fireworks explode behind my closed eyes, and I melt into his touch. Without hesitation, our kiss turns heated as our mouths part, and he plunges his tongue into mine. His hands grip onto the back of my legs as he hoists me into the air. Instinctively, my legs wrap around his waist as he shoves me against the wall. Our tongues duel fervently as I grind my center against the denim of his jeans where I feel how affected he is.

Crew's mouth leaves mine as he leaves a trail of nips and open-mouthed kisses along my jaw and down my neck, where he sucks my skin into his mouth. His hands roam over my body as his thumb flicks the metal piercing through my nipple. Tilting my head back, I let out a moan, as I don't bother being quiet as I knew the music from the band would drown out the noise.

Wetness gathers between my legs as I feel my panties dampen. I want more, but realization comes crashing into me. Squeezing my legs around Crew's waist, I push my body away from him. His lips leave my neck as dark, hooded eyes find mine. Our chests heaves, and our lips are swollen from the rough kisses.

"Fuck, Rebel," his voice is husky and raw. "Everything okay?"

I nod. "Everything is perfect."

"Then why'd you stop?"

Tipping my head down, I rest it on his shoulder as my lips find his neck for a peck. "As much as I want to see where this goes, I don't need my brother to come looking for us."

Crew groans as he lowers me. He starts to step away but I reach out and grab his arm, stopping him. "I want to continue this, but we need to be more careful right now. My brother's Bret-senses are at an all-time high, and there's the whole you-play-for-my-dad's-team. But what if we..."

Crew quirks his brow while I pause, mulling over the words. Chewing on my lip, I look up at him through my lashes. "I have a proposition for you."

"I'm listening, Rebel."

That damn nickname. I swear it does something to me every time it leaves his lips. It's like he can see me and while it touches on my rebellious streak, he knows that by me rebelling, I'm trying to find myself.

"Things are a little complicated between us being roommates and you being on the football team, but I can't deny that there's a connection between us. Right?" Crew nods, a mask falling over his face where I can't read him. "Okay, I think we should explore that connection. But there's a catch."

"And what's the catch, Bret." Reaching up, he trails a finger down my cheek eliciting goose bumps to break across my skin.

"The catch is we do it exclusively and...secretively. It has to stay between us. I don't want drama with—"

My words are cut off as his lips crush into mine with a searing kiss. It's short but impactful. "You think we can pull it off?"

"I think if we want this, we have to."

He hums. "If that's what it will take for me to be with you, then let's do it. You, me, us, we're the only ones that have to know."

"Us," I murmur. "I like the sound of that. Now get out of here, and I'll be behind you shortly."

His lips find mine one last time before he sneaks out of the closet door.

A boyfriend wasn't on my plans for this school year, but the heart wants what the heart wants.

CHAPTER 14
CREW

T he first home game of the season always hits differently. As I stand in the tunnel waiting for our time to run onto the field, the crowd's roar vibrating with the energy radiating from my teammates seeps into my skin. It's a sea of red, white, and powder blue as I look out at the sold-out crowd.

Coach Campbell stands in front of us as he fires us up with one last pep talk. But I barely hear him. My mind is already on the field as I wait for the marching band to play our introduction song which we run out to each week. Tilting my helmet-covered head, I welcome the cracks in my neck as my gloved fingers itch at my sides. Adrenaline courses through my veins, and I can't wait to be on the turf.

Cannons sound as smoke fills the air in front of the tunnel. Harris, Grant, and JP lead us out of the opening. The roar of the crowd only grows as we jog out. Once we reach our sidelines, my eyes scan the fans, taking in the blur of faces. I fight the urge to look at the end zone where the student section is, knowing my eyes will latch on to familiar green eyes. As much as my mind drifts to Bret, now is not the time to think about my girlfriend.

Girlfriend.

It still feels weird to think she made things official with us two days ago. Keeping it a secret isn't something I wanted to do. I hate that I'm hiding her because a girl like Bret shouldn't be kept behind closed doors. She deserves to be seen. But I get her hesitancy. Not only is she my roommate, which could potentially cause issues between all the roommates, but there are also issues with the whole team.

Could I have picked a more complicated girl to fall for? Not only is she my teammate's sister, a teammate who has made it abundantly clear that she's off limits, but she's my coach's daughter.

If you look up complicated in the dictionary, you will find a picture of Bret and a picture of me.

Love this for us. But no matter what the risk is, she's worth it.

Hands slap my helmet as Harris screams in my face. "You ready, Riggs?"

"Hell yeah!" I shout back, pushing against his chest. Harris continues slapping the helmets of the starting offense as he gets everyone psyched for the game.

Within a few minutes, the captains are walking across the field as I stand on the sideline with my helmet in one hand and the other grips the neckline of my jersey. The announcer works the fans, and the crowded stands erupt in cheers.

I stand on the sideline with the team as the special teams take the field for kickoff. The White Stripes' "Seven Nation Army" blares from the speakers as the crowd jumps in their seats.

It's loud.

It's crazy.

It's game time.

"Goddamn, I'm going to miss this next year." Grant's voice is loud next to me as we wait for our turn on the field. We play offense together—me as a tight end and Grant as a wide receiver.

"You could just flunk out spring semester. Come back and play with us one last time."

He laughs. "Yeah, Riggs, that'll be the day. I'm pretty sure if I fail out, my dad will kick me off the team."

"Yeah, you're probably right. It'd be nice to get to play with you guys again next year."

He shoves my shoulder as the crowd cheers at something our defense does. "Don't be getting all soft on me now."

"Nah, not me. We've got some ass to kick."

"Yeah, buddy!"

The defense comes running off the field and gives shoulder bumps as they jump in the air. They were able to hold the opposing offense to a quick three-and-out. Jogging onto the field, I find my position on the left side, lining up near the opposing team's bench, between the offensive tackles and Grant, our wide receiver. Harris takes his position under center as he calls out the play before waiting for the play clock to wind down.

The ball is snapped, and as Harris steps back into the pocket, I block the defender in front of me creating a gap for Xavier Boyd, Quinton's younger brother, to run through. It's a quick five-yard play. Jogging into position, I do the same thing as I did before. Football is a lot of repetition.

Lineup in position. Ball snaps to the quarterback. Block the defender in front of me. Repeat.

On third down, Harris calls out a new play with ten seconds left on the play clock. With my toes behind the line, my fingers twitch in anticipation. The ball is snapped as Harris drops back. I take off like a rocket, cutting through defenders as I find an opening.

With a slant movement, I turn to the sideline as the ball sails into my waiting arms. Spinning against the defender, I slip past the waiting defender. Tucking the football into my arms so that it's secure, I pump my legs as I rush toward the end zone. I'm five yards shy when I'm taken down.

Jumping to my feet, I'm greeted with congratulatory slaps against my helmet. The hollow knock and metallic clang echo inside the enclosed space. The jolting sound cuts through the background noise, a sudden reminder of the game's intensity.

Resuming my position on the outside, we repeat the motion. Only this time, Harris slides back and throws the ball into the end zone to a waiting Campbell.

"Drink up!"

The ping-pong ball splashes into the plastic cup of beer. Harris stands on the opposite side of the table from me with a shit-eating grin on his face. The fucker is kicking my ass at beer pong. He's dropping shot after shot, just like he threw for five touchdowns in our victory.

We've been at this party for three hours, and I don't think there's an end in sight. The Baseball House—where Cody Jacobs and three of his teammates live—is throwing the rager and bodies fill the space from room to room. A DJ has set up a table in the corner and has been keeping the party bumping with banger after banger.

Bret and Chloe dance on the makeshift dance floor in the living room where couches used to be. She hasn't been far from view, but when I texted her earlier, she insisted I celebrate the win with the team since she isn't drinking tonight.

I can safely say that I have. A happy buzz fills my system as the alcohol courses through my veins. Reaching for the red cup, I chug the piss-warm beer. In high school, we would play with water cups and chug our beer from a can, but here it's unsanitary beer in cups.

JP nudges my shoulder as a goofy, drunk grin spreads across his face. He's been hitting the hard liquor, and he's on his way to black out.

"You're carrying this team, bro." His words are slurred.

"No shit. Are you even conscious?"

His eyes flicker as he tries to focus on my face. "Barely."

Patting his shoulder, I turn my attention back to the game. JP and I have five cups to hit still while Harris and Cody have two. It's not even a competition anymore.

With a flick of my wrist, I let the white ball fly through the air. Golden liquid splashes in the air, and I smirk. "Drink up, bitch!"

Cody tsks and waves his finger. "Now, now, don't get so cocky, young pup."

"Oh god." I scrunch my nose. "Don't let that one stick."

The guys all laugh, and I groan. For the first two years of college, I was the "class clown" of the group, and I've had my fair share of embarrassing moments. The guys are never going to let me live down some of them.

JP holds the ball in the air, swaying on his feet, and launches the ball toward the cup. Or what must be a blurred version for him since he missed the white rim by a mile.

"Did I make it?"

Harris bends over, clutching his stomach, and howls out a laugh. "Yeah, man. You nailed it."

In two quick shots, the game is over, and I find myself chugging the two glasses they knock out. The warm, hoppy suds slide past my lips. With the back of my hand, I wipe the few droplets that slip free.

JP meanders off, and I hope it's to find someone to unlock the third-floor crash pad to pass out. The guys keep their finished attic locked for close friends to sleep over if needed. Harris and Jacobs scoot past the spectators as they make their way over to me. The three of us stare out at the dance floor where Bret and Chloe dance with a group of people. Guys try to slide their way behind the girls, but they don't let them. Instead, they twist until they dance against each other.

"How's it living with the coach's daughter?"

"It's not bad. Between everyone's schedules, it's like we hardly see each other." I slide my hands in my pockets as I resist the urge to run out on the dance floor and pull my girl into my arms. But we can't do that.

It feels like I've been tethered to Bret since last Christmas. I'm glad she's finally giving us a chance, even with all the complications.

Harris takes a pull on the bottle he's holding. "She's pretty fucking cool."

"That's what Wildflower was saying. Although, there's no way in hell I'd trade places with you guys. She's temptation, and that's a dangerous thing, boys."

"I'll be back." I give the guys a nod as I step out of the conversation. Sliding past sweaty bodies, I'm slapped on the shoulder and congratulated as I pass people. Bret's forest green eyes connect with mine as I flash her a wink before climbing the stairs. There's a bathroom on the main floor, but I'm sure it's lined up out the back.

Taking the steps two at a time, I'm relieved when the upstairs bathroom is vacant. A hand reaches out as a body slides between the wooden door as I go to shut it. "It's about time you snuck away."

"Rebel," I groan as I peruse the girl I've been watching from afar all night.

She's dressed in a unique oversized T-shirt that hangs long down her body. Light-washed shorts with frayed edges top her olive-toned, long athletic legs. Only the frayed edges of her distressed shorts can be seen beneath her shirt. In true, typical fashion, Bret has a pair of sneakers on her feet.

"Those are the same shoes you wore the day you moved in."

Her head tilts as she checks which shoes she's wearing. "You remember?"

"Of course, I remember. Rebel, I remember everything about you. Last winter when you came to the Christmas party, you were wearing a green sweater dress that matched your eyes. Military videos make you cry, especially when soldiers come home. You're not a pet person, but you love cat videos. Cinnamon is your favorite flavor, especially cinnamon rolls and Cinnamon Toast Crunch. You'd rather spend money on a new pair of sneakers than high-end makeup. You want to be an athletic director and fight to make sure girls are given the same opportunity as guys in sports programs. Oh, and you're kickass at video games."

"Okay, okay." A laugh bubbles out of her as she wraps her arms around my neck. "I guess you do remember things about me."

I nod, reaching my hands around her and propping her onto the counter. Our height difference isn't too far off and with her on the elevated surface, we are now sitting at eye level.

"Great game out there. I've been waiting all night to tell you in person."

"And I've been waiting all night to do this." Bending down, I capture her mouth with mine, which she graciously accepts. In a fluid of motion, our hands find each other. Her warm hands slip beneath my shirt as she slides them up before scrapping her short nails against my skin.

My hands move underneath the long tee shirt as I toy with the button on her shorts. Her head nods in silent permission as I flick the button through the loop. Tugging on the band, she slides her butt closer to the edge so that I can drag the material down her legs. She toes off her sneakers to free her legs entirely from the confines of her shorts as I drop to my knees.

"Now that's quite the view." Her fingers glide through my hair as I stare up.

"If you think that's a view, you should see it from my angle." I smirk as my lips find the soft spot of her knee as I kiss my way up her thigh. As much as I want to savor this moment, I know our time is limited. One of these nights I'm going to get to enjoy Bret Campbell in slow, languid movements without rushing and the fear of getting caught.

Hands leave my hair as she reaches for the hem of her shirt and tugs it over her head. She reaches behind her back and frees her breasts from her black bra. The straps slide down her arms before finding a spot on the floor beside her shirt. Within minutes, she's sitting on the edge of the counter wearing only a scrap of lace.

"You're so fucking beautiful." She blushes slightly before she spreads her legs wider, giving me the perfect view of her lace-covered pussy. My mouth waters at the anticipation of what's to come. Slipping my thumbs beneath the material, I work the lace down her legs before it finds the same destination as the rest of her clothes.

Sitting back on my legs, I take a moment to soak in Bret in all of her flawless, naked glory. This is the first time I'm getting a chance to look at her in the light. Black ink pops against her tan skin. The metal piercings contrast against her pink, erect nipples. Indents on her stomach showcase the abs she works hard to maintain. But next to her bare pussy is black ink that has me pausing.

With my finger, I graze the words that are tattooed below her panty line near her hip bone. "Lucky you."

A devilish smile paints her face. "You can thank Olivia for that."

I quirk a brow waiting for more, but she shrugs one shoulder. That explanation is good enough for me. I'm not really in the mood to talk right now anyway, as my cock twitches in my pants, reminding me what I'm in the middle of.

Leaning forward, my lips kiss her soft skin. I lightly trace my tongue over the ink as I make my way down her body. Goose bumps are left on the trail that I make as I place open-mouth kisses across her thighs and right above her pussy. Her legs widen, and her head falls back as she lets out a moan. I pull her closer to the edge and drape her legs over my shoulders. Fingers weave their way into my hair, guiding me to her center.

"Take what you need from me," I mumble the words against her flesh.

Bret rides my face seeking friction against my stubble as I continue finger fucking her. With every pump and every flick, she's closer to falling over the edge. Watching Bret come apart might be the hottest thing I've ever experienced.

I want so desperately to be inside her. To feel her pussy grip my cock as she explodes around me. But now isn't the time.

My mouth finds her clit as she palms her breasts and pinches her nipples. I flick my tongue against her while I stroke my fingers deep inside her.

"Oh god, I'm going to come." The raspy words only spur me on.

Pumping harder, I twist my fingers while I bite down on her sensitive bud. "I'm coming, I'm coming. I'm—" Bret's voice trails off as she fights the scream as her orgasm rips through her. With my free hand, I cover her mouth to help muffle her screams. Her hips grind against my hand as she rides the euphoric wave.

When I'm certain she isn't going to give us away, I remove my hand from her mouth as I remove my fingers inside her wet heat. Her come drips down my hand, and my cock aches to be touched by her. But he'll have to wait.

Bret's naked chest heaves as pink blotches coat her flawless skin. With droopy eyes and a lopsided smile, Bret pulls me to her. "That mouth of yours."

Placing a kiss on her lips, she licks the seam of my mouth. The taste of her coating her tongue, and she hums in appreciation.

"Rebel, we've gotta get out of here. People are going to start to wonder where we disappeared to."

"It's a big party. We could easily find a bedroom and lock ourselves in it for the next hour, and no one would know we were missing."

Resting my forehead against hers, I leave a soft kiss on the tip of her nose. "As much as I love that idea, the only bedroom I'm locking you in is either yours or mine. Preferably mine so I can smell you every time I fall asleep."

"Then take me home, Crew Riggsby."

CHAPTER 15
Bret

As I walk through the bustling campus on this early Tuesday morning, black coffee in hand, I make my way to the brick business building where my sports management classes are held.

Sports management is a unique field of study for women, but it's one I'm very passionate about. In high school, there was an imbalance between the boys' and girls' programs. We weren't given the same access to weight training equipment and gym time. Even our game schedule was never to opponents that matched our skill level. While I understand there is a difference between boys and girls, I want the opportunity to showcase that women deserve the same opportunities as men.

There's a vibrant energy floating around campus this morning—chatter and laughter bubbles around me as I take the cobblestone sidewalks. The air around the quad almost feels lighter. Is there something going on I don't know about? Or is this what normal people feel? The type of people whose past hasn't been haunted, who don't travel with a dark cloud floating above their head. I feel my face mirroring theirs with each head nod and tight-lipped smile.

It's been a month since I moved to Texas. Slowly, over each day, the walls I've constructed are crumbling. The relationships I'm forming feel genuine. And for the first time in a long time, I feel like I belong. Arizona was a stepping stone for fake friendships, aside from Olivia, but these friendships feel real. They don't feel forced just because I'm the coach's daughter or their friend's sister. I feel like I actually matter to them.

Crew is a big part of that, but I refuse to let him be the only reason for my shift. Feelings are hard to fight, especially when they are as strong as they are between us, but at the end of the day, I'm still here to learn about myself. I refuse to let myself fall into the same pattern I did in Arizona, where I let a guy control me to the point he shaped who I was.

This morning, when I woke up, the boys were long gone for their early morning practice. A text from Crew was waiting for me. It was such a minor gesture, but it brightened my morning instantly. I'm a total simp for a good morning text. In our quiet apartment, I could sit with myself for a more extended meditation session than I usually would. I took the time to focus on my goals and really talk to my inner self. Savasana didn't feel as heavy as it usually would. In fact, everything about this morning felt lighter.

Olivia was right. I needed a fresh start surrounded by family.

Climbing the few steps at the front of the business building, I push my way through the glass doors. The inside completely contrasts with the exterior, which I love. Central Texas is an old campus. It's been around for over a hundred years, but when they remodeled all of the buildings, they incorporated a modern feel to the interior while keeping the older charm of brick on the exterior.

Students mill around the open space of the lobby, where a stock market ticker runs on the wall. I pass a group of guys dressed in business attire—dress pants and button-up shirts. I've heard some classes require students to dress as if they were showing up in an office. I think it's great practice, but I'm glad my classes don't require that. We have the rest of our lives to dress professionally.

Tonight is my first intramural game, and since today is my long day on campus, I'm already dressed in the clothes I'll wear for the game. This is why I'm thankful I have the freedom to wear what I want for class. I'm dressed in white lightweight basketball shorts that hit mid-thigh with a black Michael Jordan Chicago Bulls jersey.

Taking the stairs two at a time, I make it to the third floor, where my classmates wait for the doors to open for the lecture hall. The doors open within minutes, and students begin funneling inside the mid-sized room. Clutching my backpack straps, I bounce down the stairs until I sit closer to the front, but not in the front row. Sliding down the row, I find a vacant seat in the middle.

Slipping my backpack free from my shoulders, I place it at my feet as I sit. After removing my laptop, I log in and find my Word document for note taking while waiting for the professor.

Right on time, our professor, a former Major League Soccer executive, enters the room and takes his place behind the podium. He adjusts his iPad until it's projecting on the large screen, and he's ready to dive into the day's lesson in sports ethics and laws—a topic I find quite interesting.

"Good morning," the professor greets, his commanding voice silences the large room. He's the only professor I have who doesn't use a microphone. His deep, booming voice is loud enough. "This morning, we will dive into scandals in the sports world."

Flipping the screen, the title of an article appears as he directs us to a case study that was available on the online portal. The room falls silent as we read the article. The scandal was something I was familiar with, but as I read the article, new details came to light. Many people admired the athlete, and when the news came out, it rocked the sports world.

After a few minutes, Professor Delgado interrupts the silence. "All right, now that you are familiar with the case, let's discuss. What are your initial thoughts?"

Hands raise around me, but I hesitate. Professor Delgado calls on someone. "I think it's greed."

I roll my eyes while the professor asks the student to elaborate.

"Everything is about money, and it's a proven fact that when an athlete is the best, they gain better sponsorships and contracts."

The professor moves from behind the podium and leans against the desk, arms crossed over his chest, as he observes the class.

"That's an interesting take and very possible. Does anyone else have an opinion as to why an athlete may turn to doping."

Again, hands raise, but this time, I don't hesitate as my hand shoots into the air. Professor Delgado points to me. My heart rate increases as my palms grow balmy, and the attention of the class turns toward me. Public speaking is not my favorite thing. In fact, I'd rather be the silent observer, but this topic needs a different perspective.

"What about the mental health of the athlete?"

"Oh, great, here we go," some douchebag behind me interrupts. "There's always one who has to bring up mental health as a reason."

A few whispers and chuckles follow, but I refuse to acknowledge them as I keep my attention on the front of the room where our professor stands. He gives me a "go ahead" twirl of his fingers.

"Mental health is a valid reason. Let's take college athletes, for example. Most athletes are eighteen to twenty-two years old, experiencing independence for the first time without parental guidance while juggling the pressures of the game they love. There's a culture surrounding sports to win at all costs because fans and the media will let you know of their disapproval if you don't. These athletes are always under stress to perform at their best, to never make a mistake, and to win at all costs. Social media and keyboard warriors have entered the athletes' space, and the pressure has only grown with it. God forbid a team loses, and so-called fans are calling for players to be traded, to be benched, and, as fucked up as it is, to 'kill themselves.' There are jokes about putting athletes on suicide watch if they make a mistake that costs the game. Newsflash, one mistake isn't the reason for a loss. Sure, in that moment, it might seem that way, but a missed tackle or a turnover causing the opponent to score can all be factors in why a team loses, not one missed field goal. The stress has reached an all-time high with the entitlement of the fans and so has the desire to be the best, which has only increased the temptation to doping."

Silence falls over the room as the professor watches me, and an uneasiness rolls down my spine. Did I say too much? But just as I'm starting to doubt myself, a curve starts on Professor Delgado's lips, morphing into a smile.

"Ahh, that's a very unique approach in more of the athlete's mindset." My cheeks heat as more heads snap my way.

Professor Delgado returns to his place behind the podium as he continues the lecture. I settle in and begin to type away on my keyboard, notating key points. An hour later, as class starts to come to an end, he flips to the last slide of his presentation.

"Your next assignment will be to create an educational campaign to prevent doping in sports. As sports management majors, it is important for you to understand the reasoning behind an athlete's motivation to dope, as well as regulations and consequences."

He clicks to the next slide with all the assignment details, and I allow my fingers to fly over the keys as I type out all of the details as he speaks. "With the assignment, you should create a comprehensive and impactful campaign targeting both athletes and the broader sports community. I want to give you the freedom to be creative with this assignment. You can approach it any way you think will be most effective."

On the screen is a list of ideas ranging from poster designs to social media strategies, a presentation plan that includes videos with interactive polls, and alternative approaches that could include documentaries, podcasts, or designing an app.

My brain begins to spin as I think of how I'll complete this assignment, but the one thing I know is that I'll be raising awareness of mental health struggles among athletes.

"Whichever strategy you decide on, there should be an overall theme to your presentation, whether it be gaining more monetary benefits, mental health pressures, wanting to be the best in their sport, or whatever the case may be. Remember, the goal of this assignment is not just to complete it for a grade but to create something that could be used in real life to make a genuine difference in the sports world. There will be a detailed rubric and some examples of effective campaigns to help guide you on the portal. You will have four weeks to complete this assignment, but don't wait until the last minute. If you have any questions, please feel free to email me or schedule a meeting with me during office hours. Good luck."

And with those parting words, Professor Delgado dismisses class. Shutting down my laptop, I slide it into my backpack before heading down the row. A few lingering people remain, and I can feel their eyes tracking my movements. But I don't pay them any attention. I still have over five hours left in my school day before I can work my problems out on the basketball court.

"There she is," Dylan, one of the guys on my team, greets me as I make my way across the court to our bench on the sideline.

Kyrie, another teammate, nods. "S'up, baller?"

"Hey, guys!" I give a small wave.

Finding a spot on the bench, I sit and unlace my sneakers before reaching inside my gym bag and pulling out my basketball shoes. Sliding my stocking feet inside the black sneakers, I adjust the tongue before tightening the laces until they're snug on my feet.

Tonight, my team is one of the six playing in the first time slot. When I read over the schedule, I was surprised to see how many teams there would be in the intramural league. There are three time slots, with sixteen teams playing every Tuesday night. When I pulled into the lot, I was shocked to see how many cars were parked.

The echo of dribbling basketballs fills the air, mixing with the crowd's buzzing as they filter into the stands. Kyrie stands in front of the bench as he introduces all of the players on the team. It turns out that I'm the only girl on the team, but Dylan keeps bragging about the first time watching me play.

The other team steps foot on the court first, and we follow suit. All twelve of us shake hands as the referee reminds us that while this game is to be played following the regular basketball rules, we are to have fun still. Once he goes over the rules, a player from each team takes their place on the bench.

Lucky for me, I'm starting. The other team is all males, which is fine. Kyrie takes his position at center court with the other team's tallest player as we wait for the jump ball. I'm standing to the side when a player from the other team steps up next to me.

"You sure you're ready to play with the big boys, princess? I heard the volleyball team is looking for players."

Determination courses through my veins as I pinch my face in annoyance. "Don't worry."

The referee tosses the ball in the air as Kyrie easily outjumps the other guy. He swats the ball to one of my teammates and we all take off down the court. I'm first to make it down to our side of the court, and as I run toward the hoop, Dustin whips a bounce pass toward the basketball. Snatching the ball flawlessly, I easily make the layup, allowing my team to get on the board first.

My defender mumbles something about it being a lucky shot. It's too bad for him. He has no idea what he's in store for. His insecure masculinity is going to be put to the test.

Dylan forces a turnover and passes the ball to Dustin, who dribbles the ball up the court. I find my position on the left side. Jabbing toward the center, I rub my defender off my teammate's shoulder as I free myself outside the three-point line. Dustin passes me the ball as my defender catches up.

He waves his arms between us as he takes a step back, allowing the distance between us to grow. "Go ahead, princess. I'll even give you extra space to dribble in."

Fuck. This. Guy.

With a glance at the hoop, I position my fingers across the ball's seams. My eyes find my defenders as my feet leave the ground, and I release the ball toward the hoop. With a flick of my wrist, the ball spins in a perfect arch. Swish. The ball sails into the net as I hold my arm in the air, allowing my follow-through to be over the top, and I wink at the defender.

"Oops, sorry. Looks like you might want to play defense."

The first half was a lot like the opening minutes. Our team continued to play as a team, while our opponents were more interested in showcasing their own skills. Their cockiness kept them in the way of succeeding.

The referee blows his whistle, signaling the end of halftime. Stepping foot onto the court, I adjust my ponytail as I scan the crowd. A red CTU hat catches my attention, and familiar brown eyes track my movement. My lip curls as I fight the grin desperate to break free.

Crew freaking Riggsby is at my game. Sitting in the back corner to avoid drawing attention. And he just winked at me. Be still my heart.

Kyrie nudges my shoulder as he steps next to me. "Ready to put this in the bag?"

"You bet. I had no idea how competitive this league was."

"That still okay?"

"Hell yeah. I'm living for this." I nod toward an opponent who is stepping out onto the court. "Did you see the face on that asshole when I drained that three in his face?"

"I think everyone saw that."

"That's what happens when you make dumbass comments that girls can't ball."

The whistle sounds again, and I take my place on the left side of the court near the three-point line as I wait for one of the guys on my team to bring the ball up the court. The dumbass I was just talking about is guarding me, and his arrogance is suffocating.

It's a very entertaining event. Music plays from the speakers as an announcer walks around the gymnasium, interviewing fans and cracking jokes. The intramural program is designed to not only get students playing basketball, but at the end of each semester, the organization puts on a charity tournament, where proceeds benefit a different organization each semester. This year's contributions will be donated to a youth center a few blocks away that needs an updated basketball court.

As the final buzzer rings out, Kyrie lands a jump shot underneath the basket. Cheers erupt as we make our way over to the bench. Sweat coats my skin as my lungs feel the slight burn from running up and down the court. My muscles felt alive as their memory of the game quickly took over.

"Nice game out there," Kyrie compliments the whole team. I'm squeezing a stream of water into my mouth. The douche from the other team stepped up his game and overcompensated his defense. I had to work harder in the fourth quarter, but it wasn't anything I couldn't handle.

We gather in a line beside our bench, and I scan the crowd of moving bodies searching for a familiar face as we wait for the other team. When we start moving, I stick my hand out and congratulate the other team on a good game.

Mr. Douche has a smarmy grin on his face. "Nice game. I didn't realize girls could actually play ball."

Dylan steps into the guy's face as I step between the two. With a hand on Dylan's chest, I look back over my shoulder. "Thanks. I'll be sure to use your toxic masculinity as fuel for my next game."

"Everything all right over here?" the referee asks as he approaches the situation.

"Everything's great." I toss another smile and return to the bench, Dylan hot on my heels.

"You should've let me punch him."

I shake my head as I sit on the bench. "Nah, he wasn't worth it. I scored sixteen points on him. That'll eat him up more than your fist."

"You sure about that? I'd make sure to land a good one." I chuckle, unlacing my shoes.

A shadow falls over it, and my first reaction is Crew. But as I land a brimming smile on the person above me, it quickly morphs into shock, and my smile slips slightly from my face.

"Grant?"

"Hey, little sis."

"Little sis?" Kyrie pauses. "You mean to tell me we have one of *the* Campbells on our team?"

"Shit, no wonder the girl can ball," Dustin adds from beside me.

Grant crosses his arms over his chest as he eyes my teammate while I suppress an eye roll. "Yeah, which means y'all better behave."

The guys all nod, and this time, I let my eyes roll. "Dad is waiting out in the hallway. We thought we'd treat you to dinner."

Zipping my gym bag, I toss it on my shoulders as I fall in step beside my brother, who tosses his arm over my sweat-soaked shoulders. Grant's body stiffens slightly. I follow his gaze and find Crew waiting, his back against the wall. "The hell you doing here, Riggsby?"

"Watching my roommate play ball." His reply is quick and confident. He doesn't give away that we are dating in the slightest.

Grant's jaw tightens as he nods.

"We're going to grab dinner with Dad. Do you want to join?"

Crew slips his hands in his pocket and pulls out his phone. "Nah, that's okay. I just wanted to swing by and catch the end of the game. See you back at the apartment."

My attention latches on to Crew thumbing away on his phone, and insecurities creep in. Is he texting a girl? What if he finds a girl who doesn't have the baggage like I do?

Shaking those thoughts from my head, I nod. "Yeah, that sounds good. Thanks for swinging by."

With a terse nod, we walk away in opposite directions, and I'm left feeling guilty for hiding my relationship with Crew.

But it's for the best.

At least, I hope.

CHAPTER 16
CREW

"What's up, Riggs?" JP sits at a table inside the private room of The Benjamin Liberty Library, where the football team has a weekly mandatory study session. The library was quieter than usual on a Wednesday evening, but that's how I like it. The fewer people inside, the less attention it brings to the football team. Not all of the team members show up at the same time on the same day, most study times revolve around everyone's schedules.

Pulling out a chair opposite him, I toss my backpack onto the table next to my cup of peanut butter and mocha iced coffee. I'm the type of person who shows up for class with an array of drinks stemming from some kind of caffeine, a bottle of water, and a protein shake of some sort. Tonight I'm going with only two options: coffee and a water bottle.

A few guys filter into the room, taking seats and pulling out textbooks. I followed suit and removed my agricultural finance textbook from my backpack along with my notebook and laptop. Tonight, I've got a hot date with a case study. As I start skimming over the notes from class, Harris drops down next to me with a huff.

"Tyler, you're late," the monitor overseeing our study tables says from where she sits in the back corner, her nose in a book.

Instead of replying, Harris let out a huff, which sounded more like a growl.

"Everything okay, man?" I ask, my voice barely audible so as not to get yelled at by the monitor.

Harris removes a stack of anatomy flashcards and a sports physiology book from his backpack and places them on the table, aggressively garnering the attention of the monitor. "Just a shitty quarterback's practice followed by another shitty media day. I'm so tired of the bullshit questions about how I'm overrated according to fans online hiding behind their screens and if it was a fluke we won the championship last year. Like Jesus Christ, I'm doing the best I fucking can."

Running my hand down my face, I let out a sigh. "Damn, man, that's rough. You know you're the best quarterback I've ever had? Bret was right when she told you that your football IQ and work ethic are unmatched."

"Thanks, man. I'm just tired of the media vultures."

JP snaps his head up from where he's reading. "They're unhinged this season."

Reaching out, I squeeze Harris's shoulder and give him a reassuring smile. "You're not alone, man. Don't let the pressure get in your head. Shut the shit out and focus on your game. Just be you, and we'll be right there with you."

Nothing else is said as we all return our attention to our assignments. Harris spends the next hour flipping cards as he memorizes anatomy parts. JP reads through his marketing textbook and takes notes while I read over financial statements from a large agricultural firm.

For my agricultural finance class, we have to analyze financial statements and identify key ratios, assess the farm's economic health, and provide recommendations for improvements.

Deciding to pursue a degree in ag business was an obvious choice for me. Our family farm in Silo Bay is the second largest farm in our county, right behind Drummond Acres, and one of the top farms in the state. I've always known my future would be to work for the family farm, and I wanted to make sure I knew I could continue growing our business bigger and stronger for future generations.

Even though I know my ending is Silo Bay, it's still uncertain when I'll take things over. I still have two years left at CTU, and there's the possibility of going pro. Right now, my mom and grandparents are still running things and neither have any plans to step aside, which is fine with me.

And then there's my brother. As the firstborn son, Jett is supposed to be the first in line to take things over. However, he never showed interest in the farm when he was home. Now, he's been gone chasing wars and fighting the good fight for years while avoiding the responsibility at home.

Finally, the monitor announces the hour-and-a-half study session is over. Draining the rest of my water bottle, I place my items back into my backpack. I'm almost to the door when Harris nudges my shoulder. "Wanna go get a few reps in at the gym?"

"Sure, man."

"JP?"

JP situates his backpack on his shoulders as his hands clasp the straps. "Nah, man. Gotta work."

The two of us walk down the main stairs. The sun has long since set, and the library is lit in a warm glow from all the lamps and chandeliers. The Benjamin Liberty Library is one of the original buildings on campus, with its unique brick craftsmanship and a wall of stained-glass windows.

"JP has been working a lot," I muse.

"Yeah, I guess his sister was accepted into a music camp next summer, and it's pretty expensive. JP wants to make sure she can go, so he's been picking up extra shifts when he can."

"Damn. I mean, how cool for his sister, but that's a lot on him."

Harris nods. "It is. I guess his mom hasn't been getting the hours at her third job like she thought."

I hum in response. JP is one of five kids, and he's a prominent provider for his siblings. His dad bailed when he was ten and since then, his mom has been balancing two to three jobs to make ends meet. As hard as his mom works, things are still tight, so JP works when he can and then sends money home.

A vibration from my pocket has me reaching for my cell phone as I land on the main floor. Harris leads the way, opening the door for me as I read my sister's text message. It has a picture of her bottle-feeding a new black-and-white calf.

Saylor: Look at this cutie who arrived this morning!

Me: Why is he on the bottle?

Saylor: Weird. I thought I was texting my fun brother, not my grumpy one.

Me: Sorry. I just got out of study tables. I didn't know we were calfing already.

Saylor: I guess I can forgive you. This little guy came a little early, but he's doing fine.

Me: He is cute.

Saylor: Well, of course he is. He's a Riggs-by calf.

Me: That's right.

Saylor: Miss you, brother.

Me: Miss you too.

Saylor: How's things with Bret?

Me: Nothing is going on with me and Bret.

Saylor: If you say so.

Sliding my phone in my pocket, I shake my head. Silence falls over us as we walk the vacant sidewalks toward the football facility. Harris is lost in his thoughts and I let him stew with them. Tyler Harris is one of the best guys I know. He's insanely intelligent, dedicated, and caring. Harris is the person you want in your corner. This is why I'm letting him fester in his thoughts until we get to the weight room, and then I will snap him out of it.

Another vibration from my pocket has me reaching for my phone. I fully expect it to be more pictures from Saylor of the new calf, which is why I'm surprised to see 'Rebel' flash across the screen.

Rebel: *image of her lying in bed from the neck down, only wearing a lace bralette and matching panties.*

Rebel: Sitting alone in this quiet apartment, I can't get you out of my mind.

My jaw drops as I stare at the image. Running my hand down my face, I scratch at my close-cut beard.

> **Me: Fuck, Rebel. I want to blow this workout off with Harris and come home to you.**

> **Rebel: I'll keep my door unlocked.**

> **Me: Good. I'm starving.**

> **Rebel: Starving? Want me to order you food?**

> **Me: Starving for you. My tongue is missing your taste, Rebel.**

> **Rebel: Mmmm...maybe you should skip that workout.**

Pocketing my phone, I push open the door and find Harris leaning against the wall, arms crossed. "Am I keeping you from a hot date?"

"No." Startled, I try to keep the tremble from my voice. Does he know about us? There's no way. We've been keeping things down low.

He drops the conversation as we walk further inside the football facility lobby.

Hank, the night guard, glances up from his paperback. "Good evening, boys. What brings you here tonight?"

"Thought we'd get a workout in and work off some steam." Harris gestures with his head toward the hallway which leads to the weight room.

"You know, back in my day, we'd find a lady friend to help with that."

We laugh, taken aback by the older man's comment: "Yeah, well, tonight I need to be alone with my thoughts."

"I saw that interview with that idiot reporter. Don't let them get to you, Mr. Harris."

"I'm trying not to, Hank."

Hank turns his attention back to his novel as we walk down the hall. Each time I come in here, I still take in the magnitude of this space. I love looking at all the trophies, awards, and highlights from past players. It keeps my motivation high and my desire to keep winning at the forefront of my mind.

I pull open the glass door to the workout room as Harris enters. The space is empty, and the smell of cleaning solution hits my senses. An empty gym is the perfect place to quiet the mind.

Tossing our backpacks to the side, Harris switches on the sound system as Def Leppard plays through the speakers.

"Now you're talking," I say, sitting down on the leg press while Harris takes his position on the shoulder press machine.

We fall silent as a cacophony of sounds fills the air from the beat of the music and the clanking of weights from the machines. After a few rounds, I glance over at my friend and see his look of determination and frustration.

"Dude, your thoughts are drowning out the music."

He grunts as he pulls the metal bar down and the pulley raises a heavy amount of weight. "I got a call from my mom before practice today."

"Ah, that explains the shitty practice." Dropping the weight back, I place my feet on the ground and rest my bent elbows on my knees.

"Yeah. I guess she met another new guy, and she's moving again." He pulls the metal bar down again, grunting at the exertion.

"Damn, man. How many times is that now?"

"Five," he grits.

Harris's mom is a mess. Since he moved to CTU freshman year, his mom has moved five times now. Each time, she calls and begs him to come home to meet the new flavor of the month. He tries to keep her at arm's distance to not create unnecessary drama for him, especially if the media were to catch wind. And that's part of the problem, too. He never knows if the guys are legitimately interested in his mom or are looking for a way to get closer to him and the payday he'll get when he becomes a professional quarterback.

Dragging my fingers through my hair, I let out an exasperated sigh. "Sorry, man."

"It's all good. Nothing I'm not used to."

"Still fucking sucks."

He chuckles. "That it does."

"Listen, I know you want to work off your stress, but I don't think this is what you need right now."

"Gentlemen." A voice sounds from the doorway, startling us. Turning our attention, we spot Coach leaning against the doorway, his arms folded across his chest. "As much as I love to see the determination, what the hell are you guys doing here?"

I nod. "Hey, Coach."

"I needed a workout, and I talked Riggsby into coming too."

Coach's stoic expression doesn't give anything away. Instead, he places a foot in front of the other and makes his way over to us. He leans against a machine opposite Harris. "I get it, but I also don't need my QB hurt. Go home, Tyler. Get some rest, and come back tomorrow focused."

With a deep inhale, Harris nods. We both stand from our benches and start toward the doorway where our bags are. Coach Campbell follows us before he pushes open the doors and waits for us to exit.

The three of us walk toward the lobby, no words being said. I can feel the frustration seeping off of Harris, and while I know he wants to push his body to the limit to feel some semblance of control, I also know that Coach is right. He doesn't need to risk an injury because he's pissed off.

"Night, gentlemen," Hank calls from over his novel.

"Night," we all reply in unison.

As we exit the main doors, Coach turns to walk in the opposite direction. He doesn't get too far before he pauses and calls out to us. "Tell my girl her ol' man says hi."

And with that goodbye, he just reminded us that we are living with his daughter.

The girl I'm falling for...hard.

When I enter the apartment, sounds from the TV fill the otherwise quiet space. I set my backpack in my doorway before entering the living room while Harris stops in the kitchen.

A street racing movie is playing on the screen while Bret lounges on the couch, her nose in a paperback. Tonight must be the night for everyone to read. I stand quietly for a moment while watching her read her book. Her legs move together as she flips to the next page. Moving close, I lean over and read the word "cock" on the page. Is my little Rebel reading a dirty scene?

"Hey, Rebel." Bret startles and lets out a squeal as she slams her book shut. She turns around, and her face is red.

"Shit, Crew. How long have you been standing there?"

"Long enough to read the word cock on your page." I didn't think her face could blush more, but I watched as her cheek color deepened. Sliding between the couch and the coffee table, I plop in the corner seat of the sectional, kicking my legs up onto the table. "What's your book about?"

She's trying to avoid eye contact with me, and I smile at how flustered she is. Harris comes into the living room, interrupting our moment. "Hi, Tyler."

"S'up, Bret?" Harris moves to the opposite side of the couch and takes a seat. "*The Fast and The Furious Two*?"

"Only the best one." Bret turns onto her side and tucks her hands beneath her cheek as she watches the movie.

Glancing to my left, Harris is engrossed with the movie while chowing down on a cold meat sandwich. The dude looks rough as hell. Sliding my phone out of my pocket, I open our message thread.

> **Me: Is my girl feeling spicy?**

I feel her phone vibrate against the couch's material. The movie drowns out the sound. It's not long before mine alerts me of a new message.

> **Rebel: I don't know what you're talking about.**

> **Me: Don't lie, Rebel. I saw you clenching your thighs together.**

> **Rebel: Maybe I was just thinking about last night.**

Me: Repeat tonight?

Rebel: If you're lucky *wink emoji*

Bret rolls over until she's on her back facing me. Her toes nudge my leg as my attention turns to her. "Hey, I have to create an educational campaign for one of my classes. I have an idea in my head, and I was wondering if you could help sketch it out?"

"I'm not the best at sketching anything other than animals, but I can try it."

"Thanks." Her lips tip up in a smile and flutters erupt in my chest. It's the same smile she flashes me when we are alone.

Late last night, after Bret arrived home from dinner with her dad and brother, she snuck in my room after our roommates had gone to bed. The two of us fooled around before she fell asleep in my arms. I had to wake her early this morning before the guys woke up so she could sneak back into her room.

I can't wait until we don't have to hide our relationship anymore. There isn't a better way to start my day than by waking up with her in my arms. But if keeping our relationship a secret is the only way I can have her, then I'll take that secret to my grave.

CHAPTER 17
Bret

Me: Good luck! I'll be cheering you on from home.

Crew: Don't get too crazy with the girls.

Crew: Or if you do, send pics

Me: *eye roll emoji

Me: I think I'm going to take a nap before they come.

Crew: Sleep in my bed so my sheets smell like you when I get home.

Me: And what do I smell like?

Crew: Sweet, seductive, warm, and, best of all, like mine.

Me: *image of me lying in Crew's bed. His navy sheets draped over my bare chest, showcasing the swells of my breasts.*

Crew: For fuck's sake. Now I have to adjust my dick in the dining room.

Crew: But you look good in my sheets, Rebel.

Me: *kiss emoji

An hour later, I'm woken by the sound of my phone's alarm going off. Tonight the guys have an away game, so instead of being home alone with the shadows and insecurities, I decided to text the girls for an impromptu girls' night in. I'm proud of myself for going outside of my shell and initiating a night in with girlfriends. When I asked if they'd be interested, the girls were enthusiastic about the idea.

Tonight, the group chat is leaving the chat.

The girls are coming over around five for dinner before kickoff at seven-thirty. Glancing at my phone, I resist the urge to text Crew. After our flirty conversation this afternoon, he's all I can think about. Not only am I the girl who doesn't want to be a distraction before a game, but I don't want to risk getting caught since he's around the team. Earlier, when I sent him another photo, I made sure my face wasn't visible. I've never been one to send nudes or sexy pictures to a guy, but there's something about Crew Riggsby that makes me want to live life on the edge.

Maybe it's the thrill of getting caught? Whatever it is, I'm here for this new, bolder Bret.

Tossing my hair into a claw clip, I flip on the handle to start the shower. I then press play on a playlist on my phone, which connects to the tiny Bluetooth speaker sitting on a shelf in the bathroom I share with Crew.

I try to keep the bathroom as clean as possible, even though I'm a total hot mess. I'm the type of girl who keeps her makeup in her bag, but the bag hangs out on the sink, and my skincare products sit next to the sink because what's the point of always putting everything away when I use it every day? Crew, on the other hand, is the organized to my chaotic life. Every one of his products has a place in the bathroom, and if I didn't see him come in and out of this room, I'd think he'd never used it. But I'm trying to be better.

While I wait for the water to warm, I stare at my reflection in the mirror. There's a glow around my face that wasn't there before. Slowly, my light is starting to come back into my eyes. Is this what happiness feels like? It's been so long since I was actually happy, not the fake kind, but the real kind. The kind that makes food taste better and colors shine brighter.

My phone has been radio silence from he-who-shall-not-be-named for weeks. A part of me is waiting for the other shoe to drop while the other part of me is hoping that this is what life is going to be like from now on. Maybe he finally got bored with the chase and the threats now that I'm states away. And he has no idea where I am.

Steam fogs the window, and I take that as my cue to get in the shower. Stepping inside, I let the hot water melt my skin away as I pour body wash onto my loofa and lather the sudsy liquid. Scrubbing my skin, I let my mind drift back to sitting on the dock in Silo Bay. Something about that place called to my soul. There was such a sense of community between the volunteers who welcomed us to Sunset Shores and the people who created signs along the road for Crew's homecoming. It's the type of place you read about or watch in movies. Small towns in the Midwest have magic to them, and this place has sucked me into its orbit.

I could see myself living there.

A ding sounds through the speaker, interrupting my thoughts. Turning off the nozzle, I step out of the shower and wrap my body in a fluffy navy towel. One thing Crew and I seem to share is our love for the color navy.

There's a text waiting from in the 'Bestie Babes' group chat.

Chloe: We're here, girl!

Me: Coming!

Glancing at the clock, I realize I was in the shower for way too long. Leaving the bathroom, I jog across the floor and unlock the door.

"Damn, now that's my kind of greeting," Brynn jokes as she takes in my towel-covered body.

Holding the door open wider, I gesture for Brynn, Chloe, and Macy to come in. "Sorry, I lost track of time."

"We're a little early," Chloe says, slipping out of her sneakers and placing them beneath the entryway table.

I follow the girls into the apartment after I lock the door behind us. "Oh, I invited our friend Savannah. I hope you don't mind."

"I don't mind," I say, shaking my head. "I met her at the party last weekend."

Chloe places bags down on the dining table while Macy pulls out a chair. Brynn takes the opportunity to peruse the apartment, poking her head into the guys' rooms. "I'm going to throw on some clothes." I gesture over my shoulder. "You guys make yourselves at home."

"Be careful what you wish for. I told her to make herself comfortable in my dorm one day, and the next thing I knew we were moving in together," Macy jokes.

"Ha. Ha. You're so funny." Brynn rolls her eyes. The three of them have such a fluid relationship with their playful banter and inside jokes. I'm really thankful that they decided to take me under their wing. Leaving the room, I dig through my clothes until I pull out an oversized CTU football hoodie and athletic shorts. The girls are all in comfortable CTU clothes, which is perfect for our night in to watch the game.

Back in the living room, bowls are spread across the table. Glancing inside, I find tortilla chips and taco dip, sliced vegetables and veggie dip, and a white mixture that reminds me of the icing from Dunkaroos with bear-shaped crackers next to it.

"Holy shit, this spread looks amazing. You did not have to do all this."

Chloe turns her head from where she's sitting on the couch. "It was seriously no big deal."

"And the guys told us to not let you cook so..." Brynn's words trail off as she shrugs.

Chloe tosses a pillow at Brynn. "Don't be rude to our host."

"Oh please." Brynn adjusts the pillow onto her lap. "Bret's one of us, which means she's fully subject to all of the asshole comments."

My heart warms at her compliment of being part of them. "I mean, I was going to order a bunch of appetizers when I ordered wings." Moving around the girls, I find an open spot on the couch to settle down on. Placing my legs underneath my body, the cushions mold around my bent knees as I relax into the nook between the backrest and armrest.

"Let me call Steve at The Eagles Nest. He'll make sure to bump our order so we get it before the game. I assume you want it delivered?"

I shrug. "It doesn't matter to me."

"Make sure you get garlic parm for me, please," Macy requests.

Chloe glances up from where she's typing away on her phone. "I want to try their luau barbeque."

"What's that?" I ask.

"It's a new sauce. I guess it's like a barbecue sauce with hints of pineapple."

I scrunch my nose. "I'll pass on that."

"Oh my gosh, please tell me you're a pineapple girl."

"Like by itself. Not on pizza or in cottage cheese like my mom." I shiver at the thought.

Chloe gasps, clutching her heart. "Pineapple goes on pizza, and that's a hill I'll die on."

A giggle breaks free as I watch her dramatics. "Okay, okay. Do they have a buffalo ranch?" Brynn nods. "Perfect. I'll take that."

"Ohemgee, it's like I'm ordering for the guys with all the wings to satisfy everyone's sauce craving." I watch as she types a hundred miles an hour on her phone before smiling. "Food is ordered. Steve said he'll have his delivery driver bring it to us when it's ready."

A natural silence falls over the room as we all cozy up on the over-sized couch. ESPN plays on the TV with an afternoon football game. I like that there isn't an awkward need for conversation. Glancing around the three girls, I can't help but smile at how different we all are. I love how not one of us decided to dress up for tonight's game. Each one of us are in our own comfortable style. Chloe's wearing a powder blue matching loungewear set. Brynn's outfit is an oversized jersey with Quinton's number on the back with a pair of navy bike shorts peeking out underneath. Then there's Macy. She's the craziest out of all of us. I mean, who wears jeans to lounge around in? Crazy people, that's who. She has a cropped, uniquely designed CTU hoodie on, and I'm assuming it's one that she designed herself.

I've heard a lot about her one-of-a-kind designs where she mixes and matches fabrics to create custom tops. Photos of her designs are shared on many fashion social media accounts. The girl is *talented*. I already have a design in mind whenever Crew and I take our relationship public.

"Anyone want a drink?" I stand from my spot and move around the table.

"What are our options?" Brynn asks.

Macy scoffs. "As if you didn't pack tequila."

"Actually, I didn't." Brynn sticks her tongue out at Macy, who laughs.

"I think we have a bottle of tequila in the freezer. JP has some kind of whiskey, and we have plenty of beer, seltzers, Coke, and water."

A knock at the door interrupts our conversation. "Let me grab that."

The girls discuss which drinks we are drinking tonight while I go to answer the door. The drink dilemma is crucial. It could be a shots kind of night, a margarita on the rocks kind of night, or a chill canned alcoholic beverage kind of night.

Unlocking the door, I twist the handle, fully expecting the delivery driver to be here with the wings. Instead, a petite girl with light brown and blonde balayage hair stares back at me. "Savannah!"

"Hey, girl!" She steps inside the door and wraps her arms around my shoulders for a quick hug. "Thanks for having me over tonight."

"Oh my gosh, of course. I'm glad you could come. I didn't have your number, or I would've invited you myself."

As I shut and lock the door behind us, we step farther into the room. "We'll change that tonight."

With a smile, we walk into the living room as shouts of greeting fill the air. Brynn jumps up from her seat. "Okay, now that you're here, let's take a selfie before we get the night started."

We giggle as we settle around the couch, finding our positions for the perfect selfie. Brynn is in the middle with her arm in the air, the front camera of her phone facing us.

"Squish tighter." And we do until our faces nearly smash each other, laughter pouring out of us. Brynn must like where we are positioned. "On the count of three, everyone yell 'Brynn is pregnant.' One." *Click.*

Our jaws drop as we realize what she just said. Screams fill the air as we all squeeze the platinum blonde in front of us. Chloe and Macy start crying, tears pouring down their faces as Savannah and I smile brightly at our friends.

"You bitch, I can't believe you've been keeping this a secret!" Chloe cries.

Brynn slips out from under our arms and slides her jersey up over her hips. A tiny bump shows on flawless skin. "I'm due in January."

"Wait." Macy's eyes widen. "That means you're—"

"Twenty-one weeks," Brynn interrupts. "This has been the hardest secret I've ever had to keep from you guys."

"Wow, B. There's a little jelly bean in your belly." Chloe reaches out and rubs Brynn's tiny bump. The smile on her face is contagious as she radiates a beautiful glow.

"I had no idea you and Q wanted kids so quick," Savannah adds from her spot on the couch.

Brynn lets out a nervous laugh. "Funny story. Remember when I got sick last spring after the NFL draft? Well, turns out the antibiotics messed with my birth control, which I should have known, but..." She shrugs. "Anyway, we were quite shocked when I missed my period."

"Oh my gosh, that's like my biggest fear," Savannah muses, and Chloe hits her with a pillow. Sav's eyes widen and bounce up to Brynn's. "Shit, I'm sorry."

"No, girl. Don't be sorry. Believe me, we have been in shock and denial for weeks. Now that we're well out of the first trimester, we're over the moon to start our family."

"I'm super happy for you." I stand and give my newfound friend a big hug.

"Thanks, Bret." Brynn hugs me back before looking at Macy. "And this is why I won't be having tequila."

Macy chuckles as she settles back into her spot on the couch. "Looks like it's a seltzer kind of night."

"I'll take a beer if you have one," Sav says, and I nod.

"Do the guys know?" Curiosity piqued my interest, so I know if I must keep it a secret.

Brynn shakes her head. "Q is going to call them up tomorrow. I told him I had to tell my girls first because even though I'm a married woman now, it's still chicks before dicks."

We all laugh as I head to the kitchen to grab drinks. Turns out it's going to be a canned alcoholic beverage—and water—kind of night.

"Get him! Get him!" Brynn roars at the TV from where she's leaning on her elbows. CTU is down by three in the fourth quarter. Our wings are long gone, and the snacks have been moved from the dining table to the coffee table.

Tonight is exactly what I've needed. The girls have filled me in on all of the campus gossip, the best places to eat and get coffee, a local florist who has the best floral arrangements, a hidden gem boutique with the cutest clothes, and everything in between.

When I left Arizona, I only had Olivia. Making friends is challenging, especially when you have the suitcase-sized baggage that I have, but the girls have reassured me that we all have our own shit. No matter what I'm going through, they will always have my back, and whenever I'm ready to talk about it, they will be there for me.

"Oh my gosh," Sav shouts, snapping me out of my thoughts.

I watch as Grant breaks a tackle and runs toward the end zone. He scores, which puts us up by three with three minutes left. Our kicker comes out onto the field to attempt the extra point. Hands clasped under my chin, I mumble a silent prayer. The ball is snapped, the kick is up, and it's good. I jump on my feet and raise my arms.

"Damn, girl, it's like you're out there playing." Brynn flips her hair over her shoulder as she adjusts her position.

"Listen, I live with three of those men, and I don't need them all grumpy when they come home."

"Finally going to take advantage of your situation and have yourself a little reverse harem action?" Chloe waggles her eyebrows as three other heads whip in my direction.

"First of all, no. Second, my brother almost killed me after that comment at dinner, and last," I say, ticking each point off on my fingers. "Crew caught me reading that book you lent me."

Chloe erupts in a full-fledged cackle as she grasps her stomach. "Please tell me it was a sex scene."

"Girl, it was right when the main character finally gave in to letting both guys in her bed. So yeah, I was pretty riled up when he and Tyler came home."

"Should've taken advantage of the situation." Brynn smirks. "The hormones have me riled up all the time. Long-distance phone sex just isn't the same."

More laughs and giggles sound. It's been the constant soundtrack of our night. Leaning back in my seat, I bounce my knee as I watch the clock tick down until the clock finally hits zero. The Eagles scraped that win out by the skin of their teeth.

"Okay, movie time!"

Reaching for blankets and pillows, the five of us snuggle together on the huge sectional couch and watch a movie until we all eventually drift off to sleep.

CHAPTER 18
CREW

The first month of school is officially over. September has transitioned into October. If I were back in Ohio, I'd enjoy the changing foliage as leaves take on golden-brown hues and temperatures start to drop, entering cool, crisp days.

But alas, I'm in Texas, where fall isn't a season.

Practice this morning was brutal. Coach had us outside running through drills as if it were summer camp and we were conditioning before moving us inside the facility for a light scrimmage. The team has been on a roll, as we are still undefeated for the season after winning our first five games. While we've won games, the scores have been close, which Coach isn't too happy about. It turns out that since winning the championship, we've plastered targets onto our backs.

Cleats click sharply against the pavement as we jog from the indoor practice facility to the locker room. Groans and grumbles filter into my thoughts. Between football and the coursework for year three as an agricultural business student, I feel drained. Last season, we seemed to find more time to party, but as classes get more challenging and external factors begin to weigh in on everything, fun seems to be taking the back burner.

I follow the guys into the locker room and immediately start stripping out of my sweat-soaked T-shirt, followed by my compression shirt.

Conversations start as I pull out a change of clothes before making my way to the showers. I'm halfway to the showers when an idea pops into my head. A slow smirk slides across my face, and I rush through my shower.

Shoving through the doors, the Texas sun greets me as I move across the parking lot toward my truck. Thumbing through my contacts, I hit the name I was searching for as the phone begins to ring. Unlocking the door with my fob, I climb into the pickup and start the ignition, waiting for the call to go through.

"Hello?" Her voice is a hushed whisper as it connects to the Bluetooth.

"Rebel, what's your schedule look like?" Tilting my head against the headrest, I close my eyes. I think I could sleep for a week if the opportunity presents itself.

"I'm almost to my first class. I have a full day. What's up?"

"Dammit. I was going to see if I could steal you away for the day."

She hums. "I think I can make that happen."

"Really?" I can't contain the excitement in my voice.

"Yeah." She giggles. "Anything for you."

Rubbing my chest, her words brighten my day. I think it's safe to say I'm gone for Bret Campbell. I'm just waiting for her to catch up.

"See you back at home."

"See you soon." We hang up, and I shift the truck into gear before peeling it out of the parking lot.

Once I'm back at the complex, I rush out of the truck before climbing the stairs two at a time. I'm desperately trying to beat the guys home to steal Bret away without them being any wiser. It's a little after nine, so I caught Bret before her first morning class, and we can spend all day together. I have the perfect day in mind and am excited to finally take my girl on an actual date. As much as I love our stolen kisses and late-night sleepovers, I'm ready to spoil her.

The door opens before I have a chance to turn the knob, and standing in front of me in a band T-shirt with some kind of sheer lace long sleeve underneath, destroyed denim shorts, and Doc Marten boots is my girlfriend.

She looks over my shoulder and skims the parking lot from where she can see. The coast must be clear because Bret grabs a fistful of my shirt and pulls me into her. Her mouth finds mine as her hands move to the back of my neck. Her fingernails scrape my skull as she skims through my hair.

I reach behind her thighs and lift her. Her legs wrap around my waist instantly as I move us inside the apartment, kicking the door behind us as I press her against the wall. Our tongues continue to duel, and the moan she lets out has my body responding. She grinds against me, and I'm fighting the urge to take her into my bedroom. Slowing down, I pull back slightly and pepper her skin with tiny kisses.

"Dammit, Rebel. As much as I'd love to see where this goes, I want to get you out of here before the guys come home and question us." She sighs, and I smile, placing one last kiss on her lips.

She slides down my front and cups my erection through my shorts. "You sure I can't take care of that for you?"

"Later, baby." I groan, tipping my head to the ceiling. "Let me change my clothes, and we can head out."

Bret tips her head. "Where are you kidnapping me to?"

"It's a surprise, but plan on being gone all day." I jog off to my room with a quick peck to her forehead.

The almost hour-and-a-half drive to San Antonio has been smooth, as traffic has been light. Bret has been playing DJ on her phone as we've enjoyed a mostly silent drive. It's been comforting not to feel like we need to fill the drive with conversation. We talk when something pops into our minds, but the conversation never feels forced.

It turns out Bret is a big music fan. I assumed that, but it was confirmed when she played DJ. Her playlist ranges from Mac Miller to Cage the Elephant to MGK and even some classic rock, which I am a big fan of.

I watch from the corner of my eye as Bret leans forward to read the road signs. "You're taking me to San Antonio?"

"I am. Have you ever been?" She shakes her head, and I smile at the fact that we'll both be able to experience something new together.

Navigating through the city streets, our eyes bounce from each side as we take in the new city. People mill along the streets as cars merge. The GPS guides us down the busy road as we search for a Tex-Mex restaurant to stop at for lunch. I didn't grab anything to eat after this morning's practice, and I'm starving. My stomach has been growling for the last thirty minutes.

We find a taco joint on the west side of the city. Turning into a parking spot, we both move to get out of the truck. Bret raises her arms above her head as she moves her body side to side, stretching. The two of us meet in front of my truck, and I reach for her hand, which she instantly takes. Bringing our joined hands to my mouth, I plant a soft kiss against her knuckles.

"Damn, it feels good to hold your hand in public." Her eyes shimmer as her dazzling smile widens.

Crossing the street, I hold open the door to the restaurant. As we both step inside, we're transported back in time. The older wood decor looks to be original, and we read sign after sign praising the establishment for its puffy tacos, whatever those are.

"Welcome y'all," the hostess greets. "Just the two of you joining us for lunch?"

"Yes, please." Bret tucks a loose strand of hair behind her ear as the hostess gathers menus before leading us to the table. She places the menus down and informs us the waiter will be right with us.

Scooting her chair closer to the table, Bret opens her menu and begins perusing the items. "I'm so hungry I think I could eat a whole cow."

"Now that's something I'd like to see." I chuckle, reading over the menu.

"Don't doubt me, Crew Riggsby."

"I'd never."

A few moments later, the waiter appears with glasses of water. Sitting them down in front of us, he smiles and welcomes us. "What can I get y'all?"

Bret twists so her attention is on the older gentlemen. "We are first-timers, and I'm dying to try a puffy taco. Can I get three beef tacos with lettuce and tomato and a side of rice?"

The waiter nods as he writes down her order before turning his attention to me. "I'll do two beef, one barbeque, and one chicken puffy taco with rice, beans, and french fries."

Bret quirks an eyebrow at my order. "I'm starving."

Our waiter leaves, and we scan the room. It's a unique space with antique jukeboxes, artwork, and even an old car on the inside.

"If you could have any food for the rest of your life, what would it be?" Bret leans her elbow on the table, head resting on her hand as she stares at me. Her eyes are alive with a light I've never seen before.

Tapping my fingers on the table, I ponder all of my options. "Damn, that's a tough one. I guess I'd say a burger."

"Really?"

I shrug one shoulder. "Yeah, I mean, you can fix it up in so many ways. Add a fried egg for breakfast, load it with lettuce and tomatoes for lunch, and slather on the barbeque and bacon for dinner. The possibilities are endless."

"Valid point."

I tip my head toward her. "Your turn."

"Smothered burrito," she answers without hesitation, and I laugh at how fast she says those two words.

The waiter arrives, and our conversation pauses as he sets down the multiple plates. The savory smell immediately hits my senses, and my mouth salivates. The tacos are piled high with meat, lettuce, tomatoes, and cheese.

"These look amazing." Bret's eyes widen as she reaches for a taco. Mouth wide, she shoves the tortilla into her mouth and moans around the bite as shreds of lettuce and pieces of tomato tumble onto her plate. I'm stuck watching her, mesmerized by how she doesn't hold back. Bret Campbell is a girl who likes her food. Just don't ask her to cook it.

A few hours later, Bret and I find ourselves below the street level as we meander around the San Antonio Riverwalk. Tourists bustle along the crowded sidewalks, milling in and out of stores, stopping to gaze at colorful murals, or sitting at cement picnic tables. Popular chain restaurants and bars line the buildings as bridges take you to and from each side of the river.

"I've got a question for you." Bret tilts her head in my direction from where we are walking hand in hand. "What's the funniest joke you know by heart?"

I quirk an eyebrow at her. "Damn, Rebel, you're really putting me on the spot today."

Moving us off the walkway, I pull her into me so that her back is to my front as we watch a boat pass by. She rests her head against my shoulder as we enjoy the silence. Leaning closer to her ear, I whisper the joke. "Why do quarterbacks tell obvious jokes?"

I pause and wait. Bret takes a moment before she shakes her head. "So they don't go over their receivers' heads."

A giggle bubbles out of her as she turns in my arms. "Oh, Crew, that was terrible."

"Yeah, but it got you to laugh."

"That it did." Bret leans up on her toes and gives me a quick peck on the lips. We both smile at each other, and I'm glad I was able to steal her away for the day.

"My turn. If you could spend the day with three people, dead or alive, who would they be and why?"

"Shit, you thought *you* were put on the spot." Bret nibbles her lips as she ponders the question.

The two of us lean against the metal railing, basking in the late afternoon sun as smells from the many restaurants filter around us. Soft music plays from the speakers attached to light poles.

"Mac Miller, so I can thank him for being a musical genius and for his lyrics, which always get me out of my head, Paul Walker for blessing us with the Fast and Furious franchise, and Pat Summitt for being an icon in women's basketball." I hum. "I just realized all of those people are dead, which is terribly depressing."

"You picked some great people to meet."

She smiles. "What's next?"

"Ice cream."

Her emerald eyes widen. "Ice cream? How are you hungry?"

"Rebel, there's *always* room for ice cream."

Reaching for her hand, the two of us resume our stroll down the Riverwalk in search of an ice cream parlor. We pass tables with umbrellas of the Texas state flag, parents corralling their children, and unique craftsmanship with Spanish mosaic details. A storefront with a large waffle cone sign comes into view.

"I knew we'd be able to find ice cream." Reaching for the handle, I pull open the door, and the air conditioning blasts us as we enter, sending a chill down our spines. Bret shivers, and I wrap my arms around her shoulders, tucking her into my side.

After we order our treats—caramel ice cream for Bret and chocolate peanut butter for me, both in waffle cones—we weave through the crowd until we find a vacant bench.

Watching Bret's pink tongue flick out and lick up the creamy treat has me needing to adjust my pants. She twirls her tongue as she laps up the melting ice cream before sucking the top into her mouth.

Her laugh interrupts the moment. "How are you holding up over there?"

My eyes snap to hers as a smile breaks free on her glowing face. "Were you doing that on purpose?" She nods. "You're going to pay for that, Rebel."

"I hope so." She winks before returning to enjoying her cone in a much less seductive way. The rich chocolate mixed with the creamy peanut butter coats my tongue.

"Not that I want to put a damper on this day, but how has everything been with you know..." My words trail off.

Bret's shoulders stiffen slightly. "It's been radio silence."

"That's good, isn't it?"

She shrugs, and I'm surprised by her gesture. "I mean, yeah, of course, it's great. I'm also worried that it's just a fluke, and I will spend the rest of my life looking over my shoulder."

My hand squeezes into a fist. "I promise that as long as I'm by your side, you'll be safe, Rebel. No motherfucker is going to make you feel less than safe by tormenting you."

"Thank you." Her words are soft as she lays her head on my shoulder.

For the rest of the afternoon and into the evening, Bret and I explore San Antonio. We visit The Alamo and the world's largest pair of cowboy boots. She takes selfies and pictures throughout our journey. I've loved watching her let her guard down and laugh in ways that fully encompass her. She radiates a sense of happiness as she's unabashedly herself as we spend time in our little bubble. Neither one of us has a care in the world. It was the perfect day, and as the sun started to set, I hated that our time was ending, at least for today.

The bright Texas sun began to lower in the sky, replacing blue skies with golden hues. Reluctantly, we climbed into my truck and started our journey home. Both of us were completely exhausted but filled with joy.

As we approach the campus exit, I hear a seat belt unclip. Doing my best to keep my eyes on the road, I glance over and find Bret moving around in her seat. With her elbow propped on the center console, she adjusts herself until she's leaning into my space.

"Rebel, what are you doing?" Concern is evident in my voice as my eyes bounce for the dimly lit road to my girlfriend.

Instead of using words to reply, her hand palms my dick over the zipper of my shorts. My nostrils flare at the implication of what she's planning. Before I can say anything, her delicate hand finds my waistband as her fingers work to unfasten my button. Blood rushes to my cock which is straining against the seam, begging to be released.

"Rebel," I groan.

"Relax, Crew. You concentrate on not crashing, and I'll concentrate on getting you off." Bold Bret is my favorite Bret.

Her hands slide inside my shorts and underneath my boxer briefs. As she works my shorts down, I try to lift my hips to allow for the fabric to free and slide. My cock springs free, and her hand wraps around my growing erection.

"Fuuuck."

I'm mesmerized by the way she pumps my cock in her hand as she manages to hold herself steady with her elbow. Her hand, wrapped around my cock, moves up and down in a twisting motion as she jacks me off. Images of her licking her ice cream flicker in my head, mixed with the anticipation of road head, has my cock leaking. If I'm not careful, this moment will be over before it even begins, and I'm not ready for that.

Bret's lips find my neck as she sucks the skin into her mouth while her hand continues to work me over. She trails kisses from my jaw down my neck to where my T-shirt meets my collarbone. Her position shifts over the center console, removing her lips from my neck as she lowers her head. She licks my thick dick from root to tip as I tip my head back against the headrest, and a moan leaves my lips.

Swirling her tongue over the crown, she laps up the moisture gathering at my tip before her perfectly plump lips wrap around the head of my cock as she sucks my length into her mouth. I hit the back of her throat, her underestimating the size of me, and she pulls back slightly.

"That's it, Rebel. Your mouth feels so good." She moans around me as I remove a hand from the steering wheel to brush her hair out of her face. I want to watch her suck on my cock.

Her head bobs as he sucks me deeper into her mouth while her tongue flicks at my crown, and her hand pumps where her mouth doesn't reach. Bret gives excellent head. Using my free hand, I run my fingers through her loose hair, allowing the tendrils to twist around my fingers. Gripping the back of her head, I help her bob up and down on my cock.

A deep moan leaves her pretty lips as saliva drips down my shaft. She uses the moisture as lube as she continues to moan as I jerk my hips.

"I bet if I reached inside your shorts, I'd find you drenched. Does sucking my cock make you wet, Rebel?" She nods her head as she hums—the vibration spurring my impending orgasm. I can feel my balls tighten at the need to come.

"Such a perfect, pretty mouth. Fuck, Rebel, I'm going to come."

Her head nods, encouraging me to come in her mouth. And with another long, hard thrust into her mouth, I'm spilling inside her. Bret's tongue continues to trail up and down my shaft as my orgasm bursts, coating the back of her throat. When she's swallowed every last drop, she pops off my cock. Leaning on my shoulder, she smiles at me, an evil gleam in her sparkling eyes.

"Thanks for the perfect day."

CHAPTER 19
Bret

"Dammit, you guys are home."

Our heads turn from where Crew and I are playing a heated battle of Grand Theft Auto. JP stands at the table and tosses his backpack onto the surface.

"Well, hello to you, too, sunshine," I greet him sarcastically.

JP scratches his face as he lets out a sigh. "Sorry, I didn't mean it like that."

"You didn't mean it like you were pissed to see the sight of your favorite roommates?" Crew quirks a brow as JP narrows his eyes.

Patting the seat next to me, I toss JP an extra controller. "C'mon, big man."

"Big man?"

I adjust my legs so they are tucked underneath me. "What? You can call me baby girl, but I can't call you big man? Sounds a little hypocritical to me."

JP's large frame plops on the cushion next to me, causing my body to sway. "All right, *baby girl*, close out of this game and hook me up in a new one. But only for a little while, y'all have to make yourselves scarce in an hour."

"What the hell for?" Tyler grumbles as he joins us on the sectional with a fresh sports drink.

JP's thumbs fly over the controller as he flicks through options on the screen. "I've got a study group, and we are all meeting here. We're prepping for a large test and don't need the interruptions."

"So, the three of us are supposed to sit quietly in our rooms?" Crew taps a couple of buttons on his controller.

"Yeah, so keep the porn to low volume, jack off. I heard your TV the other night when I went to get a drink of water. And do you have to watch screamers?" JP cracks, his eyes never leaving the screen.

My eyes, on the other hand, widen as I try to keep my breathing under control. I feel my pulse tick up as my vision blurs. Keeping my head straight toward the screen, I fight the urge to look over at Crew. Is he freaking out right now too? Or is he Mr. Calm, Cool, and Collected?

"C'mon." Tyler tosses a pillow at JP. "You've got Bret blushing."

I feel all three sets of eyes on me as I try to keep my breathing in check. But it's JP who speaks up first. "Don't tell me you don't watch porn."

Head snapping in his direction, I find a relaxed JP watching me. His legs are spread wide—he's got the whole manspread figured out. He rests his back against the cushion, one arm across the top of the couch and the other holding a dangling controller. It's as if the topic of self-pleasure and porn watching is a daily conversation. And hell, to these guys, it might be.

"C-c-can we just get b-back to the game?" I stumble over the words.

"Sure, Bret. But we'll table this discussion." JP clicks resume, and the video game starts.

Meanwhile, I'm not worth a shit at the realization we could've gotten caught. Thank God we sleep with the locks locked. But I make a mental note to keep the screams quieter.

With JP kicking us out of the living room, we cram into Crew's bed to watch a movie. Neither of us wanted to leave the apartment or spend the evenings alone in our rooms, so we decided to curl into bed together for a movie. It's a weird, intimate moment, and one we don't plan on making a habit.

Tyler was going to sit in the desk chair, but I convinced him that there was plenty of room for all three of us. I might have been a little zealous at the spacing. Being the smallest of the three, I'm forced into the middle. Crew is sandwiched against the wall since his bed is pressed against it while Tyler has the most room so he doesn't fall out of the bed.

"I vote for a Fast and Furious movie."

"Of course you do, Bret," Tyler mumbles while he wiggles around, trying to get comfortable. "What's your obsession with those movies?"

"Paul Walker," Crew and I say at the same time. Heat spreads across my cheeks as I hope Tyler doesn't read too much into the answer. His eyes squint as I catch him looking over at Crew from my peripheral vision.

"I asked her the same question a couple of weeks ago when she was watching it that night when we came home late."

"Oh yeah, I forgot you had it on then." Tyler nods. "Which one do you want to watch tonight?"

"Four." Crossing my arms over my chest, I wiggle into the covers. Heat radiates off the two giants in the bed with me. Chloe would have a field day if she saw us right now.

Crew clicks around with the remote until the opening scene fills the screen. Thursday nights are the only evening that all four of us are home. It's one of my favorite nights since we can all be together, laughing and cracking jokes at each other's expense. Despite JP throwing a wrench in our plans, we still made the best of the situation.

Warm hands meet my thigh as fingers gently trail over my skin. Goose bumps erupt over my skin as I twitch at the contact. Soft, wet lips find the delicate skin of my neck as another set of lips kiss my shoulders.

Shock and excitement course through my veins at the anticipation of having not one but two guys kissing me. One set of lips continues trailing open-mouth kisses down my neck, nipping at my collarbone. Chills roll down my spine as my panties grow wetter. Hands roam over my body before one hand slides underneath my T-shirt and the other grazes over my shorts-covered pussy.

I chew on my bottom lip as I lie there, letting the guys explore. A thumb flicks my metal piercing as my nipples harden while another hand slips underneath my mesh shorts. His finger traces a line over the wet material of my panties.

"How wet is she?" Tyler asks while he plays with my nipple piercing, sliding the bar back and forth, causing a tingling sensation to soar straight to my clit.

Crew moves my panties to the side as he traces my opening, gathering my arousal before rubbing circles over my clit. "Soaked. Aren't you, Rebel?"

All I can do is nod. Words are lost as my senses are overwhelmed by the hands playing my body like an instrument. Crew's lips find mine as he plunges his tongue into my mouth. At the same time, he pushes two fingers into my pussy. I moan into the kiss. He begins pumping his fingers inside me, the sound of my arousal filling the room as tension coils as the impending orgasm starts to build.

Tyler kneads my boob at the same pace as Crew moves inside me. But all too quickly, and on the brink of detonating, Crew's fingers slip free. His dark, hooded eyes find mine as he slides down my body, and Tyler's mouth replaces Crew's as he parts my lips with his tongue. Reaching behind his head, I grip his brown hair and maneuver his head to a position that deepens our kiss.

I'm wanton with desire at having these two men. Never in my wildest dreams would I have thought I'd share my body with these two.

With his fingertips, Crew grips my mesh shorts and dark purple thong and rips them down my legs in one go. Tyler's lips leave mine as he licks and sucks the flesh along my pulse point. My legs quake as Crew parts them. He hums in appreciation as he takes in my bare pussy. Lifting my shirt and bra, Tyler frees my breasts as they bounce slightly. His warm, wet mouth closes around a pointed bud as Crew laps at my arousal. He nibbles my swollen clit. Rolling my hips forward, I grind against his face, loving how the friction of his stubble builds my impending climax.

The edges of my vision start to blur as my stomach swirls and my orgasm builds. My body jolts from my near release as my eyes fly open and the body next to me startles.

Holy shitballs, was that a dream? A *dream*? Please tell me I did not just have a very vivid wet dream of my two roommates and I having a *threesome*. My pulse is racing as my heart beats rapidly as I try to calm my breathing. I will kill Chloe for giving me that book with the actual reverse harem in it.

Mortification cascades down my body like a bucket of ice water. Heat spreads over my already warm body as I tug the sheets up to my chin. Risking a glance, I look over to my right, where I find Tyler's stormy eyes staring down at me.

"You okay?" his rough, gravelly voice asks.

I nod. And if it were possible, my cheeks redden even more. Slowly, I tilt my head to the left, where a smirking Crew is watching me. The asshole knows exactly what I was dreaming about. It's like he has a front-row seat inside my brain.

Embarrassed, I chew on my lip as I turn my attention to where Paul Walker and Vin Diesel are hauling ass through a tunnel inside the desert. Guilt swirls in my brain at the realization I just fantasized about my boyfriend and his friend.

My attention whips to the door, where a single knock sounds before the door springs open. Assuming JP is coming in after his study session, shock takes over my body as my brother's head pops in. His eyes widen before turning into slits as he takes in the scene before him. I'm not an idiot and can imagine the sight of his little sister in bed with his teammates would be alarming.

"What the *fuck* is this?" Grant rages into the room as the guys shift uncomfortably from where they lie.

Tyler moves hurriedly. His feet tangle in the sheets as he tumbles onto the floor. "It's not what it looks like."

"No." Grant waves his arms out before him, gesturing toward the bed. "It doesn't look like my sister is lying in a bed between two guys who are half naked?"

"Okay, it looks exactly like that." Tyler raises his hands as if they will defend him from my brother's death glare. I should probably jump in and protect him.

"We were just watching a movie." That squinty-eyed glare finds mine, and I refuse to cower.

"Yeah, okay, this isn't my first night in college." Grant's arms cross over his chest.

"Wait, are you admitting to having a threesome?"

"N-n-n—" He trips over his words before shaking his head. "Don't turn this around on me. We are talking about you right now."

Yawning, I stretch my arms above my head before climbing from underneath the covers and sliding out of bed. "I'm bored with this conversation." As I step around Tyler, who is still sitting on the floor, I tap him on the head. "Thanks for the sex."

"Wha-what? N-no, man, we didn't have sex." Tyler stumbles over his words as I step out of the room. I feel guilty for putting Tyler in the spotlight, but my big brother needs to chill out a bit.

JP is sitting at the table with four other people, open textbooks spread in front of them. He quirks a brow as I walk through the room, and I flash him a wink as I enter my room. Grant is hot on my heels as he slams the door behind me.

"That's what you have to say for yourself?"

Whipping around, I fling my arms out. "What do you want me to say, Grant? The three of us were, in fact, watching a movie since our fourth roommate is having a study session in the main room."

"Then why didn't you answer your phone? I called and texted." Grant places his hands on his hips, and now he resembles our father so much.

Walking over to my nightstand, I reach down and hold up my phone. "Because it was on the charger."

His nostrils flare as he slowly nods his head. "Oh."

"Yeah." My eyebrows raise as I stare back at him.

He runs his fingers through his hair. "I just worry about you. This semester has been a lot more hectic than I thought it would be, and we haven't had the opportunity to spend any time together."

"I appreciate you wanting to look out for me, but I'm not a little girl anymore." He starts to interrupt, but I hold my hand up. "But that doesn't give you the right to come in here and accuse me of sleeping with your teammates."

Even though I *am* sleeping with one of them. Guilt swarms in my stomach as the words taste like bile slipping from my lips.

He sighs, glancing around my room. My eyes track his, and I pray there isn't any sign of Crew in my room. We've been careful not to leave things behind, and since I don't have social media anymore, I don't have to worry about slipping up and posting something.

"How about this," I start, approaching my brother. "We find a time in the next week to spend time together, just the two of us."

He tips the corner of his lips up in a soft smile. "I'd like that."

Eating the space between us, I throw my arms around him. "I love you, big brother."

"I love you, little sis."

With a final squeeze, I break our hug and playfully punch him in the arm. "Wanna go kick the guys' ass in NBA 2K23?"

"Oh, fuck yeah."

A wide grin slides over my face as Grant tosses his arm over my shoulder and leads me out of the room

CHAPTER 20
CREW

Jett: Happy 21st, little bro!

Saylor: Happy 21st! Drink up for me!

@saylor-riggsby has tagged you in a photo
@ctueaglesfb has mentioned you in their story
@qboyd31 has tagged you in a photo

The blaring sound of my alarm has my arm swinging to the side to grab my phone. Sliding my thumb against the screen, silence falls over the room. It's Monday morning, and my body is not ready to start this week. The team had a tough away game against a scrappy opponent. We kicked it into gear during the second half and pulled out a forty-two to seventeen victory.

Stretching my arms in the air, I tilt my head from side to side before rubbing the sleep from my eyes. Tossing the covers off my body, I sleepily leave my room and go to the bathroom I share with Bret. We arrived at the apartment yesterday and found Bret on a cleaning spree. Music blared from her speaker, and all of the windows, including the sliding glass doors, were open. She insisted she didn't want our help, and my body was too sore to argue.

Scanning our shared bathroom, I notice all of her items are missing from the counter. Everything is tucked away in its place. It's very unusual for her to put her things away. As much as my chaotic mind strives for order, I don't push her on the state of our bathroom. Instead, I let her do what she wants since it's her space too.

Pulling open the drawer to grab my toothbrush, I find a sticky note sitting on top. Gripping the yellow paper, I read over her handwriting as a yawn breaks free.

I smile as I read over how she signed the note with the nickname I gave her. Tucking the paper in my pocket, I reach for my toothbrush. As I brush my teeth, I can't help but think about how crazy this school year has been.

Bret showing up at our doorstep was not something I would have imagined happening, especially because she's our new roommate. As frustrated as I was that she showed up and lied about her name—okay, she didn't *lie* per se, but she definitely withheld information in our friendship—I'm thrilled she's here. This year is challenging with the pressure of football and classwork, not to mention the homesickness that hits me in waves, but having Bret here has been a saving grace.

Even with her dark past and an asshole ex who caused unnecessary drama in her life, she isn't letting it ruin her. The girl is always wearing a smile, cracking jokes, and leaving a trail of warmth wherever she goes. She might not see it, but I sure as hell do.

Opening the bathroom door, I scratch at my chest hair and stumble into the living room, still half asleep. My feet trip over each other as I take in the living room. Between the coffee table and TV stand are piles of inflated balloons. Turning toward the dining table, I find a big cutout photo of myself jumping in the air for a pass. A construction paper sign is taped to the image, saying, "21 and ready to tackle the booze!"

I walk toward the kitchen and hope Bret is waiting for me, but I find it empty when I round the corner. My shoulders deflate a little, but it's still early, and Bret is never up when we are. Heading back into my room, I get ready for the day.

I'm walking through the nearly empty parking lot after I've wrapped up my last class of the day. It's been a long day, but good. After practice today, the guys all sang Happy Birthday to me. It was a horrible rendition, but all that mattered was the thought.

Tina, the cashier in the cafeteria, heard it was my birthday and gave me a huge cookie for free. And my phone has been blowing up with messages all day. Now I'm just ready to go home, see my girl, and call it a day. We'll save the partying for the weekend since it's a Monday night.

Reversing out of my parking spot, a call comes through the radio. I hit the phone button on my steering wheel to answer.

"Happy birthday to my favorite middle child." Mom's voice is like a breath of fresh air.

I chuckle as I stop at the light and flick on my signal. "I'm your only middle child."

"Therefore, my favorite. Have you had a good birthday?"

"It's been pretty good. It's Monday, so nothing crazy is going on." Pushing down on the accelerator, I turn toward the apartment complex.

"I'm glad to hear you're not having a wild party. You've always been my good child."

"The bar wasn't too hard to reach."

Her laugh fills the car. "No, Jett sure gave us a run for our money. Have you heard from him today?"

Leaning my elbow against the windowpane, I rest my head against my fist. "Yeah, he sent me a text. Any idea when he's coming home?"

"No idea. Hopefully soon." She pauses, the weight of my brother's absence weighs heavily on her. "But we're not going to let that dampen your birthday. I can't believe it's been twenty-one years since we brought you home from the hospital. Your dad would be so proud of the man you've become."

A lump in my throat grows. I miss my dad so damn much. His death weighs heavily over the family, but day by day, we've learned to move forward. We'll never forget him, but life doesn't stop because he's no longer with us. Birthdays and holidays always seem to hit the hardest.

"Thanks, Mom," I choke on the words.

"Oh, sweetie, I didn't mean to upset you."

Easing onto the brakes, I signal as I turn into the apartment complex. I guide the truck along the path to our building. "You didn't upset me, Mom. It's just hard not having him here."

"You know he's watching over you and has the best seat in the house for your games."

"That he does." Turning the wheel, I pull into an empty parking space.

"Well, anyway, I won't keep you. I just wanted to call and wish you a happy birthday. I love you, sweetheart."

I smile. "I love you too, Mom. Tell the family I said hello."

We disconnected the call, and I switched the ignition off. Gripping the handle, I pull it toward me and open the door. Sliding out of my seat, I reach for my bags before shutting the door behind me.

Climbing the stairs, a somber mood tries to pull me under, but I fight to keep the feeling away. Slipping my key into the lock, I twist the knob as the front door opens. I'm met with a pitch-black apartment and complete silence. Apparently, I'm going to spend my birthday alone. Crossing over the threshold, I flick the light switch on.

Shouts of "Surprise!" ring out, and I startle. Clutching my heaving chest, I fight to catch my breath as I bring my soul back to my body.

"Holy fuck!"

Closing the door behind me, I take in the not-empty apartment. Shades of green and blue streamers—my favorite colors—hang from the ceiling as more balloons have invaded our space. Heads of my friends peek out from the kitchen doorway, my bedroom doorway, and the living room. A sign on the entryway table reads *"entry fee one shot"* with disposable red plastic shot glasses filled with amber liquid. Holes surround some of the glasses where people have taken a shot upon entry.

"Grab a shot!" Bret's cheerful voice sounds from down the hall. I watch as she bounces toward me as someone switches on the music, and 2 Chainz's "Birthday Song" starts playing through the speakers.

Reaching for a glass, I hold one out for her as I pick up one for myself. "Only if you do one with me."

"I'm never going to make it to the Eagle's Nest," she mumbles but takes the cup from my hands.

"Wait," Brynn shouts as she comes rushing toward us. She holds her phone out. "You two get together so we can take a picture of the birthday boy taking his first *legal* shot. We all know Riggs isn't new to alcohol."

Chuckling, I watch as a nervous Bret sidles up next to me. Tossing my arm over her shoulder, I pull her closer but still at a friend's safe distance. Holding our shots out, we hold them in a cheers position while Brynn snaps the picture. "Got it. Now drink up, bitch."

"Happy birthday, Crew." The two of us tap cups before shooting the shots. The warm liquid hits my tongue as I swallow the cinnamon-flavored liquor. We're in for a wild night if we start with cinnamon whiskey.

Licking my lips, I shiver. "Did you plan all this?"

"What are secret girlfriends for?" she shrugs, flashing me a playful smirk.

"Riggsby!" Harris shouts over the music. "Happy fucking birthday, man!"

Nudging Bret's shoulder in a silent gesture of endearment, I walk toward my best friend, who's standing in the hallway opening, arms outstretched. We pull each other in for a quick, friendly embrace, our arms crossing diagonally over each other's backs. We seal the gesture with a few taps to the back before stepping apart with easy smiles.

JP and Grant step up to us, both slapping me on the back. "Did all you fuckers know about this?"

Harris and JP's guilty expressions are the only answers I need. Grant points his beer bottle toward his sister. "She just told me last night."

Flicking my gaze from my friends to my girl, I watch as she tilts her head back and laughs at something Brynn says. Brynn rubs her belly over her tight T-shirt, and I notice her tiny baby bump for the first time. I still can't believe she and Q are having a kid. He called us a couple of weeks ago and told us the news. It was the day after Bret had all of the girls over while we had an away game.

"Drink up, motherfucker." Cody shoves a can of beer into my hands as he slaps my back. "Happy twenty-first, man."

Popping the tab, I chug the ice-cold light beer. Cody chuckles. "You're going to have a fun practice tomorrow."

"That's tomorrow's problem."

I mill around the party for the next hour, surrounded by twenty or so of my closest friends. I drink beer after beer and shot after shot as music plays the soundtrack of our night. Plastic cups and cans litter our apartment. No wonder Rebel was busy cleaning yesterday. A happy buzz has infiltrated my system, and I can feel the floppy grin spread across my face. Everything seemed a little brighter and a little funnier as the world felt pleasantly blurred.

I'm leaning against the doorway when I feel a woman's body lean into mine. Instantly, I know it's not my Rebel. Glancing down, I find Brynn staring up at me. "You're glowy."

She chuckles. "Thank you, I think? I brought the birthday boy another shot, but I'm unsure if you need it right now." I shrug, flashing her a dopey grin. "There's our golden retriever."

I quirk a brow, and she nudges my side. "Your what?"

She smiles. "Every time you get drunk, you become the human version of a golden retriever. Your eyes spark with joy, and you always have this huge smile plastered on your face. You become so affectionate, always throwing your arms around us, doling out hugs, and giving us high-fives like you're just so thrilled to be around us. Not to mention your energy as you bounce around. It's infectious and absolutely adorable."

"If I'm a puppy, can I live with you and Q?" Leaning down, I rub her belly and take on a baby-talk voice. "And, of course, the little sprout, too."

"Oh my god, Riggsby." She wraps her arm around my waist for a side hug. Hugging her back, I rest my arm on her shoulder as we observe the party.

Bret stands with her back to the balcony doors as her body is angled toward the TV. She has a whisk in her hand as a makeshift microphone as she reads off lyrics on the screen. The Killers "Mr. Brightside" plays as Bret attempts to sing the lyrics. Thankfully, she balls better than she sings. I watch her bounce as she dances to the beat, waving her arms and holding the whisk to her face.

Brynn taps my chest, pulling my attention away from Rebel. She smirks up at me when my eyes land on her. "Don't worry, Riggsby, your secret is safe with me."

I quirk my brow, and she hands me a plastic shot glass. "Happy birthday, Riggs." Shooting the cinnamon whiskey, my lids close, and I smile, feeling completely carefree.

Who said Monday night birthdays suck?

This has been the best night surrounded by my favorite people. The hangover waiting for me is going to make my Tuesday terrible, but that's tomorrow's concern—nothing a few iced lattes won't cure.

CHAPTER 21
Bret

The month is flying by. After Crew's birthday on the sixteenth, it's been nonstop schoolwork and studying. Eat, sleep, basketball, and study. Then repeat. But now that midterms are over and Halloween weekend is here, it's time to let loose and blow off some steam.

Not only am I looking forward to dressing up and partying with my friends, but I'm also super excited because it's the weekend when Olivia flies in. *Finally*.

We've been planning outfits and sending links back and forth as we determined this year's Halloween costumes. The Eagles Nest is throwing its annual Halloween party Saturday night after the guys' early afternoon home game.

Glancing at my phone, I check the time and her flight checker for the hundredth time. If I don't sit down, I'll pace a hole in our floor while I wait for her rideshare to drop her off. She refused to have me drive and pick her up, saying it was a waste of time. Olivia Reed is forever Miss Independent.

The rapping of knuckles on our door startles me. Bounding down the hall, I whip open the door. Squeals erupt as I come face to face with my best friend. I take in the beauty before me dressed in her signature grunge style.

Liv stands a few inches shorter than me. Her long legs are covered in open fishnet stockings, a leather miniskirt and Doc Martens. An oversized tee is tucked into the front of her skirt while her silvery-white hair hangs down her back in loose curls.

I throw my arms around her shoulders while hers wrap around my waist. We rock back and forth, neither wanting to let go. She all but tackles me as we stumble against the wall.

"I freaking missed you, bitch." Liv pulls away, a brimming smile on her face.

"I missed you! Come meet everyone." She grabs her small suitcase and follows me into the kitchen.

"Hey guys, this is my bestie, Liv." I flick my hand toward the two in the kitchen. "Liv, these are the guys."

"Tyler," he introduces himself as he wipes his hand off and reaches out for her to take it. He tips his head behind him, gesturing to where JP is talking on the phone. "That's JP."

Olivia smiles as JP gives her a nod. Liv and I move away from the kitchen and into the living room, where Crew is stretched out on the couch watching ESPN. "Crew, this is Liv."

At the mention of her name, Crew whips his head in our direction as he springs from his spot and moves to us. Liv and I don't have a chance to react before he throws his arms around my best friend and pulls her in for a hug.

"Thank you for saving our girl." His words are whispered, but I don't just hear them. I feel them. He remembered everything I told him all those weeks ago. My chest squeezes at him thanking her for being there when I was at my lowest of lows.

Olivia wraps her arms around his middle and squeezes him back. Her eyes find mine, and her face softens. The two have a moment, and I can't help the wobble in my chin as tears spring in my eyes. My two favorite people just met, and the sincerity in Crew's voice has me shaking.

The two pull apart, and I watch as Olivia takes a black manicured finger and wipes the smeared liner from her wet lashes.

"Well, fuck." Liv's voice cracks as she gives us a watery smile.

"Did Crew tell one of his stupid jokes already?"

Liv opens her mouth to respond, but I send her a quick, subtle shake as I cut her off. "You know Crew."

Tyler gives a tight-lipped smile and nods as he moves past us and into his room.

"He's hot," Olivia blatantly says. "Which position does he play?"

"Quarterback."

She hums. "I've never hooked up with a quarterback."

"Don't sleep with my roommate." Olivia moves past me, but not before she leans over and whispers. "But you're sleeping with *your* roommate."

She's got a point.

"So, what's the plan for tonight?" she asks, sitting on the couch in the opposite section from Crew, his legs spread wide to accommodate his large body.

"I don't have any plans. We can do whatever you want. There's a party tomorrow night after the game, and that's all I know." I step over Crew's legs and sit in a space between his spot and the corner where Tyler sits.

"I'm fine with staying in." Liv shifts her shoulders.

"Yes, let's do that, and you can catch me up on all things Arizona."

"It's still hot and dry as fuck."

Crew shifts in his seat, running his palms down his athletic shorts. "Rebel told me you did all of her tattoos."

"Have you seen my favorite one?" A subtle smirk spreads across Liv's face. I stretch my legs out and attempt to kick my bestie. She giggles as she mimes, zipping her lips closed.

Crew leans forward as he looks at Liv. "But yes, I have seen it." He says the words in a whispered rush just as Harris comes out of his room.

"You guys in for the night?"

We all nod.

"Want to all watch something and hang out?" Turning, I lean on my shoulder and shout toward the kitchen. "JP, do you have to work?"

He comes around the corner. "Nope. I'm home tonight."

I clap my hands. "Good, then it's settled."

"I'm going to go change into something comfortable." Liv stands and slides around the table. "Which room is yours?"

I point toward my room.

"Hey, Bret, want to watch *Fast and Furious Four*?"

A half smile spread across Tyler's lips, and I could punch him. The days after our movie night in Crew's room and my vivid dream were incredibly awkward. I could barely look at Tyler without blushing and fumbling over his words. I can't believe he's bringing it up right now, especially in front of JP.

Crew chuckles from beside me, and I hit him in the face with the pillow I had on my lap. "You both suck."

"Wait, what's wrong with *Fast and Furious*?" JP bounces his head from Tyler to me and then to Crew. "Does this have anything to do with you three cozying up to each other and pissing Grant off?"

"Oh my gosh, nothing happened." I cover my face.

"Wait, did you all hook up, and no one told me?" Liv props her hands on her hips as she joins us. Tilting my head back, I rest it against the back of the couch cushion.

Tyler laughs. "I'm just fucking with you, Bret."

Lifting my hand, I wave my middle finger toward him as everyone chuckles.

Assholes, the lot of them.

"How's living with three guys? Are you surviving?"

"Pshh, more like thriving. She keeps it interesting here," JP muses.

"Especially when she decides to cook," Tyler supplies, nudging my leg with his foot.

Liv smacks her legs as she jolts forward. "Oh my god, please tell me you didn't let her cook."

"One time," Crew says with his pointer finger in the air as he shivers.

"Is this why you always cooked for us?" I direct the question to Liv.

"Aw babe, you're pretty to look at, but you suck at cooking."

Everyone laughs again as JP smiles. "I'm so glad I missed that dinner."

"How's living above the tattoo parlor?"

Liv practically glows at the mention of her shop. "I love it. The guys have all been super cool. Dex said I should have my chair by the end of the year."

"Dex is the owner?"

She nods. "He's the one I'm renting the apartment from."

"That's badass, girl," JP compliments. "What's the most badass tattoo you've done?"

"I did this insane leg piece on this woman last week. Flowers went from below her knee to her ankle, where a skull rested in the center, and a snake weaved throughout the floral designs and rested on top of the skull." She reaches for her phone and starts scrolling before turning it toward JP.

"Holy fuck." His jaw drops as he reaches for her phone. "Can you do my next piece?"

"Toss it here," I say, holding out my hands. The phone lands, and I zoom in on the design as Tyler and Crew look over my shoulder.

"That's impressive." Crew's voice is laced with awe.

"I don't have any ink, but I'd let you design something for me," Tyler adds.

"Thanks, guys." Liv blushes. She's never been one to take compliments. "Plan a trip and we'll make a weekend out of it. I'm sure Bret's ready for fresh ink."

"Always, babes."

As the TV played in the background, we fell into easy conversation. Our sectional became the hub of our stories, which were filled with banter and laughter. Everything felt right inside our apartment as I was cozied on the couch with my best friend and roommates, who felt like family.

"Oh my god, this is amazing!" Liv shouts over the roar of the crowd as we toss our hands in the air, trying to draw attention to the cheerleader who is tossing T-shirts in the air

The Texas sun beats down on us as we stand among enthusiastic fans in the student section. The fight song plays, hyping the crowd up as we wait for the team to run into the field. Both of us are dressed in Macy Miller's exclusive designs. Liv paired her cropped tee with another leather skirt, while I chose baggy denim jeans with the knees ripped out.

"Welcome to your first college football game," I shout, tossing my arm over her shoulder. "Don't blame me for the addiction."

The band quits playing as silence and vibrant energy fall over the stadium. The crowd, including us, turns our attention to the massive screen on the opposite side of the field. The screen flickers to life as a soaring eagle flashes across the screen, as high-energy music pulsates through the speakers with palpable energy. Quick cuts of past games fade in and out of the screen. The crowd roars with each new clip as the anticipation builds.

The clips flash from game highlights to moments of training camps and practices as the players hit each other. Their faces were sweat-soaked and full of determination. My dad's face moves onto the screen as he gives speeches to the team kneeling before him. "Give it everything you've got," his voice booms and mixes with the music as his fist is held high. "Every play. Every day. Leave it all on the field!"

The video pans to the almost sold-out stadium today before finding the tunnel where the team waits to run out onto the field. Cannons shoot fiery red explosives into the air as the team runs out onto the turf. Shouts erupt, causing the stadium to rumble.

"Holy fuck, I have goose bumps." Liv points to her skin where raised bumps cover her arms.

Scanning the players on our sideline, I find my brother surrounded by Tyler and Crew. The three of them hold their helmets at their sides as they laugh and joke with each other, looking relaxed and ready for kickoff.

Both teams jog out onto the turf field and take their positions. Fans are on their feet as the kickoff song plays "Seven Nation Army" by The White Stripes, causing everyone to jump in place. The sound of the music intertwines with the sound of feet on metal and roaring cheers is a cacophony of noise.

Liv's eyes are wide as she takes in the scene. I've been to dozens of football games, but the start of one never gets old. There's such palpable excitement swirling around. I can only imagine what she's thinking as she takes it all in for the first time, what I wouldn't give to experience a football game for the first time again.

With the ball sailing in the air, it's officially game time.

We stand among the crowd of students as we watch the game unfold.

I have to admit that everything has finally started to feel normal again. I no longer feel uncomfortable as I stand among a group of boisterous people, feeling lost, alone, and uneasy. Having Liv here and after a month of healing, everything feels right in my life. After months of fearing my shadow, I'm finally living life again like normal twenty-year-olds should.

The first quarter flies by in a blur. For some reason attending games live always makes the time go faster. Instead of the commercial break lull on television, breaks are filled with entertainment either on the field or in videos on the Jumbotron, making the interruption feel quick. No one in the student section sits, at least around us, where we stand shoulder to shoulder, screaming our lungs out as we watch our defense stop the Tigers from scoring. Tyler scores for us as he leads the team down the field before rushing three yards into the endzone with a quarterback keep.

"He's so hot," Liv yells beside me as I shake my head. Tyler is beautiful, and if it weren't for Crew, he would be my type, which is the opposite of Olivia's dark and broody who dresses in too much black and leather.

As the second quarter progresses, I find myself glancing around more. The feeling of needing to look over my shoulder hits me, and I feel unease wash over me like a tidal wave. It's a familiar feeling I haven't felt in a while. My mind has to be playing some kind of sick joke on me.

Yeah, Bret, it's just a twisted game. It's only because Olivia is here and emotions from the past have been at the forefront of your mind.

Looking around the sea of bodies, I'm met with unfamiliar faces who offer tight-lipped smiles whenever I make dreadful, awkward eye contact. The student section roars with cheers as I snap my head toward the field. The ball is flying through the air from where Tyler has thrown it down the field. Just when I think the pass will go out of bounds, number eighty-eight lifts his arms high as he leaps in the air. Crew's supersize allows him to get just enough space between him and his defender. I watch with bated breath as he's able to bring the ball down with the grip of his fingertips.

Touchdown! Now that's the kind of catch that ends up on Sports Center.

I jump with the rest of them as we share high-fives with everyone around us. Liv and I tap aluminum beer bottles as we celebrate another scoring drive before halftime. Our section is wild as cheers continue, and the extra-point kick flies through the uprights.

"Guess who's getting laid tonight." Liv leans in close before tipping her bottle to the sidelines, where teammates walk by Crew and tap him on the helmet.

I nudge her shoulder because, yes, she's probably right. Adrenaline is constantly pouring through his veins after games.

"No, but seriously," she shouts. "This is incredible!"

"I told you!" I nod enthusiastically. "This is why I wanted you to go to games with me in Arizona."

"We'll go to more together, especially once all your hot, talented friends make it to the pros."

"Deal." We clink drinks while the final seconds in the half tick down.

Halftime arrives, and the band takes the field, lining up in formation for the spectacular performance they are known for, as my stomach growls.

"Wanna go fight the crowd with me and grab a pretzel?"

She nods, shaking her bottle. "Let's grab more drinks too."

Squeezing down our aisle, we make it to the stairs, where we have to climb Everest to reach the top. Brynn gave me her front-row tickets to use today. I have to say, the seats are phenomenal, and I need to figure out how she got them so I can secure them next year after she graduates.

Weaving through the crowd, my senses are filled with the smells of freshly popped popcorn and hot dogs as I search for a concession stand without a giant line. Between the noise of excited fans and my happiness radiating around me, I feel like I am walking on a cloud.

"I'm going to grab our beers," Liv says, gesturing to the little convenience store across the aisle from the stand. "Order me a pretzel with cheese, too?"

I nod before joining the long line of hungry fans, which seems to move at a snail's pace. When I finally have our pretzels, I turn to search for her in the sea of red, white, and powder blue, and that's when everything stops.

My body freezes like I've just been struck by Elsa's icy powers.

Just beyond the crowds of people, my eyes lock onto a figure standing a few rows away. My heart stops, and a chill causes my spine to stiffen as my blood freezes, and a cold sweat breaks out over my body.

It's *him*.

The man who has made the last year a living, breathing nightmare. The real-life boogeyman who is no longer hiding beneath my bed but staring me in the eyes.

Noise fades away as the roaring sound of my blood pumping fills my ears. My stomach clenches as I'm hit with an onslaught of terror that I thought was in my past. The feeling of security from moving states away vanishes in an instant. I'm thrown back in time to being weak and naïve. The urge to blink forces me into a dilemma of wanting to see if this is a dream or risk blinking and losing sight of him.

This can't be happening. Did he follow Liv to get to me? Oh my god. What if he's been stalking her this whole time, hoping she'd lead him to me? And we just played right into his game.

Panic rises in my chest, my breathing coming in short, sharp gasps. Nausea sweeps over me as my hands holding the pretzels begin to shake. My legs feel like lead. It's as if they're cemented to the ground. The corners of my eyes start to dizzy as my vision tunnels.

I feel exposed and vulnerable. The sense of security I've been building begins to crumble around me like shattered glass.

"Bret! Bret!" A panic-filled voice starts to make its way through my hearing. I begin to blink rapidly as my vision focuses on panicked eyes staring back at me. Liv snaps her fingers in front of my face, trying to get my attention. "Bret. *Babe*. It's *not* him."

Slowly, her words start to sink in the more she repeats that it's not him, not the monster.

"You're okay." Her voice is soft and calming. "I'm here with you."

My focus starts to come back as she continues to talk me through the panic attack. I'm forever grateful that she came with me to a few therapy appointments at the beginning. My therapist showed Liv how to talk me through any sort of unease or panic attack.

Her head bobs in front of me, and I'm unsure if she's reassuring me or herself. "I know you're scared right now, and that's okay, but you're safe. You're safe here with me. Now, take slow, deep breaths. Let's do them together."

We breathe in through our noses and count to four—which she does for me. Holding our breath for another four counts before she encourages me to exhale through my mouth as she counts to four again.

My body starts to relax as my heart rate slows and the trembling subsides.

"How are you doing?"

I nod, eyes still bouncing around the faces who stare back at me as if I'm crazy. And hell, maybe I am. Perhaps I'm the girl who loses her shit out of the blue.

"I'm fine." The words come out shaky.

"Good." Liv rubs my arm. "Keep focusing on your breathing, slow breaths. Can you tell me five things you see?"

I take a few more measured breaths and list five things I see. "A weird eagle hat, a TV, the team store, pretzels, and beer."

Liv offers me a reassuring smile. "Good, babes. Want to head back to your place?"

"No." I shake my head. "No, he's not taking this away."

"That's my badass bestie." She squeezes my forearm. I didn't realize she was still holding. "Come on."

Olivia leads us back to our seats, where the game has resumed. Ripping a bite from the golden-brown pretzel, I chew the salty dough and stare straight ahead. The rest of the game is a blur. I go through the motions whenever the crowd cheers, but my mind is no longer present. I've cast a black cloud over our day, and guilt eats away at me.

As the final whistle blows, we stand and clap. The boys pulled off a landslide victory, which keeps the Eagles undefeated. I'm barely able to muster the energy to celebrate.

"Come on, babes," Liv says as another warm smile spreads across her face. "Let's head home."

Home.

Home used to be a cute, quaint two-bedroom apartment in Arizona with my best friend. But he ruined that for me. Now, home is hundreds of miles away in an oversized, four-bedroom apartment with three football players.

It takes some time to get out of the stadium as everyone is funneling through the same exit. As we maneuvered our way to where we parked, I couldn't help but look over my shoulder. Liv reaches her hand out, and I gladly give her the keys to the Jeep.

The drive home is silent as the GPS guides Liv back to the complex. Every shadow seems to hide a threat, every car behind us a potential danger. Exhaustion nips at me from the after-effects of the panic attack as fear gnaws at the back of my mind.

CHAPTER 22
CREW

"Listen up, men," Coach begins, his voice echoing off the walls. The locker room has been a flurry of noise from the excitement of adding another 'W' to the schedule. Our gear has been stripped off, and we stand around in undershirts and uniform pants. Coach Campbell makes his way to the center of the room. His face is a melody of pride and tenacity. With a clap of his hands, the room quiets as our attention goes to him.

"What you did out there was nothing short of spectacular. You played with heart, with grit, and with the kind of determination that wins championships. But as we've seen all season, this was just one game. One step in the journey. Targets are on our backs. I know it's Halloween weekend, and I know you men won't be staying in. Celebrate tonight, but on Monday, we get back to work. This is our foundation, and we build on it each week. Stay hungry, stay focused, and stay humble. Keep pushing each other to be better. Have fun and be safe. Now let's go enjoy this moment!"

As Coach wraps up his speech, the locker room erupts in chaos. We all start whooping and hollering as we jump up and down, giving each other high-fives. JP plays a celebratory hip-hop song, which has him breaking out in his signature dance moves. Some of the guys join in, as I stand back laughing.

"There's nothing better than a good ol' fashion ass-kicking," Grant shouts, slapping my back.

"Hell yeah!" My voice comes out hoarse from the yelling.

Grant moves on to the next guy as I start stripping out of my pants, grass, dirt, and grim stick to my sweaty body. I punch the four-digit number into the keypad of the school-issued safe that comes in each player's locker. Reaching inside, I dig out my phone and tap the screen, expecting Bret's text. It's a little habit she's started. Hours before each game, she sends me a good luck text and, immediately after, a great game message of some variety. After scrolling through all of my notifications, I was surprised that she hadn't texted yet. Maybe she and Olivia are waiting outside for us.

Speaking of Olivia, when she walked into our apartment last night, she was not what I expected. The girl standing before us was grungy and badass. Bret has spoken so highly of her best friend, and I knew she wouldn't be anything short of amazing. But seeing how confident and tough she was, I was thankful Bret had someone like her in her corner.

Sliding my phone back into the safe, I grab my toiletry bag and hit the shower. As soon as I step inside the shower and under the hot spray, my body sags with relief. I should schedule a time for some physical therapy but not tonight. The water cascades down my body, and I watch as the water turns a brownish-gray color. I watch sweat and grim wash down my body and swirl around the drain. Voices echo around me as I tilt my face under the warm stream and I let myself breathe.

Grabbing a dry towel off the ledge, I pat my body down before wrapping the cotton towel around my waist and stepping out of the stall. One of my teammates grabs my shoulder. "Nice job out there, man."

I tip my head and thank him. The main locker room is still a hive of energy as the music continues to blare, and our social media team captures some clips of players who are still clothed. As much as I appreciate the banter and celebrations, I'm ready to see my girl, get some food, and start pregaming for the Halloween party, preferably in that order.

Fully dressed in clean clothes, I gather all my gear as I look around the room. Through a window, the coaches are gathered around a table, no doubt going over the game and preparing a strategy for next week. Coach Campbell catches my eye as he gives me a nod. Instantly, I feel like I just got the approval of a father.

After losing my dad, it's been hard not to have a man in that role. My grandpa tries, but he's not huge on technology, which makes calling him hard. Don't even get him started on video calls. I'm not sure if it's because Grant is on our team or if that's just Coach's personality, but he constantly reassures the team that he's proud of them and that his door is always open if we need anything, *anything*. Of course, he's a total hard ass when he needs to be, but there's something comforting in his praise.

"See you back at the house?"

Harris nods. "Yeah, man, I've got to do some press before I head out of here."

"Good luck with that." With a wave over my shoulder, I slide my bag over my shoulder and push through the doors. Scanning the faces, I don't find bright green eyes and jet-black hair. Or hell, even Liv's silver hair would stand out in the crowd.

Sliding out my phone, I pull up my messages, but there is still nothing.

> **Me: Hey, Rebel. Are you still at the stadium?**

With a few nods to people waiting, I walk down the crowded hall as I'm hit with a tinge of pain in the center of my chest. It's been so long since I've had someone waiting outside for me. Jealousy strikes me in waves, and it doesn't help that I have to hide my girlfriend from the world. One day, I'll be able to have her in the hall and she'll be waiting for me.

The back parking lot is still full as I'm one of the first to leave, which is pretty standard. As much as I love a post-game party, I need to unwind in my own space unless it's a night game. Then I'm ready to party until the morning. Climbing into my truck, I slide my phone out one last time. There's a message waiting for me.

> **Rebel: This is Liv. We got back a little over thirty minutes ago. Bret is sleeping. Sorry, I should've texted you earlier.**

> Me: Thanks for letting me know. I'm heading back now.

Liv likes the message, and I reverse out of my space. Bret's sleeping? Did she drink too much at the game? And if she did, that's odd because she's not a huge drinker.

What would usually take me less than fifteen minutes to get home ended up taking me thirty minutes due to all of the traffic.

The apartment is still quiet when I step inside. Leaving my keys on the hook in the entryway, I toss my bag in my room as I go further into the living room. Bret's door is closed, and I see Liv sitting on the couch. She glances up and offers me a tight-lipped smile. It's not anywhere near as happy as it has been.

"Hey, Liv." I sit on the couch opposite her, my legs spread out wide as I sink deeper into the sofa.

"Good game. Although I don't know much about football, what I did understand is that you made an insane catch."

"Thank you. Was it fun?"

Her face falls as she clenches her jaw. Yeah, something is definitely wrong. "The football game was so much fun. It was my first game, and I can honestly say I can't wait to watch one again."

"But..." Worry has me leaning forward and resting my elbows on my knees as I watch her.

"But there was an incident." Her voice quiets as she chews her bottom lip. Raising my brows, I encourage her to keep going. "She's okay, and I'm totally breaking the best friend code, but Bret said she confided her past to you." I nod, and Liv continues. "During halftime, we went to get food, and while we were in the crowd of people, Bret had a panic attack."

My eyes widen as my stomach drops. "What happened?"

"She thought she saw *him*, but it wasn't him. The guy resembled her ex, but I saw the guy who startled her, and it wasn't him. But her brain convinced her it was, and she spiraled. I was able to talk her down from the panic attack, but it took a lot out of her. I tried to get her to leave, but she wanted to stay for the rest of the game."

I run my hands down my face as my head drops between my shoulders. I hate that some asshole continues to torture her. He's not even in Texas, but he's twisted her brain so badly that she can't mentally escape him.

"Why didn't she ever report him?"

Liv lets out a long sigh. "She was scared. He's done a good job of being seen without leaving a trail. Bret's afraid she doesn't have enough proof, and then there's the stigma of it all."

"The stigma?"

"He's on the football team. There are always accusations around the team, and she didn't want to cause unnecessary drama when she didn't have any proof. Not for her, for her brother, or her dad."

He's on the football team. We might play them in a few weeks, depending on how the conference shakes out. How is she going to handle that? And I know her dad and her brother. They would want the fucker to pay even if it did cause drama on their end. Coach Campbell would burn the whole world down for his daughter, and hell, so would I.

Rubbing my temples, I stare out the balcony door and watch branches dance in the breeze. "I want so badly to protect her, but I don't know how I can do that when she won't tell anyone we're together."

"I see how you look at her and how you two act when no one is watching. Keep being her anchor, Crew. She's been through so much, and you're helping. It might not seem like it right now, but Bret is the happiest I've ever seen her, and that's including how things used to be before the douchebag."

Keep being her anchor. I nod. Of course, I can be her anchor. I'd be anything she wanted me to be. My heart belongs to Bret. It's been with her for a long time, and each day that I'm with her, she takes a part of my soul, too.

Hours later, I'm still pondering how to make Bret's life a better place. A place where she doesn't have to live in fear of the shadows. A place where she feels *safe*. Since I've been home, we've bumped into each other a few times. We all sat and ate takeout from a barbecue joint Quinton got me hooked on.

I've tried to get her alone a few times, but she's avoiding me. I even openly confessed I was thinking of staying in for the night. I wasn't going to, but if that's what Bret needed, I wanted to give her the option.

Everyone looked at me as if I had grown a second head, so clearly that was out of the question.

Now I'm standing in front of the mirror attached to my dresser as I assess my outfit. The snug navy material fits every contour of my body, and if I'm not careful, my lower half will break through the stitching. A gold belt with an eagle's crest is wrapped around my waist, and gold accents hang off my shoulders, resembling the eagle's wings. Deep red gloves and wrist guards line my wrist. I even bought the matching deep red boots with a gold eagle crest.

I can't believe Harris, JP, and I are doing a group costume. No doubt some heads will turn in our direction either because of our badass entry or because they have no idea who the hell we are. Running my fingers through my hair, I finish styling the longer strands on top of my head.

My phone vibrates against the dresser, and I see a new message from the group chat.

Roomies

Rebel: You ladies done yet?

JP: Listen here, this shit is tight.

Me: We didn't think through how thick our thighs are.

Rebel: Mmm thick thighs

Rebel: OMG, that was LIV!

> **JP: Uh-huh, sure. Whatever you need to tell yourself.**

> **Me: Harris?**

> **JP: He's having a diva moment.**

> **Harris: Fuck off. This costume better get me laid.**

> **Rebel: Are we ready for a roommate reveal?**

> **Harris: ...fine.**

Leaving my phone on my dresser, I open the door and stride toward the living room, my patriotic cape blowing behind me. Placing my hands on my hips, I puff out my chest while keeping my chin held high. The sound of a door opening makes me look to my left as JP emerges from his room.

I stand still, watching him adjust the high-tech blue and silver suit. The details on the suit are incredible. Armor plates are designed to sit on the chest and shoulders, giving the costume a futuristic look. His eyes are covered by a mask with reflective lenses. His stoic expression, paired with the mask, adds an intimidating edge to his costume. I can't imagine how he feels if I thought my suit was tight. It looks like a second skin as if it were made for him, making him look like a real-life superhero—or villain.

As he moves into the living room, we both size each other up. Our expressions stay neutral. He walks around me, and I turn, never giving him my back. It's as if we are preparing for battle. With our chests puffed out and our heads held high, both of us crack at the same time.

"Dude, your costume is sick."

JP laughs. "Mine? Have you seen yourself? It's no wonder you're the face of The Seven."

The other two doors open as the girls' voices filter in, but I can't help the booming laugh that escapes as I catch a glimpse of Harris walking out of his room. JP turns at the sound of my voice, allowing a gap to form between us. The girls start laughing as we take in the group's final member.

"I swear to god, if this costume doesn't get me laid tonight, JP, I'm going to kill you in your sleep." Harris's voice is stern and deadly serious as we all continue to laugh at his costume. It's not because it's terrible by any means but how ridiculous the superhero who wears it is.

"This is great," Liv says between gasps of air as her boisterous laugh continues.

Harris stands before us, wearing the signature green and gold suit that clings to his frame. It's a good thing all of us are in insane shape, considering each suit shows off everything, and I mean *everything*. The sleeveless jumpsuit is cut off at his shoulders, and a scale texture covers the entire suit, giving it the full aquatic vibe. Brown-scaled gloves stop below his elbows.

But the best thing about this suit is that around his waist, hooked into his belt, is a...

"Is that an octopus?" Bret's eyes widen, and that's when my mouth drops. I was so caught up in Harris coming out dressed in a superhero costume with an octopus covering his dick that I didn't even have a chance to check out the girls.

Bret and Olivia are both in matching costumes. Everyone was sticking to a theme this year. My breath catches in my throat as I take in her body. Her boobs spill out of a black lace-covered corset which exposes her olive skin as it trails beneath a black skirt that has some kind of girly material hanging off it. Fishnets cover her long legs, sparking an image in my head of them wrapping around my waist. A ribbon is crossed over her calves, connecting to black ballet shoes and another piece is tied in a bow around her neck. Her black hair is tied on the top of her head and her stunning face is covered in black and white makeup to give the illusion of a skull.

She looks fucking incredible. Sexy and badass. And I get to call her mine.

Bret must feel me watching her because her emerald-green eyes find mine where a blush no doubt covers her cheeks beneath the skull makeup.

"I cannot believe you three are going as Homelander, A-Train, and The Deep." Liv shakes her head. "You guys missed the perfect opportunity to turn Bret into Starlight."

"But she has black hair," JP points out.

"Yeah, well, she can wear a wig because there's no way she'd go as Stormfront, she sucks."

"Wait, you know *The Boys*?" Harris steps closer to where we are all gathered in the room. I still can't take him seriously.

Liv pops her hand on her hip as attitude pours from her. "Of course I know *The Boys*."

"Marry me?"

"Smooth, Harris."

"What's *The Boys*?" Bret asks timidly.

JP mocks, stumbling backward as he feigns shock. "Oh hell no. You mean to tell me you've been living with us for almost three months, and you don't know what *The Boys* is?" Bret shakes her head. "Tomorrow, when we're hungover as fuck, no one better make plans because it's going to be a Cousin Jimmy's and *The Boys* kind of day."

"Deal."

Liv pulls out her phone and instructs us to get together. The guys and I do what she says as she takes our pictures. This continues for the next ten minutes before we climb into the rideshare that will take us to The Eagles Nest.

The rideshare driver parks in front of the bar, and as I open the back door of the SUV, sounds surround us—car engines and laughter. The outside of The Eagles Nest is filled with people waiting their turn to enter the packed bar. Once again, I'm glad that I am on the football team and JP works here throughout the week.

The girls giggle behind us as I follow JP and Harris to the entrance. Vibrations from the bass hit us as the music seeps out from inside. Neon lights flicker, and flashing lights shine through the glass as we enter the building. The Eagles Nest is always the place to be on campus, but Halloween night is epic. The annual party attracts students and locals alike with the costume contest, entertainment, and cheap drinks. This year, the bar hired a famous DJ instead of their typical local band.

"Who's ready for a wild night?" Harris asks over his shoulder.

"Me!" Liv shouts, prancing around and full of giggles. She started pregaming before we left with the cinnamon whiskey. Somehow, we didn't polish off all the bottles for my birthday.

As I look around at my friends, I can't help but smile at our super-hero costumes and the sexy, dark ballet dancers who joined us. I knew it would be a challenging adventure when I accepted the scholarship to play at CTU. I never thought I'd meet some of my best friends, curate my favorite memories, and form a family not created by blood.

Forming a single file line, I feel a hand brush against mine. Looking over my shoulder, green doe eyes stare up at me from behind her black and white skull makeup. Her fingers slip into mine as she gives my hand a few quick squeezes before her hand slips free. As small of a gesture as that was, the discreet movement reassured me that we were okay and so was she.

Stepping into the bar, a wall of music hits us in full force. The DJ on the main stage is playing a pop and hip-hop mash-up. Laughter and conversation mix with the loud music, making the space deafening. Heads turn our way, taking in the new arrivals—us—as we do the same. Vampires, nurses, police officers, Barbies, and costumes of everything in between stand wall to wall. The smell of beer and sweat-soaked bodies fills the air creating a fragrance that should be called bad decisions.

Tonight feels like it's going to be a good night.

"Drinks?" JP yells, and I nod. "What do you want?"

"Shots and beers!" Liv yells, her body already moving to the beat of the song. She grabs Bret's hips and starts moving them for her. Bret giggles as she shoves her best friend off her before tossing her arms in the air. She moves her hips as a carefree mask slips into place.

JP disappears to the bar as the four of us continue going farther into the bar toward the crowded dance floor. I have no idea how we will find a place to dance, but people start to part as they recognize our quarterback.

Yeah, I'll never take for granted our football team perks.

A vacant high-top table sits off the side of the bar and dance floor, and I swear Harris breaks out in a sprint to snag it before someone else. Bret's hand glides against mine again. God, I desperately want to pull her in front of me and use my hands on her hips to guide her. I've been dying to get my lips on hers since she came out of her room dripping sex appeal. Now I'll have a front-row seat for every guy in this bar trying to pick her up, and I won't be able to do anything about it.

"This place is crazy!" Liv shouts as we all lean against the high-top. She's standing opposite Harris as Bret and I stand between the two. Our backs are to the wall as we face the dance floor. Bret takes advantage of our position and lines her leg and hip up until they are plastered against mine. She leans away from me to keep up the appearance. But Liv gives her a knowing look.

"Time to drink up!" JP places a tray of shots on the table, followed by a bucket of beers.

The girls clap their hands as excitement rolls off their faces. Everyone grabs a shot and hoists it in the air. JP opens his mouth to spout a cheer, but Harris speaks up first.

"Here is to honor. Here's to getting on her, to staying on her, and if you can't come in her—"

"Come on her," Liv and Bret finish, both girls cracking up as the guys and I stare at them.

We shoot the cinnamon whiskey and enjoy the burn that coats our throats and warms our bodies. Everyone shivers before staring out at the dance floor to assess the situation. I take the opportunity, while everyone is distracted to lean down to Bret's ear.

"I've got you tonight, Rebel." Her emerald eyes sparkle in the flashing lights as she tilts her head in confusion. "I'll watch over you so that you can have fun."

Realization dawns on her as she flashes me an appreciative smile that has her eyes softening.

"Let's go dance!" Bret reaches for a beer, twisting off the cap on the aluminum bottle. She takes a long swig. She subtly hits my hips with hers as she's moving around Liv. As she passes her, Bret smacks Liv's ass before grabbing JP's hand. "Dance with me!"

The two start maneuvering through bodies.

"You bitches get me!" Liv yells, reaching for a beer and grabbing my hand. She pulls me around the table, where she drops my hand for Harris's. We bounce off dancing couples as we find the other two.

With my adrenaline pumping, confidence from my costume seeping into my subconsciousness, and the vibrant energy in the bar, I have a feeling tonight will be a night we'll never forget...or remember.

CHAPTER 23
Bret

The blaring sound of an alarm startles me from my deep sleep. The awful noise triggers the jackhammering to fire up in my brain.

"Olivia Kate Reed, if you don't shut that alarm off now, I will smother you." I groan from my side of the bed, where I'm wrapped in layers of blankets.

Grumbles sound from beside me as the blankets tug and rustle. Finally, the horrid alarm shuts off.

"What time is it?" The words come out in a croak. My mouth feels like the desert, and I grimace as I try to keep my tongue from sticking to the roof of my mouth. Slowly, it frees itself like a sticker peeling away from glass. Trying to swallow, my throat feels like sandpaper.

I need water. Desperately.

"Time for me to head back to Arizona." Liv groans and sadness seeps through me. I'm not ready for her to leave, not yet.

Rolling over to my side, I blink my heavy lids as remnants of last night stick to me. Mascara is clumped up in my lashes as morning goop sticks to the inner corners of my eyes. The pitch-black room starts to come into focus the more I blink. I feel my long hair move as I find my new position, and I can already tell it's sticking up all over the place as if it were a tangled rat's nest. My skin feels sticky from sweat, and there's no doubt I smell like a dirty bar from all the alcohol seeping from my pores.

Liv cuddles closer to me as I wrap my arms around her as she acts as the little spoon. Her hand trails up my thigh. "Babes, are you wearing any clothes?"

Glancing under the navy comforter, I'm met with the sight of skin. "Uhhh..."

"Bret!" She chuckles, smacking my ass. "You're such a brat."

"I seriously don't remember stripping my clothes off."

Burrowing myself deeper into my covers, I continue lying there. Liv's warmth radiates through the covers. I've missed this—time spent with my best friend.

"And your naked ass isn't moving..."

We both shake with laughter. Our giggles are loud enough that we don't hear the knock on the door as it's pressed open.

"What the hell is going on here?" Turning our heads, we find a shirtless Tyler leaning in the doorway, arms crossed over his chiseled chest.

"Wanna find out?" Liv's voice drips with seduction while Tyler's eyebrows hit his hairline.

"No." I shake my head, rolling away from Liv but keeping the sheets gripped tight underneath my chest. "I don't have any clothes on."

Tyler's eyes widen. "Well, I...was just letting you know we made hangover pancakes if you guys are hungry."

Liv sits up, pulling the covers with her. I frantically grab for them before I flash my roommate. "What are they, and why do they sound amazing right now?"

"They're just thick, fluffy pancakes to help soak up the booze."

"Count me in!" Liv bounces from the bed and looks back at me.

"Let me find some clothes." She nods as she walks to the edge of my room and flicks on the light switch. I groan as the overhead light blinds my eyes. Blinking through the bright beam, I sit up, clutching my sheets as I take in the state of my room. Only when I sit up does the room begin to spin as I'm hit with a bout of nausea.

Clothes spill out from my dressers as parts of my costume are strewn across the floor. Tossing off my covers, I will my legs to work. On shaky legs, I stumble over to the dresser, pull out a pair of boy shorts and find an oversized hoodie.

As quickly as I can, I rush through, brushing my teeth and getting the stale taste of last night out of my mouth. Staring at my reflection in the mirror, I watch the foam build around my mouth as I attempt to brush my tangled hair with my opposite hand—thoughts of last night flash in my mind.

We had been at the bar for an hour or so, all of us on the dance floor, with Tyler and Crew sandwiching Liv and me as we moved to the trendy club music. JP had a constant rotation of girls grinding against him. Chloe and Cody joined us. She wore a tight pale pink mini skirt with a pastel floral corset top. Her honey-blonde hair was braided with strands of baby breath and daisies pinned in her hair.

On the other hand, Cody was dressed in cargo pants, a tight white T-shirt, and a green apron. The flower and the florist. It was seriously the cutest costume and from what I know about Chloe, it fit their personalities perfectly.

Stepping out of the bathroom, I follow the sound of laughter to the living space, where I find my best friend and two of my roommates gathered around the table. Black clothing is spread chaotically around the floor and down the hallway.

"There she is." JP claps. "The great flasher."

Rubbing my eyes, I stare at him. "Flasher?"

"Yeah, baby girl." JP grabs a pancake from the stack and sets it on his plate. "You don't remember?"

I shake my head as I glance around the three. Tyler averts his eyes as Liv smirks around a mouthful of pancakes.

"You started stripping out of your clothes as soon as we walked in the door. There is literally a path from the front door to your room."

Groaning, I cover my face with both my hands. "I need caffeine if we are rehashing last night."

Passing pieces of my clothes in my hunt for coffee, I can't help but shake my head. I'm notorious for stripping out of my clothes after a night out, but I was hoping drunk me would get the memo that I live with guys, and it's probably not the best thing to do. Rounding the corner to the kitchen, I'm met with the hum of the coffee maker as the dripping sound of the brewing coffee hits a ceramic mug.

Leaning against the opposite counter with a glass tumbler filled with an iced coffee, the color of the sand, is my hunk of a boyfriend. His unruly blond hair stands on its ends as he rests his head against the cabinet above the counter he's leaning against. I take a moment to scan my eyes over his half naked body while his eyes are closed. Crew's thick, muscular body is on full display as his arm muscles bulge from where they're crossed over his chest. A prominent V trails below the gray sweatpants he's wearing, and I can't help but admire how snug those pants are in all the right places. The fabric squeezes his thick thighs as the outline of his dick is evident through the light-colored material.

Noise still filters from the dining room, and I hastily eat up the space that separates us.

"Hey, boyfriend," I whisper the words as I fling my arms around his neck.

Crew's eyes fly open as he quickly glances to the doorway before unfolding his arms and pulling me against his chest.

"Hey, Rebel. How are you feeling?" Tilting my head up, I look into his tired chocolate-brown eyes and admire the golden flecks spread throughout. He bends down as our lips find each other. It's a quick kiss. Neither one of us wants to risk getting caught as we separate from each other.

"I feel like I was hit by a truck." He chuckles, and I cringe. "Apparently, I stripped out of my clothes last night."

Crew's lips tilt in a smirk as he reaches behind me for the white mug. "I didn't mind the show. Although I'm not a fan of sharing my naked girlfriend with the rest of the group."

"Sorry," I cringe, taking the mug from his outstretched hand.

Warmth seeps from the hot, rich, black coffee, and I savor the heat against my palm. Nothing is better than a steamy cup of joe in the morning, especially when you feel like death warmed over.

"Nah, don't be." With a kiss to my temple, Crew steps around me, and I follow him out of the kitchen toward the rest of our friends. He gestures for me to take the empty seat next to Liv while he sits in his desk chair, which is already in the room.

Sitting down, I grab my fork and stab two cakes, plopping them on my plate before reaching for the maple syrup. The glass canister is warm to my touch as I pour the sweet amber liquid over the golden-brown pancakes. "Warm maple syrup?"

"Obviously." Tyler nods. "When do you have to leave, Liv?"

"Never," I mumble around a mouthful.

"I wish, babes." She leans her head until it's resting against my shoulder. "I need to leave by one."

JP glances at his watch. "Baby girl, that's in like thirty minutes."

She shrugs, adding another pancake to her plate. "These are amazing. Someone needs to send me the recipe."

"I can do that." Tyler nods.

The next fifteen minutes are spent eating layers and layers of pancakes, laughing about our drunken antics, and begging Liv to become an Eagle. At five till one, my best friend stands in the living room hugging my roommates goodbye.

It's weird how effortlessly she fit right into the mix. There was never any awkwardness among the group. It's as if she's always been here. But that's Olivia Reed for you. The girl with an edgy exterior but a selfless heart who meshes in with whatever crowd she's around.

After she hugs JP, she moves to where I'm leaning against the hallway wall. With a pout on her face, Liv spreads her arms wide. "Babes."

I reach for her shoulders and pull her into me. "Thank you for coming and for everything."

"I'll always have your back, my twin flame sister." Pressing a kiss on my cheek, she pulls out of my embrace. "See you soon."

"See you soon."

Liv is not a believer in goodbyes. She says they're too final, and as long as she's breathing, there's no such thing as goodbye or the end.

Turning, she stares down the over six feet tall walls of muscles standing before us. Her stern expression would make anyone cower. "Now, you guys better take care of my girl." In the briefest of seconds, her eyes flit to Crew. "She's been through hell, but you guys are good for her. Protect her, or you'll have me to deal with. And I *know* some people."

Nudging my shoulder against hers, I shake my head. Her phone chimes from her back pocket. "That's my cue. Thank you for an epic weekend."

"Come back anytime." JP smiles at Liv as she reaches for her bag.

Giving me one last hug and a wave over her shoulder, my best friend vanishes out the front door.

With Liv gone, the apartment felt colder and emptier. It's as if a dark cloud has settled over apartment eight-thirty-four and soured my mood. Not that I've been in the best mood, thanks to the awful headache that ibuprofen and sports drinks won't cure. I spent time tidying up the apartment by storing leftover pancakes, cleaning the dishes, and wiping down all hard surfaces. Somehow, in an apartment full of grown adults, we managed to get syrup all over the place.

Once the kitchen was spotless, I grabbed all the fabric scraps from my costume last night. I still can't believe I stripped out of my clothes once I crossed the threshold. Getting back to the apartment is a bit of a blur and I really, *really* hope I didn't try to make any moves on Crew, especially in front of our roommates.

The guys all retreated to their rooms at my insistence. I can't cook so the least I could do was clean up. But as I was bending down to pick up the last piece of clothing, I caught a whiff of myself and shivered.

I headed to the shower and peeled out of my clothes. For the next thirty minutes, I stood under the hot spray and let the water wash away the night before. I lingered longer than usual as I savored the burn against my skin, hoping the water would absorb in my very dehydrated body.

Freshly showered and feeling somewhat better, I padded back to the living room, where the guys had emerged from their rooms. All three of them were in their self-designated spots. Sports drinks lined the coffee table, all of us needing the extra electrolytes. Settling on the couch between Tyler and Crew, I reached for a blanket on the back of the sofa. I cozied into my spot as JP queued up *The Boys*, keeping his promise of bingeing the show together.

Hours and almost a whole season later, our bodies are molded into the cushions. Aside from some of the gruesome details, the show isn't half bad. After being introduced to The Deep in the show and seeing Tyler dressed as him last night, I clutched my stomach from laughing so hard. The character is self-assured, insanely cocky, and somewhat comically pathetic.

The sun has long since set and the golden hue has transitioned into darkness, the only light coming from the glow of the TV. JP dozed off a while ago, his soft snores are occasionally heard in the show's quiet moments. Tyler, who is curled up in the corner of the sectional, rests his head on a pillow opposite us as he watches the show. His eyes occasionally droop as everyone still feels the effects of last night.

With everyone else preoccupied, Crew and I have slowly erased the gap between us. His thick thigh rests against my bare skin. A thrill runs through me with each brush of his arm against mine. With a subtle glance at him from my periphery, I notice the slight smirk toying at the corner of his mouth. Carefully, and oh so smoothly, his fingertips run down my hip and underneath the waistband of my boy shorts. The fluffy throw blanket is a shield, keeping his movements concealed from wandering glances.

With a slight squirm, I wiggle my hips to help him get to my aching center. His soft touches allow for the unspoken connection between us to become electric. Two fingers run down my slit as I feel my arousal coat his digits. My heart races as desire coils low in my belly. I fight the urge to throw caution to the wind and straddle his thick thighs and the erection pressing against the mesh of his shorts.

Crew keeps running his fingers up and down my wetness as I struggle to keep from squirming. It feels so damn good to be touched by him and the risk of getting caught only intensifies the moment. I never considered myself an exhibitionist, but the more we sneak around and risk getting caught, the more I want to test those boundaries. Fighting to keep my attention on the show before me, my vision blurs as I focus on his strong fingers.

How is he keeping his attention straight ahead and with a straight face?

The struggle to breathe is real as my heart rate intensifies. Crew gathers my arousal until his fingers are coated before bringing the wetness to my clit. Working my nub in circular motions causes my body to respond. Chills run down my spine as my nipples harden to almost painful peaks. The urge to touch them grows as my fingers itch to soothe the ache.

Everything fades away, leaving just the two of us in our own electrified bubble. As he strokes my sensitive bundle of nerves, his masculine smell invades my senses and the urge to straddle his lap intensifies.

I want him. I need him. The intensity of my craving for Crew Riggsby is almost overwhelming.

My fists clench as my fingernails leave little crescent moons indented in my skin.

The orgasm continues to build with each scrape, pinch, and pull. I fight to keep control so our cover isn't blown, but the more he works me, the harder it is to fight the desire threatening to take hold of me.

As if he knows what's about to happen, Crew rubs faster against my clit as he applies more pressure.

Oh my god. Oh my god. Oh my god. I repeatedly chant the words in my head, fighting the urge to scream from the delicious feeling.

I can't fight the orgasm any longer as my body shutters in release. At the same time, something jarring happens on the screen, causing Tyler to jump. My jerky movements as I came were timed perfectly, as if I was jumping with the show.

Crew Riggsby is a genius—a perfectly timed sex god.

The rise and fall of my chest start to slow as my body floats back down from where my soul shattered with that mind-blowing orgasm. With one last swipe of his fingers, Crew removes his hands from my pants. I watch from the corner of my eyes as he subtly brings his fingers to his mouth and sucks my arousal.

Holy. Shit.

CHAPTER 24
CREW

L eaves crunch as I walk along the cobblestone paths from the football facility to the quad. The crisp morning air stings my hot cheeks as I adjust my cap and pull my hoodie tighter against my exposed neck. Texas still doesn't feel like the fall I'm used to but the morning air is crisp for CTU.

As I get closer to the academic buildings, the campus is slowly coming to life. This morning's practice was grueling, which I knew it would be. Coach made sure we worked out all the alcohol in our systems from this weekend by sweating it out through our pores. I was thoroughly drenched and smelled terrible. Thank God for locker room showers. My muscles ache from the weekend's partying and rotting away on the couch all day yesterday. Factor in this morning's drills, and I feel like I was battling a freight train.

Laughter filters around me as I pass a group of people. One of the guys gives me a nod. "Nice game, Saturday."

"Thanks, man." I jerk my head up in the same motion. The feeling of being basically a celebrity on campus always catches me off guard.

As I climb the steps to the business building, I scan the faces, looking for a tall, black-haired beauty. Our class schedule is similar, and since we both major in business, the odds of running into each other are high. When I don't spot her immediately, I move down the hall for my first class of the day—Agriculture Marketing.

I pull open the door to the small lecture hall, slipping into a seat near the middle. Our professor is already in the room getting his items arranged for class. Reaching inside my bag, I do the same as I pull out my laptop and a notebook. Removing the pen from the spirals, I twirl it around my fingers, patiently waiting for class to start. Other students file in and sit as the room buzzes with chatter. Professor Ramirez clears his throat as silence falls over the room.

"Good Monday morning!" he enthusiastically greets. "Today, we'll be discussing the latest trends in agri-marketing strategies. By a show of hands, how many of you have heard of precision agriculture?"

A few hands go up, and while I know what it is, I hate being called on to explain things. Words can be tricky for me. While I'm smart, words get jumbled from my brain to my mouth.

Professor Ramirez calls on a girl in the front. "Precision agriculture involves using technology, like GPS and remote sensing, to optimize field-level management regarding crop farming. It's about increasing efficiency and yield by understanding the variability within a field."

"Exactly." He claps. Professor Ramirez is very passionate about agriculture, which is evident in his mannerisms. "How do you think this can be marketed to consumers?"

I thought of a farm in a neighboring town and how they mapped their property for some kind of simulator. With that knowledge, I decided to jump in. A sly smile slides across our professor's face as surprise from me raising my hand registers. "What do you have for us, Mr. Riggsby?"

"You could market through a video game. It's no secret that video games and apps are still all the rage. Gamifying the process could help consumers understand the complexities and benefits of modern farming techniques."

With arms folded across his chest, Professor Ramirez raises an eyebrow. "Video games? Please elaborate on how this game might work."

Sitting up straighter in my seat, a new thrill runs through me. As much as I love football, nothing compares to my love of agriculture. It's been instilled in me since birth, and while I'm enjoying time away from the farm and seeing what else the world has to offer, I'm itching to get back to where it all started.

"The game could simulate a farm where players use precision agriculture tools to manage their crops. By creating a fictional farm, players will experience reality by making decisions based on weather patterns, soil conditions, and pest management. These are real variables that farmers must know how to handle and adapt to. The goal of the game would be to maximize yield while maintaining sustainability. Players could see the direct impact of their decisions."

The girl next to me begins nodding enthusiastically while she bounces her pointer finger in the air. "That's a great way to raise awareness of sustainable practices. And you could educate people who might not have exposure to farming. It could raise awareness and educate how important farming is to civilization."

"And you can incorporate challenges or difficulties on each level," a voice sounds from behind me, causing everyone to shuffle in their seats. "Players could solve real-life problems like drought, flooding, and pest infestation. It would make the game not only educational but fun and engaging."

"I am impressed," Professor Ramirez says, standing at the front of the room with a beaming smile.

Conversation continues around us as others give their opinions on how precision agriculture can be marketed. Some suggest transparency in farming practices, while others suggest direct-to-consumer sales, which cuts out the middleman. For the next hour, the class comes alive as the conversation flows into new territories as we express challenges in agriculture.

"What a thrilling conversation full of different perspectives, but intriguing nonetheless. For our last major assignment of the semester, you'll work in groups to develop a full marketing plan for your chosen educational component. Think about who you want your target audience to be, distribution channels, and promotional strategies. And remember, creativity is key."

He pauses, gathering his notebooks as time ticks closer to the end of class. "I know the video game idea is fun, but other ideas exist. Choose your groups carefully that balance skills. A proposal is due by next Friday." His final words are said in a rush as students gather their things.

Glancing around the room, my attention snags on the guy in the back who talked about the difficulty levels. He points to himself and then to me. I nod and join the scurry of people trying to find their groups.

"Care if I join you?" the girl sitting beside me asks.

I nod. "Sure, I'm Crew."

"Lauren."

"Eric," the guy from the back introduces himself. The three of us funnel out of the classroom.

"Sounds like a lot of work," Lauren says as she walks beside me.

While it will be a lot of work, I feel a renewed sense of purpose. This is why I came to school here.

"Yeah, but things like this can make a real difference." My mind is already spinning as excitement to start the project has my fingers twitching.

The three of us exchange numbers and start a group chat to discuss meeting times. It turns out that Eric is on the wrestling team, which makes finding a time that much more challenging. Between two athletes and a girl who works part-time, our schedules clash.

Moving through the line of students as we make our way down the hall, my eyes land on a broad smile coming toward me. My eyes trail up denim-clad legs, a sliver of skin peeking out from her cropped long sleeve. Her hair is pulled through a cap, and she looks happy. Her eyes flick to the girl next to me, and I see her eyebrow arch in confusion. It's slight, but I catch it.

Is my girl jealous?

"Can you guys send me your schedules, and I'll work with my boss to come up with a date that works for the three of us?" Lauren asks, clutching her books against her chest.

I nod while Eric agrees. "See you guys Wednesday."

The two of them go their separate ways as I wait on Bret. She stops, the toes of our shoes touching, as I smile down at her. "Morning, Rebel."

"Morning." Her smile never leaves her face. I love seeing her happy. Her smile is like coming up for fresh air. "Who's your fan club?"

"New group assignment for a huge project."

Turning on her toes, she takes her place next to me as we move out of the crowded hall and into a more secluded corner of the business building's lobby. "Looks like it'll be even harder to get alone time with you."

"Speaking of alone time." I wiggle my eyebrows.

"Crew Riggsby, I am not going to have public sex with you."

I scoff. "We'd find a storage closet."

She slaps my chest as she giggles. At the same time, I fight the urge to grab hold of her fingers and pull her into me.

"Have any plans tonight?"

She hums as her bright green eyes stare up at me. If we aren't careful, someone is going to see us. At this point, I hope someone does. I'm tired of having to watch my glances and touches. But I respect Bret's decision to wait. She doesn't want to cause animosity on the team, and I appreciate her decision.

"I don't think I have any."

"Good. What time are you done?"

"Six thirty."

"I'll pick you up out front of the Union." Bret glances around before quickly leaning up on her toes and pressing a chaste kiss to my cheek before she bounces away.

Turning, I watch her leave and can't help but think how grateful I am that she's in my life.

As the day winds down, I find myself back in the quad as the sun sets. Mentally exhausted, I move around students who are looking forward to heading home for the night, all to start this over in the morning. Veering off on a separate sidewalk, I spy Cody and Chloe lying underneath a tree. He's leaning against the tree while Chloe sprawls out in the grass. Her head rests in his lap as they both read. One of these days, that'll be me and Bret. Well, not precisely that particular scenario, but the open public display in a natural setting.

The door of the Union is held open for me, and I thank the girl who leans against the glass as I enter. I beeline for the coffee bar, desperate for a caffeine fix. The day plays over in my mind and all the homework and assigned reading I need to do. Everything feels overwhelming right now. The football season is ramping up with important games as we approach the end of the season and the battle to play in the championship is on us. Final projects are being assigned for classes as we prepare for final exams in the coming weeks. I love it, though. This is everything I've ever dreamed of, but it's fucking exhausting.

Stepping up to the counter, I ordered a small, hot black coffee and an iced peanut butter and mocha coffee. When I have my drinks, I take the stairs off to the side and walk through the basement toward the front of the building, hoping to avoid anyone eating dinner in the cafeteria. I didn't want to explain why I had two coffees in my hand. Climbing the stairs back up to the main level, I sit off to the side of the main entrance and wait for Bret.

Pulling out my phone, I pass the time by scrolling through Instagram. Saylor posted a video on her story of Grandpa being chased by that damn rooster. He's the meanest sonofabitch on the farm. The rooster, not Grandpa. Although, he is a tough old man and not one you want to piss off.

Hearing Saylor's laughter, an ache forms in my chest. I wonder how things would have been if Dad hadn't died. Would Jett and him have been able to mend their differences? Would he be home and not running away from the farm? Would I?

My mind filters back to the project we were assigned in agri-marketing. The idea of turning our family farm into a video game excites me. It's a potential new revenue stream that not many people have tried. Football might be my present, but farming is my future. A future where I want Bret standing beside me.

"Sorry," she huffs, startling me back to reality. "Class ran over."

Standing, I give her the cardboard cup. "What's this?"

"Thought you might need a caffeine fix."

She reaches for the cup, and I watch her hands wrap around it, her shoulders scrunching as she inhales the steam billowing from the lid. "God, I love you."

We both pause, eyes wide as we stare at each other. Time stands still, and neither of us knows how to navigate these waters. I've never had a girl tell me she loved me. I thought the first time I heard those words,

I'd be hit with panic, that a cold chill would run through my veins at those three words.

But that's not what I feel. It's the complete opposite. Warmth spreads through my chest, my heart beats faster, and a smile spreads across my face.

Meanwhile, Bret's eyes are wide, her mouth floundering. I can see the wheels spinning in her brain as she internally panics. Are we there in our relationship? Who knows. But now that those words have been uttered into existence, I feel it.

"I love you, too." I interrupt her mental meltdown.

"Crew, I-I-I..." She trails off, her chest heaving. "You what?"

"I love you, Rebel." I nudge her shoulder as shock morphs her features. "Now let's go get some dinner, woman. I'm starving."

She nods, her shoulders sagging in relief at the topic change. I lead us through the glass doors and down the aisle of cars until we reach my truck. We both climb inside and silence fills the cab the whole way to the restaurant.

Downtown parking is smooth sailing this late on a Monday evening. Most commuters are home for the night, so I navigate through the streets and find a parking lot not far from our destination.

Bret and I step out of the truck, and her hand finds mine. I give her a few reassuring squeezes as she looks up at me. Flashing her a wink, I guide us down an alley.

"Did you bring me down here to kill me because I could think of ways you could do it on campus."

I scoff. "Absolutely not. There's no way I'm getting rid of my favorite person that easily."

"Could have fooled me," she mumbles as she scans the vacant street. A brown wooden door is ahead, with a dumpster further down the alley. Ivy runs up the red brick exterior where a small, lit sign above says *Osteria Bella*.

Ushering Bret inside, we are met with a dark hallway, light from the outside illuminating the space. The floors are lined with worn carpet, and the smell of fresh-baked bread and garlic permeates the air.

"Italian?"

CHAPTER 25
Bret

Crew smiles down at me as he places his hand on the small of my back. The warmth from his large hand grazes my exposed skin, and I melt into his touch. Since we clearly entered the back door, I follow the worn carpet down the hallway.

What is it with this man and finding hidden gems?

An older woman sees us from where she's standing at the front. We watch as she gathers menus in her hand before waddling toward us.

In the small, quaint space, tables sit close to each other. Each one is covered in a red and white tablecloth, giving the restaurant a family-style theme. In the center of each table is an LED candle and a small bouquet.

"Welcome, welcome," her thick Italian accent greets us. "Two?"

"Please," I say with a warm smile as I reach for Crew's hand. I can't get enough of his touch now that we aren't on a busy college campus. My body craves his constant connection.

The woman leads us to a booth in a corner. She places the plastic-covered menus and napkin-wrapped silverware on the table. Soft Italian music plays from above as chatter from other patrons creates the ambient soundtrack for the night. Taking our seats across from each other, I glance around at the dimly lit room cascaded by the warm glow of lamps and candles.

"I'm Nina. First-timers?"

We nod.

"Welcome to my restaurant. My papa started Osteria Bella when I was six in 1954. All of the items on our menu are authentic family recipes. If you have any questions, please ask away, but in the meantime, what can I get you to drink?"

"I'll have a Coke, please."

Crew asks for the same as Nina moves away from our table before visiting with another.

"This place is so cute."

"So is the view." Crew's husky voice has my attention turning across the table, where he winks at me.

"Charming, Crew."

"Why, thank you, Rebel."

Opening the menu, I take in the multitude of items listed. I'm grateful when I see that the descriptions are in English since the names are in Italian, which wasn't one of the languages I studied in school. A comfortable silence falls over our table while we both browse the extensive menu. Reaching my leg out, I feel Crew's leg and run my sneaker-covered foot up and down his leg in slow, soothing movements.

I still can't believe I blurted out that I loved him. At first, I was going to brush it off with a generic, 'I love you for buying me coffee,' but the way my cheeks heated, I knew he knew it was more profound than that.

A few minutes later, Nina returned to drop off our drinks, basket of breadsticks, and house salads. Both Crew and I laughed as we ordered the same dish—lasagna bolognese.

"Are you excited for next week's game?"

Next week is Veterans Day, and to honor our servicemen and women, there's a rumor that CTU is releasing new jerseys and that there will be a ceremony at halftime. No one has seen the new uniforms yet. I'm sure the athletic department is waiting until next week so the media can run wild with coverage leading up to the big game.

"Yeah, it should be a good time." His voice is low, and as he glances to the side, I can tell the topic is making him uncomfortable. I didn't even think about what this would mean for him. Not only was his dad a veteran, but his brother is also currently serving. I'm sure the stress of the day weighs heavy on him.

Crew sits with his elbows on the table, his head resting on his folded hands. He almost looks comically large in this booth. I can't help but take in his sharp jawline, which he keeps trimmed into a very close-cut beard that nearly resembles stubble. The scratch of the hair always feels delicious against the sensitive skin near my center. Just the thought has me clenching my thighs as heat pools in my belly.

"Thank you for taking me to dinner." I blurt the words as his head whips in my direction.

"Anytime, Rebel. I know it's hard to find time to steal away, and it's going to be even harder the closer we get to December between the games and assignments I have coming up."

I sip Coke from my straw before placing the plastic cup down. "Seriously, don't sweat it. We'll make it work. It's not like we don't live together or anything."

"That's true."

Nina returned with hot plates of pasta, and we thanked her. We both unwrap the paper ring on the napkin and pull out our forks. I cut into the oversized square-shaped layered pasta. Melty cheese hangs from where I pull the forkful from the rest of the dish. Steam pours from my fork as I bring it toward my mouth and continuously blow, hoping to cool the pasta down. Crew, on the other hand....

"Oh my gosh," he mumbles, trying to cool his mouth. "It's so hot."

Soft giggles escape. "She said it just came from the oven."

Risking a bite, I place a mouthful of the pasta, meat, and tomato sauce mixture onto my tongue and moan as the flavors hit my tastebuds. I watch as Crew reaches for his Coke. With a swallow, I see moisture gathering in the corner of his eyes. He places his fork on his plate while reaching for another breadstick. I shake my head as I watch the trainwreck before me.

"Will you be able to go home for Thanksgiving?"

He shakes his head no as he rips off a piece of bread. "It's a lot to travel back and forth when we have the big game the Saturday after."

The big game is what college football has dubbed the rivalry between CTU and Lafayette. Both teams and their fans absolutely hate each other. I'm excited to attend my first rivalry game. I've always watched it on TV from Arizona. Now, this year, I'll get to feel the atmosphere of hatred as the desire to win swirls in the air.

"Would you, um, like to come home with me for Thanksgiving?" I hesitantly ask.

"I go every year." He smirks, his fork hanging from his hands.

My mouth flies open. "Shut up!"

He chuckles. "Yeah, Rebel, your mom makes mean pies."

"Oh my god, her pecan pie."

"Forget the nuts, give me the pumpkin." Crew scoops another forkful. "The guys and I all ride up together."

"That's so cool."

"Yeah, we're really fortunate your mom does this."

Every year for Thanksgiving, my parents open the house to anyone on the football team who would like to come and have a home-cooked meal. She and my dad, with the help of some family, cook the entire meal. She said it wouldn't be a home-cooked meal if she ordered catering.

"Controversial topic…" I trail off, letting the suspense build. "What's your favorite Thanksgiving food?"

"Easy. Green bean casserole."

"No way!"

"Is that your favorite too?"

I shake my head. "Second favorite. Sweet potatoes are my favorite, but only the ones roasted in a skillet with butter with spoonfuls of brown sugar melted on top."

"God, those sound delicious."

"They do." I lean back from the table and play with the napkin resting in my lap. "Although the thought of food right now." I shiver.

"That was the best lasagna I've ever had." His eyes snap to mine, panic evident. "Don't tell my mom that."

"Don't worry, your secret is safe with me."

Reaching across the table, I place my hand on top of his. He flips his hand over and laces our fingers together.

Nina dropped off the check after asking about our meal, which we gushed over. Twisting, I reach for my purse. "Bret Addison Campbell, don't you dare reach for your wallet."

A thrill runs through me at his harsh voice. Something about it elicits fire straight to my core.

"You know I can contribute to our dates, too."

"I know you're capable, but my mother would rip me a new one if she knew I didn't treat my woman."

Grabbing the check, Crew stands from the bench, his height towering over the table. He reaches for my hand, which I gladly take, as he pulls me from my seat. His hand never leaves mine. Not as he paid. Not as he leads me out the doors. And not when he walked us down the street to a gelato shop Nina told us about.

Spending time with Crew is effortless, like sliding on my favorite oversized sweatshirt and curling up with my favorite movie. There's a natural ease to our conversation, a rhythm we've quickly fallen into despite the newness of our relationship.

A peace I had long since forgotten settles over me. It's a peace that has been absent for way too long. I watch Crew animatedly tell story after story, his eyes brightening as my favorite smile stays plastered on his face. There's never any pressure to fill the silence with conversation. And I take that as a comforting sign.

I'm surprised at how at ease I have felt with Crew. It's a feeling I've felt since the moment we've met. There's safety in Crew's company, especially wrapped in his muscular arms as he plants soft kisses along my temple.

Crew drives us back to campus, and we park next to my Jeep in the nearly empty parking lot. Leaning over the console, I seek out his lips in the dimly lit cab. The only light filters in from a parking light near our spot.

Before I let things get too heated and we move to the back seat, I pull away. "Thank you for tonight."

"I'll follow you back to the apartment." He winks as I slide down. Shutting the door behind me, I glance over my shoulder as Crew waits for me to leave.

As I drive back to our shared apartment, I smile at the headlights in my mirror. For once, I didn't feel concerned about the person trailing behind me. Tonight, the man I love is following me home.

And later that night, when the apartment is dark and quiet, I slip into his room and crawl under his sheets. His strong arms pull me close as his nose rubs against my loose hair. Both of us find comfort in each other.

"I love you, Crew."

He hums, his lips kissing my neck through my hair. "I love you, too, Rebel."

CHAPTER 26
CREW

Me: I'm Batman!

Rebel: Why did I just say that in my head in a dark, raspy voice?

Me: You're cute

Rebel: You and those winks.

Me: What's wrong with them?

Rebel: They do things to me.

Me: Good luck tonight, Rebel!

One thing I never thought I'd attend in my life is a Halloween-themed intramural basketball game. Today is officially Halloween, and there isn't a shortage of costumes on campus. Although I'm glad we celebrated Saturday night because there's no way in hell I'd wear a costume to class. It's not that I'm not a fun guy, because I am, but it's absolutely ridiculous to wear the gear as you sit behind a desk all day. I've sat next to the Hulk, a female Harry Potter, a police officer, and some kind of Disney princess today. It's weird.

Even though I find dressing up on Halloween dumb, I'm still sitting in a crowded gymnasium dressed as Batman—the things we do when we're in love.

In love.

I am still basking in the glow of Bret confessing her feelings. The icing on the cake was when she crawled into my bed late last night and whispered those words again. When the warning alarm went off, she curled deeper into my side. We risked getting caught, but it was worth it. Luckily for us, she didn't need to leave my bed for class until well after the guys and I had gone to campus.

What's even crazier about this intramural basketball game is not only are the fans wearing costumes, but so are the players. My girl-friend is warming up by jogging up and down the court dressed as Lola Bunny from *Space Jam*, thanks to Macy's helpful sewing skills. I've got to give it to her. At least she found a cartoon character wearing a basketball uniform. One of her teammates is dressed in all green from his socks to his shorts to his long-sleeved fitted tee, which has a giant 'G' printed on his chest and an orange beanie on his head. He went as the water bottle version of a popular sports drink.

At least Bret's team had the right idea finding costumes they could still play in, while the other team took the theme seriously. Players on the other team wear masks, gloves, and capes. How the hell do they think they're going to play basketball dressed like that?

A girl dressed as Barbie stands at the end of our row and points to her friend halfway down the aluminum bleacher. Everyone scoots across the hard surface to make room for her when there isn't much room to begin with.

Adjusting my large frame on the bleacher, I lean forward until I rest my elbows on my knees. The announcer taps the microphone before welcoming everyone to the game. A hip-hop song comes over the speakers as he introduces each player on both teams. When Bret told us she was playing intramural basketball, I thought of some kind of backyard pickup game. This is far from that. It's almost like the junior varsity league at the collegiate level.

Claps and cheers ring out around me, and it's nice to be the one in the crowd instead of being cheered for. Adjusting my mask, I ensure it's secure so my identity is kept safe. Tonight is about Bret, and I don't want to take the attention away from her. I also don't want to be busted by her brother if he's here tonight, too. The last time I could explain, this time might be trickier.

Tracking Bret's movements, I watch as she stretches her arms, one after the other, as she jokes around with her teammates. Since moving to CTU, I've been watching the spark come back to her personality, but there's nothing like seeing Bret on the court. When she steps foot between those lines, it's as if she's transported to paradise. A glow radiates around her as her body relaxes. Her smile is brighter, and her eyes sparkle as she bounces around.

I watch as a referee, who is a paid student, steps up to half-court as the players all take their positions for the jump ball. With the ball tossed in the air, Kyrie, Bret's teammate, dressed as the sports drink water bottle, taps the ball with his fingertips. Bret slides around the other team and grabs the loose ball. With a few quick dribbles, she moves the ball over the half-court line before launching a rocket of a pass to one of her teammates, who has cut toward the basket.

And just like that, Bret's team is up. I clap as her team all shares quick high-fives before running back to the opposite side to play defense. As Bret slides her feet in the shuffle, she turns her back to help play defense, and I notice the tiny ball of fur attached to her shorts. I can't believe she had Macy sew a bunny tail on her costume.

Bret cuts across the lane, jumping in the air to go against her opponent. She's able to steal the ball. She throws it ahead to a waiting teammate as everyone sprints to the other side of the court. Her teammate sees Bret weaving through the defense, and he throws her the ball. Stopping outside of the lane, I watch in fascination as Bret shoots the perfect shot. My smile slides free as I'm unable to contain my excitement.

My phone buzzing in my pocket startles me. Sliding it from my pocket, I see Saylor's face illuminating from the screen. It's a selfie of the two of us from last Christmas. Declining the call, I type out a quick text message.

> Me: I'm watching a basketball game. Everything good?

Within seconds, a new message pops up.

> Saylor: Ugh, ditching me for sports? It's such a Crew thing to do.

> Saylor: Yes, everything is fine. Just miss my big brother.

> Me: Miss you too, sis.

Glancing up from my phone, I watch a few minutes of the game. Bret's now guarding a guy dressed as a pirate, hook for a hand, and everything. Seriously, how does this guy think he's going to play? Commotion from the other end of the gym has me turning my head. Both Coach Campbell and Grant are standing in the doorway.

Fuck my life.

I'm so glad I found a full costume to wear for tonight. The buzzing of my phone has me returning to Saylor's conversation.

Saylor: What basketball game are you watching? Doesn't college basketball start next week?

Me: How do you know that?

Saylor: A guy I'm talking to is on our high school team, and he told me that college starts next week. I guess he has tickets to Ohio State's first game. *shrug emoji*

Me: What does talking to mean?

Saylor: The same thing it meant when you were in school, Grandpa.

Me: What's his name?

Saylor: Not doing this…

Saylor: Hey! You avoided the question.

Me: It's an intramural game.

Saylor: Ew, why?

Me: *image of Bret dressed as Lola Bunny dribbling the basketball down the court.*

Saylor: OMG stop! You've got it bad, big brother. Are you watching Bret play basketball? Why is she dressed as a bunny?

> **Me: Haven't you ever seen Space Jam?**

> **Saylor: Sure, I watched it at Tony Deluca's house…**

> **Me: …Saylor.**

> **Saylor: But why is she dressed in costume?**

> **Me: Halloween-themed game.**

> **Saylor: Please tell me you're sitting in the gym dressed as some superhero.**

> **Me: *Selfie of me dressed in an all-black Batman costume***

> **Saylor: *laughing emoji* New screensaver.**

Cheers pull my attention back to the game. I know I'm supposed to be focused and watching Bret, but aside from her talent, the game is really one-sided. I assumed that would be the case when I saw what they were wearing, but the lack of talent is astonishing when this league is pretty much a league composed of people who played in high school but didn't want to pursue the game in college.

The game goes by in a blur. Bret's team was outscoring the other team so badly that the announcer decided there would be a running clock during the entire second half to get the game over sooner. As the final buzzer sounds, Bret high-fives her teammates before lining up to shake the hands of the opposing team.

People stood from their seats as impatient students tried to rush out. Standing, I let the few people who were sitting on the other side of me pass by as I sat back down and waited for the chaos to settle. Coach and Grant still stood in the far corner, which means I'll need to safely exit from a different direction.

I watch Bret move over to the bench, where she starts shuffling things around in her bag. It's then that it dawns on me that I should send her a warning text.

> **Me: Your family is here. I'll meet you at home.**

> **Rebel: See you soon.**

Glancing over, I notice Coach has his back to me as he and Grant talk with a group of people. Taking my chance, I quickly step down the bleachers and cut around the other side. A second door in the back will lead me down a few hallways to another rear entrance. Sweat gathers on my palms as my heart rate picks up. The guilt and anxiety are starting to wear on me.

Twenty minutes later, I'm lounging on the couch when the sound of keys jiggling in the lock alerts me. "Hey," Bret's soft voice calls as she pushes open the door.

Standing from the couch, I move toward the hallway as she rounds the corner. The corners of her mouth tip up. "Well, hey there, Batman."

Reaching up, I toss the mask onto the dining table. "I can't get the damn zipper to work."

She turns her pointer finger in the air, instructing me to turn around. "How long would you have sat there if I hadn't come home right away?"

"Probably all damn night," I grumble—stupid Halloween costume.

I feel the zipper slide down my back as the material slides open. Bret trails her smooth hands back up my exposed back as she pushes the silky fabric off my shoulders. Moving until she's in front of me, Bret continues working the fabric over my shoulders, down my biceps, until she's pulling my hands free. Leaning forward, she sticks out her tongue and licks up my stomach, starting at the waistband of my boxers, over the indent of my abdominal muscles, over my chest, until she's sucking the soft skin of my neck into her mouth.

Her hands explore the path she just licked before her fingertips grip on to the one-piece costume. I watch in fascination as she slowly drops to her knees, bringing the material with her. My cock juts out as best it can while still being restrained by my boxer briefs.

In slow, calculated movements, she trails her hands up my thighs, gripping me as she goes. From her kneeling position, she stares up at me, and the view is perfect. Bunny ears sit on top of her black hair, which is pulled high on her head in a ponytail. The white and blue striped tank top hugs her perky tits and toned stomach.

My hand reaches out as I stroke her cheek with the back of my hand. "So beautiful. You look so fucking beautiful on your knees."

Her head tilts into my touch as I slide my thumb across her lips. Bret opens her mouth and sucks my thumb between her plump lips. Wrapping her lips around it, she twirls her tongue as she sucks my thumb deeper. I groan, wishing it was my cock her lips were wrapped around.

"I need to shower."

"Well then, let's go shower, baby." Bending over, I scoop Bret up in my arms and carry her the few feet to the bathroom we share. The smell of her body wash still lingers in the air.

Coconut. Vanilla. Cocoa Butter.

Everything that makes up Bret.

She wiggles out of my grip as I set her on her feet, walk over to the shower, and twist the knob. I watch Bret remove the bunny ears and make slow, calculated movements as she strips out of her costume. Before I know it, she's standing completely naked in front of me. No matter how often I get her to myself, I'm amazed at how perfect her body is. Freckles sporadically cover her body, her black ink on display, and muscles she's worked so hard to achieve.

I slip out of my boxers and grab two fluffy towels from the closet. When we both put navy towels in the closet, I couldn't help but smile at how much we both liked the color navy. Pulling open the shower curtain, I climb in over the tub's ledge. Bret watches, her intrigued eyes following the path of the water as the droplets run down my body. Her eyes on me turn me on even more.

"You gonna stand there all night, or are you joining me, Rebel?"

My voice snaps her out of her daze as she climbs into the tub. Her shoulders relax as a soft moan leaves her lips as the hot water runs over her body. She tips her head back, letting the water soak her hair. She's captivating. Mesmerizing. Beautiful.

Reaching for her shampoo, I tip a hefty-sized pour into the palm of my hand. I lather the liquid until bubbles start to form, and then I'm running the shampoo over Bret's head. Using my fingers, I work the suds into her hair. Her head falls forward until her forehead is resting against my chest.

"That feels amazing."

Her lips find my chest as she presses tiny kisses along my pecs before leaning her head under the spray. Bubbles run down her back, pooling at our feet.

"I know nothing about conditioner, and as much as I want to keep washing you, you're on your own for that one."

Her soft laugh fills the tight space as she reaches for the bottle. While she conditions her hair, I grab her loofa from the hook and apply a generous amount of body wash. Watching the soap suds up, I run the pouf over her body. I really work the soap into her skin, making sure her breasts are completely clean.

"I think my tits are clean."

"Are you sure? I think I missed a spot."

She moves further under the spray, rinsing the conditioner and soap from her flawless body. My fingertips trail over her wet skin as I glide them to the apex of her thighs. Trailing down until I'm pressing two fingers deep inside her tight pussy.

Bret gasps as she clutches onto my shoulders, holding herself upright, and her legs quake. She reaches up and slides her fingers through my damp hair while I continue to pump inside her. With a tug on my strands, she pulls my head down until our mouths meet. I groan at the contact as my tongue slides through her parted lips. I shiver at the contact, which sends electric currents straight to my cock. My erection stabs her in the stomach, and I can't wait to sink inside her.

She rocks her hips against my hand, seeking out her release. I press my thumb against her clit and feel her pussy spasm against my fingers. With a gasp, I take the opportunity to deepen the kiss as I push her against the cool wall.

"More, Crew," she pants. "I need more."

I rub her clit in a light caress as I slowly apply more pressure to her sensitive bud as she rocks against me. Water droplets cling to the end of her nose as steam billows around us. Curling my hand around her pussy, I hit the spot deep inside her.

Bending down, I suck one of her peaked nipples into my mouth and flick the metal bar with my tongue. Her muscles squeeze my fingers, and I wish it were my dick being suffocated. With one last bite down on her nipple, my palm grinds against her clit as she comes on a scream. The passionate cry leaves her throat and echoes off the shower stall. And I pray our roommates aren't home.

With a heaving chest, Bret drops to her knees. In a flash, I take in her doe eyes as she stares up at me before sucking my cock into her warm mouth.

"Fuuuuck," I grit out.

Her swollen lips wrap around my thick cock. My fingers weave into her soaked hair as I help guide her up and down my shaft—her lips suction against my crown as she flicks her tongue against the sensitive spot underneath.

"God, you look so pretty with my cock in your mouth." I moan. "It feels so fucking good, Rebel."

And as much as I love having her lips wrapped around my cock, it's not where I want to come. I need to be inside her. Pulling my hips back, my cock slips free with a pop as her eyes spring to mine.

"I need to be inside your pretty pussy."

"God, it's so hot when you demand things from me."

I quirk a brow. "Then get on your feet and bend over, Rebel. Let me see what's mine."

A sexy smirk plays across her lips as a shiver runs over her. Stroking my cock, I watch as she does just that. Bret moves to the far end of the wall, and with a confident gleam in her eyes, she bends over.

"Come fuck me," she demands from where she's staring up at me.

"Fuck." My shoulders sag as I run my hand down my face. "There aren't any condoms in here."

"It's fine," Bret says without hesitation. "I'm clean, and you can pull out...just this once."

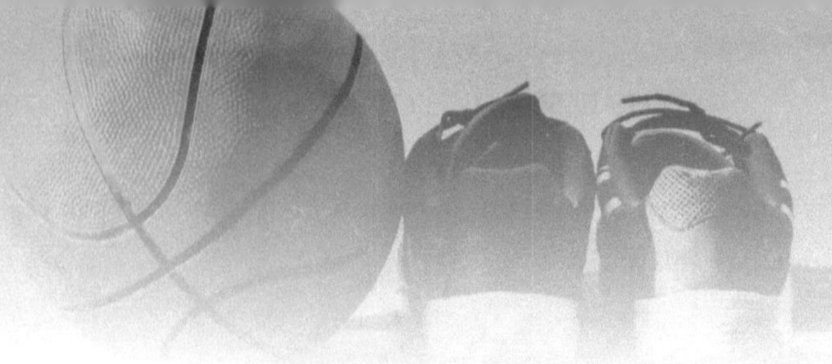

CHAPTER 27
Bret

S ex without a condom?

I've never had unprotected sex. Although I've only ever slept with one other person, but still. As scary as it is to suggest, I trust Crew. Wholeheartedly.

Crew's eyes widen as his face morphs with some kind of emotion. "Are you sure?"

I nod. "Just this once. I need your cock inside of me." I wiggle my ass in the air and watch his eyes track the movement. He growls, physically growls, like some kind of jungle cat.

His hand finds his erection as he begins stroking his shaft up and down as he walks closer. "Where do you want me?"

I feel him tap his cock on my ass before running it over my crack. The head of him taps against my tight hole. "Want me here?"

A thrill courses through me as heat coils in my belly, a mixture of nerves and arousal. Nibbling my lip, I stare up at him.

"Not tonight, baby," he murmurs. Crew slides lower through my slit as he positions himself at my entrance. Between the shower water and my arousal, I'm dripping wet. Throbbing and swollen. Needy.

With one hand gripping my hip, his tip prods at my entrance. Very slowly, he pushes himself deeper. Inch by inch until he's fully seated inside me. Pausing, he lets my body adjust to his size. With this new position and the angle, I feel full. Blissfully full.

Crew's hips begin to move as he slowly starts thrusting inside me. His movements are calculated as he glides in and out. Every time he gets close to slipping out of me, my pussy clenches around him. The feeling of having sex with no barrier feels better than I expected.

"It feels so good," I pant.

The hand that is not gripping my hip trails up my spine before he wraps my long strands around his fist. With a slight tug, he begins rocking faster.

"You take me so well, Bret," he grunts. "I'm not going to last long. Not without a condom. Touch yourself, Rebel."

Removing my hand from the ledge, I trust Crew to hold me up by his grip on my hair and hip. Spreading my palm across my boob, I palm and squeeze the flesh, using my thumb and palm to pinch my nipple. A strand of pleasure shoots straight to my clit.

I bring my hand between my legs. Slowly, I rub the pads of my fingers and work my sensitive bundle of nerves, begging for a release.

"That's it, Rebel. Make yourself come." His hand tightens around my hip to the point where I think bruises will form as a delicious pain fuels my impending orgasm. Crew's thrusts take on an erratic pace as he pistons his cock deep inside me. Each time he thrusts deeper inside me, he hits that sweet spot deep inside me, taking both of us closer and closer to the edge.

Leaning forward, I press up on my tiptoes as I grind back against him. My fingers rub harder as Crew pulls my hair and pinches my nipple. The pleasure building in my core is unbearable. With each thrust, the orgasm coils in my belly before igniting my entire being.

Shock waves pulse throughout as I quake with release. In the next moment, Crew's hips rock faster before he pulls out of me. I watch over my shoulder as he jacks himself off as warm ropes of cum land on my back.

Our chests heave as we stare at each other, trying to catch our breath.

"You're perfect." Crew cups water in his hands and rinses his release down the drain.

Knuckles rapping against the door have both of us wide-eyed, and panic shows on our faces. Tyler's voice calls through the door. "Yo, Riggs, we're going to The Eagles Nest for wings. JP is working tonight. Are you in?"

"Ye-yeah, man," he stutters his response. I'm surprised the sound of heartbeats can't be heard.

"Have you seen Bret? I saw her Jeep in the parking lot."

Shit, shit, shit.

An awkward silence falls over the room as we stare at each other, both of us trying to figure out how to avoid this mess. Looking up at Crew, I place my first two fingers down and move them back and forth.

"Fingering?" I smack his chest.

Bending one finger at the knuckle, I move it in front of the other and then repeat with the second finger.

"Walking?" I nod.

"Riggs? You hear me?" The knob jiggles and my heart drops to my stomach. He cannot come in here. Did we lock the door?

"I think she went for a walk!" Crew yells the words in a panicked rush.

"Cool, I'm going to go change my clothes. Can you fill her in if she gets back before I'm done?"

"Yeah, man."

We wait with bated breath to make sure the coast is clear. The shower water has long since cooled off. Crew twists the handle to the off position before sliding open the curtain. He reaches for our towels, and I wrap the fluffy cotton around my body.

We both step out onto the rug and Crew creeps over to the door. I reach down, gather all my dirty laundry, and toss it in the closet laundry basket. Twisting the knob, Crew peeks his head out.

"Coast is clear."

I rush past him, kissing his cheek quickly, and run into my room. Quietly closing the door, I rest my back against the wood and take a deep breath. That was way too close.

But damn was it worth it.

As I'm walking into the apartment late Wednesday afternoon, I'm met with total silence. The guys are all on campus for classes before their weekly required study session. I'm home early since my last class of the day was canceled due to the professor being sick.

Tossing my keys onto the entryway table, I walk into the kitchen. Needing an energy kick, I reach inside the fridge for a Coke. My phone vibrating in my pocket startles me. Sliding it out, I find a text from Chloe waiting for me.

> **Chloe: Hey, girl! I hope you had a great day! Would you want to hang out tonight?**

I'm caught off guard by her text. It's not that we don't get along or anything like that, it's that Chloe doesn't typically text just me outside of the group chat, although the chat has been quieter than usual.

> **Me: Hey! Yeah, I just got home for the day. Where would you like to meet?**

> **Chloe: I'll come to you with dinner! Do you like subs?**

> **Me: Love them. I'm a chicken, bacon, and ranch kind of girl.**

> **Chloe: You've got it! See you shortly!**

I no sooner lock the screen, and it vibrates in my hand.

"Hello, my favorite mother."

"Hello, my favorite daughter." We both chuckle at our typical greeting. "How's my girl?"

Leaning against the counter, I rest my hand on the top. "I'm doing good. Staying super busy."

"I figured. You must be since I rarely hear from you."

"Yeah, I've had a lot on my plate."

She tsks. "I thought for sure I'd see you more now that you live in the same city as your parents."

"Mom," I grumble, not ready to get into the lousy child guilt. "I see you at home football games."

"Uh-huh. Don't worry, your father keeps me in the loop."

"Oh, is he now? Does he have spies around campus?" I ask the question and secretly hope he hasn't spied on me. Crew and I don't flaunt our relationship on campus, but there have been longing glances and lingering touches. I can't help myself when he's around.

"He has. He said you're playing basketball again. I'd love to watch. I miss watching you run up and down the court."

Sticking my finger underneath the tab, I pop the opening on the can of Coke. "Bret Addison, are you drinking?"

"Yes, your underage daughter is going to tie one on with her mother on the phone."

"I'm not naive enough to think that you don't go out and party. I know you're out there living it up."

"Nobody says 'living it up.'" I laugh.

"YO-YO?"

"Please just stop." I shake my head. "It's YOLO for you only live once, and again, no one says that. I'm just drinking a Coke."

"Oh, honey, I wish you'd stop drinking that. Soda is so bad for you."

Bringing the can to my lips, I take a long pull as the dark, fizzy liquid slides down my throat. "Am I supposed to stop smoking too?"

She gasps. "You're not smoking, are you?"

"No, Mom."

I can picture my mom standing in her pristine kitchen, the phone resting on her shoulder, hands in soapy dishwater, her face flustered from my antics. "Anyway, did you hear that your father and I were asked to be on a reality show? Apparently, a network wants to film a behind-the-scenes glimpse at life in football families across the country, and your father was the top choice."

"That sounds terrible. Please tell me you said no."

It's her turn to chuckle. "Of course, we did as if we'd have cameras filming our every movement. There's no way."

"Thank god."

"Besides, I don't want to have to worry about cameras watching me change or, god forbid, when it's Tuesday night, and your father and I crack open a bottle of wine, lower the lights, curl up on the couch..."

I gag. "Stop, please don't go any further than that."

The laugh she lets lose vibrates through the earpiece. "Your mom has jokes, too, sweetheart."

"Remind me not to sit on the couch," I grumble, pressing off the counter and carrying the can of Coke with me to my room. Light filters in from the windows, illuminating my room. The white walls feel extra bright. I can't wait until I have my own space and I can paint the walls to darken my cave. Moving closer to the bed, I go to plop down on my mattress when a brown oversized envelope halts my movement. Sitting on my pillow, I see 'Rebel' scrawled in Crew's scratchy handwriting. A smile plays on my lips.

Mom's voice brings me back to our call. "Bret, sweetie, did you hear me?"

"Sorry, Mom."

"It's okay. I was just talking about Thanksgiving prep. Are you coming home this year? What about your roommates? They come every year."

"Yes, Mom, the four of us will be there."

"Aw, honey, that makes me so happy."

A knock on the door draws my attention away from my mom, who is rambling about the menu and how many pounds of potatoes she has to order. Considering how many men will be at the house, it's ungodly.

Leaving my room, I head to the front door, where I look through the peephole. Chloe stands on the other side, wearing a purple dress and holding a plastic bag. Turning the lock, I open the door.

"Hey!" Chloe greets.

"Hey, come on in." I step aside, welcoming her inside as I shut the door behind us. "Mom, my friend came over for dinner. Can I call you later?"

"Of course. I'm holding you to that returned phone call."

"Yes, Mom." Rolling my eyes, I shake my head.

"Love you, honey."

"Love you, too, Mom." Ending the call, I let out a long exhale.

I love my mother, I really do, but the constant contact can get overwhelming. Even though I haven't actually taken the time to call her, she sends many text messages. Grant says she does the same to him. I told Dad she needed a hobby away from us kids and her role as a coach's wife. She needs to find something that makes her happy so she can focus on that.

Chloe is standing by the dinner table, pulling out packages of subs. "I'm so sorry. I didn't realize you were on the phone."

Shaking off her apology, I go to sit next to her. "Don't apologize. Thanks for grabbing dinner. As excited as I am to have you over, I'm slightly surprised."

"Yeah, I might have an ulterior motive." Chloe scrunches her nose as her cheeks pinken.

Quirking my brow, I pull out a chair, sit down, and start unwrapping my sub. "I knew it."

"I promise I want to hang out with you. We haven't had a chance to spend one-on-one time together. I mean, dancing at the bar doesn't count."

We both dig into our subs—mine a toasted chicken, bacon, ranch on Italian and Chloe a toasted meatball sub on Italian. I groan as the perfectly seasoned chicken hits my tongue. There's just something about a CBR that makes my stomach happy.

"This is so good," Chloe mumbles around a mouthful.

I nod my head in agreement. Silence falls over the table as we both spend the next few minutes devouring our subs. I must have been starving because I inhaled this sandwich as if I were one of the guys.

Wiping her face with a napkin, Chloe breaks the silence first. "So, have you met anyone on campus?"

"Met anyone? I've met lots of people."

She wiggles her brows. "No, like, *met someone*."

My face heats as I glance down at the remainder of my sub. Only the end of the bread remains. I'm so tired of sneaking around. Keeping secrets will be my death, and after last night's close call, we are bound to get caught.

We are so close to the season being over. Just a few more weeks, and I can admit to the world that I am Crew Riggsby's girlfriend. Then I will have to deal with the repercussions of keeping our relationship a secret from my dad and overprotective brother.

"Oh, um, I'm not really looking for anything right now. I declared this year the year of Bret."

She eyes me skeptically. "Uh-huh."

I shrug, gathering our wrappers and shoving them into the plastic bag to throw away later. We both move from the table to the couch. I take the end where I bring my legs up to sit cross-legged on the section in Crew's spot. Chloe moves to the corner spot, where she tucks her legs underneath her and adjusts her dress to avoid flashing the goods.

"Speaking of guys, thanks to your book and your constant need to mention my so-called reverse harem fantasy, I had the most embarrassing thing happen to me."

Leaning forward, Chloe's eyes shine as excitement crosses her face. "Oh my gosh, please tell me you propositioned your roommates."

"No." I shake my head. "The other night JP had a study session, and Crew, Tyler, and I watched a movie in Crew's bed. Well, I fell asleep between them and had the most erotic dream with both of them."

"Oh my gosh." Chloe chortles, her gleeful laugh erupting around us. "How was it?"

"I mean." I shrug, wiggling my eyebrows.

"That's the best thing anyone has told me in a long time."

"Oh, and then my brother walked in on the three of us in bed."

Tears pour down her face as she clutches her stomach from laughing so hard. Chloe wipes her face as I shake my head. The whole situation could have been avoided if she wasn't planting reverse harem seeds in my brain. Silence falls over the room as Chloe fights to pull herself together.

"Are you good at keeping secrets?" I snort, choking on my spit, and start spluttering everywhere. Chloe stares at me with shock written all over her face. "You okay, girl?"

Patting my chest, I nod. "Ye-yeah, I'm good at keeping secrets."

Chloe continues to eye me wearily. "Okay, perfect. I need your help with something."

"What's up?"

"You know that we host family dinners on Sundays…"

"Yes, Chlo, I have been at every Sunday dinner since I moved here."

She reaches for her phone before scooting closer to me. "Well, I was thinking about throwing Brynn and Quinton a surprise baby shower next Sunday. Q has a bye week, and he's flying in for the weekend, so it's perfect."

"Aw," I gush. "That's such a cute idea. I know I'm a newbie, but having a friend who's having a baby is really cool."

"You say that because you don't have to live with her. Brynn Wilder is the strongest girl I know, and right now, she cries about everything. She's a hormonal mess." She snickers as I cringe. "After she announced the birth control malfunction, I made Cody go back to using condoms because I was super paranoid the pill wouldn't work. He had to talk me off the ledge by promising me that if I ever go on any medication, he'll wear a condom, but not until then."

"Not ready for kids?"

Horror flashes across her face. "Oh no, I don't even know if kids are in my future. Cody and I both have struggled with shitty parents—my mom and his dad—and it makes me nervous to have kids. I refuse to have unprotected sex."

I nod, my thoughts trailing back to last night. Last night, when Crew and I had unprotected sex. We were caught up in the moment, and I was so desperate for him that I didn't want him to stop. It's probably the most irresponsible thing I've ever done—dread pools in my stomach at realizing how stupid I was. Based on my cycle, I should be in the all-clear, but accidents happen. And much like Chloe, I am so not ready for babies. Hell, Crew and I can't even be in public. How would I announce that I'm pregnant? My palms are sweaty, and my chest squeezes.

"You okay over there?" Chloe's voice pulls me back into the present.

"Totally, I just pictured being in Brynn's shoes, and my anxiety skyrocketed," I tell her.

Chloe scrolls on her phone before passing it over to me. I stare at the screen and take in the perfectly curated secret Pinterest board. Scrolling through the images, I absorb the color scheme of creams, tans, greens, and oranges. Table decorations of baby booties, eucalyptus runners, neutral baby onesies, and vases of baby's breath. Games, food, and photo backdrop ideas.

"Holy shit, this is amazing," I gush as I continue to scroll. "What do you need my help for? I think you've got this planned."

She blushes, almost embarrassed at how organized she is. "I was wondering if I could ship things to your apartment and if you wouldn't mind helping me set up?"

"Are you going to have it at the house?"

She nods.

"How are you going to get Q and Brynn away?"

"That's the tricky part. The two hide away in her room whenever Q visits, barely coming up for air. I talked to Macy, and she said that she and Gregg would come up with something."

For the next hour, the two of us scroll through our phones, searching for decorations and baby items we can order that will arrive in time. A reality show Chloe is addicted to is playing in the background as our soundtrack for the night. Everything about this moment feels like a dream come true. Warm fuzzies flutter in my stomach to be a part of a family. This CTU group has different personalities, but they all share one thing—their love for each other.

CHAPTER 28
CREW

Everything about this day feels different. It's not even nerves because we are playing a good team. As we approach the final weeks of our season and maintain our undefeated record, more hype surrounds us. With this week's game being on Veterans Day, the university has planned a few ceremonious events to honor our servicemen and women.

It's weird being around military appreciation days since my dad died and my brother is away serving our country. Growing up, my dad would come to school with us on Veterans Day since our district put on an assembly every year. With them both gone, it feels weird to celebrate them when all you want to do is *honor them* but in person. Don't get me wrong, I'm proud of my brother for serving our country and fighting for our freedoms. I just miss him. I want to fix our relationship and feel like I have a brother in my life.

Sitting on the bench before my locker, I lace up my cleats before wrapping my feet with tape to keep the laces in place. Jitters don't normally flutter in my stomach. I rarely suffer from pregame nerves, but something in the air tells me today is different. I can't put my finger on why, though.

One different thing is our jerseys. The athletic department upgraded our home jerseys for today's particular game. The white and powder blue digital camo uniforms are sick as fuck. Our white helmets even have matching camouflage inside the CTU letters.

"Yo," JP says from his locker across from mine.

The guys and I all turn our attention to him. "I had the weirdest fucking dream last night."

Grant pauses from where he's taping his shoes a few lockers down from mine. "What was it?"

"We were all playing football, but we were dressed like chicks."

I shrug, glancing around at the other guys. "It doesn't seem that weird. Were we in like dresses?"

"The hell do you guys get into in your apartment that wearing dresses isn't that weird?" Grant scoffs, disgust and confusion morphing his features. "Please don't tell me y'all parade around wearing my sister's dresses."

"First off, I've never seen your sister in a dress," Harris chimes in. "And second of all, don't be saying shit like that. It takes one of these fuckers to overhear, and we have a whole rumor on campus."

I chuckle. "That's not what I meant either."

"Anyway," JP drawls, regaining our attention. "We weren't wearing dresses but tutus, like ballerinas wear, and cheerleading skirts."

"Bro, that's weird as fuck," Harris says.

"Thank you." JP waves his hands in front of him.

"Maybe you've fucked too many cheerleaders, so now you're going to become one." Grant howls, causing the room to laugh.

JP tosses his sandal at Grant, who catches it. He bounces over to our big defenseman and gives playful punches on JP's pads.

"Man, fuck you," JP grumbles as laughter fills the room.

I turn to lock up my safe and double-check I have everything as the coaches file in from the attached conference room. Coach Campbell claps his hands, commanding our attention.

"Gentlemen," he starts, glancing around the room and making eye contact with each of us. "Today is a special day. I won't stand up here and tell you what you need to do out there because you already know. I will tell you not to let today's ceremonies distract you from playing our game. Let's go out there and show them what we're made of."

Cheers erupt as we clap our hands, forming a huddle around Coach.

"Eagles on three," Harris yells over the chaos. "One, two, three."

"Eagles!" we chant back before funneling through the doors, our helmets in hand.

The sounds of our cleats clinking against the tile echo down the hall as we jog toward the tunnel. Lights from media photographers flash around us as adrenaline rushes through our veins. Helmets go on as we line up inside the chute and wait for our signal.

Coach stands at the opening inside the tunnel as our captains surround him. Coach raises his hand in the air as we bounce on our feet in anticipation of what's to come. He drops his arm as we run onto the field.

The packed stadium erupts in cheers as we follow the male cheerleaders who hoist our flags high in the air and lead us to our sideline. The announcer continues to hype the crowd up as we find our places. Since there were more pregame ceremonies than usual, we were immediately directed to line up for the national anthem.

With my left hand hanging at my side, I grip my helmet and place my right hand over my heart. An up-and-coming country singer takes the field as she has the honor of performing the national anthem. As she belts out the lyrics, military members hold the giant flag on the field, and I stand tall as thoughts of my father and brother flash through my mind.

Even with all the distractions, the noise from the sold-out crowd, and the emotions of playing in front of the veterans we are honoring, we never wavered. As soon as the ball was kicked off at the start of the game, we played with heart and tenacity. We played the way we trained by putting on one helluva show for our fans.

As the referee blows his whistle, signaling the end of the half, we jog off the field. Sweat poured down our faces. The score is in our favor as we lead by seventeen. Our kicker hit a thirty-seven-yard field goal as the first half ended. I turn, ready to jog off the field as usual, but Coach stops us. Everyone looks around in confusion.

"We're staying on the field," Coach says. "It's an extended halftime. Once the ceremony ends, we'll go back for a normal halftime."

Scanning the crowd, my eyes land on Bret. She's standing in the front row of the student section with Gregg, Macy, Cody, Chloe, and Brynn. Quinton is home for the weekend, but he's down here on the sidelines somewhere. Perks of being a famous alumnus. I swear she can feel me watching her from forty yards away. I watch her emerald eyes scan the sidelines until they land on mine. Our eyes connect, and her features soften.

The announcer's voice echoes through the stadium, startling her. "Ladies and gentlemen, please direct your attention to the fifty-yard line. Please join me in welcoming our honorary veterans."

The crowd falls silent as a respectful hush envelops the stadium. My heart pounds as I stand shoulder to shoulder with my teammates. My makeshift brothers. It's been three years since I've seen my real brother, and the absence never fully fades away.

A familiar knot tightens in my stomach as anxiety starts to creep in. Having a loved one overseas never gets easier. Even though I've continued living my life, I never forget about him. I wonder what he's doing right now. Is he hunkered down in a bunker? Is he on a mission? Or is he at camp waiting for his next assignment?

Veterans begin to walk out from our tunnel and make their way to the makeshift stage. They're greeted by a thunderous round of applause as everyone in the stadium thanks them for their service. I clap along as I feel a wave of sadness.

Three years ago, when Jett was home, he looked so different. Serving in a war will do that to you. But while he joked around the table, his eyes also showed sadness. Is he happy? Does he miss the family like we miss him? When he hugged me goodbye, he told me he would do better at staying in contact, especially since I was heading off to college. But life has a funny way of throwing a wrench in your plans. I'm sure he's doing his best to keep in touch with the occasional email, and at least he wished me a happy birthday this year.

Photographers and members of the media shuffle around the field, capturing the ceremonious events. Some turn toward the team to capture us in our special uniforms.

The announcer's voice cuts through my musings. His voice softens, filling with emotion as a wave of restless energy radiates around me. "And now, ladies and gentlemen, we have a special guest. Please welcome Staff Sergeant Jett Riggsby, returning home after eight years of service."

My world stops. Did I hear him right? Did he just say Staff Sergeant Jett Riggsby? My breath catches as I try to swallow the lump of emotions that wells in my throat. My heart is racing, my palms are sweating, and my vision blurs. Blinking, I try to clear the tears that are gathering in my eyes. I'm not a crier, but goddamn, this might do the trick.

I'm so caught up in everything happening around me that I didn't even see him step on the field. It's not until Coach Campbell is clapping me on the shoulder pads, and my teammates are staring back at me as they move. The gap they make lets me see clearly.

My brother, dressed in his uniform, is making his way toward me. He looks just like I remember, only a little broader and with a little more wear on his face. My knees buckle as I fight to keep upright. Dropping my helmet, I pinch my forearm because there is no way that this is actually happening. My chest tightens, and my chin quivers as I keep the sobs from bursting.

Realizing that this is reality, I take off, pushing through the guys who clap me on the shoulders as I move past. My vision tunnels as I jog onto the field and eat up the distance between me and my brother. Everything blurs around me—faces, noise, everything is gone as I race toward him.

When I'm finally standing before him, Jett's wide smile that matches mine takes up his face. Arms wide, we both pull each other in for a hug. Holding him tightly, he hugs back just as fiercely. "You're really fucking here?"

"I missed you, little bro." His voice is thick with emotion and has a raspier tone, which wasn't there before.

I can't fight the tears any longer and let them stream free. Fuck the crowd and anyone who sees it. All I care about is that Jett is here. He was home, on US soil, safe.

"Are you home for good?"

"Figured it was about time."

A weight I didn't know I was carrying slipped away. No more worrying about where in the world Jett was stationed. Gone was the gnawing fear if he was safe and in one piece. All of the worry was gone.

The crowd's cheers funnel back into my ears, but only as a distant hum. We pull apart, our eyes damp from tears as we both take each other in.

"Fucking look at you." He beams. "You're not that tiny shit any-more."

"Yeah, good luck with beating me up now."

"I'm proud of you, Crew." His voice cracks, and emotion clogs my throat.

"Need a tissue?"

"Fuck off." He playfully shoves me. "Now go. You've got a game to win, and I've got a game to watch. It's about damn time I caught one of your games in person."

This is no longer just a game anymore, it is a reunion, a homecoming.

"This one time." Jett pauses as he takes a long pull of the beer dangling from his fingers. "Crew was in a phase where he refused to wear pants."

I groan. "Why do you have to do this?"

Tossing his arm around my shoulder, he pulls me against him in a half hug. "That's what big brothers are for. They make fun of their younger brother in front of pretty girls."

Jett, Bret, and I all went to a pizzeria off campus. It's not Cousin Jimmy's. This place has wood-fired, inventive, hand-tossed pizzas. The rest of the guys all went to The Eagles Nest, Bret only tagged along because Jett insisted the female roommate not be left out. Whatever that means.

"Anyway," Jett drawls out. "Back to my story. We were at my aunt and uncle's when Crew decided he was tired of wearing his pants. He stripped out of his jeans and took off running through the backyard, where all of the family was gathered. Dad took off running, but Crew refused to stop. He hopped the fence into the pasture, bare ass and everything. When Dad started climbing after him, Crew here thought it'd be funny to jump on the back of a ram, which took off running through the field with a half naked Crew."

Bret's booming laugh has heads whipping in our direction. The two of them have clearly hit it off. Jett has been telling story after story while drinking beer after beer. There is a pile of bottles in the center of the table.

"Does Mom know you're home?" I ask, sobering the mood.

He nods. "Yeah, I called her when I returned to US soil. I'm flying out tomorrow afternoon to head home."

"She's going to be glad to see you." He hums as I take another bite of pizza. "What are your plans?"

"Brother, not tonight." Jett lolls his head toward Bret. "So tell me, how did a pretty girl like yourself end up rooming with my brother?"

Bringing her cup to her mouth, she takes a long drink of her Coke. Bret offered to be our designated driver since she didn't want to use her fake ID in an actual restaurant.

"Funny story, actually. I used my real name, and with my major and extracurricular activities, the guys assumed I was a guy and accepted my email inquiring about the room."

"Oh, that's great," Jett chuckles. "So what's your major?"

"Sports management. I'd love to be an athletic director."

She glances over at me, and I wink at her, which causes her cheeks to pinken just like I knew they would. Everything feels right tonight. My brother is home, and my girl is having dinner with us. Jett keeps giving me weird glances, and I wonder if he's catching on to the sparks swirling around Bret and me.

"That's cool." Jett whips his head in my direction. "You guys should plan a trip to Silo Bay over spring break. I think you'd like it."

"I was actually there when the team rolled through earlier this fall."

He taps his chin with his pointer finger. "That's right. I heard all about the town's golden boy returning home."

Rolling my eyes, I shake my head. "Please, just wait until they pull something together when you show up tomorrow. They will be rolling out the red carpet."

Inhaling half a slice of pizza, Jett wipes the grease from his mouth with his napkin. "More like barricades so the troubled Riggsby boy doesn't step foot in city limits."

Now, he might be onto something. Jett Riggsby was notorious for causing all kinds of hell. From spray painting road signs to throwing parties in abandoned houses to being a menace whenever he could. He and his group of friends were trouble, but no one said anything about it since they could never actually prove it was them. Not to mention, their football team was incredible all four years. They were practically local celebrities who paved the way for my class to follow in their footsteps.

"Excuse me." Bret wipes her hands as she stands. "I need to use the restroom."

Jett and I both nod as I watch her walk toward the hallway where the bathrooms are.

"So, how long have you been screwing your roommate?"

Spluttering the beer I was drinking, golden liquid dribbles onto the table. Glancing from the beer to my brother, a knowing smirk plays on his lips. "Shut up."

The asshole chuckles. "Seriously, Jett, you can't say shit. She's Coach Campbell's daughter."

He laughs harder. "You've really stepped in it this time. Banging the coach's daughter, wow."

"It's not like that," I grumble. Scanning the room for any wandering eyes. "We're dating but keeping it a secret."

"C'mon, Crew. What are you doing?"

I sigh. "It's a long story. It's a twisted, complicated story, but we're going to tell everyone. She just wants to wait until the season ends so there aren't any problems on the team."

"How the fuck do you think they're going to react when they find out you've been together for months?" He hisses the question.

"Don't you think I don't know that? Huh?" I lean forward, turning my head to stare directly at him. "I said it was a long fucking story, and we tried to avoid things, but it just happened. Now fucking drop it, you dick."

Reaching for his beer, he finishes the half-full beer. "I'll drop it, but I'm telling you it won't go over well."

I watch Bret weave her way through the tables, her face beaming as she looks at our table. "What'd I miss?"

For the next hour, time seemed to slow as the three of us sat at a secluded table, laughing and telling stories. It was at that moment I realized how complete I felt. Of course, I wished the rest of my family were here, but there would be time for that. Right now, with my brother home, I feel hope. Hope for a future I've dreamed about since I was a little boy. A dream of running my family's farming business with my own family and my brother by my side.

Tonight was a celebration of more than a game. It was a celebration of family, resilience, and the unbreakable bonds that tether us together.

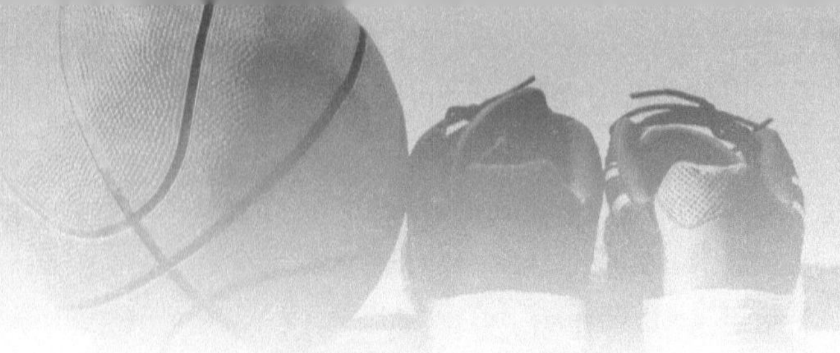

CHAPTER 29
Bret

"Where do you want these?" I ask Chloe, holding up a stack of cardstock. Scanning over the cards, I chuckle as I read the questions.

'Who will be the more fun parent?'

'Who will be changing the first diaper?'

'Who will be thrown up on first?'

'Who will want more kids?'

I've been at the townhouse Chloe shares with Brynn for the past two hours, helping her transform their backyard into a surprise baby shower for Quinton and Brynn. Cody, her boyfriend, has been here, too. He's been assigned to be the heavy-lifter/Mr. Fix-It, so whenever we need something moved or hung, we yell for him.

Chloe has rented plastic tables and chairs scattered around the backyard. Each table is covered in white fabric table linens with a strand of eucalyptus running down the center. Three tall vases are placed evenly down the center of each table, mixing greenery, baby's breath, and faux orange picks. Places are set with white tableware with clear coasters resting in the center of each plate. The coasters read *"a baby is brewing."* She wanted the party favor to be something cute that both the guys and girls could use.

With the help of her dad, Scott—who happens to be a Michelin-star chef, Chloe has prepared all of the food. When I offered to help, the three yelled "no" at me. Apparently, Chloe informed her dad about my lack of culinary skills. Scott offered to give me cooking lessons the next time he was in town. He's been in Arizona working at a new restaurant he opened at a spa, one that he's adamant all of us girls attend on him.

Did I mention that I love Chloe's dad? He's a lot like mine—cares a lot for his daughter.

"Oh, you can just set those on the gift tables." Chloe is putting the finishing touches on the backdrop she made. It's a foam board, and she cut the top in an arch and painted it white. A collection of ombre-colored orange balloons is attached to the foam board, creating the perfect backdrop for photos.

Turning around, I take in the backyard. "Chloe, this looks incredible."

"It does," Cody adds, carrying a wicker chair over to Chloe. She points to where she wants it, and he sits it down before kissing her temple.

Adjusting the chair to where she wants it, Chloe steps back, places her hands on her hips, and observes her work. With a satisfied nod, she smiles brightly. "Thank you both for all of your help. I seriously couldn't have done it without you."

"What's up, my favorite people?" JP's booming voice comes through the kitchen and out the patio doors. He walks through the open doors and pauses. "Holy shit, this place looks dope."

And it does. The gender-neutral, "little cutie" theme is perfect. Shades of oranges, white, and green are scattered around as far as the eye can see. Real and faux oranges are sprinkled in with the decor to capture the whole 'little cutie' theme. Instead of a traditional banner, Chloe has hung onesies across the top of the patio door.

"Damn, no wonder you had to leave first thing this morning." Tyler follows JP through the door and snags a handful of sliced green peppers from the veggie tray.

Crew comes through the door holding a stack of gifts. "Did you guys forget something?"

"Oh shit, totally forgot about the gifts." JP laughs, grabbing a couple of wrapped gifts from the stack Crew is holding.

Chloe points to the table on the patio. "You can put all of those there. Let me go grab the appetizers."

"Need any help?" Tyler asks.

She shakes her head no. "I've got it. You guys just mingle. We only have thirty minutes until Macy is supposed to have them home."

"How'd she get them out of the house?"

Cody watches Chloe as she walks inside the door before turning toward us. The boy is smitten with his girl. "Gregg invited Quinton to golf nine holes, and Macy convinced Brynn to go too."

"I'm sure Brynn loved that." JP chuckles, popping a tomato in his mouth.

"She's been texting me the whole time, letting me know she's in misery, especially since she can't partake in the alcohol portion of golfing," Cody informs us.

"Yeah, because half of golf is drinking." Tyler chuckles.

Chloe enters the backyard carrying a large tray with bruschetta, and fresh basil and warm garlic waft behind her. My mouth waters as I inhale the delicious scents. More voices come through the townhouse and funnel through the patio door. Savannah follows my brother and three other guys who I've learned are Cody's roommates—Hudson, Ty, and Niko. And it's Ty, not to be confused with Tyler, my roommate. Although, I've learned I'm the only one who calls him Tyler—he's Harris to everyone else.

Everyone hugs and gives special handshakes in greeting while Chloe instructs everyone to put their gifts up, grab drinks, and help themselves to food. Twenty minutes go by in a flash as Chloe receives a special text from Macy informing us their car is a few minutes away.

What's nice about today's surprise party is that Brynn and Quinton know that the weekly family dinner is still taking place, so we don't have to worry about hiding, but they have no idea they're walking into their baby shower. My eyes find the gift table, which is overflowing with presents. Gift bags and wrapped presents of every shape and size cover the table.

Laughter filters to where we are all standing, waiting patiently. Nerves and excitement blossom in my belly as the anticipation builds. Chloe stands front and center as everyone else casually gathers around her.

Macy is the first to walk out, a massive smile on her face. And then out steps Brynn, looking over her shoulder, laughing along with Quinton and Gregg. She's dressed in a baby blue ribbed dress that hits mid-length, a matching sweater covers her arms, and white sneakers cover her feet. The dress hugs her seven-month baby bump perfectly.

When she turns her attention to the yard, she halts, hands flying to her mouth.

"Surprise!" we all yell as she bursts into tears.

Quinton steps up beside her, lips tipped up in a smile as he wraps his arms around his wife. Brynn is overcome with emotion as Quinton helps her down the few steps.

"Oh my god, you guys!" she says, emotions clogging her throat. "You bitch, this is why I had to be forced to spend the afternoon watching freaking golf?"

Macy shrugs. "How else was I going to get the two of you out of your room?"

"Chlo." Brynn's lip pouts as her shoulders soften.

"Like it?" Chloe asks tentatively.

Erasing the space between her and Chloe, Brynn throws her arms around her best friend's shoulders. "Like it? I love it!"

"Nice job." Crew nudges my shoulder from where he moved next to me. I smile softly at him.

Quinton goes over to the group and does the whole handshake/pat on the back thing guys do while Brynn goes around hugging everyone. She pulls me in last, hugging me tightly. "Thank you so much for helping Chloe."

"Of course. You look beautiful."

"Please, I look like a beached whale."

Quinton sidles up next to her. "Don't talk about my woman like that. She's growing the next football star."

"Or cheerleader," she retorts with a wink.

Chloe disappears back into the kitchen as she instructs everyone to grab their plates and make their way inside for dinner. The aroma of home-cooked Italian dishes wafts through the air as everyone groans in appreciation. Platters are filled with roasted chicken and vegetables, garlic-butter angel hair pasta, spaghetti and homemade meatballs, a garden salad, and garlic bread. Apparently, Brynn can't get enough pasta, which is why Scott and Chloe made a variety.

With plates full, everyone gathers around the perfectly decorated tables. Laughter and the clinking of silverware mingle with the conversations as everyone enjoys the delicious dinner. Sharing jokes and stories while grilling the soon-to-be parents.

As dinner starts to wind down, Chloe passes out the cardstock games to everyone. The first game she had us play was a typical prediction game where everyone had to guess the date of birth, statistics like height and weight, gender, and so on. She said she'd keep the cards, and whoever got the most right would win a gift card to The Eagles Nest or something similar.

Now, the next game is interactive. Open conversation and laughter surround the tables as everyone jokes while they answer the questions. While everyone is filling out the cards, Chloe stands and moves between the two tables as Quinton grabs two chairs for him and Brynn to sit on. Chloe instructs them to switch one shoe and to sit with their backs to each other.

"Okay, guys, I'm going to ask Q and B the question, and without seeing each other, they'll raise a shoe of the person to whom they think the answer applies in the air."

"Then we'll mark off who was right on the card?" Hudson, one of Cody's roommates, asks from beside me as Chloe nods.

Leaning forward with a pen in hand, I wait to see if I'll be checking off or crossing out my answers.

"Look who's acting all studious," Grant chides, teasingly elbowing me in the ribs. I stick my tongue out as he chuckles.

"First question, who will be the most fun parent?"

Both Brynn and Quinton raise Brynn's sneakers in the air.

"Oh c'mon," JP grumbles.

"Did you seriously not pick Brynn?" Cody chides.

"Don't be one of those dads that loses his cool when he has kids."

"I'll keep him young." Brynn winks, the suggestive tone not lost on anyone.

Chloe brushes a strand of hair out of her face as she reads another question. "Who will be the first one to get peed on?"

"They do that?" Quinton gasps.

We all shrug as Chloe looks at Q. "I mean, they can't control it."

Brynn and Quinton both raise Q's shoe, and we laugh. He's obviously going to be the first one to get peed on if he's not expecting it to happen. The game continues as everyone adds their commentary along the way. Everyone's playful side came out to play as jokes and digs didn't go unnoticed.

Savannah and Grant tied with the most correct answers. When she looked over at him, I couldn't help but notice the slight blush in her cheeks as her eyes seemed to glow. I'm adding that in my mental bank to bring up later. Right now, I am not in a position to talk about anyone's relationships when I can't even bring up my own.

As Chloe titters around, ensuring everyone has everything they need, Brynn and Quinton glowed as they walked around the group, enjoying conversations. Their smiles grew wider as the night went on, their happiness radiating. While everyone is busy, I take the opportunity to start gathering all of the dishes from the tables. On my third trip inside the kitchen, I have a shadow on my trail. Scraping the dirty dishes into the sink, I rinse them off before placing as much as I can into the dishwasher.

"Hey, Rebel." His hushed voice sounds raspy.

A soft smile plays on my lips as I scrub the pan covered in hardened marinara sauce as he sidles beside me. "Hey."

Opening and closing the drawers around the sink, Crew finally finds the right one as he pulls out a towel. Rinsing the pan, I pass it over to him to dry. Everything about this interaction feels domestic as I glance out the window and watch the group mill among each other.

"I can't believe Q is having a kid. It feels like yesterday when he showed me the ropes on campus."

"You two were pretty close." The words come out as a statement rather than a question.

"He kind of stepped into the big brother role for me. I was pretty dumb and naïve. The small-town kid who's never been in a big city with parties and girls at the ready." He glances over at me. "Not that I was with a lot of those girls."

I give a soft laugh. "It's fine, Crew. You can talk about all the babes."

"There was never '*all the babes.*'" He taps his shoulder against mine as I stare up at him. We fall into a routine as I wash and he dries, making our way through the pile of dishes.

"Do you want kids?"

The question startled me as I dropped the soapy plate I was holding. Luckily, it didn't break in the sink. Leaving the plate in the sink, I lean forward, gripping the edge of the sink and staring out the window.

I used to think about having kids all the time. Growing up, I'd play pretend with my dolls and make Grant be the dad while I was the mom. We'd dress up our babies, pack little diaper bags, and push the kids through the house in little toy strollers. I used to beg my mom to let me take my baby doll with me wherever we went. Even as I got older and outgrew pretend play, I'd still think of kids. I enjoyed babysitting throughout junior high and when I could in high school.

Then, when I started dating he-who-shall-not-be-named, I started picturing the white picket fence and picture-perfect family with two kids, a boy and a girl. But as things got worse, that dream started to fade. Everything started to drift away—my hopes, dreams, and ambitions.

But now, with Crew standing here next to me and as our relationship evolves, that dream begins to flicker in my mind. I can see kids again in the future. Only this time, I want a house on a farm. A place where I sit on a swing on a large wraparound porch, sipping lemonade as my slew of kids play in the front yard. They'd stand and scream excitedly as their daddy returned from a long day of working the fields. He'd bend and scoop all the kids up in his giant arms before carrying them up the stairs to me. He'd place them on their feet and tell them to scurry off because he needed to see his woman. And with a welcome home kiss, he'd sit next to me as we watched the life we've built play out in front of us.

"Yeah, I want them."

He bobs his head up and down. No words are said as he dries the last of the dishes, and I wipe down the counters. Glancing around the room, it sparkles and shines. You'd never think that just minutes ago, this room was lined with dishes to feed our little family.

"Hey, there you two are." Chloe jogs into the kitchen, pausing to take a look around. "Wow! You guys did not have to clean."

"It was the least we could do after you did everything."

She loops her arm through mine as she leads us out of the kitchen. "Please, girl. I could not have done it without you."

Everyone is sitting around waiting for us to join the group again. I don't miss my brother's glare as he watches the three of us. His nose flares as Crew steps out behind us. "I found them. They completely cleaned my kitchen."

"Thank god we don't have to do that," Cody grumbles from his seat.

Chloe rolls her eyes. "It's time for presents!"

Moving over to the table, I reach for my packages for the happy couple. "Okay, but I have to go first."

"Girl, you didn't have to get us anything," Brynn says, facing me. Her smile is bright, and her pregnancy glow casts an almost halo-like effect around her.

Bouncing over to the mom and dad-to-be, I place one box in Quinton's outstretched hand and the other gift in Brynn's before sliding out of the way. She tries to balance the box around her belly but struggles. With a huff, she tells Q she'll just wait to open hers until he's done.

Slipping his finger beneath the envelope flap, he breaks the seal and pulls out the card. As he opens the card, something lands on his lap. He grabs the item before tipping his head back and laughing. Placing the ring on his finger, he twirls the white embroidered key chain with an image of New Balance 608 sneakers with an embroidered "Dad Life" below.

"This is great," he howls. Q holds it up, and everyone chuckles at the unofficial-official pair of dad shoes.

Placing the card and keychain on the small table Chloe placed between the chairs, he unwraps the gift. As he removes the top layer, his eyes flit to mine. "You didn't."

I wink as he continues to open the gift. Murmurs of "what is it?" come from the group. Flipping the top of the box, Quinton pulls out his very own pair of "dad sneakers."

"Oh my god, you're going to look so hot in those," Brynn says.

JP whoops from his seat. "Leave it to the sneaker queen to get our boy some dad kicks."

"How'd you know my size?"

I shrug nonchalantly. "I have my ways."

"My turn!" Brynn shouts eagerly.

Q thanked me as he placed the box on the floor before helping his wife unwrap her gift. Ripping open the paper, she moves tissue paper out of the way before pausing, her hands hovering over the items. Her eyes snap to mine as tears escape her blue eyes.

Slowly and gently, she begins pulling out items. A clear, round decorative piece fixed to a wooden block is on top of a cream-colored crochet blanket. Doves flying through the air with clouds and the sun are engraved in the acrylic. A wooden-handled rattle with a soft shade of tan crocheted dove's head and a matching baby lovey made with soft fleece and the same style crochet dove finish the package.

"This is perfect." Emotion clogs her throat as she gently places everything back in the box. She hands it to Quinton as she gets out of her chair and waddles her cute self over to me. She puts her hands around my shoulders and pulls me in for a suffocating hug. "Thank you so much."

"You're welcome. Crew told me the story, and I thought you'd like to have doves looking over your sweet baby." She sniffles before pulling away. She waddles back to her seat after a quick peck to my cheek.

The rest of the evening is spent with more laughing and crying as all of the gifts are unwrapped. Everyone seemed to have the same idea for Quinton—lighthearted gifts to help ease their nerves, which come with welcoming their first baby. Brynn's gifts were a mix of sentimental and the essentials. Chloe gifted a journal for Brynn to write letters to her baby and track growth and other significant items. While the practical items were a variety of adorable gender-neutral outfits, bottles, a baby monitor, bedding, and everything in between.

Everyone shared the same excitement as we watched. As the evening starts to come to a close, Brynn stands from her chair and gets our attention.

"Thank you all so much for coming to shower us with all of your love. Chloe, thank you for planning the surprise. I should have known something was up with how you've avoided me." She winks at her bestie, who feigns innocence. "It's no secret that Q and I have had our issues with our parents. But one thing is for certain—you are our family. In the four years that we've been at CTU, our group of friends has meant more to us than that. I can't imagine life here without you all in it."

"Which makes this next part so fucking hard." She pauses, looking up at Q as she grips his hand. "After talks with Q and my counselors, I'll graduate at the semester's end."

Shock ripples around the group as Chloe's eyes well up with tears. "Wait, what?"

"I was able to work a few things out by taking an extra class this semester, but I have enough credits to graduate. Besides, you guys don't want a baby cramping your style."

"Uncle Cody doesn't care about his style." Q groans as Brynn chuckles.

"Q will be in the off-season, and I'll have our baby. It's just time to say goodbye. My time at CTU is over." A sob rips through her chest as she says her last word. Everyone stands and makes their way over to them.

Even with the heavy news, the day has been nothing short of perfect. These people discovered each other at a time when no one knew who they were. Friendship blossomed as a familial bond grew more profound in the time spent together. And as final hugs of goodbye are given, the love shines through as we all wait with anticipation of the arrival of our newest member.

CHAPTER 30
CREW

I never thought I would say I was happy to be in a bland, dull, quiet study room at the campus library. After a very emotionally heavy weekend, which included the surprise reunion with my brother and Brynn announcing she was moving, I was exhausted by Monday morning. We all knew it wouldn't be long before Brynn moved, but no one expected it to be in a month.

As happy as I am for everyone, it feels weird that our little family is starting to break apart. It was inevitable, with our group consisting of people my age and a year older, but you don't realize how fast time goes until you're staring the end in the face. Brynn graduates this winter, then we'll lose a good chunk of our group next spring. Cody and Chloe, JP and Grant, and Gregg and Macy will be calling their time at CTU over.

At least I'll still have Harris.

And Bret. How has it been only three months since she came strolling back into my life? Three months of turning my world upside down with her perfect, high-pitched throaty laugh. Her green eyes remind me of my hometown lake and are now left unguarded. The confidence she has to crack jokes and bust our balls as if she's been a part of our CTU family for years.

Everything about Bret being here feels normal, as if this was her destiny to begin with. The more I'm with her, the more I crave her.

Her energy, her spark, her heart. With the season almost over, it won't be long until I can claim her and shower her with my love out in the open.

I didn't realize how much I was floating through the motions of class, football, and partying until she arrived. Bret Campbell might have come here needing an escape, a place to feel safe, but in doing so, she's given me a purpose outside of the mundane. Day by day, I'm starting to find myself through her—the real Crew Riggsby with a passion outside of football and the family farm.

"Earth to Crew." Lauren's elbow nudges mine from where she sits next to me. The motion startles me, causing me to jump in my seat as my attention is returned to the present.

"Shit," I say, shaking my head. "I didn't mean to zone out."

"It's fine," Eric grumbles from his spot at the whiteboard. The guy has black and blue circles under his eyes. He mumbled something about extra conditioning to drop weight for his weight class on the wrestling team.

Leaning back in my chair, I scan the colorful notes on the board. "Where were we?"

Lauren sighs as she skims over her notes. "We are trying to decide the overall game design and concept."

"I think we need to focus on the core mechanics and features," Eric adds. "We should map out the player's journey from the very beginning to mastering the technique using precision agricultural techniques."

Flipping through the pages of my notebook, I read back critical points from the lecture when we first discussed the video game concept. "I agree. I think the very beginning should start with basics like seed selection, planting, and watering. Will the player focus on cover crops or only on natural watering processes?"

"Oh, I like that." Lauren scribbles something in her notebook while Eric jots the ideas down on the board. "Then, as the game progresses, we could introduce concepts like soil analysis and the benefits of drone usage."

Snapping my fingers, I point my finger at her as I lean forward in my chair. "Exactly. Drones are all the rage, and there could be substantial benefits of using drones with farming."

As the conversation continues, a thrill runs through me. This is why I chose to go to college and get a degree rather than staying at home and just taking over the family business. I wanted to learn, expand my knowledge, and continue to grow the agricultural industry.

"Let's assign tasks," Lauren pipes up. "We have two weeks to finalize everything, and as much as this is a group project, we all have our strengths."

Eric and I nod as I stand from my seat to take a picture of the whiteboard for my reference.

"I think it's safe to say you should run with the education aspect, Crew."

"Yeah, I agree," comes from Lauren. "This was your idea to start with, and you seem to have the most knowledge of what should be included. Could you reach out and find some success stories?"

I nod, mentally going through the list of topics to explore. "I know someone who has had their farm mapped, I can try to contact them."

Lauren looks over at Eric, and a sheepish expression highlights her face. "Eric, if it's all right with you, I'd like to focus on the marketing. Video game design isn't something I'm super confident in—but I can try if I need to."

Eric shakes his head as Lauren's worry eases. "I'm what you call a video game connoisseur."

"Great, looks like we've got all the areas covered." I clap my hands together as I gather my notebooks. "I'll be here Wednesday night at six for mandatory study tables if you guys want to meet up."

"Sounds good," Eric and Lauren both say.

As we gather our things, Eric erases the whiteboard before the three of us leave the private room. Excitement swirls around us as we exchange conversations on our way out of the library and go our separate ways.

I'm halfway to the union when a large, black arm is thrown around my shoulders. "Wassup, Riggs?"

"Not much, Big Man."

JP groans, and I chuckle. "Wicked woman. She better not let that stupid nickname stick."

"I've already changed your name in my contacts."

"You heading in for food?"

I nod as we step around people. Girls pass by with flirtatious smiles.

"How come I haven't seen you hooking up with anyone this semester?"

"Maybe I'm keeping it away from the apartment."

"You think Campbell has a problem with it? She's never seemed bothered when I bring girls back."

"I don't think she cares. She told us from the beginning she wouldn't cramp our bachelor life or however she worded that."

Glancing out of the corner of my eye, I take in my friend. From the outside, he seems to be the same Jeremiah with his clean fade, beaming smile, and dressed to kill. But on the inside, turmoil is raging in JP's mind. "Everything been okay with you?"

"Shit, Riggs, hit me with the Dr. Phil question." He sighs, staring out in front of us.

His eyes reflect a variety of emotions. And just when I think he will ignore me, he lets out a deep sigh.

"Things are rough at home. My mom is trying, but my siblings are getting older, and the expenses are piling up. I can't sit here, with a full ride at my dream school, and not help them chase theirs. Jessa is a junior and was asked to attend a camp this summer. It's expensive as hell, but she has a chance to receive a scholarship to go to Juilliard. The school for performing arts. I can't let her miss out on that opportunity."

He pauses our conversation as people pass by. Claps on our shoulders and congratulatory remarks are made as they walk by.

Hoisting his backpack higher on his shoulders, JP continues. "Then there are the twins. Jalen and Jacoby are in the eighth grade. Their class is going to Washington DC, this spring, so there are extra costs associated with that. My little sister, Juniper, is growing like a weed, and her body style is different from Jessa's, so her hand-me-downs don't fit. It's just a fucking lot. It's hard to be here when they need support in Houston."

"Fuck, man," I sigh. "Is there anything we can do to help?"

"Hell no. I appreciate it, man, but we aren't a charity case." Anger rolls off his shoulders at the implication that we help him.

"That's not what I meant, and you know it. Besides, we're a family here, and family has each other's backs. No matter what. Don't carry the world's weight on your shoulders when there are people here who will bend over backward to help you."

With a terse nod, the conversation is dropped. JP flings open the doors to the union as I follow him to the cafeteria.

Voices echo off the walls as we near the cafeteria. Everyone is inside during their lunch breaks. The smell of chili wafts in the air, and a hunger I didn't know I had rumbles in my stomach. The smell of simmering spices invades my senses as I'm transported home. A crockpot full of Mom's home-cooked chili simmers while the flavors mingle together. Fresh cornbread bakes in the oven as we sit on the couch with football playing in the background. Sundays were for chili and football, and we gathered around as a family.

Walking through the crowded cafeteria, I head straight to the soup station and ladle a steaming scoop of chili into a bowl. I chuckle at realizing it's Texas-style chili, which means no beans. In Ohio, our chili is half beans with a mixture of black, kidney, pinto, and ranch-style pinto beans. With a chunk of cornbread, I head to the cashier to check out.

Glancing over my shoulder, I find that JP has found a group of ladies to chat with. Since he's occupied, I enter the seating area and scan the room for someone to sit with. My eyes land on the Campbell siblings, Grant and Bret, who are sitting across from each other in what seems to be a heated discussion. As I reconsider sitting with them, Bret's emerald eyes land on mine. I hold her gaze and read the rescue flag she's waving. The decision is made, and I steel my shoulders to join them.

"Am I interrupting?"

"Yes," Grant grits out while Bret says, "No."

"S'up guys," Cody greets as he slides up behind me.

He and I take the open seats at their table as relief flashes over Bret's face.

Bret

The universe is out to punish me today. Not only did I sleep through my alarm, but I managed to shut my finger in the bathroom door, spill my hot coffee all over the kitchen, and barely make it to class in time. Everything about this day has been wrong. And to make matters worse, as I scanned the cafeteria for something greasy to eat—thanks, period—I stumbled into my grump of a brother.

No, I literally stumbled into him. As I was turning around from grabbing a Coke, I ran right into him. His nostrils flared as frustration covered his face.

"Sorry," he grumbles.

"What's got your panties in a knot?" I ask, closing the door to the refrigerator and carrying my tray to the cashier.

Tina, the usual cashier, isn't here today, which is a bummer because I could use one of her famous cookies, which she reserves for her favorites. And since Grant is one of her favorite people, I've become one, too.

"It's been a shit week." The sound of Grant's voice startles me as I walk through the seating area in search of a table. I forgot he was following me.

Dropping my tray on an empty four-seater, I plop in the chair. "It's only Monday."

"Yeah, and I'm over it." He pulls out the chair across from me as I take in his grilled chicken sandwich and a huge salad.

Lifting my burger to my mouth, a small smile touches my lips as Crew pops into my head. The juicy, thick burger loaded with tomatoes, ketchup, mustard, and extra pickles reminds me of our conversation in San Antonio about what it would be like if we could eat one food for the rest of our lives. Chewing a mouthful, I use my napkin to wipe up the dripping ketchup.

"Want to talk about it?" I say around a mouthful.

Grant scoffs. "Oh, now you want to talk? Addy, I've been trying to get you to talk for weeks."

"If you're going to be a dick, there are other tables."

Setting his sandwich on his plate, he rubs his hands up and down his face. His shoulders sag as he hangs his head forward. There's no denying my brother is a grump. He's always been broody and easily frustrated, but this Grant is entirely different. Deciding to drop the bratty little sister act, I reach out and grab his forearm.

"Grant." His name is a whisper on my lips. "What's going on?"

Eyes that match mine stare back at me. With a long exhale, he purges his frustrations. "Dad has been grooming me all season for a position he will have an opening for on his team next season. The job is mine as long as I want it. And I do, Addy, I want the job, but there's so much pressure. Not to mention senior year classes and other shit I'm dealing with."

"Does the other shit have to deal with a certain brunette with a killer smile?"

His eyes snap to mine as he glares at me. Looks like I hit the nail on the head. "Jesus, please tell me Savannah hasn't been running her mouth at girls' night to my sister."

"No, she hasn't said anything. I was just making an assumption, which you just confirmed."

"Am I that transparent?" I shrug, taking another large bite of my burger as I clutch my stomach.

Cramps knot and twist deep in my lower belly. All I want to do is go home, curl up in a ball with a heating pad, and eat a bag of chips. Most people crave chocolate when they're on their period, but I want all of the chips I can eat. Specifically, salt and vinegar and barbecue chips, mixed in a giant bowl so every bite is a surprise.

Grant skeptically stares at me. "What's your deal?"

"Period." He gags as I roll my eyes. "Anyway, we are discussing your problems today, not mine."

"Sav and I have been off and on for three years. Neither one of us wants to make things official. She's not here to get her M-R-S degree since she plans to move home to Kentucky, or so she says."

"And what's the position Dad has you training for?"

He uncaps his Coke and takes a long drink. The two of us have an unhealthy obsession with the dark soda. "He wants me to start next year under the wide receiver coach."

My mouth drops open. "Holy shit, that's huge."

"It's the dream, you know. So in all my free time"—he rolls his eyes—"I've been basically doing the role of a quality control assistant without the actual title. It's been Dad's way of testing me. After our games, I have until Tuesday to produce a report with player performance analysis with individual player stats, detailed player evaluations, and game performance analysis where I break down each game-by-game and third down and red zone efficiency."

"That's *a lot*," I muse, shoving a fry in my mouth.

"That's not even everything. He wants reports on opponents with a detailed analysis of their defensive backs and defensive schemes. So basically, on top of practices, fighting with Sav, my own reports, and assignments for class, I'm unofficially interning for Dad."

"Sounds like you might have to put this thing with Savannah on the back burner, especially if it's more stress on top of everything."

Grant leans back in his chair as his eyes flit around the room. "It's hard when she's all I can fucking think about."

I understand where you are coming from, Grant, more than you know. The heart wants what the heart wants, no matter how complicated the situation may be. At the end of the day, it's up to the mind to figure out how to make it happen.

Of course, I don't tell him that. That truth would open a whole other line of conversation, and I'm not ready for that can of worms.

"Enough about me and my bullshit. Everything going well with you? I mean, I'd love it if you'd tell me why you're here, but considering you've evaded that conversation, I'm gonna drop it. Just know I'm here if you ever need to talk."

Resting my elbow on the table, I lean forward and stare at my brother. Dark circles live under his eyes, and his hair is messy and mussed as if he's run his hands through it all day. Growing up, Grant has always been my best friend, confidant, and protector, but everything changed last year when I pushed him away when a rage of desperation told me to scream at him to get his own life and stop acting like a helicopter parent.

The look on his face was as if I'd reached inside his chest and ripped out his heart. If I would have slapped him across the face, I think it would have hurt less. Of course, I've apologized, and he's said he forgives me, but we aren't the same. Now, here I am, sitting across from him, lying to his face about my life at Central Texas University.

I'm the worst little sister. And once again, I pray to the heavens that he'll forgive me again when everything comes crashing down around me.

"Thank you for respecting that, and I'm still sorry about everything." Moisture wells in my eyes as I stare up at the ceiling, blinking away the tears.

"Don't, Addy. It's in the past." He grabs my hand and squeezes. A soft but stoic look passes over his face.

Clearing my throat, I offer him a small smile. "Yes, the past is in the past, and I have to say that I love it here. Everything about CTU feels like home. I'm truly happy here."

"You definitely fit in, that's for sure."

Taking a long drink of my Coke, I lean back and scan the room. Standing at the edge of the seating area is a man I'm desperate to run to—a man I want to throw my arms around and claim right here in the dining hall. I want to stand up on my chair and shout that Crew Ryan Riggsby has stolen my heart. A heart I thought was hardened. Dark-chocolate eyes land on mine. I feel my pulse tick as a smile plays on his lips. Briefly, his eyes flash to the back of Grant's head, and I watch Crew steel his shoulders and start making his way toward us.

"Am I interrupting?"

"Yes," Grant grits out while I say, "No."

"S'up guys," Cody greets as he slides up behind Crew. The guys sit at the table and the bubble between Grant and I is broken.

Idle conversation fills the table as the guys talk sports. Something about their fantasy football league and their predictions for who will win the Super Bowl this year. I zone out as I scan the faces in the dining hall. I watch as couples openly hold hands. As groups of guys give each other claps on the back as they greet each other. A table of girls throws their heads back in laughter. I enjoy the chance to observe and people-watch. For once, I did not feel like I needed to scan the room for familiar eyes that made up my nightmare.

Shouts and chairs scraping against the tile interrupt my people-watching. Attention forms around a table a few sections away from us. JP stands chest to chest with a man who is built bigger than him. A sobbing girl stands between them. You can feel the tension radiating from the men as JP tries to convince the guy he didn't know the girl was taken.

Oh, the drama.

In seconds, Grant, Crew, and Cody are on their feet and moving to the commotion. All I can do is stand by and watch as the guys try to sort out the issue before exchanging punches.

As calm as things seem to be for me, it looks like we should focus on our other roommate.

CHAPTER 31
Bret

Arriving at my parents' house for Thanksgiving dinner is nothing short of overwhelming. Cars line the driveway, forcing us to park down the street. It's been a few years since I've been home for one of my mom's famous Thanksgiving dinners, and it seems the guest list has only grown in size.

JP practically jumps from the SUV as Tyler shifts the car into park. Apparently, Thanksgiving is JP's favorite holiday. He woke everyone up by yelling, "Wakey, wakey! It's Turkey Day!" from the living room at seven o'clock this morning. The Thanksgiving Day Parade coverage was blaring from our TV starting at eight thirty.

With coffees in hand, the four of us lounged around all morning, watching float after float before we switched the channel to the first NFL game of the day. It was a very chill, very basic morning until we all had to get ready for the four o'clock dinner at my parents' house.

"Bro, would you chill? The food isn't going to be gone." Tyler shuts the driver's side door as the lock sounds beeping.

JP glances over his shoulder as he's already quite a few feet in front of us. "But Mrs. C makes the best mashed potatoes."

I shake my head. My mom makes good mashed potatoes, but dinner isn't served until five. She instructs everyone to get to their house at four to allow plenty of time for everyone to settle. Someone is always running late, so to avoid her plate getting cold for hosting duties, she tells everyone the start is at an earlier time. I think it's kind of genius.

Passing the next-door neighbor's driveway, we follow the sidewalk past the perfectly manicured lawn my parents pay a landscaping company to maintain. The two-story white brick house stands out against the black trim and green bushes in the flowerbeds—another thing the landscaping company takes care of. As much as my mom loves to garden, with my dad's coaching schedule, they've resorted to hiring some help around the property. Their home sits on an acre in a gated community thirty minutes from campus. A mixture of CEOs, doctors, retired NFL players, and even a celebrity or two live in our community.

We followed a few people up the front steps, where my mother stood inside the door, welcoming her guests. Her brunette hair is slicked back in her signature chignon bun. The brown plaid dress clings to her and accentuates her frame. She's dressed as a dutiful housewife, simple and stylish, prepared to host a lovely dinner.

With the slightest of touches, I feel Crew's fingers slide against my hand. Glancing up, he flashes me a subtle wink as he creates more space between us. It's the smallest of gestures, but it warms my heart. It's his way of saying that he's keeping his distance, but he's still thinking of me.

"My favorite daughter!" Mom's excited voice welcomes us as it's our turn to enter the house. With arms open wide, I step into her embrace.

"Mom, I'm your only daughter."

Pulling back, she holds me at arm's length, taking in my appearance. Today's outfit is out of my go-to comfort zone. A burnt orange sweater vest hangs off my exposed shoulders and is slightly tucked into my black, cropped flared jeans with the knees ripped out. My sneakers were exchanged for black-heeled booties, which I rarely wear anything heeled. And my long black hair is curled voluptuously down my back.

"You look lovely, darling." Mom's eyes bounce from mine to where my three roommates stand. "All of you look so handsome."

And they do. JP is dressed in dark-washed denim and a lightweight cream sweater, which contrasts with his dark skin. Tyler is wearing khaki dress pants and a navy polo shirt, while Crew is wearing medium-washed jeans and a plaid shirt. He looks like the country boy he is.

"Please come in. There are coolers lining the back patio filled with everything under the sun. Make yourselves at home." Mom steps aside as each man bends down and hugs her as they thank her for hosting.

Following the guys, we made our way through the entryway into the open living room, which led into the large kitchen. Every surface was covered in burnt oranges, browns, and creams, as all of the fall decor was placed in the perfect location, creating an inviting and cozy atmosphere. The air smelled of an array of scents, from pumpkin-scented candles to the roasting turkey.

Groups of people mill around the space, spilling out to the backyard where tents and tables are placed. Familiar faces of relatives and family friends greet me, some pulling me in for conversation. Comments on my hair, questions on where I've been, and everything in between are asked. And while I knew the shock of seeing me would have people flocking toward me, I was hoping to find a table in the corner and just people-watch.

"Bret, sweetie, there you are," Mom interrupts my conversation with a nosy family friend looking for the scoop. She's the type who acts incredibly sweet, hoping you'll open up to her, and then spreads your gossip around town. I welcome the interruption from Mom.

"Excuse us," I tell the lady as I turn toward Mom, who smiles politely as she ushers me away. We weave through the crowd until she finds a quiet spot inside the kitchen away from eavesdropping ears.

"Sweetie, your father and I would like you to meet friends of ours' son. He'll be joining us for supper and is a medical student at CTU."

Mentally processing the news, I quickly rack my brain as I try to figure out how to get out of this. I'm not interested, and my parents don't know I'm dating.

"Oh, I-I…That's nice of you guys, but I'm…I'm kind of seeing someone."

"Nonsense. Sweetie, how are you kind of seeing someone?"

"It's complicated."

"Oh." Her face softens as she places a gentle hand on my forearm. "Bret, no guy should ever make you feel like your status with him is complicated. He should want to be fully with you or without you. You're too good of a woman to settle for complicated."

"Mom—" I start, but I'm quickly interrupted.

"Bret, honey, believe me. If a guy wants to be with you, he will climb the tallest mountains, jump the widest rivers, and hike the hottest deserts just to be with you. And as much as I love you and your independence, can you please do us a favor and meet Duncan? It doesn't have to go anywhere, but when I told Kathy about you, she insisted the two of you meet."

Dad steps into the kitchen, a bright smile on his face, causing the conversation to lull. "Bretster!"

"Hi, Dad!" I greet him, stepping into his waiting arms.

"Did you know our daughter is seeing someone?" Mom asks as I let out a deep exhale. Having my dad on my back about this is not what I need right now.

Only a few more weeks, I repeat to myself.

Dad pulls back and stares down at me. "I haven't heard anything about my little girl having a new boyfriend. Hopefully, he's better than the last one."

I scrunch my nose as I outwardly cringe at his comment. Not because it isn't the truth, but just the mere mention of he-who-shall-not-be-named has my body on high alert. "Can we not do this today?"

"Sure, kiddo," Dad says, giving Mom a pointed look. A silent conversation passes through them. "Dinner looks to be ready. I was going to thank everyone for joining if you want to come outside."

I follow my parents through the back door for my first chance to escape since we arrived forty minutes ago. Sliding my phone out of my back pocket, I notice a waiting text from Crew.

> **Crew: Need me to rescue you?**

> Me: Not now, but I might need to take you up on that offer later.

> **Crew: Everything okay?**

> Me: Loaded question. But since we still have to keep things under wraps, my mom has arranged a blind date for me...today...

> **Crew: Oh, Rebel, this is going to be fun to watch *smirking emoji***

My mom's elbow gently nudges my arm, pulling my attention from my phone to where my dad stands.

"Good evening. On behalf of my wife and I, I would like to thank you for joining us for our annual Thanksgiving dinner. This is the sixth year we've hosted it, and each year, our attendance gets larger and larger. We are grateful for every one of you. There's plenty of food, so please, no one leaves here hungry."

I watch as my parents stand in front of their guests, smiles brimming, as they look like the perfect couple. I know their marriage isn't perfect, but they've been a great example of what love should look like for my brother and me, so I don't understand why my mom decided to force some guy onto me. The only thing I can think of is that this son of their so-called friend is a member of the boosters or a high-end donor to the football team. It's the only thing that makes logical sense. My parents have never inserted themselves in my dating life. In fact, I feel like it's always been the opposite, with them not wanting their "baby girl" to leave the nest.

I'm thankful that Crew understands and considers this night a joke. His own form of entertainment. Now, if only it were my joke.

Spinning around, Mom's voice has me pausing in my steps. It's too late to retreat to the safety of the tent where the food has been set out.

"Kathy, I'd love for you to meet my daughter, Bret." Mom points in my direction as if I wasn't obviously her daughter. "Bret, sweetie, this is Kathy, John, and their son, Duncan."

"You're really tall," Duncan blurts as he visibly takes in my height. He's a few inches shorter than me—even without heels, I'd still be taller than him.

"Thanks, I think." Taking his outstretched hand, our handshake feels more like a business greeting than anything that is supposed to feel semi-romantic. There are definitely no sparks that run straight through my body. My pulse and heartbeat stay at the same rhythm. There are absolutely no reactions to the man in front of me. Not like there are when Crew is simply in the same room as me.

"Why don't the two of you run along and fill your plates, get to know each other?" Kathy muses. Her eyes have stars in them as if she's just introduced her son to his future bride. News flash, Kathy, never going to happen.

With an outstretched hand, Duncan gestures for me to lead the way. I walk toward the food and throw a tight-lipped smile at Kathy and John. Hopefully, if I pile enough food on my plate, I'll be too busy eating to carry on any sort of conversation.

Long tables fill the inside of the large tent. Each table is decorated as if we were attending a wedding reception and not a Thanksgiving dinner. Cream tablecloths, vases of fall-shaded flowers, pumpkins, and scattered leaves run down the center over the top of a burlap runner. In the far corner is a line where the food is being served buffet style as people eagerly fill their plates with a medley of options: roasted turkey, mashed potatoes and gravy, sweet potatoes, green bean casserole, cornbread, and everything in between. My roommates are all gathered at the front of the line, no doubt being the first in line to make sure JP receives plenty of Mom's mashed potatoes.

My chest ached to be with them. To openly hold Crew's hand as we waited in line. Instead, I'm stuck with Dr. Boring.

Dr. Boring was, in fact, boring. The entire time I tried to eat, he shared detail after detail about his residency. News flash, Duncan. Nobody wants to listen to stories about bodily fluids at the dinner table—a holiday dinner, no less.

Wiping my face with the cream linen napkin that matched the tablecloth, I turn to Duncan and paste on a very fake smile. "If you could excuse me, I need to use the lady's room."

"Of course. Remind me when you come back to tell you about this patient I had this week who…" I don't allow him the chance to finish his sentence as I very rudely, but desperately, escape the table.

My eyes scan the tent and find my parents preoccupied with their table guests. Dad pulls at the collar of his shirt, no doubt ready to put on a T-shirt and kick his feet up for the night. A large screen plays the NFL game, which has captured the attention of most men. Seeing how everyone is occupied, I take the opportunity to sneak out of the tent.

The grass crunches beneath my heeled feet as I follow the path to the side of the house. Mentally crossing my fingers, I pray the side door is unlocked so I can sneak inside. Twisting the knob, I let out a sigh of relief when the door pushes open. Voices carry from the living room, where guests mingle, as I sneak up the back staircase. Reaching the top, I beeline down the hall to where my bedroom waits. Pushing open the door, the familiar room has a smile breaking free.

Dark gray walls filled with records and posters greet my eyes, and my shoulders sag at the familiar sight. The eggplant-colored bedding calls to me as I inhale the familiar scent, which resembles male cologne. I love that my mom continues to spray the room with the same bottle of cologne each time she dusts.

Trailing my fingers over the picture frames, my heart bursts at the memories. Pictures of Grant and I throughout our childhood, family pictures from traveling to different cities to watch Dad coach and frames of Liv and me in Arizona. Small fragments of time that have helped shape me.

A soft rap on the door has me glancing over my shoulder. My lips tip as I take in long, muscular legs hugged perfectly by denim, a brown plaid shirt button against a taut, muscular chest, light blond hair trimmed in a tight, stubbly beard, and chocolate-brown eyes that swirl with sparkling gold flecks.

"Hey, handsome."

"God, Rebel, I can't go another minute without touching you. Seeing you with that tool and being unable to claim you in front of our friends makes me want to go all caveman." Crew steps slowly into the room. His eyes scan the space, and I'd love to know the thoughts swirling around inside his brilliant mind.

With his front brushing my back, he reaches his arms around my waist, and I melt into his touch. His fingers trail over an image of me in a frame from my senior year of basketball. I'm standing tall and lanky with a basketball resting on my hip in the crook of my arm, my smile wide, my long, brownish-blond hair is in two braids, and I'm wearing my team's black and blue uniform.

"So this is teenage Bret."

I nod.

"She's cute. I totally would've been into her in high school."

Turning in his arms, I look at him as we are nearly eye to eye, thanks to my shoes. "Oh, she totally would have been into you."

He hums. "Is that so?"

With a terse nod, I lean forward, clutching his blond hair as he clutches me. I seal my lips against him as he moves his hands and grips my face. Everything about being alone with Crew Riggsby in my parents' home is risky. But I love the thrill of sneaking a boy into my room. Leading me backward, Crew moves us until the back of my knees hits my bed.

He groans as I press my body against his as he takes control. Before I can second guess anything, I'm losing control. It's as if I'm starved for Crew Riggsby. I can't get enough of him. He's the air my lungs are desperate to breathe. Tongues tangle as we explore each other's mouths. Chests heaving against each other, he grips my jaw as he consumes every inch of my greedy mouth.

Moisture gathers as arousal soaks through my panties, ruining them. An ache builds deep in my lower belly, and before I know it, I'm in his arms. My center hits his waist as I feel every inch of his growing erection. He thrusts deeper into my mouth before I pull away and kiss his neck. Fire builds as I feel how needy I am to come from his touch. If he keeps kissing me the way he is, I may come from that alone.

"Move to the bathroom," I mutter against his neck. He glances around before finding the door in the back and carrying me inside, setting me on the sink. A soft glow from the built-in nightlight cascades enough light to see each other without giving away our location. His lips are back on mine as his kiss fuels the ever-stoking fire.

"Crew," I rasp out between kisses. Those mocha eyes I love so much darken into a deep umber as the tension continues to swirl around us. In this moment, in this dark bathroom, it's only him and me. We're the only two souls in the universe. Two souls desperately searching for a place to call ours.

"If I'm going to watch you entertain another man, it's going to be after I make you come on my tongue."

Body vibrating with the need for more, I reach out and cup his hard cock through his pants. Moaning against my mouth, he gives my mouth a final exploration before he trails kisses down my throat as he thrusts his hips into my hand. His kisses turn carnal as he bites my exposed shoulder before dropping to his knees.

What is it with us and bathroom sinks?

Unclasping my jeans, I lift my hips as he pulls the denim down my legs with my black lace thong. He pulls off my booties as he removes my jeans, leaving me wholly bared to him.

"I'll never get used to this fucking view." I stare down at the gigantic man as he takes in his view. His large frame should make him intimidating, but he's only ever shown me adoration, and he's never afraid to get on his knees for me.

Desire, love, and appreciation lace his eyes as he admires me. No one has never made me feel so seen, so worshipped, and so loved than Crew Riggsby.

Reaching up, Crew grips my ankle as he places open-mouthed kisses from my calf to my above my knee. His tongue licks a path up my thigh before swirling around my clit and capturing it between his teeth.

"Oh, god," I moan as the sensation feels so good. Sucking with fervor, he begins devouring me as my back arches and nearly forces me off the sink.

His chuckle is a welcome vibration against my center as he drapes an arm across my hips, holding me in place. With his free hand, he slips it beneath my sweater as he begins tweaking my nipple. The sensation builds as I feel the precipice closing in.

"You taste so perfect, Rebel." He licks down my center before plunging his tongue into my opening, his nose brushing my clit. "So fucking perfect."

With hard flicks of his tongue against my clit, he pinches my nipple, which has me nearly screaming my release. Head tilting toward the ceiling, I begin to chant indecipherable words as Crew keeps his pace before biting down on my clit.

Wave after endless wave of pleasure rolls through me as he sends white-hot pleasure coursing through my body. Slipping his hand from my boob down my stomach, his tongue continues to lap at my arousal as he draws the orgasm from my body.

"Look at me." His words are rough, strained. Chest heaving, I try to catch my breath as I meet his hooded gaze. "I love you, Bret."

"I love you, too." Crew stands and cups my face in his hands before leaving me with one last toe-curling kiss before stepping away. I stare at his erection pressing against his zipper and want to take care of him desperately, but time isn't on our side. Not that he would let me do that. The man is insatiable when it comes to getting me alone and devouring me.

Sliding off the counter, I bent down to slip my thong and jeans back on before doing the same with my shoes.

"I'm going to sneak out of here and head back downstairs. Are you good?"

"Yeah, I'm going to clean up in here. Maybe my supposed date has left."

He lets out a deep chuckle. "Don't count on it. He has googly eyes for you."

Rolling my eyes, I groan. "God, don't remind me."

With a parting wink, Crew leaves, and I'm left alone. Cleaning up the bathroom and fluffing my hair to make it look less manic, I spritz an air freshener to get the smell of orgasm out of the bathroom.

I make my way back to the party and dread the conversation I will be forced to endure.

This year, I have a lot to be thankful for. I am grateful for a fresh start away from drama and scars and for the friends who quickly became family. Without them, I do not doubt that I still would have worked on finding myself, but they've brought out a new side in me—a more unrestrained side.

And for that, I'll always be thankful for my year at Central Texas University.

CHAPTER 32
CREW

The locker room was a whirlwind of noise and chaos, the air charged with a mixture of frustration and determination. We are up by one touchdown against our rival, the Lafayette Gators, as we play in the season's biggest game. There is no love lost between our two schools, as each year, we battle it out for bragging rights until the next season. Currently, CTU is on a five-game win streak against the Gators, and we have no desire to end that streak today.

From where I'm lying on the trainer's table, I watch as my teammates pace the room, their cleats clinking against the tile, while others sit with their heads between their shoulders. The energy is palpable as everyone is feeling the pressure to win. The sound of ripping draws my attention as I glance at my feet where the athletic trainer works on taping up my ankle.

With two minutes left in the half, I jumped for a catch and came down wrong on the defender's foot, tweaking my ankle. The trainer wanted to work on it then, but I refused to leave the field until halftime. There was no way I was showing my cards to the defense and letting them think I was hurt.

"We need to tighten up our defense." JP sits with his elbows resting on his thighs as he stares around the room.

"The blitz is killing me," our center adds.

Grant stands up from his locker bench and moves over to the whiteboard. Uncapping a marker, he jots down x's and o's, symbolizing our offense and defense. He points his pen as he taps the marker against the board. "We've got to exploit their weak side, and we've got to tighten up our defense to stop giving them easy yards."

Internally, I smile as I watch my friend take charge and coach us based on what he's seen on the field. Grant Campbell has the coaching gene like his dad. He has a way of seeing the field, understanding the players, and providing feedback in a likable manner while still making sure the point isn't missed. Grant will make an excellent coach one day.

The coaches enter from their adjoining conference room. Coach Campbell claps his hands as the room silences, and he captures everyone's attention. "Gather around and listen up!"

"We've got to stop letting them push us around out there," our defensive coordinator says. "This is our house, and they're controlling it like it's theirs."

"It's a dog fight out there, men. One that they're more hungry for." Coach's voice is stern with a mix of authority and encouragement. "This isn't how we play our game. We're playing theirs, and we are lucky the score isn't worse."

Other coaches give their feedback as we work out our game plan for the second half. The trainer finishes taping my ankle and helps me get my cleat on my foot, where she added an additional wrap of tape. Luckily, it isn't anything serious, and I can continue playing in the second half. Last season, I got a real sense of winning, and I'm hungry for it.

"This is what we work for." Coach's voice breaks through my thoughts. "Rivalry games are challenging. They bring out the best in everyone and our desires to win. We have to keep fighting and dig deep, men. These games are won by heart and grit. Who has the drive to win?"

"We do!" Harris shouts, standing on his feet. His eye-black is smeared down his face from sweat. Everyone follows his lead as we circle up. "This is our house! This is our game! Eagles on three. One. Two. Three."

"Eagles!" Cheers follow our shouts and screams as we work to hype each other up.

As I walk down the aisle, Coach stops me with a hand on my shoulder. "You good, Riggsby?"

"Hell yeah, Coach!"

He slaps my shoulder pad. "That's what I like to hear."

Jogging through the tunnel, we enter the field with the crowd's roar. A new energy buzzed around our sidelines, and the halftime pep talk was doing its job as a new determination set in. With the fuel of the boisterous crowd buzzing in our helmets, we were ready when the referee blew his whistle, signaling the start of the third quarter.

As the ball sailed high in the air, Xavier Boyd stood in the end zone as he waited. Catching the high kick, he took off like a rocket, weaving through the crowds of players, all desperate to get the most out of the play. Taken down on the forty-three-yard line, it was time to line up for our first chance on offense.

Grant slaps my helmet as we run out together. Taking my position on the far side, my fingers twitch as I wait for the ball to be snapped. Harris's voice cuts through the noise as he counts us down. The ball is snapped, and I lurch forward to block the defensive back. With a slant route, Grant is open down the middle, and we pick up a quick five yards.

The opening drive continues this way—short plays to pick up a few yards each down as we work the clock in our favor. With us controlling the score, we have the patience to take our time. The moment of desperation hasn't hit us yet. After running a full six minutes off the clock down on the four-yard line, Harris snaps the ball as I push the defender closer to the end zone before spinning and catching the flying ball. It was a textbook play from the trust I have with our quarterback. We both knew I'd get open. All Harris had to do was have the ball in the air waiting for me.

Tossing the ball, I break out the dance moves as I celebrate the touchdown. The guys all run over to me and smack my helmet, causing the noise to ring in my ears.

"Hell, fucking, yeah!" Harris yells as he jumps on me.

"I told you, I got you." I chuckle as we jog off as the special teams take the field. More cheers and congratulations are said as I unclip my helmet and walk toward the bench.

With the extra point sailing through the uprights, we take a twenty-one to seven lead with less than nine minutes remaining in the third quarter.

As the game progresses, the tension on the field is tangible. The Gators have brought the game within four points as we head into the fourth quarter. Our defense is struggling to keep the Gators' offense in front of them. Adrenaline courses as tempers flare. More than once, we've had to step in and break up heated discussions on the sidelines. Everyone wants to blame someone else. Lafayette has done their job of getting into our heads.

Taking the field, it's not long before I'm jogging back off. Their blitz couldn't be held, as the added pressure of the collapsing pocket had Harris throwing an interception.

"Keep your head up, Harris." I nudge his shoulder as he moves to the sideline, head hanging between his shoulders. "That wasn't your fault back there."

His eyes flick to mine, and I can see his frustration. If I know Harris as well as I think I do, I know he's blaming himself. He's letting the inner voices take over. The demonic voices are telling him he's not good enough, that last season was a fluke, and that he's overrated. They are all bullshit things the media has been feeding him for the past four months. Lies that have started breaking down his spirit.

It's Lafayette's turn to control the clock. With a mixture of short runs and passes, the Gators start working their offense to take as much time off the clock as possible. Anxiety swirls in my stomach as I pace the sidelines. With each pass, I watch with bated breath as I pray we force a turnover. JP stands on the line in his defensive back position as he fights for position.

"That's a hold! That's a hold!" My voice is mixed with my teammates as we yell that a blatant hold on JP wasn't called. The crowd erupts in chaos as they boo the missed penalty. With Lafayette on the seven-yard line, I squeeze the face mask of my helmet I'm holding as I watch the ball soar through the air. With an outstretched hand in the end zone's back corner, we watch as the Gators' wide receiver brings down an insane catch. On his tiptoes, he secures the ball without stepping out of bounds.

Fuck.

Coach calls the offense together as Lafayette sails their extra point, putting them up by four. We have to score a touchdown to win.

"This is it," he begins, looking each of us in the eye. "Remain calm, quiet the noise, and focus on our game. No matter what, you've worked your asses off. Now, let's go win this fight!"

Clasping my chin strap and jogging onto the field, I felt like I was gearing up for a battle. A battle to win the war and keep the people happy. Our teammates, our coaches, our fans, and the university. Everyone is relying on us right now. The pressure is suffocating as I fight to keep the shaking from my hands. Chest heavy and determination in my eyes, I stare at the defensive back lining up across from me as he prepares to make the final minutes of the game my own personal hell.

With every snap, every yard, the anxiety tightened its grip on my chest. Our drive down the field was a desperate race against the clock, every yard a tiny victory. The sideline buzzed with anxiety as the crowd worked to hype us up, but I drowned it all out. I had to focus on what was in front of me. Even if he was a six-foot-six, two-hundred-and-sixty-pound muscle wall determined to make my life miserable.

Harris dropped back as Grant and I ran our routes as the final minute ran down as if our lives depended on it. Cutting toward the sidelines, I braced myself for the inevitable crash of the defender's body as I watched a perfect arched ball sail through the air in our last attempt to get out of bounds and stop the clock.

Jumping in the air, I climb an invisible ladder and stretch with all my might to catch the ball. Too bad the defender went with me. As the ball descended toward my outstretched arms, the defender's wingspan was simply longer than mine. I watched as the ball bounced off his fingertips and sailed out of bounds. Crashing to the ground, hope deflated as disappointment crushed my soul.

The final whistle blew, signaling the end of the game and our winning streak against the Lafayette Gators. An almost silence covered the stadium as everyone stood stunned. My body slumped where it was lying on the ground, and I took a few deep breaths before getting to my feet. Glancing around the field, I was met with disappointed teammates who stood with their shoulders slumped, mirroring mine.

In the blink of an eye, everything we worked for was simply over. Our chance of getting to the national championship game was gone. The promise of playing for another conference championship looks to have vanished. Now, it's a waiting game to see how the other teams do this weekend. Devastation crushes my soul.

All the hard work, all the sacrifice, it felt like it had all been for nothing.

This loss hurt.

CHAPTER 33
Bret

An eerie cloud has hung over our apartment for the past three days. The guys are still mourning the devastating loss they experienced on Saturday. Standing in the student section, my heart broke for them as time passed. I sank to my seat and sat there, mouth ajar, staring at the field. Shock filled the stadium as everyone looked on with disbelief.

My heart hurt for my dad, who gave his everything to his team. My brother, who played his last rivalry game against Lafayette and whose chance at being back-to-back champions vanished. My roommates worked their asses off, even if they refused to think that. And for my boyfriend, who did all that he could but couldn't secure the pass.

In my heart, I knew it wasn't the missed pass that cost us the game. The play ended the game, but there were many more moments that shouldn't have happened.

What's frustrating is that the guys will only get a bowl game, and they are already acting like their season is over—especially JP, whose time at CTU will end with a bowl game instead of a national title game.

Even though life as we know it felt over, we still had to carry on. This week is our final week of classes before finals next week. Assignments are due, lectures are spent reviewing, and studying fills everyone's free time. Factor in the depression weighing heavy on my roommates, and it's as if I live alone.

Cranking the volume on my Jeep, I let MGK play as my soundtrack while I drive from campus to the sports complex. Tonight is the charity intramural basketball tournament. With scheduling conflicts and the league only taking teams with winning records, the tournament consists of eight teams playing a single elimination tournament in one evening. Based on the schedule, it will be a long and exhausting night, but it's for a good cause.

Shifting the gear into park, I reach for my gym bag and step out into the evening air. Cars coast through the lot, searching for a place to park. Doors shut and locks sound as I walk toward the sports complex. Pulling open the door, I'm met with a small line of people who are being directed to pay for admittance. The entry fee and any donations local businesses have contributed to the community center are being donated. Avoiding the line, I nod at the front desk clerk, who recognizes me from the hours spent on the court. He returns the gesture and wishes me luck as I pass by.

Inside the gymnasium, a cacophony of sounds greets me. Students file onto the metal bleachers scattered around the courts. Music plays from the speakers as an announcer walks around the gym, providing commentary and cracking jokes. The sound of basketballs hitting the court and sneakers squeaking provides another layer to the atmosphere. It's loud, it's chaotic, but it's going to be a fun night.

My eyes scan the courts until I land on Kyrie's tall frame, warming up on the back left court. Weaving through the sea of people, I sit on the metal bench. The coldness sends a shiver through my body.

"S'up, girl? Ready to ball?" Kyrie asks as he dribbles the ball toward the bench.

Reaching inside my bag, I slip off my street shoes in exchange for my basketball shoes. Leaning down, I tighten the laces as I look up at Kyrie. "Hell yeah. It's going to be a long night."

"I hope you brought your jump shot," Dylan muses from where he joins me on the edge of the bench.

"You know it."

"Thatta girl." Dylan tightens his laces as we wait for the rest of our team to show.

Standing to my feet, I bend down to touch my toes as I feel the delicious stretch of my hamstring muscles. Leaning from one foot to the other, I allow the stretch to deepen until the muscles feel relaxed.

"All right, all right," the announcer says as he approaches me.

Pausing my warm-ups, I place my hands on my hips as I watch Monty, our announcer, step closer to me. His entire being is upbeat and full of energy, making him the perfect emcee. "We've got CTU royalty with us tonight. Bret Campbell, can you tell us what's your go-to excuse for missing a shot?"

"I don't miss." My words come out as confident and cocky, just as I intended, which causes Monty to step back.

"Oh shit, girl, you just went there." Flashing him a wink, he steps around me, asking Dylan a question as I resume warming up. It's not long before the buzzer sounds, and we step onto the court.

The student referee stands at half-court, but before he has a chance to toss the ball into the air, the crowd erupts in chaos. There are cheers and shouts, clapping and whistling. Following the noise, I find half a section filled with my friends. JP, Tyler, Crew, and Grant stand shirtless, their chests spelling out my name, as Brynn, Chloe, Cody, and his roommates stand holding signs. A soft chuckle leaves my mouth while tears fill my eyes as I read the signs they hold.

"You're Dunkin' Awesome!"

"Keep Calm And Break Ankles!"

"My Friend Is A Real Baller!"

This is everything I've ever wished for—friends who feel like family, who welcome you with open arms and cheer with you. Transferring to CTU has been the biggest blessing. I've found myself while creating a life I'm proud of. I took back *my* life and found my happiness.

I give a subtle wave to my fans as I line up around the center circle. With the ball tossed in the air, the game officially started.

For the next three hours, I push my body to the limit. While the games aren't that deep—it is intramural—the desire to win kicks in every time I step foot on the court. After we trounced the first team, our opponents only got stronger as the evening progressed. Chest heaving, I fight the exhaustion as I guzzle down water. I thought I was in shape, I really did, but after two back-to-back games, my body is feeling it. It's a welcoming pain, but a pain no less.

"You good, Campbell?" Kyrie asks from where he stands in front of me.

"I thought I was in shape, but damn, that last team was tough."

"You are good, don't doubt that. It's like they had some kind of freaky superpowers. I don't remember them being that good the last time we played them," Dylan says from beside me.

"I'm glad I wasn't the only one who thought that."

The gym lights gradually start to dim around us as the crowd's murmurs interrupt our conversation. As darkness and shadows cast over the room, I laugh to myself at how serious the rec department and student activities committee took tonight's charity tournament. It's been a fun and lively environment, and I cannot wait for next semester's league to start.

A hush falls over the crowd as a thrill of anticipation fuels the air.

"Ladies and gentlemen, welcome to the main event." Monty pauses as the sound of bells ringing plays over the speaker. "Who's ready to witness a helluva championship game?"

The roar of the crowd echoes off the wall as a thrill seeps into my bones. This is what I miss most about playing—the energy that courses through the crowd as the tension builds for what's to come. And even though this entire league has been for fun, I appreciate the seriousness all of the athletes have expressed. While it is fun, the competitiveness runs deep.

"We've got an epic matchup tonight between our top two teams in the league. If you've been here before, you know these players bring the talent. So, let's turn up the volume, fill this gym with energy, and give these athletes the atmosphere they deserve. Now on your feet while we announce our players. Let's get loud, CTU!"

Chaos ensues as the fans feed off Monty's vibrant energy. Strobe lights flash as our opponents are announced first.

Flashes of red, white, and blue light up the court, moving with the beat of the hype music blaring from the speakers. As Monty makes his way down our lineup of players, I sit on the bench, watching my knee bounce. It's not from nerves but from the adrenaline ready to break free. My second wind is here, and I'm ready to put on a hell of a show. My friends showed up to support me, and a show is what they'll get.

"Put your hands together for Bret Campbell."

Jumping to my feet, I jog across the court to where my teammates are gathered at the foul line. I hear my name shouted as JP's booming voice can be heard above the crowd.

The shiny wax floor shimmers from the play of lights, each flash heightening the anticipation. It was a visual symphony, setting the stage for a great matchup.

As the gym lights flicker back on, my team huddles together as Kyrie hypes us up. With the blow of the whistle, it's game time.

Stepping foot inside The Eagles Nest, I'm met with cheers from my friends.

"Champion!" JP shouts from his cupped hands.

Shaking my head, I can't help but feel the wide smile spread across my face, along with a blush from being the center of attention. Kyrie nudges my shoulder as we walk through the almost empty bar to where my friends are gathered.

The championship game was a battle from tip-off to the final buzzer. While both teams wanted to win, mainly for bragging rights—but also for The Eagles Nest gift card, it was a lighthearted game as everyone cracked jokes and poked fun at each other. At one point, my ribs hurt from laughing so hard instead of exertion. Our team ended up winning by ten points, but the game went back and forth, which kept the crowd fully involved.

JP sent out the bat signal, informing us that we were all going to The Eagles Nest to celebrate and that he wouldn't accept any excuses for anyone not to show up. Even with my body exhausted and covered in sweat, I couldn't fight the elation at the invite.

"I'm glad you joined our team. You're a helluva baller, Campbell."

Nudging his shoulder back, I smile up at him. "Thanks for letting me. It's been a weird year for me, and this was the best therapy."

"Ball will do that to you."

Niko, Cody's roommate, stands as he and Kyrie clap backs. Moving around the table to an empty seat, my brother reaches his fist out for me to bump. "Sure was fun watching you play again. I still don't understand why you didn't take that scholarship."

"Whoa, hold up," Tyler interjects from where he's sitting across the table, a beer bottle in front of him. There are a few buckets spread across the table. "You had a scholarship, and you turned it down?"

Shrugging, I reach inside for an aluminum bottle. Carrying the bottle, I twist the top and take a long pull of the ice-cold, hoppy liquid as I sit between Brynn and Hudson, another of Cody's roommates. "I wanted to keep ball to myself. I didn't want to go to South Carolina and lose the love and enjoyment of the game."

"Shit, South Carolina," Hudson whistles.

"Besides, if I would've gone to South Carolina, I wouldn't be here with you guys."

"Here! Here!" Brynn shouts, lifting her water glass into the air. Bottles are tapped as B slouches into a pout. "Someone drink a beer for me, please."

"I've got you, B." Cody tips his bottle in her direction.

"You're my favorite, Cody." She winks as he blows her a kiss back.

"Don't make me call my boy," JP chimes up.

"Oh, please do." Brynn smirks. "I love jealous Q."

"Jealous Q, probably got you into your current situation," Grant snarks.

Conversation flows as platters of food are brought to our table. I don't hold back as I pile on a huge portion of nachos, mini tacos, and wings. Hunger has taken over my body as she craves sustenance. From where Brynn sits, she taps around on her phone, which is connected to the bar's music system. It definitely pays to know Brynn and her connection to the owner. She plays an alternative song from the early 2000s with everyone bopping their heads.

For the first hour of the night, everything is perfect.

But, like all good things, everything must come to an end.

A heaviness falls over my lids as exhaustion threatens to take me under. We've been at the bar for two hours, but no one has made the move to leave. Instead, we are dancing to the music Brynn has queued up for us from the bar's TouchTones.

For the first time this school year, everyone is at ease. The stress of tomorrow will wait.

I watch Brynn throw her head back in laughter as her round belly sticks out. She's thirty-one weeks, and in a few short weeks, life as she knows it will change.

My brother stands among his teammates as they chat among themselves, occasionally jumping in to dance with us girls. He's soaking up his time with his friends—his brothers—because their season is quickly approaching the end, along with his time at CTU.

Crew glances over every once in a while. His eyes scan my features as a smile plays on his lips. The movement is subtle but reassuring nonetheless. Our time of keeping our relationship a secret is almost over. Even though dread pools in my stomach as the conversation with my brother—since he deemed me off-limits—will no doubt be rocky.

At the end of the day, my big brother only wants what's best for me, and it's safe to say that Crew is what is best. His heart is so big, and he loves without question. I've witnessed the love he has for his family and his friends. He protects the people he cares about and never takes his time with them for granted. He's learned the hard way that tomorrow isn't always promised.

I watch Chloe flail her arms around, doing some crazy dance she saw on social media. I can't help the bark of laughter that erupts deep inside me. Chloe is the most down-to-earth girl I've ever met. She has such a soft and kind heart. I've loved getting to know her this semester. Her eyes flick to her boyfriend's, and I swear the love they share can be felt in the room. That's how powerful it is.

Brynn groans. "I've got to pee again. I swear this little bean enjoys jumping on my bladder."

"I've got to go too!" I shout over the music as I turn on shaky legs. I've had more than my fair share of beers tonight. But with a nearly empty bar and my favorite people around me, I figured, why the hell not? Tonight, I'm letting my hair down—figuratively—and enjoying college.

"You okay, Bret?" Brynn intertwines her arm with mine as she leads me to the bathroom.

I tip my head down and rest it on the side of hers. "I'm wonderful."

"That's my girl." Pushing open the door, we are met with a clean but dingy bathroom. There are only two stalls in the women's room, and I let Chloe and Brynn go first. Standing in front of the sink, I splash cool water on my makeup-free face. I stare at my reflection as the droplets run down my heated skin. My eyes look brighter and more alive. Even tinged pink, the color has come back into my features.

Gone is the scared little girl too afraid to look over her shoulder. The time spent in therapy and working through my struggles has paid off. For the first time in a very long time, I feel happy, energetic, and full of life. The drive to chase my dreams is back.

A buzzing in my pocket pulls my attention away from my self-reflection. Sliding the phone out, I glance at the lit screen, fully expecting to find a flirty text from Crew.

A chill runs down my spine as I read the notification alerting me of a new message from Unknown Number. Swiping a trembling finger across the screen, I unlock the display and face the monster lurking at the edge of consciousness.

> **Unknown Number: You thought you could run and hide from me, little kitten. I'll be seeing you soon.**

> **Unknown Number: *photo attached***

The attached photo was taken from the tournament and posted on CTU's social media channels. There I stand front and center, surrounded by my teammates holding the charity check from tonight's game. I don't understand how he found the photo. Does he have some kind of alert set up for my face?

Feeling the ground shift beneath me, I clutch the sink with my hands—one still holding my phone. The room starts to shrink as I'm flooded with memories of how I used to feel with Chad. My vision blurs with unshed tears as I work to keep the rising bile from projecting onto the mirror. The mirror in which I was just admiring how far I'd come. In a matter of one single text, I'm thrust right back into that scared, cowardly girl.

I can almost hear his smooth, charming voice as it spews venom at me. His manipulative words were always his weapon of choice. My hands tremble, the weight of the phone almost burning my hand.

How could I be so stupid to allow myself to be photographed?

How could I be so reckless?

I practically gave him a tracking number, pinging straight to my location.

Blood pumps through my veins as my heart pounds. The beats are coming so aggressively that it feels like it could beat out of my chest.

Seconds feel like hours as my brain spirals with all the ways I could have prevented this.

Why did I have to come here? Why didn't I run farther? I should've gone someplace across the country—like Vermont—someplace where I knew no one.

Instead, I practically invited a monster into this incredible group of people. Their family is no longer safe, and it's all because of me.

Chad has never shown any physical violence. I don't think he has the balls to hit me, but desperate times lead to desperate measures. For the last four months, I've kept him away from his *kitten*. What if I only escalated things?

What if he comes after my brother? Or Crew? Oh God, what if he comes after Brynn? I just unleashed a monster and put her precious unborn baby in danger.

A vise wraps around my chest, the pressure building with every passing second. Each breath comes in shallow, rapid succession as if my lungs won't expand. Heart pounding erratically, in wild frenzied beats, sends shockwaves through my entire body.

"Bret! Bret!" Brynn's panicked voice barely slips past my pounding pulse. Chloe reaches out, and I can feel her delicate fingers as she tries to get my attention. My head lolls, and my vision rolls as I fight to focus on the girls. With icy fingers, the anxiety grips my heart, sending cold, numbing fear outward.

"Crew." His name comes out in a nearly silent, raspy voice.

"What, honey?"

"Crew," I say between pants. "I need Crew."

Brynn turns and rushes out of the bathroom as Chloe stands beside me. Her mouth moves, but I can't make out anything she's saying. The pulse throbbing in my temples blocks out all the noise around me. The weight in my chest grows heavier as if someone is stacking boulders on my lungs. The suffocating feeling consumes me.

Black dots fill my vision as the edges begin to blur, darkening with each fight for air. Every breath feels like a struggle, and my lungs cannot get enough air from the shallow breaths. The anxiety courses through my veins in sharp points, sending ice along its path as my body shakes with fear.

I try to focus on the breathing techniques my therapist taught me, trying to get my body to relax, but it's easier said than done.

I try to ground myself in the present with each breath, but nothing works. I am stuck, sinking, drowning in fear. The pounding of my heart and the weight in my chest are constant reminders of the terror that lurks in the shadows, waiting to pounce.

CHAPTER 34
CREW

"You guys ready for the season?" Grant leans against the bar, a bottle of beer dangling from his fingers.

Out of all of us guys, he's the most responsible. He's the dad of our group, always making sure we are on our best behavior at bars and parties, keeping our heads focused on classes, and never letting the outside world infiltrate our team dynamics. But as the night goes on, I can't help noticing how heavily he's been drinking. I know tonight is a night to celebrate and our feelings are still raw from the loss this weekend, but he's tying one on.

"Fuck yeah, we are," Ty, Cody's roommate and teammate, answers. "The talent we lost last year was replaced with even better players."

"It should be another good season." Cody's eyes never leave the dance floor where his girlfriend dances with Brynn and Bret. The girls are in their bubble, and none of them has a care in the world as they move their bodies to the beat of the music.

"Hopefully, you have better luck than we did," Harris grumbles.

The chip on his shoulder might as well be a bag—party-sized. I can't say I blame him. The media has been blaming him for our loss which is absolute bullshit. He didn't throw the ball wide or too high. The defender merely got lucky by getting his fingertips on the ball. Not one play or person should be held responsible for our loss. It was a cumulative effort to piss away that lead.

Leaning against the bar, I nurse the beer I've been holding for a while as my teammates and friends continue their conversation. My body has been wound tight since we arrived at the gym. Something about watching Bret weave her way through defenders as she pulls up for jump shots with so much finesse does things to me. Seeing her in her element, so carefree, has me itching to praise her.

I can't wait to get her home. To devour her. To worship her sculpted body that she spends hours at the gym perfecting.

Chloe sidles up in front of Bret as she grabs her hips. The two dance in a seductive rhythm, which causes Brynn to laugh so hard that she's clutching her baby bump. An easy friendship has formed between them, and I'm happy to see Bret at such ease. There was no doubt in my mind she'd fit in with the girls, that's just Bret's personality, but to witness the camaraderie, the inside jokes, and the love between the girls has me rubbing my chest.

A few songs pass by as the girls leave the dance floor for the bathroom. I'll never understand a girl's need to pee with a group. My attention comes back to the group of guys who are discussing the girl JP is hooking up with—the same girl who didn't disclose she had a boyfriend and almost caused a fight in the middle of the dining hall.

All of the noise in the bar fades away as my eyes land on a distressed Brynn moving as fast as her pregnant body will allow. Panic covers her face as all of our heads whip in her direction. Cody stands taller, alerted by her evident distress, his instinct to protect her apparent, as we watch her eyes widen with fear.

"What's wrong?" His voice is husky. "Brynn, is it the baby?"

With a terse shake, she looks in my direction, which is also near half of the guys, including Grant. Tears well in her bright blue eyes, causing the hair on the back of my neck to stand. Brynn's not a crier.

She doesn't wear her emotions on her sleeve, but right now, all of her cards are showing. Pain. Fear. Panic. "She needs you."

Cody cups her face as he tries to get her to calm down. "Who needs us? Is it Chloe? The baby?"

Her head shakes as she sucks in a lungful of air. "It's Bret. She needs you."

Grant starts to move, but Brynn places a hard hand on his chest, stopping him. Her eyes flick to mine, and I see the war battling in her eyes. It's at that moment that I know she knows. Hell, she's been suspicious this whole time, and she's afraid to out us. "Crew, she needs you."

Puffing out his chest, Grant turns to me. With his hands fisted at his sides, I see the anger radiating from him in waves. The suspicion he's been cautious of is coming to light. "Why the *fuck* does *my* sister need *you*?"

"Listen, man..." Heads whip in my direction as I just admitted to there being more between Bret and me. Two words. Two words that have our entire world crashing down. A secret we've worked so hard to keep was exposed in a matter of seconds.

"We don't have time for this." Brynn grabs my hand and pulls me behind her. Taking off in a jog, I can feel the turmoil brewing behind me like a Midwestern storm on a hot summer day as pressure systems crash against each other.

Pushing through the door, I hear Brynn outside the door fighting with Grant. One thing about Brynn is that she will stop at nothing to protect the people she loves. I can't focus on what's going on behind me because panic seizes my ribcage, crushing my lungs as all of the air is expelled as I take in the sight in front of me.

Bret's chest heaves violently as I watch her fight for air. Her breaths come in rapid, shallow gasps, each one more desperate than the last, as if she were drowning on dry land. Her hands cling to her shirt in tight fists as her body trembles. The color she had been getting back on her face is completely drained, leaving her looking like a pale ghost.

Erasing the space between us, my heart lurches to comfort her shattered soul. "Rebel, baby, I'm here. Fuck, baby, look at me."

Wide, panicked, stricken eyes stare up at me as she follows the sound of my voice. "Bret, I need you to focus on me. Baby, I'm here. You're safe."

I rack my brain for all of the information Olivia texted me after she left on how to walk Bret through a panic attack. After she had witnessed her freak out at the football game, Olivia wanted to make sure that I knew all of the tips Bret's therapist had taught her. We spent an evening on FaceTime together, and she walked me through step-by-step directions on how to ease the situation before it turned catastrophic.

"I know you're scared right now, but everything will be okay. Just focus on me. Focus on how I'm breathing. Can you try to take slow, deep breaths with me?"

Bret gives a quick, tight nod.

"Good, baby. Ready? Breathe in through your nose...one, two, three, four. Release...one, two, three, four." We repeated the process four more times to slow down her breathing. Chloe is still in the room, but she's melted into the background. Everything about this moment feels vulnerable, and I'm sure Bret's feelings are the same as her insecurities are ripped out of her.

"I need you to tell me five things you see."

Her eyes bounce back and forth as I see the panic still coursing through her beautiful emerald eyes, ones that are now dull and dim. "Sink, mirror, paper towels, you, beer poster."

"Great job, Rebel. How about four things you can touch?"

Her cute nose squishes. "Cold sink, soft shirt, silky shorts, and the hair tie on my wrist."

We continue the motions until she's listed off three things she can hear, two things she can smell, and one thing she can taste. Slowly, she starts to come down from the panic attack. Her body sags with exhaustion, but I refuse to let her fall in this bathroom. Reaching behind her back, I scoop her in my arms and adjust my hand behind her knees until she's secure. Bret goes limp in my arms as she tucks her head against my shoulder.

"Is she okay?" Chloe's soft voice whispers from behind us.

With a tight-lipped smile, I offer a small shrug. "She will be."

"You really love her, it's clear as day."

"I really do."

"Keep her safe, Crew." I nod as I push my way through the doors.

Grant, Brynn, and JP are waiting in the hallway opening to the dance floor.

"She okay?" Brynn's concern is evident in her voice.

"She will be. I'm taking her home."

"Like hell you are." Grant steps in front of me, but JP steps between us this time.

"You two can hash this shit out tomorrow. Let him take her home. We've got her, Grant."

Anger morphs his features and seeps into his green eyes, which resemble Bret's flare. He's pissed, and if it were up to him, the clenched fist he has at his hip would be meeting my face.

"Take me home," her tiny voice interrupts the standoff. Brushing past Grant, I carry Bret across the dance floor toward the exit. Walking past the guys who stare at me as if I've grown two heads, I nod goodbye as I exit the building. JP and Harris are hot on my heels, with Bret's keys and her wallet attached.

"I've got her Jeep," Harris shouts as he moves toward where I'm parked.

Digging the keys from my pocket, I toss them to JP. "You good to drive us?"

"I'll be fine." Climbing into the truck's back seat, I situate Bret on my lap. Her death grip around my neck hasn't softened one bit. The five-minute drive home feels like forever as I whisper consoling words and reminders that she's safe as I pepper her head with kisses.

Tomorrow I'll figure out what the fuck caused the panic attack. I'm tucking my girl into my bed and wrapping my arms around her tonight. I'll be the shield to protect her from the nightmares while reality waits.

With every nightmare, every startle, and every gasp for air, I'm there for her all night long, calming her down and consoling her. Sleep never consumes me. Each time I start to drift off to sleep, images of her standing in that bathroom flood my vision.

Her distress was palpable. I could feel it as soon as I stepped foot inside the tiny two-stalled room. It was heartbreaking to witness, a stark and painful reminder of how fragile life can be. The light dimmed from her eyes, and my heart shattered to see her in pain.

CHAPTER 35
Bret

The flickering of my eyelids pulls me from the few hours of sleep I managed to get last night. Attempting to roll, my body is met with the resistance of a heavy arm draped across my middle. Snapping my eyes to the arm, I feel my heart tick in panic as familiar blond hair and a large hand greet me.

Crew nestles his face in my hair, free from my hair tie. Warm lips find the spot where my neck and shoulder meet as I melt into his front. My head pounds as my stomach rolls. I feel like I'm hungover, and while I may be, I know the alcohol isn't the cause. Last night's panic attack was the scariest one thus far. I thought I was going to die from a heart attack right there in a college campus bar.

The beating of my heart increases as I remember *why* I was experiencing an attack on a night when I was supposed to be having fun celebrating with my friends. Fighting Crew's hold, I roll over until I'm facing him. Brown eyes peek through the slits of his eyelids as he watches me.

"You wanna talk about it?" His deep voice is husky with exhaustion. The dark circles under his eyes tell me he didn't sleep last night. Guilt swirls in my belly at the thought of him losing sleep over me and my fucked-up situation.

"Hefoundme." I rush the words out before I lose my nerve. Crew whips his head back as if I slapped him.

"What do you mean *he* found you? How?"

Closing my eyes, I rest my forehead on his bare chest, unable to make eye contact. "I don't know how, but the school posted a photo from the charity tournament. He must have some kind of facial recognition or my name in a search that'll trigger an alert if posted online."

"Bret, I think it's time to look into your options."

I stiffen at his admission. I know he's right, but deep down, I'm terrified of what's going to happen. I'm scared no one will believe me and my character will be questioned, which will drag my parents and brother through the mud. No one needs that kind of drama, especially my dad, who's already facing issues with the media.

"Baby, I know it's hard, but last night was really fucking crazy. I thought—" His voice breaks as he swallows a lump of emotions. "I thought I was going to lose you last night."

Springing my eyes up, I meet his gaze and find moisture lining his mocha irises. My heart breaks at the sight of the vulnerability that meets me. "I'm sorry I put you through that. It must've been awful for you to witness."

"Rebel, you have nothing to apologize for." He cups my face, brings his lips to mine, and presses into a searing kiss. I melt into the kiss, thankful to have found him.

Pulling away, I roll away from him before sliding out of the covers. I'm still dressed in my athletic shorts. My jersey has been removed, leaving me in a sports bra. Crew rolls to his back, the sheet clinging to his waist, as his broad, muscular chest is completely exposed. I stare at the cross above his heart—the pure heart that cares deeply. I wonder if his dad was watching over him and saw that we needed each other in our lives.

"Where are you running off to so early?" His eyes are closed as his bent arm rests over his face.

"I need to go have a conversation with Grant that I should have had months ago." Moving back to the bed, I kneel on the mattress, resting my hands in my lap. Crew's eyes peek open as he watches me. "I'm sorry for dragging you into this mess, putting you in the middle, and asking you to keep us a secret. I never should have done that. It wasn't fair to you, Crew."

He sits up, the sheet falling away, as he moves closer to me. Cupping my face, he gazes down at me from where he kneels in front of me. "Bret Addison Campbell, you have nothing to apologize for. I would do anything for you. Hell, if you wanted to keep us a secret forever, I would have done that. Selfishly, I loved having you to myself."

"I don't deserve you, Crew Riggsby."

"That's just it, baby. You deserve the whole damn world, and try as I might, I will ensure you have everything you want in this life. I love you."

"I love you, too." Pulling him in for a hug, I squeeze him tight as I bury my face into his chest, and I let a few tears break free. Crew isn't in a hurry to break our connection, he lets me take all of the time I need to regroup. Once I feel ready, I slip out of his embrace and out of his door.

The apartment is quiet as I walk down the hallway toward my bedroom. Skipping the shower I desperately need, I change into a pair of joggers and an oversized hoodie. Looking at the logo, I see it's one of Crew's, and I debate changing out of the Silo Bay Hawks sweatshirt.

Fuck it. I could wear a ballgown or a plastic bag, and Grant would find a reason to hate it. He's going to be livid no matter what I show up in, might as well wear what I want.

After a fast trip to the bathroom, where I empty a full bladder and scrub last night's stale beer taste from my mouth, I grab my keys and slip out of the apartment.

Twenty-five minutes later, I'm standing outside Grant's town-house doors with two coffees in hand. Rapping my knuckles on the metal door, I wait for him to open it. When I think he isn't going to open, he swings the door open. I'm met with a disheveled Grant whose hair is sticking out in a hundred different directions and a scowl mars his features. His nose flares as his eyes flash with anger.

"Addy," he grits my name through his teeth, which causes my chin to wobble. I can't explain the wave of emotion that hits me. Maybe it's the realization that I've caused more pain in our already strained relationship or the fact that we are growing further apart each day. Our lives are going in different directions, leading farther and farther away from each other.

Grant's eyes soften slightly as he holds the door open wider for me to enter. Crossing the threshold, I hand him one of the steaming to-go cups from a local coffee shop, which is why it took me so long to get to Grant's. Fresh cleaning scents welcome me as I move further into the open space. A large sectional faces a TV with an ottoman in the middle. A smaller kitchen sits off to the left, facing the living room. Not a decoration or personal detail is in the sterile space.

As I sit on the leather couch, the door shuts behind me with a slight slam. I bend my knees in front of me, burrowing into the corner of the armrest, and hold my legs.

Grant sits opposite me, legs spread wide as he rests his coffee in his hands. Silence falls over the room, neither of us speaking. I am still trying to figure out where to even begin. Would he rather hear about the panic attack? What brought me to CTU? Or my relationship with Crew? The number of white lies and secrets stacked up, their height almost resembling Mount Everest.

With a deep exhale, I meet Grant's stare. "Where do you want me to start? I have no idea where to even begin this conversation."

"I don't fucking know, Addy. Maybe try the beginning? The part I've been begging you to talk to me about." He runs his hand through his hair as he rests against the back of the couch. "It's been nothing but secrets since you arrived. I'm glad to have you here, but it's been nothing but secrecy."

"That's my right, Grant. I told you I would tell you when I was ready."

"How long have you been fucking my teammate? My *friend*?" I reel back as if I'd been slapped. His tone drips with so much disgust I think it would have hurt less if he would have called me a slut.

"I guess I deserve that," I whisper before resting my chin on my knees. "If I start telling you everything that's happened, I need you to do me a favor."

"I'm not sure you're in the best position to ask for favors."

"Grant, I'm not fucking joking. I need you to sit in that spot, remain calm, and let me tell you everything. No interjecting with rude comments or asking me a thousand questions. It's hard for me, okay?"

"All right, Addy. I'm not making any promises, but I'll try."

Bringing my to-go cup to my lips, I savor the burn of the rich, dark roast as it coats my tongue before traveling down my throat, warming the path as it goes.

"There's been a rift between us since last school year, and I know it's my fault. I hate how our relationship has started to deteriorate. I always assumed it would be inevitable, but I thought it would be when you found a wife and you'd start doing things with her family instead of ours. Little did I know that I'd be the one to find someone and fuck everything up."

"Ad—"

"Grant, please." He nods reluctantly. "When you and Dad came to visit, you both met Chad. I should've listened to you then and believed everything you said. You'll never know how deeply sorry I am for listening to a boy I'd just met over my best friend."

For the next ten minutes, I shared with Grant all of the problems that came from my relationship with Chad. I leave out some of the details. There are just some things a brother doesn't need to know, like his sister with a handful of pills, because that version of me is long gone. Even with the events from last night, I know deep down I'm not that scared girl looking for a way out.

Anger seeped from Grant, and a few times, he stood from the couch and paced the room. His hands stayed clenched at his sides the entire time, his nose flared, and he muttered indecipherable words. When I shared what happened last night, he threw his remote. I never realized Grant had such an anger issue. Maybe he should have played defense so he could hit more things.

"I'll kill him," he roars from where he's burning a path in his carpet. "I'm not kidding. I'll fly to Arizona right now, find the small dick motherfucker, and I'll kill him."

"Okay, bro." I roll my eyes. "You and Crew won't be killing anyone. I'll handle it."

"You'll handle it? It's been a year, Addy. A year of this asshole tormenting you, forcing you to change your plans, and leaving you scared of your own shadow. The buck stops now." He's right, I know he is, but I'm scared of the repercussions. "Why do you have that look on your face?"

"Because I'm scared of what will happen." He shakes his head, and I can tell he doesn't understand. "What if they can't prove any of the incidents, and I look like the girl who cried wolf? What if they drag you and Dad into the mix? That kind of negative press isn't good for either of you, not when Dad's facing shit from his loss, and you're looking to be hired on."

"Who gives a shit about us? I know Dad would feel the exact same way. You come first, Ads. No job is more important than your safety, so stop using us as an excuse. Let's talk to someone to see if you have enough evidence. The university has a ton of lawyers on retainer. Let me figure out what we need to do to stop this guy. Maybe even threatening to go public or bring attention to the dean at Arizona will cause him to back off. But let me handle that."

Silence falls over the room as we both process the information overload. My forehead rests against my knees as the urge to curl up and fall asleep hits me. Emotional baggage is heavy, and when you unload the piles of trauma it can feel like a weight is being released, freeing you, while also feeling completely drained as all of the sensations course through your body, leaving you on an adrenaline crash.

"I love him, Grant." Nostrils flare, and his eyes turn into slits as he glares at me. "I'm in love with Crew. It's not something we planned, but it was inevitable."

"Inevitable? Do you hear yourself?" Leaning forward, he places his elbows on his knees and stares at me. "You spent the last twenty minutes talking about how you thought you were in love with a guy who was playing mind games on you. Then you transfer schools without telling anyone and move in with my teammates after I casually brought up that some of my friends were looking for a place to live. You're here for five minutes and fall in love again. Do you even know what love is?"

"It's not whatever game you're playing with Savannah. And I didn't jump straight into bed with him as if he was a complete stranger, fuck you very much." It's my turn to get angry as I feel my body heat rise from my blood boiling.

"You were at the same party I was at last Christmas. You witnessed my time spent with Crew. Anyone with eyes could see that there was chemistry with us, but I was in a relationship with a piece of shit. I friend-zoned him so fast his head spun. When I came here, I had no idea he was one of my roommates. It's not like I had this grand plan to move here and trick your teammate into falling for me.

"I wanted to fight it. I tried, but you can't fight love, Grant. It happened, and I was the one who told him we had to keep it a secret. It was my idea to hide us from the world. If you want to be mad at someone, be mad at me. And you definitely have no right to be mad at JP and Tyler—they knew nothing."

"Bullshit. There's no way those two didn't know about you two."

I shake my head, pushing a loose strand of hair from my face. "They really didn't. I heard them talking about it last night. The guys are just as pissed as you are."

"I don't think they're just as pissed."

"You know what I mean." He nods as the conversation lulls. I watch as he processes all of the information shared today.

Grant stands and makes his way around the sectional. I watch as he goes into the kitchen and grabs his phone. His thumbs fly over the keys as he types before scanning the screen. Walking over to the fridge, he holds open the door.

"I don't know about you, but I'm hungover as fuck and then all of that"—he waves his hand around the air in a circular motion—"I could use a sports drink. Want one?"

"Please, red if you've got one."

"Saved the cough syrup flavor just for you." He tosses me the bottle as he takes his place back on the couch, his nose glued to his phone. Whatever he's reading must be intriguing.

Twisting open the orange cap, I take a long chug of the red liquid as I savor the fruity drink.

"Okay, I've got an idea." It turns out that Grant was reading information on legal proceedings and ways to improve my security measures until things with Chad end.

Grant researches as I jot down essential findings for the rest of the afternoon. Both of us nurse hangovers—mine is emotional, and his is very much from the alcohol he consumed last night. By the time I'm ready to drive back to my apartment, the two of us have created a plan of action.

It has me hopeful that everything will finally come to an end and that I can return to enjoying my life.

CHAPTER 36
CREW

The last day of classes went by in a blur. I think it's safe to say that the anxiety I've been feeling all day was crippling. Not only have things been tense in our apartment since our secret was revealed, but the tension is wound so tight I'm surprised it didn't detonate. The group of teammates I view as brothers won't acknowledge me.

The drills were punishing, and the walkthrough was spent going through the motions—no banter, no celebrations, only the necessities. I felt like I had been banished from the team. And for what reason? Loving the coach's daughter because that's what the truth is. Along the way, I fell headfirst into Bret Campbell, and my love for her runs deep. There isn't anything I wouldn't do for her. She's more than a fling, a hookup. She's the woman I want to stand beside for the rest of my life.

Bret brings calm to the chaos of being a student-athlete. She makes me feel seen when I feel like I'm floating through the mundane. And if Grant would give me two seconds of his time, he would know that, too.

At the beginning of our relationship, I was terrified to tell her brother. Scared of what his reaction would be. But with everything out in the open, I couldn't believe how childish I had been. I never should have been afraid of confronting him. As a big brother myself, I would have wanted to know that my sister was being treated with respect and shown what it's like to be with a man who loves her and shows her how valuable her worth is. That's precisely what I've given Bret, and if he can't see that, he has to live with that.

The only good thing about this day is that the video game concept Eric, Lauren, and I have been working on for the past four weeks has passed the class with top honors. Professor Ramirez was so impressed with our presentation that he informed us he would contact a friend of his who might be interested in purchasing our concept. Talk about a breath of fresh air in an otherwise shitty day.

Climbing the stairs to the apartment, I'm ready to spend the night in my room to avoid the awkwardness of our home. The other day, when Bret left and spent the entire afternoon with her brother, I sat the guys down and tried to explain everything. It was obvious that they were pissed. I mean, I can't blame them. For the last three months, Bret and I had been sneaking around, sharing secret touches and glances all behind their backs.

Since then, everyone has been steering clear of everyone. Even Bret has been quieter than usual. She explained that her conversation with her brother went fine, but fine doesn't mean you should avoid your boyfriend.

With a deep exhale, I push through the door and prepare for battle. Tossing my keys on the table, I step further into the apartment and find Bret and Harris cooking in the kitchen. Well, Bret is supervising from where she sits on the counter. She smiles warmly at me while Harris spares me a glance before returning to the vegetables he's cooking. Soy sauce and garlic waft from the sizzling pan.

Leaving the two in the kitchen, not wanting to interrupt their bubble since it seems they've managed to sort out their issues. Harris doesn't appear to be giving her the cold shoulder he's given me the past two days. He must be reserving all of the ice for me.

Stepping inside my room, I toss my backpack toward my desk and fish out my phone from my pocket. Flopping on my bed, the bland walls feel smothering as if they are closing around me. Suffocating me, leaving me fighting for air.

Scrolling through my messages, my thumb hovers over my brother's name. Since he returned home a few weeks ago, Jett's been making a genuine attempt at fixing our relationship. He sends a text every day.

Some days he's updating me on life in Silo Bay. The town prepared a welcome home parade, which I knew they would do something. Streets were lined with people waving the American flag as the high school band, with the help of the local police station, helped escort Jett into town. It was a true patriotic display welcoming home a local hero. While almost everyone has welcomed him home with wide arms, others aren't so quick to forget the trouble he caused in high school. Oh, the joys of small-town life.

Other days, he's sending me updates on Riggs Cattle and how the farm is doing as winter knocks on Ohio's doors. He shares the financial projections and the steps he and Grandpa have taken to prepare for winter calving. There are also updates on how much Grandpa and the rooster do not get along. Those stories always make me laugh. I still can't figure out why Grandpa keeps the bastard around. Jett talks about mending his relationship with Mom and how he disapproves of Saylor's friends she's running around with. It's comical how he stepped into such a protective big brother role, considering the trouble he and his friends caused around town.

More times than not, Jett has reached out to simply ask how I'm doing. If classes are going well or if I'm prepared for a game. He also asks about Bret and if I'm ready to admit to everyone that she's more than just a friend. It doesn't help that Mom and Saylor have been feeding him their theories. I've got to love the meddling women in my life.

> **Me: You were right.**

Closing the screen, I no sooner lay it on my chest before it vibrates. Holding the screen in the air above my face, I swipe open the new message.

> **Jett: I usually am, but what about this time?**

> **Me: My secret relationship with Bret blew up in our faces.**

> **Jett: I told you. Secrets always come around and bite you in the ass.**

> **Me: Yeah, well, my teammates aren't speaking to me, and I'm 98% certain Grant wants to punch me.**

> **Jett: As he should.**

> **Me: Well fuck you too.**

> **Jett: Listen, I'm saying if my friend were sneaking around with my little sister, I'd be pissed too. He trusted you and welcomed you into his life, and you betrayed that trust.**

Well, fuck. Reading that text message felt like a punch to the gut.

> **Jett: Give him time to cool off and then talk to him. Explain that it's more than just a casual fuck. Tell him how you feel about her. Don't be afraid to be vulnerable. It'll all work out in the end, little brother.**

> **Me: When the fuck did you become so wise beyond your years?**

> **Jett: I've had my heart broken before...**

> **Jett: Talk later. Grandpa is fighting with the fucking rooster again.**

Tapping the phone against my chin, I ponder his thoughts. Giving Grant space seems like the best option. However, I have to deal with him every day, and we leave for the conference championship game tomorrow. I want to win Saturday, and I don't want the animosity I caused seeping onto the field. This is what Bret's biggest fear was with our relationship, and it's come to full fruition.

Commotion from the living room snaps me from where I'm lost in my head. Raised voices and shouts have my feet hitting the ground as the terror that Bret's ex has stumbled upon our apartment. Ripping open the door hard enough to feel like I pulled from the hinges, I face a heated Grant.

His attention turns from Bret to where I'm standing. I barely have time to recognize the anger—and hurt—in his eyes before he storms toward me. His steps are quick, like a bull chasing a matador's waving red flag. Refusing to back down, I wait for the verbal lashing. Only the verbal spars never come. Grant's fist flies through the air, slamming into my jaw like a freight train. My head snaps back at the jarring, unexpected hit as I stumble backward. Pain erupts across my face.

Gasps fly from Bret's mouth as curses come from Harris and JP from where they're standing a few feet away. Their sounds barely register as the shock causes my brain to delay for a few seconds. The bitter and metallic taste hits my taste buds as blood coats my tongue from running over the spot where he cracked open on my lip.

Wiping the blood off my lip with the back of my hand, I stare at the man in front of me, stunned. My teammate. My friend. My brother.

Grant's chest heaves as his fists remain clenched at his sides. His eyes stare back at me, and it's then that I see more than anger. This punch wasn't intended to hurt me. It was the final display of how he felt. Betrayed.

Everything my brother said was right. Since I've known him, Grant has done nothing but try to protect his sister. He's lost sleep worrying about her, missing her, and wanting to watch over her, hating that she was hundreds of miles away. He warned us, wanting her off limits to his teammates who have only shown him our fuckboy ways time and time again. Even if I wasn't one of the guys who hooked up with every girl under the sun, I still laughed and joked around with the guys. I'm not saying I've been a saint by any means.

As crimson blood drips from my lip, I realize that I have to prove myself to him. I have to show him that Bret was never another notch on my bedpost. While she was supposed to be off limits, her heart called to mine, and she stole it from my chest.

On the field, my job has always been to provide the pass protection, but in loving her, my job is protecting her and keeping her safe. She's the end for me.

Bret's sliding in between the two of us, tears streaming down her face. The sight has my knees quaking. "Stop," she pleads, but his eyes never leave mine. "Grant, please."

The glare he sends would have a lesser man cowering in the corner, but I refuse to back down. I know he's pissed, but I'm all in with her. "I love her, man."

Grant's body thrums as his fists clench again. He takes a step toward me, which causes Bret to place her hands on his chest. Harris comes between us, and JP moves behind Grant. "C'mon, man," Harris says. "Go cool off. You need to get ice on your hand, or you won't be worth shit Saturday."

"Fuck the game," Grant hisses. This entire season is imploding, and I can't help but feel like the catalyst.

JP pushes Grant, encouraging him to move toward the door. "Enough. Harris is right. You need to chill the fuck out."

Jerking his arm free, Grant casts one last look over his shoulder as he stares at Bret. With a disappointed head shake, he leaves our apartment. Bret breaks down, sobs ripping from her chest as I pull her into my arms. Tears soak through my shirt, and I feel her heartbreak.

Is this going to be the end of us?

Are we going to withstand this storm?

"Here." Harris stands before me, holding an ice pack in his hand. "Put this on your face before you bruise."

Taking the cold gel pack, I place it on my jaw and rub circles on Bret's back. Her sniffles quiet as her red-rimmed eyes stare up at me. With tentative fingers, she traces the cut on my lip.

"I can't believe he punched you."

"You understand how much your brother cares about you."

"Listen," JP sympathetically says as he returns to the living room. "You need to fix this. I'm not going out like this."

Queasiness covers Harris's features as he nods in agreement. One thing Tyler doesn't do well is conflict. He's the peacekeeper, and I can tell he's struggling with everything. I nod at JP, and he moves past us to his room.

Harris's eyes scan over to where I'm consoling Bret, and I can feel the storm raging battle in his mind. With wide eyes, he gives me a look to confirm what JP had said.

"Let's go to bed, Rebel." She nods as I lead her to my room.

We both quietly strip out of our clothes as we climb into bed. Sliding under the covers, we lie skin-to-skin. No words are said as she curls against my chest, and I wrap my arms around her, cocooning her to my body. Our thoughts swirl around the room as no words are spoken.

Why does it feel like we've taken five steps backward?

I shouldn't be here alone. A part of me knows that deep in my soul. It's not safe, not when four days ago, I received a threatening text message promising that he'd find me.

Especially after the scathing letter Grant sent him, threatening to report him to the dean and campus police. Hopefully, with the threat, Chad will back off. The letter was only the first step in our plan. We hope it will buy us some time until we can gather all of the evidence. A friend of Grant's is a pre-law major and is helping us formulate a plan. She gave us tips on what documentation authorities would need to proceed with legal actions.

We were able to comb through my phone storage and find enough damning evidence from text messages, voicemails, and photos of unwanted gifts Liv had sent whenever she found items on our front rug to present a case if need be. Grant is hoping the letter will be enough to have the small dick asswipe—his words, not mine—shaking in his boots.

Four days.

It's crazy how much can change in ninety-six hours. Everyone is out at The Eagles Nest one minute, drinking, dancing, and finally relaxing after a stressful semester. The semester was filled with fresh starts, new beginnings, stresses, and excitement. But with one text message, the blissful bubble we found ourselves living in bursts. Leaving nothing but pain, turmoil, and betrayal.

A panic attack so intense I thought I was dying had me calling out for Crew. Of course, it would. The terrifying feeling of not being able to breathe forced my hand to beg for the one person I knew who could save me.

I never realized how much I'd destroy the one person who always had my back. Who's protected me and only wanted the very best for me.

My chest squeezes as guilt threatens to consume me. Taking a few deep breaths, I try to ground myself before I spiral into a panic attack. One this week was more than enough. Wiggling deeper into the couch, I snuggle tighter into the thick blanket I'm wrapped in. Flicking through the channels, I search for the sports network where the game is.

The boys left yesterday afternoon for the conference championship game in Arlington. I promised everyone that I would be fine. Somehow, my voice wasn't convincing because they arranged for Cody to check in on me. Every fifteen minutes, I have a check-in text from Cody or Chloe. Occasionally, Hudson and Ty, Cody's roommates, will check-in, too.

While I appreciate the concern, I want to rot on the couch as I enjoy an evening alone to wallow in my emotions. The animosity in the apartment has weighed down on us like a crashing wave threatening to pull us under. It looks like the whole "doesn't do drama" line, the one I placed in the email I sent Tyler when I was inquiring about the apartment, was a flat-out lie. Since I stepped foot in central Texas, all I've caused is drama, just like I did in Arizona. Chaos seems to follow me, causing stress in innocent people's lives.

I like to think that everything is Chad's fault. However, I'm not naïve enough to believe that the drama I've caused isn't anyone's fault but mine. I decided to transfer without telling my parents. I showed up at the front door of three guys, and I had led them to assume I was a male roommate. I decided to pursue Crew when I knew that it would only lead to problems, and it was my idea to keep our relationship a secret once again, knowing that the magnitude of that white lie would destroy everyone around us if it weren't handled correctly. Exposing our relationship amid a panic attack in front of our friends wasn't handling the situation correctly.

It turns out at twenty, I'm still as childish and immature as I was at sixteen. No amount of convincing on my part would prove otherwise. I thought I could handle things my way, but I couldn't. Instead, I made the wrong decisions and destroyed everything in my path like a tornado swirling through Oklahoma, ripping friendships off their foundations and flattening any semblance of independence in my wake.

Swiping at my cheeks, I wipe away the moisture that has gathered. My fingers itch with the desire to pack everything up and run. Run far away from Arizona, from CTU, and civilization. Maybe I'll find a college in Alaska. I'd welcome the frigid tundra with open arms.

The announcer's voice interrupts my pity party as I turn my attention to the game. Almost the whole first quarter has passed, which I've missed because I was lost in thought. Truthfully, it's hard to watch, knowing how much pain I've caused the team.

The cameraman pans to the Eagles' sidelines, where my dad stands in the middle of an offensive huddle. Anger radiates from his body as he screams at the players. The angle switches to Erica Adams, an ESPN sideline reporter. I'm too stressed to take in her always fashionable sideline outfits.

"This is not the same team we've seen earlier this year and last season. You can feel the tension. No longer moving in sync, but now as if they're fighting against each other, not with each other."

"I couldn't say it better myself, Erica. Something has clearly gone wrong behind the scenes, and it's tearing this team apart."

What happened was I blew into town and wrecked everything like a category-five hurricane. The wave of emotion hits me full force, and I find myself sniffling into the pillow. I watch through blurred visions as another missed catch has the team turning over the ball again.

A heated conversation occurs on the sideline between my brother, my boyfriend, and my roommate. An offensive coordinator moves toward the commotion as he angrily breaks up the quarrel. He grabs Crew by the jersey and pushes him toward the bench while he points down the sideline, where Grant follows his finger. Both guys stomp to their designated areas.

Minutes pass as the defense tries to salvage the shit show of a game. As time winds down and the halftime whistle blows, CTU is down twenty-four to three.

"You've got to wonder what will happen in the locker room. The chemistry that made this team formidable has all but vanished. How does Coach Campbell fire up his team and fix the turmoil among his players?"

"That's a good question, Stan. Erica Adams is on the field with the man himself."

The camera changes as my dad's tall frame towers over Erica Adams as she stands on the edge of the field while the team runs to the locker room. The worry lines on my dad's face seem more profound as his eyes reflect frustration and disappointment. Once again, the stress in someone's life directly results from my decisions.

Flickering on the edge of my vision, my flight or fight radar is flashing. My fingers twitch, my heart races, and my head spins. But as I sit here, the negative thoughts consume me as the desire to flee wins.

With bags packed and a note left on the dining table, I do what I do best...

I run.

CHAPTER 38
CREW

"**I**s this how it's going to end?" Coach's disappointed voice asks from where he stands inside the locker room. With a bowed head and his hands resting on his hips, he doesn't yell. He simply asks us a question.

The room stays silent. No one risks moving from where we sit in the unfamiliar locker room. Slowly, he tilts his head as his eyes scan the room. Coach Campbell takes the opportunity to look at everyone. The disappointment is heavy in his eyes as guilt gnaws away at me. Running my hands down my face, I cringe as I hit the bruise on my jaw.

Who knew Grant could pack such a punch? The black and purple addition to my face has drawn all kinds of curious glances. When Coach asked me what happened, I had to tell another lie. Lie, lie, lie, it seems to be the only thing I know how to do.

"Because if it is, go ahead and leave your stuff in the locker room and board the bus. There are men in this room who would kill for the opportunity to be in your shoes. Tonight, you're playing against each other instead of standing beside your teammates and fighting together."

His speech continues as I glance around the room and find long faces mirroring mine. It's my fault we are playing like shit. I caused the dynamic shift, and I fucking hate it. Grant and I have to find a way to squash our issues if we want to salvage this game.

"All eyes are on you tonight, gentlemen. I've taught you all I can. I've prepared you for the battle, but it's up to you to win the war. The decision is yours. Will you go out there and let them walk all over us? Or will you fight like the Eagles I know you are?" A slow clap begins as Coach gives us one last parting motivation.

Harris joins Coach where he stands as the rest of us huddle around. "One more half! Thirty minutes to put it all on the line! Eagles on three! One. Two. Three!"

"EAGLES!" The roar echoes off the walls, vibrating the air around us. Gripping my helmet in my hand, I turn and am met with Harris standing in my face. He reaches a hand out to stop Grant from moving past us.

"You two work out your shit, or don't bother coming back out. I'm done with your bullshit affecting my team."

Grant's shoulders stiffen as he stares at Harris's hand pressing into his chest. The tension is palpable as Harris leaves the two of us, and everyone else funnels through the locker room. With one last glance, Coach Campbell leaves the locker room with a raised eyebrow and a shake of his head.

"Look, man," I start while Grant flinches at my voice. "I love her."

His molars grind together, and I'm surprised one doesn't crack because of how tense he's squeezing his jaw shut. As much as I love Bret, it's time I put it all on the line. I should have fought harder from the beginning to give him a heads-up.

He deserved that as one of my closest friends and a person I look up to. I should have respected him more. As awkward as it is to have a conversation about my relationship with my difficulty with words, it's the only way we can try to move on. It's time for a discussion with Grant—a brother to a brother.

"You're her brother, and you want what's best for her. I get it. I have a little sister, too. I know she was supposed to be off-limits, but she's never been a game to me. She's been through hell, and I'm not here to cause her any more pain. In fact, if I could take it all away for her, I would. She's it for me. Me, her, us, that's all I want."

I watch as he stares through me from where he stands opposite me. When I think the conversation will only be one-sided, he speaks up. "It's been four days, and I can't figure out why I'm so mad at you."

His blatant honesty takes me aback—shocked by his admission and his unexplained anger.

"Watching over Bret has always been my job. Growing up, my dad taught me the importance of being a big brother and how it was my duty to protect my little sister. From a young age, we've always been close. We played together, we fought together, we enjoyed each other. She was my first friend, my best friend.

"The more we traveled, the more our bond grew. She was the one constant I could count on in a life full of uncertainty. She was always there for me, just like I was there for her. As she started getting older, the protectiveness only intensified, especially when we got to high school, and I was surrounded by horny classmates who only wanted to fuck their way through school. And when I started hearing my sister's name come out of those douchebags' mouths, the more I wanted to guard her from the fuckboys who would only use her, lose her, and destroy her. Bret's always had a tough exterior, but her heart is too good to be hardened. She loves hard and is incredibly sensitive."

He pauses, taking a few deep breaths, and runs his fingers through his sweat-soaked hair. "You're exactly the type of guy who deserves my sister's love. You're loyal, care deeply, and protect the people you love by always putting their needs before yours. I've watched it on the field, with your family, and how you interact with strangers."

An onslaught of emotions comes over me as I feel a lump growing in my chest. With a fist, I rub circles over the spot near my heart.

"For the past three years, you have been a part of my life, a little brother I never had. I know I'm a grumpy fuck, but deep down, I'm just as sensitive as Bret." He pauses, pointing a finger at me. "And if you tell anyone that, I'll punch you again."

I huff out a laugh as he continues. "I think it hurt that you didn't respect me enough to come have this conversation man to man, friend to friend, *brother* to *brother*. It made me question if you were the good person I've always held you to be, and then I questioned if you were good enough for my sister."

"Fuck, Grant. I wanted to, but Bret was afraid. She begged me not to, and I don't keep secrets and lie to my family. But I promise you, I'll never hurt her. Hell, it has almost killed me this week seeing her so torn up over everything. Not to mention the fucker who's been terrorizing her life. You have no idea how badly I've wanted to track him down and end him."

A sarcastic chortle leaves his lips. "Yeah, I have *no idea* how badly you want to end him. Of course I do. She's the person I promised to protect, and I feel like I failed her. When she told me everything she's been through in the past year, the guilt I have for not pressing the issue last year is eating me alive."

I nod as I reach my hand out and wait for him to take it. "Are we good?"

"We're good, Riggsby." He grips my hand before pulling me in for a hug. As he claps my back, he whispers, "But if you hurt her, I'll end *you*."

The two of us run out of the locker room, through the tiled hallway and tunnel, as we make it out on the field with twelve seconds remaining before the start of the second half. Harris finds us first, his face stoic as he takes in the two of us.

"You two dickheads finally work your shit out?"

Grant nudges my shoulder as he places his helmet on his head. "Yeah, we're good."

It's like whiplash watching Grant's moods. Long gone is the sensitive, vulnerable man from the locker room. Grumpy Grant is firmly in place.

"Thank fuck. Let's go win back this game."

And win back the conference championship game is what we do.

"Woo-hoo!" Harris screams as he jumps on my shoulders. "We're back, baby!"

The spark that feeds the electricity between the team was ignited. The passion and excitement are back, and it feels damn good. For the last twenty-nine minutes and thirty-six seconds, we've worked our asses off as we fought tooth and nail to take control of the game.

With the touchdown throw Harris just threw me, we've taken a thirty-one to twenty-seven lead. With the momentum shift on offense, our defense has mirrored our enthusiasm. Now, all our defense has to do is keep the Jaguars from scoring in the last twenty-four seconds.

As the clock hits zero, multicolored confetti rains down from the ceiling as our marching band starts playing the fight song. After a rocky start, we persevered and came out on top. As wonderful as the high is from winning the game, a weight has been lifted after the conversation with Grant. We celebrate our win on the field for the next thirty minutes as the conference commissioner presents our team with the championship trophy.

Freshly showered, water droplets drip from my hair as I climb the steps to the charter bus waiting outside the stadium to take us to our hotel. Sliding out my phone, I'm met with several notifications.

Mom: Congratulations, sweetie! I'm so proud of you! Love you.

Saylor: Ahhh!! MVP and Champions?! Way to go, big brother!

Jett: Glad you pulled your heads out of your asses! Proud of you, little brother!

Scrolling through the messages, I search for "Rebel." My eyebrows pinch together when I don't find a new message from her. Our last messages are from when she wished me good luck, and I confirmed she was safe inside our locked apartment.

Fear coils as the terrifying notion that something could have happened to her. Ignoring the congratulations text from Cody, I fire off a text.

Me: Have you heard from Bret lately? She hasn't messaged me since before the game.

Cody Jacobs: Yes, she messaged me around halftime, saying she was calling it an early night and that all of the doors were locked.

Cody Jacobs: She's safe, bro.

My shoulders slump in relief as I pocket my phone. Only a few more hours until I'll be home with my girl, and we can start living the life we've been dreaming about...out in the open.

****

After our three-hour drive from Arlington, the guys and I arrived at the apartment around eleven thirty the following day. Most of the guys went out to celebrate last night, while I barely made it to my hotel room before crashing. Between the adrenaline rush and the anxiety from this week's events, I was mentally and physically exhausted.

"I think I'm going to sleep for a week," JP grumbles from behind me as we climb the three stories of stairs.

"Dude, finals week." Harris digs in his pockets for his keys.

"Man, forget finals." I wish I could forget finals. Instead, I'll be busy preparing for three back-to-back full days of exams today and tomorrow. But not before I take a nice long nap with my Rebel.

Harris has the door unlocked by the time JP and I drag our asses up the wooden stairs. Silence greets us, and I huff out a laugh. Rebel must be just as exhausted as we all are. Hell, I can't say I blame her. She's been through the wringer this week, and there's nothing more exhausting than being stuck inside your head.

Moving inside my bedroom, I placed my suitcase against the wall next to my bed and put my phone on the charger I forgot to bring with us.

"Riggsby." JP's panicked voice has me turning on my heels. "You're going to want to see this..."

His voice trails off as I stride down the hallway to where he waits next to the dining table. The corners of his eyes are softened and tilted down as he looks at me. I don't like the way he is watching me. His lips press together in a line as he exhales slowly. Pity is never a good expression to see on anyone's face. A piece of paper is held between his fingers.

With an outstretched hand, I take the sheet of notebook paper from his hands. Taking my time, I read the letter word for word.

My stomach plummets as I drop the letter. It floats to the ground while I take off running to Bret's door. Her white door is standing open, which is my first clue. Moving around her room, I look for Spalding—her basketball—if he's gone, she's gone because there's no way she'd leave him behind. Bending down, I search below her bed before flinging open her closet doors. Gaps with empty hangers capture my attention before I trail my eyes over her haphazard floor.

All the color drains from my face as my knees buckle. I don't fight the pull as I drop to the ground. A hand grips my shoulder, but I barely feel it. My heart has been ripped from my chest along with my soul.

She's gone.

Crew—

You've been a safe haven when I thought safe would never be in my vocabulary again. From the first late-night bowl of cereal, I knew my heart would belong to you if only I'd give it a chance. Once I did, I felt the moment our souls tethered together. I thought love would be enough because, Crew, I love you so fucking much.

I can't bear to witness the rift I've caused in your life. I showed up at your doorstep and interjected myself in your life and uprooted the family you've built here. It's killing me to know that I'm the reason for the animosity between you and the guys, and I can't let it continue.

By the time you read this, I'll already be gone. I know this is the coward's way of leaving, but I'm too weak to say this to your face. Fate brought us back together and maybe it will again. My heart will always belong to you, Crew Riggsby.

Love,

Your Rebel

CHAPTER 39
Bret

Crew: Rebel, come home. Baby, please, everything is going to be okay. Please just come back.

Crew: Good morning, beautiful. I feel like I'm living a nightmare with you gone. Nothing is the same without you. Please just talk to me.

Crew: Please just talk to me. Tell me how we fix this. I love you, Rebel.

JP: The apartment is a total sausage fest without you. Miss you, baby girl.

Tyler: Take the time you need to focus on yourself, Bret. You've been through a lot of dramatic shit. Prioritize your meditation and find your inner peace. I miss my cooking buddy.

Chloe: Hey, girlie. I'm here if you need anything. Love you!

Staring around the dark gray walls of my teenage room, I clutch the teddy bear I've had for years, seeking the comfort it once gave me as a scared child. I'm transported back to a time when my insecurities were less tragic. When my biggest concern was how many points I'd score in my basketball game or what we were doing Friday night after school.

Now I feel like a lost little girl trapped in the space that once offered me solace, haunted and at war with my inner demons. The quiet is needed to think, but it's only made those demonic voices louder. It's suffocating, squeezing my lungs in its powerful grip. My thoughts wage war with each other, swarming like angry bees, stinging my doubts with questions I can't answer.

Why did I run?

Why is that the only option I feel whenever my back's against the wall?

Am I truly worthy of being a part of something? Or will my dark cloud consume everyone it comes into contact with?

For the past however many months, I've surrounded myself with friends and a boyfriend who have embraced me—flaws and all—as they pulled me into their world. What if everything they've witnessed was only a façade, fooling them with a version of myself that didn't really exist?

The safety I felt with them, with *Crew*, and the warmth of belonging all feel like an illusion now.

Lying on my side, wrapped in a heavy dark purple blanket, I clutch my knees tighter to my body, squeezing my stuffed bear as my mind turns against me. Is this what my life is now? It is a constant cycle of questioning every decision and every moment of happiness I've felt, trying to decipher what's real and what's being twisted in my head.

Walking the streets in San Antonio, I felt free. With Crew by my side, as we navigated the small shops with our banter and endless conversations, that was real. There's no doubt in my mind that I was truly happy. For one afternoon, we escaped reality and got lost in each other. His eyes sparkled, and his smile beamed as his admiration for me radiated from him. It was real, I know it was, but why does my mind keep playing tricks on me?

I want so desperately to love Crew with every fiber of my being. He already owns my heart as our souls are tethered together. He makes me feel whole, safe, seen, and protected. What if my demons are too much? What if my dark thoughts suck his jovialness and kindness from his soul?

Now that the insecurities I've worked to keep out of my mind have resurfaced, I can't help but feel them take root, dig deeper inside my mind. Each passing thought of doubt of being unable to be loved, questioning my worthiness, and if I have the right to happiness only branches out as the dark thoughts water the intrusive thoughts spreading throughout my mind.

An endless loop of self-sabotaging thoughts keeps me from seeing clarity as my own fears cover me in a fog.

What if I'm destined to be alone, with safety being nothing more than an illusion?

The fear gnaws at my consciousness as I slowly slip into the darkness.

Finals week was hell. Not only were the exams brutal, but it's been a full week of isolating in the comfort of my parents' home. Again, embracing my inner coward as I avoid my apartment. I had every intention of running far away from Texas but as I shifted the Jeep into drive, my thoughts drove me to my parents' home. I guess I need to be surrounded by familiar walls in the comfort of my teenage room with my parents right down the hall.

Crew continues to call me every night and message me throughout the day as if nothing has happened between us. I know it's unfair to him to be ghosted, but I need space to process. I know that Grant and Crew patched things up at the football game, and if I had continued to watch, I would have seen the shift in their dynamic. As grateful as I was that those two worked through their issues, I couldn't go home. I wasn't ready to face the music, and I might have overreacted even though, at that moment, I felt justified.

I miss home. I don't know when I started considering a four-bedroom apartment on the outskirts of campus home, but that's what we've built. Video game tournaments and cooking dinner together—or observing everyone cook together.

Tears blur my vision as the weight crashes in on me. The ball of anxiety spreads, tightening my chest. Everything hurts. The pain I've caused feels insurmountable, and I don't know where to go from here. It feels like too much time has passed, and I'm scared to admit I should have stayed. I should have fought harder against my inner demons. I should have waited for Crew to come home so we could fix things together. Him, me, us, that's what we've been saying this entire time, and when I had the first opportunity to jump ship, I took it.

A soft knock sounds at the door, interrupting yet another spiral. The door opens with a soft creak as my mom pokes her head in, hesitating to answer. I watch as her eyes land on my tear-streaked face, her face softens as she gently moves toward me as if she's cornering a wild animal. With my rage and rollercoaster of emotions, she might as well be.

"Sweetie." Her voice drips with concern, and I can feel her heart breaking. Yet another person I've hurt this week. "Bret, sweetheart, please talk to me. I'm worried about you."

Her tone has the sob I've been fighting erupting in my chest as the tears flood my vision. The truth is I'm worried too. I'm scared these thoughts will never end. I'm scared I'll find myself on a bathroom floor with no one there to save me. No one talks about how hard life is, especially when the voices start talking.

"I'm worried too, Mom." She drops on the bed beside me, throwing her arms around me. The two of us sit in silence, allowing the weight of those words to settle over us.

"Baby, please talk to me. What is going on?"

For the first time, I spilled everything to my mom. I told her about a boy I thought I loved and how he broke every part of my being. His cunning words and sharp tongue broke me and left me in pieces. How he refuses to accept there is no "us" anymore and how he won't give me the peace I am desperate for.

As hard as it is to give her a glimpse inside my head, I rip the Band-Aid off and spill the gruesome details. For so long, I've struggled with a demonic voice that tells me I'm not worthy and that I'll never be good enough. On my darkest days, he nudges me closer to the end with his vile words that everyone will be happier if my burdens aren't weighing them down.

I explained to her that my first tattoo brought pain at a time when I was numb. With the first piercing of the needle, I felt myself coming back to life. I chose a butterfly because of how it symbolizes hope and resilience, representing all of my struggles with my mental health and how I'm going to emerge stronger.

I'm not worried about the disappointment of not fitting into her perfect box. I'm not worried she'll look at me differently or judge me. Right now, I need my mom to help carry the pain. No matter how hard I try to show how strong I think I am, I'm weak with the darkness swirling around inside me. I need to be free from the burden.

Silence falls over the room, my truth weighs heavy over us. The only sounds are from our sniffling noses. It feels like we sit there for hours as I process the relief I feel to finally let it all off my chest while my mom simply processes the devastation of my chaotic words. Reaching for a tissue, she wipes her damp cheeks before blowing her nose.

"I can't believe you've been facing this alone, Bret." There's no trace of disappointment or anger in her voice, only sadness. She moves, cupping my face as her thumbs wipe away tears. "Honey, we are always here for you. I can't imagine how scared you must've been."

The thing is, I haven't faced everything alone. Sure some days it feels like it's me against the world, but the other days I've had Olivia by my side and recently Crew. It's so easy to get swept up in the feeling of being alone, but maybe the fog is starting to lift. Maybe I'm starting to see things with clearer eyes. There have been two people consistently by my side throughout this fight, and I've been so wrapped up in my hell that I haven't given them enough credit.

"You've been through so much, and I hate that you've had to go through any of it. But it's okay to not be okay. It's okay to step back and say, 'Hey, I need a break.' Bret, honey, I want you to hear me—*really* hear me when I say this," she pauses, placing a comforting hand on my forearm. "Never feel like you are a burden. You're not alone in this, in life, *ever*. Let us carry some of the load and navigate these rocky waters. We love you, Bret Addison, so much."

The dam breaks as more tears flood my vision. Wrapping my arms around my mom, I cry into her waiting arms. I've wanted to hear that

I wasn't alone for so long. Even through our differences, she *saw* me. I've always known she loved me, that's never been a question, but sometimes those burdens have felt dismissed, and maybe that's how I've interpreted them. Today, with her, I don't feel so alone anymore.

"What's going on?" my dad's deep voice asks from my doorway.

"Does this mean you've finally told them why you transferred?" My brother's voice startles me. I wasn't expecting him to be here too.

Mom's head whips in his direction, nearly knocking me off the bed. "Grant Lucas Campbell, did you know?"

"I found out last week."

"Found out what?" Dad's eyes bounce from Grant's to where Mom and I sit on the bed.

Gripping Dad's shoulder, Grant nudges his head toward the hall-way. "C'mon, let's go to the living room, and she can fill you in while I share how we are going to put Bret's fucked-up situation to rest so we can get our girl back."

Heart warming, my shoulders soften as I gaze across the room at my big brother. Aside from his grumpy exterior, Grant is the biggest teddy bear. I laugh silently, wondering if that's why I've always cared so deeply about my little teddy bear. Maybe deep down, I've always associated Grant with a teddy bear and chose my comfort animal to symbolize my brother.

I hope one day he'll be able to leave his broody shell and find someone to love. He deserves it more than anyone I know.

Three hours later, our stomachs full from cheap, greasy delivery pizza, the four of us sprawl out across the living room couches. Grant lays across the smaller couch, his feet dangling over the armrest as he scrolls through the channels. I lean against Mom, the two of us sharing a blanket. A new aura surrounds us as fresh light has been shed on our relationship. We can only hope that it continues to grow strong. Dad relaxes in his recliner, which is *his*. No one is safe if he finds it occupied when it's time for him to sit. So possessive. He scrolls through his phone, typing away. A coach's job is never over.

After mindlessly scrolling for what feels like hours, Grant finally selects a movie. A soft melody fills the room as headlights appear on the screen. The car drives down a foggy road before transitioning into sunrise over miles of cornfields. *Hoosiers* is a family classic in our home, filled with nostalgic memories of Sunday evenings huddled around like we are tonight. Bowls of popcorn rested on our laps as Dad taught us the game of basketball.

As we wait for the actual movie to start, I can't help but chortle at the memory that pops into my head. Grant turns his head and quirks a brow at me, no doubt questioning if I've lost it. "Grant, do you remember that time we were walking through the fields with Dad in Indiana, and you lost your shit when that bug landed on your finger?"

A booming laugh flies from Dad's mouth as he sits in his chair. Grant, on the other hand, sits there shaking his head. "I was six and terrified of my own damn shadow."

"Which makes it even funnier." My shoulders shake uncontrollably as tears run down my face as the laughter consumes me. It feels great to be laughing like this after this past week. "You took off screaming in such a fit. When you finally calmed down, Dad asked you if it was a bug with a white wing and then convinced you your finger would fall off."

Dad's laughing so hard he's snorting while Mom's shoulders shake so violently I'm afraid they'll pop out of her sockets. I clutched my stomach, my abs burned like I'd done a hundred crunches.

"Assholes." Grant points to each of us. "Every last one of you."

A night in with my family was what I needed. As difficult as it was to share with them my troubles, I feel relieved to know I no longer have to hide anything from them.

When Grant filled my parents in on punching Crew and the whole debacle of everything leading up to the second half of the conference championship game, Dad was disappointed in Grant's behavior. While he appreciated Grant sticking up for me, he didn't appreciate how he went about it.

Mom and I talked about my relationship with Crew. It was the first time the two of us had sat and really talked about a boy I liked, or in this case, loved. With eyes full of warmth, Mom shared some of her journey with Dad. It wasn't as black and white as I had always assumed. But it's what she told me that has stuck with me.

"You deserve to be loved, Bret, with all your fears and insecurities. Don't let those fears stop you from embracing something that could bring you so much joy. It feels scary to give your heart over to someone to trust, protect, and nourish. I'm telling you it's okay to feel fear. You're not alone in life, my beautiful girl. Leap, honey, because when you do, you'll see how worthwhile it truly is."

I'm ready to take the leap and fall headfirst into the unknown with Crew Riggsby by my side. But first, I need to put an end to my past.

CHAPTER 40
CREW

Days run together as I spend my time floating through the motions—wake up, go to practice, come home, and sulk. Everything feels off without Rebel. Colors are dull, food is bland, and life is boring. Bret's smile lit up the sky and made life brighter. Every day feels like I'm navigating through quicksand, hoping that each step won't be the one to pull me under.

I'm stuck in an endless spiral of wondering if, by leaving a note, she was breaking up with me or needed space. What in the Ross and Rachel "we were on a break" hell am I living in?

Gray skies greet me as I leave this morning's practice. The drab color matches the emptiness I feel inside. A steady shower falls from the sky, and I let the rain fall over me as I leisurely walk to my truck. Halfway there, a voice calls out behind me.

"Riggs!" Glancing over my shoulder, Grant jogs toward me. Things have started returning to normal since our little heart-to-heart a couple of weeks ago. Dread creeps in the closer Grant comes.

No words are said as I stare at him or through him. It's really anyone's guess where my mind is. "She's at the rec center."

"What?"

"Bret's at the rec center. She was planning on being there for a few hours today."

I'm confused about why he's telling me this. Is he giving me his blessing to chase after his sister? Does she even want me there? With a terse nod, I turn on my heels, leaving him confused.

"She misses you, Crew."

Slamming my door shut, I sit silently as I try to process his words. If she missed me, then why is she ignoring me? Why did she run? And why won't she come home if she misses me so much?

Jamming my finger in the ignition, the truck fires to life as I tear out of the parking lot. It's been seventeen days since I've seen her. Seventeen days after being around her vibrant soul for one hundred and three days. Yes, I've counted the days I was fortunate enough to see her smile and those where darkness has surrounded me.

My chest is on fire as I drive the few minutes from the football facility to the rec center. I can't lose her. Not without fighting for her. But I'll let her go if she's truly ready to end things. She deserves to be happy, even if that means without me.

Mom always told us that if you love something, set it free, and if it comes back, then it was meant to be. I've always hated hearing that expression because it never felt soothing. Why would I want to set something free I loved?

I'm in a daze as I make my way through the quiet recreation center. Winter break has the campus feeling eerily vacant, as almost everyone has gone home for the four-week hiatus. A ball of anxiety clogs my lungs, and fire spreads through my body from the nerves of approaching Bret. She feels like a wounded animal who will either lash out or run in fear.

The sound of the dribbling basketball feels like the beat of my heart. Each thump beats against my ribs as dread drops into the endless pit of doom. Uncertainty swirls around me as I step through the doorway. I said I'd let her decision be whatever it was, but first, she needs to hear me out. Then I'll live with whatever choice she makes.

Bret is on the first court, dribbling with desperation as she pulls up for a jump shot. Following her shot, she races to the net, where she grabs the ball and dribbles with force to the opposite side of the key. She repeats the motion, never missing a shot. Her raw athleticism shines through with every dribble, every move, every shot. I watch her muscles work as she pushes them to a new test every time she grabs the ball. Her body moves in fluid tranquility, but I can see the pent-up energy she's forcing herself to release. It's in the sharp lines of her shoulders that gives her away.

"You just going to stand there and watch, or do you want to play?" Her voice interrupts me from where I'm admiring her. She clutches the ball with a hand on her hip and waits for my answer. Stripping out of my sweatpants, I toss them to the side before reaching behind my head and pulling off my hoodie one-handed.

With a nod, Bret shoves the ball across the court to me. Catching it, I bounce it a few times from where I stand as I get a feel for the grip again. I played basketball throughout middle and high school, but it's been years since I stepped onto a court. I've long since traded the round rubber ball for an oval pigskin.

Our eyes meet as I step onto the court, and a silent understanding passes through us. She needs this—an outlet to expunge her inner workings from inside her. The pain. The fear. The destruction.

Dribbling to the spot between half-court and the three-point line, I bounce the ball to her. Catching it between her hands, she holds it to her chest before firing the ball back to me.

"Use me." The words leave my lips, deep and husky, while her eyes squint with confusion. "Take it out on me, Rebel. Work your shit out on me. *Use. Me.*"

Settling in her defensive stance, Bret squares up as she waits for me to make the first move. With the ball checked up, I jab to the right before driving to the left side. Her steps falter as surprise flicks across her determined face with my decision to go left when it's my weaker side. Only in basketball, it's my preferred side.

With each shuffle across the floor, Bret's eyes shine with a tenacity and ferocious challenge, almost as if she was daring me. Pulling up outside of the key, I shoot the basketball and watch with surprise as it banks off the backboard and lands through the hoop. Bret's wide-eyed gaze finds mine as she jogs to retrieve the ball.

That's right, baby, I'm full of surprises too.

Bret jogs to the top of the court, her shoulders tight, and I can almost hear the gears turning in her pretty mind. Bouncing the ball to me, I feel the frustration in the zip of the pass. A tight set to her jaw has me fighting the grin, desperate to escape as competitiveness rushes through me. This game was different, though. It isn't about the hustle of the gridiron but putting my heart on the line for her. I am here for her, willing to put my body through the wringer to prove I'm not going anywhere. The long run is here, and I'm sprinting to the finish with her by my side. No matter how hard she fights against me, I'm not backing down.

Determination seeps from her as she lowers her shoulder, driving into me as she moves toward the basket. Fumbling backward, I let her use me just as I instructed. Bret's body is a blur as she vents her inner turmoil with each bump into me as I refuse to back down.

You're going to need to try harder than that, Rebel.

If this is what she needs to feel alive and free, then I'll welcome every bruise she gives me.

Her jaw clenches tight as she goes up for a layup. Stretching out as she brushes into me and drives her strong body through mine, my fingers graze the ball, blocking it. With a thud, it lands out of bounds. Frustration radiates off of her. Bret slams the ball with two hands to the ground, and she roars a curse as if the word was ripping through her chest.

The two of us continue our back-and-forth game. Sweat pours down our bodies as if we were dancing in the rain. Frustration bubbles inside her like a tea kettle about to boil over. Bret drives toward me again, and her dribbling intensifies with each push. With even more focus, resembling the defensive backs I'm used to blocking, Bret explodes with more force, grit, and tenacity.

What do you have inside you, Bret?

Refusing to push back, I absorb the hit and feel her electric charge pass through me, sending a charge across my limbs. This is what I wanted—for her to use me and allow me to be her outlet, her punching bag. This pickup game was never *just* a game; it was a battle, a war against her mind.

Her chest heaves as she spins and fights to create space between us.

I'm done giving you space, Rebel. If you want it, you've got to work for it.

As if she could read my mind, I see the storm roll over her eyes as the thundering sound of her heart fueled her to exert herself. I match her step for step as she dribbles around the lane before regrouping.

Standing up slightly from my defensive stance for the briefest second, Bret smirks as she takes advantage of my weak point. Her shoulder lowers as she drives through me and barrels down the lane. I'm hot on her tail as I work to make up the distance.

But I'm too late.

Powering off her right foot, Bret drives through her body, her pain fueling her momentum as she releases the ball with one hand. I watch from where my legs pause as the ball hits the top corner of the painted-on square and it lands perfectly through the orange hoop.

Swish.

The sound of the net makes Bret bend over as she rests her hands on her knees. Head hanging, chest heaving, the sound of her sobs breaking through the quiet gymnasium. Slowly, I approach her before dropping to my knees in front of her. Trailing a soft touch down her cheeks, I gather the moisture of falling tears.

"Rebel."

Her eyes snap to mine, red-rimmed and pooled with tears. No more words are said as we continue to stare at each other.

Even without words, I can feel the cathartic release the game has brought her. If this were the end of us, at least I would know I gave her this. I could help carry the load for a short time when the world felt too heavy for her shoulders.

Bret's emerald eyes feel like home as I stare at her. Soaking in every single detail. The gold flecks around her green irises, the freckles spread over her flawless face, and her plump lips I've kissed so many times. Everything around us has faded away.

It's just her and I.

The game was never a game to us. It was always something more profound. A way to prove our connection, loyalty, and unspoken bond that called to each other last Christmas. It's been almost a year since she stepped foot into my life. Three-hundred and sixty days of waiting for the time when I got to call her mine.

Bret Campbell is the other half of my soul.

Our destiny was forged long before we met. It's as if the universe has always known we are meant to be. Everything in our lives has been a stepping stone to our union.

And in a blink, everything changed.

"I love you, Rebel." The words are soft as her eyes widen, and we both rise to our full height. I reach my hands out, nearly chest to chest until they cup her slender, delicate jaws. "I love you more than I have the words for. You're hurting, and I wish I could take it all away. If I could reach inside your beautiful head, I would pluck out each negative thought that is tearing down my girl. I would rip apart every person who dared to hurt the woman I love. I would destroy the world and never blink twice if only I could have my Rebel back."

Tears stream down her pretty face as a rope tightens around my lungs, forcing the air out as fear and insecurity creep in. Words have never been my strong suit. Confessing how I feel has always been a challenge as I struggle to relay my thoughts in a way that makes sense to others. But today, I'll try. I reach inside my soul and will the words to come to the surface. I take my last shot to bring my girl home to me.

"From the moment we looked at each other, I felt a connection to you. It's as if your soul called to mine. You being here felt like we had a real shot at pursuing my feelings, that spark whenever I'm around you. Watching the light come back in your eyes has been a blessing to witness. Your heart is pure, your mind brilliant, and your energy addictive."

Clearing the emotion from my throat, I run my thumbs over her cheeks, wiping away the tears. My chest cracks as I watch her cry.

"You've been through unimaginable things no one should ever have to endure. You've trusted and been burned, but I promise with all of my being, you can trust me with your heart. I'll protect you. I'll worship you. I'll never stop proving how much I love you and how lucky I am to have you in my life. Let me carry some of the load. Let me love you, Bret. Please come home."

Her expression flickers with a thousand unspoken emotions, a mixture of shock, love, and something deeper, more conflicted. Her swollen lips part, and I wait for the words to come, but they never do. It's as if she's at war with her heart and her mind. The emerald-green eyes I love to admire blink rapidly as she fights to keep the tears at bay. Her movements never sway as she stands firmly in place, not giving anything away.

The love is there—I feel it and see it in her softened gaze.

But it's not enough.

I see the tension in her shoulders as the war rages and her mind wins. A cold chill sweeps through me as if she's reached inside and ripped out my beating heart. The same heart that only beats for her. Bile rises as I fight the nausea of being vulnerable. For opening my heart and spilling my soul, I know I've lost her even before she says anything.

Bret glances away briefly, and when her gaze finds mine again, it's filled with sadness as she steps back. My hands slip from her face as I'm desperate to feel her again. Fingers twitching as she slowly pulls away, creating space between us as I realize she's not ready. She needs more time—time I didn't want to give her—but if I want her, and I do, I have to give her space to continue her journey. I can only hope she doesn't forget about me along the way.

"I love you, Crew. I love you so much," she chokes over her emotions. "But I have to put my past to rest. I can't move forward with you if I'm afraid of my own shadow. I have to end it."

"Let me help you."

Her face softens, giving me a pitying smile that I hate. "Thank you for offering, but I have to do this alone. I promise I'll come back to you when I'm free."

I stand there in an empty gymnasium as I watch the girl I love turn on her heels, grab her things, and rush out of the door. She never looks back. And I'm stuck wishing to go back in time. To a time when only we were there, wrapped in each other's arms, tangled in my bed.

Gathering up the pieces of my shredded heart, I take the first step forward.

The first step without her.

CHAPTER 41
Bret

The last forty-eight hours have been the longest two days of my life. After Crew showed up at the court, and we played our dueling one-on-one game, I left with an emotional hangover. The numbness threatened to consume me, but I pushed with all my might to keep my head above water. Crew's confession played on a loop in my mind. The sincerity in his words and the vulnerability in his voice meant everything to me. Each time my fingers twitched to pick up the phone to call him, something held me back like an invisible wall made of everything I hadn't resolved yet.

Telling Crew I needed more time and couldn't go home with him nearly destroyed me. The look of mourning that crossed his beautiful features nearly had me crumbling to the ground at his feet and begging for forgiveness. I wanted to take back everything and pray for him to welcome me home, but I knew I had to end things with Chad. I had to fight for my freedom, and I hoped Crew would still be waiting for me when everything was finished.

I wanted desperately to tell him my plan, but fear kept the words inside in case anything went off script. I didn't want to get his hopes up only to have them crash down around him, especially with the team leaving for Vegas to play in their bowl game.

When the silence became deafening, I kept telling myself to keep pushing forward. Even though I was causing him pain, it was pain I hoped he would forgive me for later. When the dust settles, it will only be him and me—the two of us for the rest of time.

Glancing at my phone, I realize I've probably missed the entire first quarter of the bowl game. My flight from Arizona to Vegas was delayed. Not to mention, the airports were packed with people traveling for Christmas.

Who plans a bowl game two days before Christmas?

After quickly stopping at the hotel to drop off my luggage, I hopped in the waiting rideshare to Allegiant Stadium. The good thing about arriving late to the game is the line to get in is practically nonexistent—crowds of fans mill around outside, where tents and merchandise trailers are set up. Mascots and blow-up animals line the sidewalk as small bands entertain the crowd so that those in attendance can watch the game on the outside screens.

Scanning my mobile ticket, I pass through security, where my clear bag is checked, and I place my VIP badge around my neck. Climbing the stairs, I open the entry doors as I rush into the stadium. But as soon as I step inside the black interior, I'm taken aback. Jaw slackened, I take in the incredible entry. A gigantic chandelier hangs in the sky, its lights glimmering. The black and white, modern interior feels more like an art exhibit than any football stadium I have ever entered.

As eager as I am to get to my seat, I allow myself a few minutes to walk around the stadium and thoroughly soak in the magnitude of such a venue. Walking down one hallway, black wallpaper with metallic shapes and designs line the walls as it leads to an open space with windows overlooking the Vegas strip. Casinos and resorts shine, coming to life in the night light. Following a crowd of people, I stumble across a hallway, which is, in fact, an art gallery. Portraits hang from the walls, each giving an art deco vibe. Huffing a laugh, I can't believe I'm at a game in this stadium.

The announcer announces the end of the second quarter, and I take that as my cue to find my mom. Before the halftime rush escapes their seats, I hop into the first concession line I see. With a giant pretzel and a large Coke in hand, I push through the crowd until I find the section behind our bench near the fifty-yard line. She's sitting among the crowd near the center of the field. The perk of your dad being a coach is you are given great seats. Other wives and family members circle her, but there's an empty seat next to her reserved for yours truly.

Scooting my way down the row, I plop into the chair with an exasperated sigh, startling her. "Bret, sweetie, you made it."

"Barely," I grumble around the mouthful of pretzel I couldn't resist any longer. "Traffic was a bitch."

She side-eyes me but doesn't scold me for cussing. It looks like we are both letting things go today. "How did everything go in Arizona?"

"It went as planned. Hopefully, everything is taken care of."

"That's great, sweetie. Couldn't talk Olivia into coming?"

"Oh no, I think her days of football are over. Besides, she officially has a chair as a tattoo artist at the shop, and her waiting list is over a year long. I don't see her taking any extra time off any time soon."

"Well." Mom pauses as I chuckle at her expression. I can tell she's struggling with what to say next. "Good for her."

Nudging her shoulder, I laugh out loud. "C'mon, Mom, what do you say we fly to Arizona and get ourselves matching tattoos? Hell, I bet Liv knows someone in Vegas who can hook us up. A friend of a friend sort of thing."

Scoffing, she shakes her head, eyeing me as if I'm on drugs. "Over my dead body. Did all that altitude go straight to your head?"

Shrugging, I take another huge bite of the delicious pretzel and savor the salty dough. Glancing at the big screen, I finally take in the score, mentally scolding myself for not checking sooner. The Eagles are up seventeen to seven.

"You look good, Bret."

"Thanks, Mom," I say, leaning my head on her shoulder. "I feel good."

"Happy?"

A smirk tilts my lips. "Hopefully, by the end of the game."

"He's playing an excellent game. One of those touchdowns is his."

Sitting back up in my seat, I smile as I stare out at the field, willing the time to go faster. Not that he has any reason to, but a part of me hopes he'll look this way when he runs back onto the field. I want him to know I'm here. I'm here for him.

The halftime entertainment runs off the field. I didn't even pay attention. I was too busy with what was happening in my head and my conversation with Mom. The lights flash in theatrics as the announcer announces the CTU Eagles as they run out of the tunnel. Placing my drink in the cup holder attached to the back of the seat, I stand with the crowd, clapping and cheering.

Dad glances in our direction as he flashes Mom a wink. His attention slides in my direction, and a smile spreads across his face. He gives a subtle wave. Warmth spreads through me, and for the first time in nearly a month, I feel excited for the first time in a long time. As much as I've loved my time at CTU it was always shadowed with the fear of the unknown. Now that that fear has been resolved, a weight no longer blinds me. I feel free and allowed to dream for the future.

In thirty minutes, my future will feel the same way.

Hopefully.

"Block! Block! Block!" I scream on my feet as I watch Crew protect the passing game as my brother runs down the field, the football clutched between his arm and body. He makes it fifteen yards before he comes down on the twenty-yard line.

Time moves in slow motion as we work hard to hold our lead. The team is playing like a well-oiled machine, everyone is gelled and in sync. This is how they're supposed to play. It's so different from how they played in the conference championship game—well, the first and only part I watched.

Dad glances up briefly as he looks for Mom. It's as if she's the calm to his storm, his breath of fresh air in a time of chaos.

"Time needs to move faster," I grumble as I sit, placing my hands underneath my thighs to keep them from shaking with nerves.

"Relax, it'll all work out."

"How do you stay so calm?"

"At the end of the day, it will all work out." A warm smile spreads across her face as she looks at me. "If you're going to be with a man who loves football as much as your father and has the opportunity to play professionally, you need to learn to keep calm. When their world feels like it's on fire with pressure, you need to be the one they lean on. Be the calm to their storm, sweetie. Remind Crew that no matter what, you love him for *him*. Not him as a player or him as a coach or whatever he may be. Your love for him matters at the end of the day."

I hum. "I was just comparing you to Dad's calm to his storm in my head. And why did you throw Crew into the mix?"

She pats my leg. "Oh, sweetie, even someone who is blind could see how much you two love each other."

Cheering from the crowd has both of us turning our attention to the field. Standing in the end zone, Grant throws his arms in the air in the touchdown signal as Crew sprawls on the field, his toes still in bounds. Jumping to my feet, I scream as I watch the replay on screen. The guys celebrate with claps on the helmet and shoulder pads as they jog off the field, passing the special teams.

The extra-point kick is good as the Eagles take a thirty-one to seventeen lead with a minute remaining. In a matter of sixty seconds, the Eagles will be winning a bowl game.

"Go." Quirking my brows, I stare at my mom. "Go to the gate and show the security guard your badge. Be on the field with him. Tell him how you feel and celebrate this win with him, *together*."

Blinking rapidly, I stare at the lights as I wish the tears away. Throwing my arms around her shoulders, I pull my mom in for a hug. "Thank you for everything, Mom."

"I'm always here for you, Bret. *Always*."

"I love you."

"I love you, too." She pulls away, a tear streaking her face. "Now go get your happily ever after."

Standing from my seat, I move through the fans as I fight the rush of people leaving. Excusing myself through the crowd, I finally find the gate for where I can get on the field as the final seconds tick off the clock. Red fireworks shoot out of the endzone before multicolored confetti shoots from cannons.

The guard finally lets me on the field, and once again, I find myself moving through chaos. Scanning the field, I keep bouncing my eyes back and forth for number eighty-eight.

Pushing through bodies, I feel him before I see him.

Glancing up, I find familiar mocha eyes staring back at me through the masses of football players and media members.

Nibbling on my lip, I fight to keep the grin from covering my face as I make the trek to him. His eyes never leave mine. It's not until I'm standing before him that I realize I have no idea what I will say to him.

He stands there, sweat dripping down his handsome face as he holds his helmet in his hands.

"Hi." The words come out sheepishly, and I mentally palm my forehead. Seriously, after everything, I'm going to start with "hi."

Dropping his helmet to his feet, glove-covered hands cup my cheek as he pulls my face to his. Luscious lips find mine in a searing kiss, and I melt.

Crew Riggsby feels like home.

CHAPTER 42
CREW

As the final whistle blows, I jump with my teammates on the sideline as we celebrate one last victory together.

It's crazy to think that after three years of playing together, I'm saying goodbye to teammates who feel more like brothers. Goodbyes are the worst. They're so definitive, so final. As if there isn't modern technology and travel to allow us to see each other. It isn't the same.

The thrill of winning helps ease that ache, especially when we played such a great last game together. This is how we should have been playing. We had chemistry among the team. Gone was the animosity and drama. Tonight, we went out there and played our game.

Turning to run out onto the field and celebrate with my team, I'm hit with a compulsion to look to my left. I can't explain it, but my gaze moves from straight ahead of me toward where my team is running off the field to the sidelines.

That's when I see *her*.

Dodging bodies and searching the sea of faces, she moves through the crowd as confetti falls around her. Pieces stick to her hair and skate down her face, but they never once deter her from the mission she's on. Standing in place, I mentally will her to look up.

Dazzling emerald-green eyes land on mine, and there is an explosion in my chest. The lights shine brighter, the noise is louder, and my heart beats faster.

She's here.

With tentative steps, she erases all the space between us. No one obscures her view when she's standing in front of me. That's when I see what she's wearing. Standing before me is Bret Addison Campbell, wearing *my* jersey. It is a custom jersey, no doubt made by Macy. One side of the jersey is white with a navy eight, and the other side is powder blue with a red eight. I can only assume the back has my last name on it, and the thought of her wearing my last name sends a warm fuzzy feeling deep into my marrow. The idea of making her mine, giving her my last name, makes me feral.

Her eyes bounce between mine, and I wait with bated breath for her to say something. *Anything.*

"Hi." The words come out sheepishly, and I smile at her nervousness. Only she has nothing to be nervous about. She's *here.* That's all that matters.

Dropping my helmet to my feet, my glove-covered hands cup her cheeks as I pull her face to mine. Desperate to taste her, I place a searing kiss on her succulent lips. She melts into my touch, and everything feels right in the world. Cameras flash around us, and I don't even care if they capture hundreds of pictures. I no longer have to hide this woman behind closed doors.

"Woohoo!" A shout comes from beside us.

She pulls away, a grin splitting her perfect lips as she shyly tucks her face into my chest. Wrapping my arms around her, I pull her in close as I find a smiling JP and Harris. Their bodies close in on us as they jostle us around.

"The squad's all here!" JP shouts as Bret chuckles. "Welcome back, baby girl!"

"It's good to be back."

The guys get off us as she takes a step back. She flicks her hands toward the field. "Go, celebrate! Congratulations on winning!"

"Glad our lucky charm was back in the stands." Harris winks at her before he and JP jog off.

"I'm really glad my lucky charm was here."

A blush fills her cheeks as she smiles up at me. "I love you, Crew."

Fuck, those three words. Those are the three words I've been so desperate to hear.

"I love you, too, Rebel."

"Go celebrate with the boys. I'll be waiting for you in your hotel room." She flashes me a devilish look. All of the blood starts to rush to my dick as visions of what I'm going to do to her tonight flash in my head.

"Gross." Grant moves up beside us as he flings his arm over Bret's shoulders. "Now that you two have worked out your shit, I do *not* want to hear about you defiling my sister. But I am glad to see you both smiling again."

Bret pushes her brother off of her and toward me as she practically demands we go onto the field. The confetti has settled, and boxes are being brought out with Vegas Neon Light Show Championship hats and shirts.

Two hours later, I'm swiping my hotel key and pushing through the door to a waiting Bret. Standing at the large window that overlooks the strip with a beer bottle dangling from her fingers is a freshly showered Bret. Her long black hair hangs damp down over her shoulders, giving me the perfect view of my last name on her back. She slipped my jersey back on, which hangs mid-thigh, exposing her long, smooth legs.

Tossing my bag to the floor, I stride across the carpet as she watches me from over her shoulder. With her back to my front, I pull her in tight as I pepper kisses down her neck as she sighs into my touch.

"Crew," she moans as she tries to turn in my arms. I know what she wants to say next.

Sucking the soft flesh into my mouth, I bite down, and she gasps. "Sex first, then talk."

She nods, and I allow her to turn toward me. I press her against the wall as she shivers against the cool glass. Her lips find mine as she runs her fingers through my damp hair and pulls me closer to her. Our mouths open, and my tongue slides through her lips. Both of us are hungry with desire and longing as I devour her mouth. I taste the hoppy ale on her tongue, hungry for more. My cock jerks in my sweats, growing harder with each of her flicks across my tongue.

It's been weeks since I've touched her, tasted her, fucked her, and I'm desperate to have the woman I love. She moans in my mouth, holding me closer to her as she plays with the hair at the base of my neck.

I never want to go without her touch.

My hands trail down the backs of her thighs as hunger roars through me. Gripping her thighs, she jumps in my arms as I carry her to the bed. A desperation to taste her rips through me as I gently toss her onto the mattress, where she bounces. Her hair flies around her as she lets out a giggle.

"You look sexy in my jersey, baby." I lean over the bed and kiss her lips before trailing open-mouthed kisses down her neck, over the seam of her jersey, and her flat stomach as I push the material out of the way. Her bare pussy greets me, and my eyes roll at the sight.

The "lucky you" tattoo stares up at me, and I can't help but think about how true that ink is. I am damn lucky to be hers. Skating the hand that is on her stomach, I grip the jersey and continue pushing it up.

"As hot as it is to see you in my jersey with my name on your back, I need to see you. All of you." Bret leans forward, helping me remove the stretchy fabric, and we toss it somewhere behind me. I groan as I stare down at her exposed body. I take in every inch of her in her perfect form. My lips wrap around a pointed bud as I flick the metal barbell through her dusty rose-colored nipple. The piercing still drives me wild.

She whimpers, and I feel her try to close her legs. I tsk as I grab her bare pussy, and I suck her breast further into my mouth. I'm a man obsessed as I feel her silky skin beneath my touch. I'm desperate to taste her, to worship her entire body all night long.

My fingers skim through her slit, she's soaked. Desperate for my touch. Her nipple frees from my lips with a pop. "Is all of this for me?"

"All of it. Touch me, Crew."

I hum as I bring my arousal-coated fingers to my lips. Sucking her taste off, I moan as my eyes roll. My mouth fucking waters for her. It's been way too long since I ate this pretty pussy, and I'm starving. Placing a knee on the bed, I climb over her legs before settling between them. I drop my face, hovering just above her opening as my eyes look up at her.

Our gazes lock as I watch her eyes darken with desire.

"Crew." She wiggles her hips, pushing her pussy closer to my face.

"Greedy girl."

"Stop teasing me. It's been so fucking long."

Her chest heaves at the anticipation of what's to come, and a smirk plays on my lips. Squinting, her glare turns serious. When she starts to open her mouth, I flatten my tongue and run it through her slit before swirling it across her clit.

"Fuck, Crew." Her words are drawn out around a moan.

It's the sexiest sound in the world, and my cock hardens to granite as her hands find my hair. The ache to grip my cock washes over me, and I wish I could wrap my fist around it while I taste her. There's something about eating Bret's pussy that turns me ravenous as her sweet taste hits my tongue.

With her hands fisting my hair, she glides her pussy up and down my tightly shaved beard seeking friction. Glancing up, I watch her closed eyes as her lips part before she bites down on her lower lip. A hand leaves my head and finds its way to her breast, where she begins massaging it before pulling on her nipple. The sensation spurs her on as she rides my face. Her back arches as I flick her clit before I lap up every drop of her wetness before plunging my tongue inside her.

"Oh goddd," she moans as she pushes my face further into her pussy. I chuckle at her greediness for more. My quiet girl has turned into a ravenous rebel with her insatiable need.

Her legs quake against my head, and I know that her release is close. Removing my tongue, I lick my way up to her clit. Using my lips, I suck her clit into my mouth. Her deep moan reverberates off the walls as she screams something indecipherable. Eating her faster, she grinds her hips against my face as I lap at her.

"Mmm, I'm so close. Right there, Crew. Right there!"

"I need you to come all over my face, Rebel," I tell her.

Giving sloppy kisses to her pussy as her hips buck off the bed. With a hand across her hips, I hold her in place while I devour her. Her pussy pulses against my tongue as she gets wetter, letting me know she's on the precipice.

She screams my name as my cock screams for his release as she comes all over my face. Glancing up, I watch her watch me lick and suck her sensitive bundle of nerves as she falls over the edge. Her orgasm takes control of her body as she shudders with her release.

"Fuck, I missed you."

"I missed you too." Her words are breathy as her chest heaves and her eyes droop.

She leans up on her elbows as a wicked gleam lights her face. "Get on your back, baby. It's my turn."

Collapsing in a heap of limbs, our chests heave as we both come down from our orgasms for the third time. Dark hair splays over the white pillow as I move to untangle my legs in the sheets spread haphazardly around the bed. Bret plays with the smattering of blonde hair at my waist. Everything feels right with her by my side.

As I hold her close, I realize that, just like in the game, my job is to cover the pass protection—shielding her not just from the world but also from the dark thoughts that creep in, protecting her from the battles she fights in her own mind, and guarding our future together.

No matter where life takes us, one thing I know for sure is that we'll do it together.

CHAPTER 43
Bret

4 Months Later

Standing in front of the mirror, I admire my reflection one last time before we have to leave for graduation. The black fabric clings to me, hugging every curve just right. The ruching and slight slit add a touch of texture, drawing my eyes down to where my dress flares into a playful mini skirt. I adjust the wider straps until they're sitting in the correct spot on my shoulders, providing a comfortable fit that contrasts beautifully with the elegant square cut of the neckline. I take a deep breath, feeling the soft fabric against my skin, and know this dress was made for moments like this—where I need to look and feel my best.

Four months have gone by in a blink. Between classes and assignments, the second semester has been hard to keep up with anything outside of schoolwork. Sunday dinners were few and far between. Brynn moved in the middle of December, placing the first hole in our group. But a few weeks later, their baby girl, Cleo, was born a few weeks early. Once baseball season began, Chloe traveled with the team for the second year as the lead reporter for the school's newspaper. The guys on the team were busy with the start of their new baseball season.

With the beginning of the end, the guys and I started our own traditions. We spent more nights in with video game tournaments and junk food. The four of us settled into a new norm. Instead of Sunday dinners with all of our friends, it was a takeout night where, each week, we would try a new restaurant. A lot of times, Grant would join us, too.

One thing that hasn't changed is Crew and I's dedication to each other.

After our celebration that night in Las Vegas, we spent the rest of the night rehashing my mental health break and where we went from there. I explained to him the plan my family and I created with the help of Grant's friend. With the help of campus police, we worked with local law enforcement to obtain a restraining order, and I described how I flew to Tucson to sign copies and give my statement. When the police arrived to inform Chad, he practically shit his pants from nerves. What he thought was harmless was never that for me. When the authorities threatened jail time, he wept in the interrogation room. I watched behind one-way glass and felt relief as the weight was lifted.

Chad was no longer our problem.

"Now that that mess is taken care of, what should we do for the rest of the night?" he asked, kissing my temple.

"I'm not sure if I can go again, Crew. I'm a little sore."

"Wanna go get married? We're in Vegas, after all?"

My booming laughter fills the room as I poke him in the side. "I am not pulling a Quinton and Brynn and eloping with you. Besides, I want a better proposal than that."

Rolling over top of me, Crew places his elbows on either side of my face, resting his weight. Leaving a smattering of kisses over my face, he stares down at me. "Don't worry, Rebel. When I propose to you, you'll know it's a real proposal."

"When?"

"Yeah, baby. When. I can't wait to put my ring on your finger and call you my wife."

I hum. "Say it again."

"My wife."

"Okay, let's go get married now."

"Patience."

I smile at the memory as a knock sounds from my door. "Damn, baby girl. You clean up well."

"Thank you." Turning, I take in JP as he stands in the doorway dressed in navy dress pants, a white button-down, and a navy and light blue striped tie. "You look handsome, JP."

Tears well in my eyes as I stare at my roommate. We'll watch him graduate in a few short hours as he moves on to bigger and better things. I arrived with a brother when I stepped foot at Central Texas University. Now, I've gained a whole family of brothers and sisters. It's crazy where life can take you.

"We've got to get going if you're riding with me." I nod, slipping into the black pumps I pulled out for the day.

Cocking my head, I stare up at him from where I'm clasping my shoes. "Why is it always you getting me?"

"Those two fuss over their hair too much."

"I think they're worse than me."

His eyes widen as he nods. Reaching for my purse, I follow JP to the living room, where the other two emerge. Everyone looks dapper—Harris in his dark-brown dress pants and a cream and deco-printed shirt. Crew wears black slacks that hug his thick thighs and a tailored white button-down. I feel his gaze as he takes in my outfit like I did him.

Stepping closer, Crew places a strand of hair behind my ears before leaning in. "You look breathtaking."

My cheeks heat as he places a chaste kiss on my temple. A soft smile tips the corner of my lips.

Reaching into my purse, I pull out my cell. Tapping the camera icon, I shout. "Roommate selfie!"

With a few groans, the guys all close in around me as I take a picture of the four of us.

"One more," JP adds as I lower the camera.

With it hoisted in the air, I adjust the angle. As I go to click the screen, the three of them all plant kisses on the sides of my head. I laugh, and tears well in my eyes.

"My favorite," I whisper as I look at the image.

It is *hot* inside the Central Texas Athletic Center as we wait for the graduation ceremony to conclude. I fan my face with the program as I scan over the graduates sitting in the center of the room, all dressed in navy caps and gowns.

As the keynote speaker concludes his speech on resilience and hope, he encourages the graduates to reflect on their journey at CTU and the time spent getting to this momentous day. Crew's arm stretches behind my seat as he rubs my bare shoulder with his thumb. Chills run through my spine, and goose bumps cover my skin. Tilting my head, I rest it on his shoulder.

"I'm glad my journey brought me to you."

"I love you, Rebel."

"I love you, too."

My mom smiles at us from beside me while my dad glares at Crew. He likes to act as if he's not okay with our relationship, but he's given Crew his blessing. The two met to discuss their roles on and off the field and their dynamic going forward.

Applause fills the large space as the speaker finally wraps up his speech. The moment we've all been waiting for is finally here. The graduates stand row by row, and each name is announced as they walk across the stage.

"Grant Campbell." Clapping, I watch my big brother move across the stage, shaking hands, before accepting his diploma. Pride swells in my chest as I watch my best friend achieve a degree, which puts him one step closer to chasing his dreams.

As Grant faces the audience, his eyes skim the crowd, looking for the section I texted him. I can't help but reminisce on our time together growing up. Days of playing superheroes with our dress-up capes and creating our own professional football games in the backyard. He's always been there for me, including me in his games and watching over me. Our time together is coming to an end. I couldn't be more proud of the man he's become, and no matter where life takes us, I'll always be in his corner, cheering for him.

Crew and I watch the speaker announce Cody, JP, Hudson, Cody's roommate, and Chloe. I feel so much excitement as I watch them take the first step of their future. Our lives will all take us to different places, and while it will be hard, I know we'll always have each other. The bat signal will fly whenever someone needs us. Because the thing is, the bond created in this family is stronger than whatever life will throw at us.

We're tethered together.

As the ceremony closed, Crew held my hand as we navigated the crowd. We moved toward the exit, where we told Grant we would meet him.

"That will be us next year." Crew muses in my ear.

"I can't wait."

"Oh yeah? What are you looking forward to most?"

"Silo Bay."

His head whips in my direction. "What'd you say?"

"Silo Bay." I chuckle. "You've got a farm to take care of, and I will have endless walks along Lake Drummond in the future."

"Are you saying you want to live in Silo Bay after graduation?"

"After graduation. After a few years of watching you play in the NFL. Whichever." His mouth is slack as he stares at me. It's as if I've short-circuited his brain. "I want to create a life with you in Silo Bay."

"Rebel, I fucking love you."

The bright sun bearing down on us as we step out onto the concrete interrupts our conversation. I dig through my purse for sunglasses, and my phone buzzes against my hand.

Brynn: Tell my best friends happy graduation!!

Me: Will do!

"Hey, Crew." He turns from where he is in conversation with my dad. "Did you hear Savannah's name?"

He shakes his head as I type another message.

Me: Did Sav not walk?

Brynn: Grant didn't tell you?

Brynn: She had to withdraw this semester. She'll be back next year for one semester!

Locking my phone, I drop it into my purse. I am curious as to why she had to drop out, and it runs through my head. I don't have much time to dwell on it before Grant walks toward us, gown partially unzipped and a diploma sleeve in his hand.

"Congratulations, sweetie!" Mom yells as she wraps him in a hug. Dad follows her with a handshake before pulling him into a hug.

"You did it!" I say, throwing my arms around my big brother. "I'm so proud of you, G."

"Thanks, sis. I guess I'll have to rely on Crew to look after you next year."

"Yeah, right. You know your ass is staying to help coach me."

"Ah fuck, Dad, I might need to rethink that offer. I don't know if I can coach this joker."

Dad shakes his head at their antics. In a way, it's like he gained another son with Grant and Crew's brotherly friendship.

"Bret, stand next to your brother for pictures."

For the next fifteen minutes, we go through an endless cycle of poses as Mom ensures every situation is accounted for. The spring air is hot in Texas, and I can feel sweat rolling down my spine.

"Mom," Grant grumbles as I glance around the thinning crowd. It looks like everyone got the hint and wrapped up their pictures before they melted from the heat. As I'm making a pass back to my brother, my eyes land on someone familiar standing off in the distance.

Our eyes make contact, and I watch as she startles. With tentative steps and shoulders leaning forward, she moves toward our group. Noise fades away, the bickering between Mom and Grant turns to static. I can't peel my eyes away from the girl—the woman—walking toward us.

My eyes scan over her body as my pulse thrums in my ears.

"Bret," Grant's voice finally breaks through the static. "What are you staring—"

His words trail off as he turns while Savannah approaches our group.

"Congratulations, Grant." Her voice is small and shaky.

At her voice, everyone turns toward the petite brunette. The olive-colored dress makes her bronze skin seem even more sun-kissed. A gasp leaves my mother's lips as I take in Savannah's smocked dress that hugs her every curve, including the tiny baby bump the dress accentuates.

Time seems to freeze as everyone stares at her arrival. The moment of joyful celebration transforms into the beginning of uncertainty.

The start of a surprising new story.

EPILOGUE
Bret

"D o we have to say goodbye to this view?"

Crew chuckles as he sidles up behind me. His cool skin brushes my bare arm and the familiar waves of electricity spark goose bumps.

"We'll be back soon," he mumbles as he trails kisses through my hair and down my neck, where he nibbles the sensitive skin. "Besides, I can think of a better view."

I hum, nuzzling into his touch. "And what's that?"

"You, sprawled out begging to come on my cock."

"Crew," I scold as heat flames my cheeks, but my eyes never leave the morning glow as the sun rises over Lake Drummond.

For the past three months since we graduated, Sunset Shores has been our home. Much to Crew's mom's dismay, we decided to rent a place for the summer rather than stay in his childhood room on the farm.

The pistachio green townhouse in Silo Bay overlooks Lake Drummond and the upper balcony has been my favorite place to drink my morning coffee. Birds fly overhead, their songs wishing us good morning. The mossy, damp, earthy smells intertwine with the tangy algae, and it's a welcome fragrance to my senses. It's the scent which brings me back to my first trip to Silo Bay two years ago.

A lot has happened since that visit when the coaches surprised the team with a stop in Crew's hometown.

In April, Crew and I graduated from Central Texas University and embarked on our twelve-hundred-mile road trip. Leaving campus was hard. It's where *we* began. In my time at CTU, I rediscovered myself and learned no matter how hard life gets, I have a support system that loves me and is there for me. I found a family of friends who are more like siblings and even though life has scattered us around the country, our familial bonds will keep us together.

In the weeks leading up to graduation, Crew received a phone call from a video game developer. It turns out his college professor did know someone in the industry, and after months of indecision, the developer finally reached out. After a long conversation with the rest of Crew's group and through some negotiations, the video game concept for precision agriculture was acquired for one hundred and seventy-five thousand dollars and came with a royalty share. It was an incredible opportunity and one the group couldn't pass up. Crew's concept will be a nationwide game and will be featured in retail stores across the country. The hope is to inspire the next generation of farmers.

Toward the end of April, we boarded a flight to Green Bay, where we met my dad and Crew's mom, brother, and sister because Crew decided to enter the NFL draft. For months during our senior year, Crew struggled with the decision of pursuing professional football or coming home to Silo Bay. After many conversations with his brother, Jett assured Crew he had things handled on the farm for a few years. Besides, the NFL only comes knocking once. The Indianapolis Blues selected Crew in the fourth round. Luckily for us, Indy is only two and a half hours away from Silo Bay.

Preseason games start in one week, so our time in our little slice of heaven has officially ended. Crew has been spending time at our new house during the week while he has to report for practices, and I've been soaking in the last few weeks of Silo Bay before our next adventure begins. While Crew is busy with football, I'll start as an assistant athletic director at a local high school near Indianapolis.

It seems everything is falling into place for us. Our future is looking bright, and I couldn't be more excited to look ahead. Long gone are the days of looking over my shoulder and waiting for the other shoe to drop.

"Where'd you go, Rebel?" His deep, raspy voice interrupts my thoughts as I bring my mug of coffee to my lip, savoring the rich, full-flavored coffee.

"I was thinking about how crazy the last few months have been and how excited I am to build a future with you."

"I can't believe this is our life."

"I can't either."

Silence falls over us as we watch the golden glow of the morning transition into shades of orange and pink as the sun fully rises over the blue-green lake.

"Come with me?"

"To the end of the earth."

With a kiss on my temple, he shakes his head. "No, right now. Come with me."

"We need to be at your mom's in a couple of hours."

"There's time, I promise."

Glancing down, I take in my exposed tan legs peeking out from the oversized tee I slept in. "I need to change."

"You go do that, and I'll hook up the boat for one last ride before we leave." With a smack to my ass and a kiss to my temple, I watch his chiseled shirtless back retreat into the master suite. He reaches for a T-shirt and with a wink, he disappears into the hallway.

Since we've been staying on the lake, Crew moved the Jon boat he used to ride on with his dad to the garage of the townhouse. It made the most sense to keep it here rather than running out to the farm whenever we wanted to go for a ride. Every day, whether it be the start or the end of our day, the two of us load up the boat and meander down the channel where Crew sketches and I read. Thanks to Chloe, I've become a reader and enjoy getting lost in the pages of a good story while the melodies of the bugs and Crew's scratching as he draws fill the silence.

Drinking the rest of my coffee, I bring the mug inside, where I shuffle through my clothes. Slipping on a black sleeveless dress, I slide my feet into sandals. Yes, I've become a summer dress kind of girl because we are on *vacation*. Don't worry. My sneakers and band tees are boxed and waiting to be unpacked at the new house. Twisting my hair into a messy bun, I apply a coat of mascara before jogging down the stairs.

Crew is waiting in the driver's side, his hand out the window as Creedence Clearwater Revival plays softly from the open window. The trailer is hooked up to the truck for the one-mile drive to the boat ramp.

Climbing into the cab, Crew's hand lands on my bare thigh as I get situated in a silent gesture of comfort. Shifting the truck into drive, we slowly climb the hill in the parking lot. We turn onto the road separating the businesses from the lake. Driving past Sunset Shores Grill, I remember the bus parking here for the surprise visit. Of meeting Crew's mom and sister for the first time and feeling the urge to call this place my home.

The metal gates surrounding Sunset Shores Resort come into view and I stare up at the pistachio green townhouse. Our first home together, just the two of us. A place where we've spent almost four months learning more about each other. Figuring out each other's quirks and how to coexist in the same place without roommates. The four walls. I knew my love for Crew would never change.

As we drive further down the road, I turn in my seat to stare past Crew's perfect profile—the tight set of his chiseled jaw. Disheveled blond hair from last night's *feast* on the dinner table is hidden beneath a backward hat. Since being back in Silo Bay, Crew has worn a rotation of Riggs Cattle and Silo Bay Hawks hats. The worn-out hats, especially backward, give my kitty all kinds of flutters.

If I thought I couldn't resist this man in college, it's only gotten worse. I'm insatiable.

"You're staring at me."

His voice startled me from my daydream, where I *was* staring at him. I'm not sure what has me so on edge today. Maybe it's the impending goodbye breakfast at the farm or the move we are embarking on later today. There's a feeling coursing through my body, and I can't quite explain it.

"I wasn't staring at you. I was saying goodbye to the lake."

"Liar." A slight smirk tips the corners of his lips as he squeezes my thigh.

Looking around the cab, I don't see the bag Crew always brings when we go out on the boat. "You forgot the bag with your sketching supplies."

"I thought we could enjoy the morning together."

A few moments later, Crew reverses the truck as he backs the trailer down the boat ramp. I watch from the passenger side as he hops into the Jon boat and moves it to a ramp where he ties it off before returning to the truck. Even after these weeks on the water, I haven't gained enough confidence to help unload the boat.

Once the truck is parked, the two of us make our way to the aluminum chariot, hand in hand. Extending his hand out, Crew helps me navigate to the front of the boat. Glancing over my shoulder, I watch as he confidently moves, steps onto the boat, and reaches for the starter cord.

The way he positions himself, you can tell he's done this hundreds of times—no hesitation, no second-guessing, no stress if it'll start. Wrapping his large hand around the cord, he pulls sharply, and I watch his sinewy muscles flex with the movement.

Spluttering to life, the engine roars, vibrating the aluminum body underneath us. A now familiar smell of gasoline and the exhaust mixes with the fresh, aquatic scent of the lake.

Crew's eyes flick to mine as he shoots a wink in my direction before taking the bench seat in front of the engine. A spark of admiration flits through me as I stare at the man sitting behind me. With his size, people think he's gruff at first, but they couldn't be more wrong. Deep down, Crew Riggsby is a teddy bear who enjoys the simple moments in life.

Crew reaches for the rope and slips it from the cleat as he navigates us away from the wooden dock. The greenish-blue water parts as we glide through, disrupting its glass-like state. Birds chirp and locusts call to us as we putt down the channel. Leaves transition to a golden color as their green slips away, welcoming the telltale signs of fall approaching.

Halfway down the channel, Crew shuts the engine off, allowing us to float with the current. The boat gently rocks as he moves up a row until he's at my back.

"I love you, Rebel." His words are soft as he helps turn me around so that I'm facing him. There's a new glint in his eyes, and I'm squinting, trying to decipher his mood.

"I love you, too. Are you ready for Indy?"

His face breaks out into a beaming smile as he nods excitedly. "I can't believe this is my life."

Reaching out, I rub his thick forearm. "You deserve every second of it. Thank you for allowing me to be a part of your journey."

"You deserve it, too, Rebel." I tuck my chin as an onslaught of emotions hit me. But it's Crew tipping my chin up so our eyes meet. "You've been through hell and back in a short time. Through pain and fear, you've come out on top. Bret, you're brave and stronger than you give yourself credit for. Your heart is so big, and I'm grateful you chose to love me."

"It was never a choice to love you, Crew. I knew our souls were connected from the moment I met you."

His features soften as he reaches into his pocket. It's the same pocket he keeps his phone in. But it isn't a rectangular phone. No, it's a black velvet box. My eyes widen as I stare at the man across from me.

Crew's eyes bounce around our confined space. He chuckles as he tries to go down on one knee. "I didn't think this through."

"Bret Addison, *my* Rebel." Crew clears his throat as my nose tickles and tears well in my eyes. "As we look forward to our future, there's no doubt in my mind that I want you—no, need you—standing next to me. Will you do me the honor of becoming my wife?"

My head nods before he finishes his words because, yes, becoming Crew's wife would be my biggest honor. "Yes, Crew."

I watch as Crew removes the delicate ring from the black box, and my breath catches in my throat as I fully take in its magnitude. He slides the platinum band onto my finger, the metal cool against my skin on this humid morning. The large oval diamond steals my breath away as it glints and shimmers in the early light. The stone is flawlessly cut and more gorgeous than I ever imagined. Everything about the ring is perfect—the gem is the perfect carat size, and the fit is snug as if it were made for me. Each detail is timeless, from the slender band of smaller diamonds to the dazzling solitaire stone. I can't ignore how it glimmers against my bronze skin.

I'm mesmerized by its beauty.

By this man.

At this moment.

It's more than anything I could have imagined.

Not too long ago, I thought my future was over. The idea of love was just that, an idea. But the universe had other plans. Tears spring free and slide down my face as I realize everything perfectly reflects our love—pure, encompassing, and remarkable.

I'd follow Crew Riggsby to the ends of the earth, without a doubt.

Now, I'll do the honors as his wife.

Want to know more about their future? Download a special bonus epilogue! Visit authoralexisbuxton.com/extras and get a glimpse at their future!

Not ready to leave CTU?

Ready to witness the unexpected twist when CTU's newest football coach must navigate his future with the woman who just re-entered his life, pregnant and leaving him to question everything, including if he's the father?

Check out **_The Game Plan_**, a forced proximity, marriage of convenience, coach and student romance releasing Fall 2025! Preorder today: https://mybook.to/thegameplan

Have you read book one in the CTU Eagles series? If you want banter, plenty of sexual tension, feeling all the feels, and a twist you don't see coming, check out Brynn and Quinton's story in **_The Late Hit_**.

Want to learn more about Macy and her decision to abruptly move out of the townhouse? Check out **_The Christmas Scramble_**, an emotional holiday novella.

Want to learn more about Cody and Chloe and their tension filled romance? Check out **_The Change Up_**, an emotional, forced proximity, baseball meets bookworm romance.

Don't want to wait until fall 2025 for the next book in the CTU series? Stay tuned for a **romantic comedy standalone coming early 2025**, where the _firecracker_ he can't forget thinks he's the _enemy_ as they find themselves working together at a tropical resort! Will their sparks ignite or turn into an all-out battle?

If you're craving more, join the Facebook reader group, Heartfelt Huddle Hub, for lively discussions with fellow readers and an exclusive behind-the-scenes look!

Thank you so much for reading Crew and Bret's story! If you enjoyed it, PLEASE consider leaving a rating/review on Amazon and/or Goodreads.

Acknowledgements

This book holds a special place in my heart, as it's loosely inspired by my own experiences. Writing this story allowed me to revisit those emotional, chaotic years and transform them into something healing and meaningful.

First and foremost, I want to thank my husband—your love, support, and unwavering belief in me have been a constant source of strength. You've always been my biggest cheerleader, and I couldn't have done this without you. To my two beautiful children, you are the light in my life and my greatest joy. Thank you for filling my days with love and laughter after tough days of writing.

To my alpha readers, both new and old, thank you from the bottom of my heart for being there during every stage of this journey. Your insights, feedback, and constant encouragement mean more than words can express. To Alexis, Allie, Krissy, and Jill, thank you for helping me when I struggled to write some of the hardest scenes.

A special thank you to my amazing beta reader, Brittni, for all of your thoughtful feedback and for helping me shape this book into what it is today. Your sharp eye and honest thoughts have made all the difference.

To my talented cover designer, Mel, thank you for consistently bringing my vision to life with stunning covers that always capture the essence of my stories. You have an incredible gift, and I'm so lucky to have you on my team.

To my wonderful editor, Ellie, thank you for cleaning up my grammatical messes with such grace and dedication. Your willingness to dive in and polish my words has truly made this book shine.

To my ARC team and the reader community, your enthusiasm and love for this story fill me with so much gratitude. Thank you for being the first to dive into these pages and share your thoughts.

And lastly, to every reader who picks up this book—thank you. Your support means the world to me, and I hope this story touches your heart as much as it has mine.

With all my love,

Alexis

About the Author

Alexis Buxton is an avid reader turned author. A lover of all things love, Alexis enjoys reading all varieties of romance novels – the steamier, the better. Writing has always been a passion of hers and with the encouragement of friends and family, Alexis decided it was time to follow a childhood dream. She enjoys writing romance novels with damaged characters who need a little extra love and leave you feeling all the feels.

Born and raised in Ohio, Alexis currently resides in a small, lake town in Ohio with her husband and two small kiddos. Alexis is a small-town girl, through and through.

An avid sports fan, when she doesn't have a book in her hand, you can find Alexis watching sports. She prides herself on being a Cleveland Browns fan, even on the hardest days (or years). She also enjoys going on adventures with her family, visiting breweries to try new craft beers, attending races at her local dirt track, and supporting local businesses and restaurants.

Alexis runs on coffee and chaos, but she wouldn't have it any other way.

Stay in Touch

facebook.com/authoralexisbuxton
_instagram.com/author_alexisbuxton_
tiktok.com/@authoralexisbuxton
goodreads.com/alexisbuxton